THE
STARS
THAT
GUIDE YOU HOME

THE STARS THAT GUIDE YOU HOME

JEMMA ROBINSON

The Stars That Guide You Home
First published in Great Britain in 2021 by:
DAISA PUBLISHING
An imprint of PARTNERSHIP PUBLISHING

Written by Jemma Robinson
Copyright © Jemma Robinson

A CIP catalogue record for this book is available from the British Library.

Paperback ISBN 978-1-9162023-0-6

Book cover design by: Partnership Publishing
Book Cover Images ©Shutterstock 417845992

Book typeset by:
PARTNERSHIP PUBLISHING
Barton upon Humber
North Lincolnshire
United Kingdom
DN18 5RG

www.partnershippublishing.co.uk

Printed in England

Partnership Publishing is committed to a sustainable future for our business, our readers and our planet.

This book is made from paper certified by the Forestry Stewardship Council (FSC), an organisation dedicated to promoting responsible management of forest resources.

DEDICATION

Firstly, thank you to the whole team at Partnership Publishing for taking a chance on me and my characters and for helping me to make my dream a reality.

For my Mum and brother, who never stopped me from chasing my dream and supported me all the way, even when times were hard.

For Cassie, who gave me the confidence to bring my own characters and worlds to life when I never thought that I could.

For Jan, who willingly gave her own time for free to proofread and format my original manuscript.

And for my Tonyas, who happily read each & every chapter that I sent them in completely the wrong order and gave me the feedback I needed to get it to where it is today. I hope you enjoy it just as much in the correct order!

Sophia

"Go on then." Tom grins as he swings his bag over his shoulder. "How many do you reckon I can cut down today?"

"Hmmm," I say, thoughtfully, absent-mindedly stroking Amos as he sits by my side. "Ten …"

"Ten?" he repeats incredulously, a laugh escaping his lips. "You, my dear, confuse me for some sort of woodcutting god. I am but one man."

"A great man though," I reply, and he smiles softly, bending down to brush my lips with the gentlest of kisses.

"Well, this great man may manage six trees by nightfall." He smiles. "Enough to keep the roof over the head of an incredible woman," I smile and stroke the back of his hair.

"All I need is you. Doesn't matter where we are, as long as I'm with you then I'm safe. I'm happy."

He kisses me again before pulling away, grinning.

"Just me?" he questions. "I don't think poor Amos here would be very happy about that, eh boy?"

Amos cocks his head to the side at the sound of his name and whines. Tom chuckles, rubbing Amos' head with gusto.

"I've got to go," he says, quickly kissing me once more. "Take good care of her whilst I'm gone, won't you, boy?"

Amos barks and wags his tail in response.

"He always does," I say, smiling, looking up at Tom. "Love you."

"Love you too," he replies, smiling. "I'll be back by nightfall."

With another gentle pat of Amos' head, he walks to the door and opens it. The early morning sunlight glints through as he walks out and over to the paddock, closing the door behind him.

I busy myself feeding Amos, tending to the chickens and collecting the eggs, letting the pig and the goat out into the pasture to enjoy the morning sunshine. As I walk back into the cottage, Amos looks at me from where he has settled on his blanket.

Out of the corner of my eye I spot something glinting on the mantelpiece and realise it is one of Tom's axes; a smaller one that he uses to cut down the felled trees. I pick it up to examine it.

"He'll come back for this," I say to Amos who looks across at me, tiredly. "He won't just use one of the other axes in his bag, he will have to come back for this one. Creature of habit that one. You mark my words."

Amos yawns widely and closes his eyes again, completely uninterested. I chuckle to myself as I pick up the axe and place it on the table, ready for Tom to come back at any minute. Just as the kettle whistles on the fire I hear footsteps outside.

"Told you," I say triumphantly to Amos, who still looks like he couldn't care less. "Creature of habit."

I turn towards the door, arms folded, grin on my face. As it opens, I start my victory speech.

"I knew you'd be back! Bag full of axes yet you can't work without ..." My voice dies in my throat and my blood runs cold as I see that it is not Tom at the door but three men. Three of the King's Men.

"Hello Sophia," the Captain says, as he walks towards me. "We have been searching for you for a long time. The King has been most concerned for your welfare."

Instinctively I reach behind me, scrabbling for the axe on the table, but they are too quick for me. One of the guardsmen reaches for the axe whilst the other grabs hold of me, dragging me towards the door.

"Tom!"

I scream his name, kicking and struggling against the guardsman but he keeps a tight hold of me, closing his hand over my mouth, muffling my screams. The Captain stands in front of me, shaking his head.

"Pointless. We saw your woodsman on his horse, making his way deep into the forest. He can't hear you. And even if he did, we will be long gone before he makes it back."

A growl comes from the corner of the room. Amos stands, his head lowered with his teeth bared, ready to pounce. The Captain points his sword at him menacingly.

"Stay back, beast," he warns, but as I struggle against the guard once more, Amos dives forward, clamping his jaw around the Captain's arm. He screams, dropping his sword and in the melee, the guard holding me releases his grip. I rush to the door but as I am about to turn the handle I hear a loud yelp and turn to see Amos on the floor, blood pooling from his side.

"Amos!"

I rush back towards him, but the guardsman has maintained his composure and wrenches me back. Amos looks up at me with pitiful eyes as he lets out a whimper. There is nothing I can do as I am dragged backwards out of the door and thrown into a waiting carriage. Still, I scream Tom's name until I am driven far enough away that I know he will never hear my voice again.

Ｊames

The rolling green hills and the smell of pine trees are a familiar, homely sight and scent after so many years away.

To be summoned back to the Capital by King Edmund was unusual, but most welcome. It feels good to be home. The last time I saw Edmund was before he gained his kingship and was a mere boy of sixteen. His father, King Alfred, wanted me to teach him about the world, in order to prepare him for the life he was destined to lead. Though a medical doctor by trade, I had also worked as a private tutor for the families of Lords and Ladies, teaching their children the beliefs of the old gods and the sciences of the new world, as well as politics and languages.

Edmund was a trying student at times. Highly intelligent but unwilling to listen, instead choosing to believe in his ideas alone, stating on more than one occasion that, in the end, the people would take his word as gospel when he became King.

Despite this, I was fond of him. Beneath the arrogance he could be charming and polite.

I knew that if he could channel those aspects of his personality and dispel what I hoped was the arrogance of youth, he would grow to be a great King.

The sound of the gates opening snaps me back from my thoughts, and as my carriage pulls closer to the long stretch of road leading to the palace, I take a moment to look properly at what is now Edmunds.

And the difference is marked.

Where King Alfred had maintained the traditional beauty of the building, Edmund has chosen to adorn the turrets with gilded statues of cherubs and eagles alongside draping banners of ruby and gold. Despite my reservations at this new feel to the palace I am still looking forward to reacquainting with Edmund after all these years.

My carriage slows to a stop and the footman opens the door to bow as I step out, stretching my limbs, appreciating the feel of the ground beneath my feet as I walk over to the front doors.

"My name is Doctor James Collins." I introduce myself to the footman at the door as I open my bag to retrieve the letter of summon. "I am here at the request of King ..."

"James!" Edmund's voice rings out and as I look up I see him striding over, resplendent in a red silk waistcoat and breeches, a gold chain finished with a ruby pendant resting against his chest. His dark hair falls loose from its ponytail in places, just like it always did when he was a boy.

I extend a low bow as he reaches me.

"Your Majesty."

I feel him grab my shoulders and raise me back up to look him in the eyes.

"We have known each other long enough to bypass formality, James." He smiles, "after all, I'm not sure I would be here without your integral support and guidance. Call me Edmund, please."

I incline my head respectfully. Still smiling, he claps my shoulder. "Would you care to join me for a drink?"

I smile, gratefully. "It would be an honour and most welcome. It has been a long journey."

He grins at me, then leads on past the footmen and through the doors into the Palace. Courtiers, maids and guards all stop and extend low bows or curtsies in his presence as he washes past them, up the staircases lined with carpets the colour of his favourite gemstone, towards the study that was once his father's.

Alfred died three years ago.

I still regret to this day that I was unable to attend his funeral. I was out of the country on a medical expedition with my University fellows. I only found out the news on my return four weeks after his passing. I counted him as one of my dearest friends and not to be able to be present on his final journey out of this world is something that will live with me until the end of my own days.

We reach the door and Edmund goes straight over to the drinks cabinet. As he pours two glasses of port wine from a crystal decanter, I take the time to look around the study which used to be his father's space. A lot remains the same.

The same books on philosophy and ethics still stand on the large oak bookshelf and the most comfortable ornate armchairs still take pride of place in front of the roaring fire, where Alfred and myself would often sit late into the night discussing a variety of matters. Newer additions which I have never seen before include various unrelated objects placed underneath crystal cloches; a gold button, a silver ring set with an emerald and engraving which I cannot quite make out, a trio of bronze coins. And most disturbingly, a dagger, bloodstained and muddied at the hilt.

"I see you are admiring my trophies."

Edmund's voice takes me by surprise as I turn to see him standing behind me, brandishing two goblets full to the brim with ruby-red port.

"I've been busy since I gained my Kingship, James." He smiles, handing me one of the goblets. "I have won many battles to maintain the freedom of these lands and my rights as King. Some big, some small but not insignificant. I like to take a little souvenir from each of my victories to remind myself of the glories and remind others that I am not a person to be taken lightly."

He walks towards the cloche covering the dagger, placing a hand on top of it.

"My battle with the King of Fallean. It went on for four long months. But I got his surrender in the end, taking his dagger, which had been his father's, for good measure."

"And the ring?" I ask, clearing my throat.

8

Dear Isabella,

Thank you so much for taking part in the Book Tour for "The Stars That Guide You Home."

Hope you enjoy!

Love + light,

Jemma B

"That one has the best story of all." He grins, "but it will have to wait for another time. As I have some wonderful news to share with you, James."

He gestures to the chairs and I gratefully take a seat, appreciating the warmth and comfort. Carriage riding, though by no means a rough way to travel, can get uncomfortable by the fourth day of jolting along old stone roads and forest trails.

"What is your news then?" I enquire, as I sip my port, admiring the depth of flavour with a satisfied sigh.

He gives me a knowing grin.

"Well …" he begins, placing his own goblet down on the table as he looks at me. "This may come as a shock, James. At times I can hardly believe it myself … But I am a married man."

I look at him, trying to figure out if he is being serious. Surely if he were married, I would have heard something.

"We had to keep the wedding as quiet as possible," he explains, sensing my confusion. "Sophia had found herself in a spot of trouble. We didn't want to draw attention to the fact that she was back here in the Capital."

"Sophia?" I look at him in astonishment. "As in Sophia Reynolds?"

He nods and I shake my head.

"I thought she left the Capital years ago? No one had seen or heard from her?"

"She did." He nods, "as I said, she had managed to get herself into some trouble. She had found herself living with a man who was cruel to her. He was a drunk, a violent drunk

9

who hurt her quite badly, James. Of course, as soon as I heard of this, I made arrangements to take her out of that horrific situation and bring her back here. Then one thing led to another, old feelings reappeared and ..."

He's smiling widely and I hold out my hand to shake his in congratulations. But a niggling part of me can't help but wonder about the unlikeliness of the situation. From my distant memories of Sophia, she never wanted anything to do with Edmund. Her disappearance from the Capital was thought of by most people as a desperate attempt to escape an arranged marriage, which she wanted nothing to do with.

Still, I smile back at him, clapping him on the shoulder.

Many years had passed since she left the Capital and if she had found herself in such a horrible situation then maybe she had realised that there was a better life here with Edmund after all.

"Where is she then?" I ask. "I would very much like to meet her."

Edmund frowns. "I must admit, James, that's partly the reason for my asking you here." He smiles, ruefully. "I apologise if you feel I have asked you here under false pretences."

"She's ill?" I enquire carefully, and once again he gives me a puzzled frown, shaking his head.

"No, not ill in the traditional sense ..." he begins, before breaking off. He takes a deep breath before continuing. "It is an affliction of the mind."

"I see." I nod thoughtfully.

10

"She will not leave her chamber. She hardly eats and barely says two words, even to me."

He sits down heavily in his chair. I remain standing, watching him closely.

"When did this start?"

"Not long after we were married, which is now a month ago. Everything was wonderful and then suddenly it was like she turned into this different person."

"You said that she had suffered quite badly due to this other man," I say, thoughtfully. "It is possible that old memories are returning and causing her to retreat into herself because she is frightened of what she went through."

"Would you attend on her?" he says. He looks tired, his face anguished. "To see what you think. To see if you can help her?"

"You are aware that afflictions of the mind are not my specialism, Edmund. I'm not sure how much use I will be."

"I trust you, James," he says, seriously. "I trust you and your opinion. Please."

Looking at him again, I smile and nod.

"If it is what you wish, then I will be glad to. I shall attend on her tomorrow morning and do my best to help her."

He smiles gratefully, lifting his glass to clink against mine.

I was now aware of the reason behind being summoned to the palace. It would appear there was lost time which Edmund and I had to catch up on and so we stayed up late into the night, talking and exchanging stories until the fire burnt away into embers.

The next morning I knock lightly at the door to Sophia's chamber, and after a few moments it is opened by a young girl who I assume is her Lady-in-Waiting. She curtsies and I bow, respectfully.

"My name is James Collins." I introduce myself with a smile. "I am a Doctor. King Edmund has requested that I call on Lady Sophia as she has been unwell."

She nods.

"Lady Sophia is in bed." She replies, "please, follow me, sir."

"If she is sleeping I can come back a little later on, I don't wish to disturb her."

"She ain't sleepin' sir." She shakes her head, her accent betraying her working-class roots. "She don't sleep."

She continues into the chamber and I follow, slightly perturbed by her comment.

The room is peaceful and minimally decorated, in stark contrast to the rest of the Palace. Old oak furnishings are all that adorn the plain white room and as I enter the bedchamber I see that it is equally simple, including the four-poster bed upon which I see Sophia laying.

I barely recognise her as the girl I had seen around the village many years before. That girl glowed with carefree happiness and joy.

The young woman I see before me looks as though such joy has been long gone from her life. Her face is as pale as the bed linen she rests atop of. Her red hair fans it like flames of a fire, the only piece of colour in the room.

Her green eyes are red-rimmed and wet with tears. As I reach her bedside, I bow respectfully before speaking.

"Lady Sophia, my name is James Collins. I am a doctor. King Edmund has advised me that you are feeling unwell and he wishes me to look in on you, to see if there is anything I can do to help?"

I see the girl who showed me to the bedchamber waiting respectfully at the door and I realise I haven't yet asked her to leave us.

"Miss, would you mind leaving us for a few moments so that I can assess Lady Sophia's condition?"

She looks at me and then at Sophia who silently shakes her head, her eyes fearful.

"Of course," I say gently. "If Lady Sophia wishes you to stay, then I have no objection."

I see her glance at Sophia who nods her head slightly. With a curtsey the girl makes her way over to the bedside and takes a seat beside it.

"I beg your pardon, Miss, I have not asked your name."

She offers me a small smile. "It's Annalise, sir"

"And you are Lady Sophia's lady-in-waiting, yes?"

Annalise nods.

I turn to look at Sophia, but she gives no reaction that she is even listening to what we are saying.

Medically, aside from the fact that she appears distant and visibly upset, the only thing which concerns me greatly is her right arm, which is both bruised and covered in painful looking raised blisters.

13

"May I take a look at your arm, my Lady?"

She doesn't respond, so I reach out my hands to take her arm and take it as a good sign that she is alright with it when she doesn't pull away. As I turn it as gently as I can, I hear her wince in discomfort.

"How did this happen?"

She remains silent. I once again turn to Annalise to see if she can give me some answers.

"It was like that when she arrived, sir," she answers, quietly. "I've been bathin' it in lavender water but it don't seem to be making much difference."

I smile kindly.

"The blisters need to be drained first. Then a poultice of lavender and comfrey can be used to help with infection and to calm the skin. I shall prepare one now and show you how to use it if you would like?"

She nods and I gently place Sophia's arm back down on the bed. Annalise has followed me and as I begin to work, I speak with her again.

"So, you have no idea how Lady Sophia gained the injuries to her arm?" I ask, gently, as I hand her lavender to begin taking the buds from the stalks. "They are quite specific injuries and only present in one place."

She looks worried. I stop what I am doing and turn to her.

"You need not be afraid, child. Anything you say in this room will not leave it. I took an oath as a physician to keep the confidentiality of my patients and of those who also take care of them." I pause before continuing carefully. "I know about Lady Sophia's background. I know that she was living in a horrible situation before she came here. I just want to know if this was done to her by the man she was living with then."

"Tom …"

Sophia's voice is so quiet I barely hear it. As Annalise and I turn back towards the bed I see she's tossing and turning in the bed, repeating the name over and over.

"Does this happen often?" I ask Annalise, as we make our way back over to the bed.

She nods. "Almost every day, sir."

I place a gentle hand to Sophia's shoulder.

"My Lady," I say quietly, as she comes round. "My Lady, it's okay. You are safe. It is just a bad dream. You are safe here."

There are tears in her eyes as she looks at me fearfully.

"I'm not safe. Not with him. Not here."

I look at her sadly, wondering what on earth could have happened to have made her this fearful. With a gentle voice I try once more.

"You are at the palace, my Lady. You are no longer in any danger, I promise you that. Your husband is very worried about you."

"Tom …"

She says the name again, the tears flooding down her face, Annalise looking at her in concern. She squeezes her arm gently before looking over at me.

"Would you give us a moment, Doctor?"

I'm surprised by the request, but I can see that Sophia trusts Annalise and maybe the young girl can get her to open up a little somehow. Getting to my feet I incline my head in agreement, advising her that I would be right outside when they were ready. I go and stand outside the door and I cannot stop thinking about the marked difference in the girl I remember so vividly in her childhood. Whatever is wrong with her, whatever has happened, it is likely that I will need some help from a colleague or peer to get her on the road to recovery. I'm just relieved that Edmund got her to safety when he did. I hear the click of the door handle behind me and turn to find Annalise standing there.

"I fink she is ready to talk, sir," she says, and I follow her back into Sophia's chamber where I see she is now sat up, her head propped up with pillows, her hands twisting at the bedsheets as she looks across at us. She looks first at Annalise, who seems to nod in encouragement, and then to me.

"Annalise says that, as a Doctor, you swore an oath?"

Her voice is soft and gentle, still tinged with her earlier tears.

I nod as I walk over to the bed and take a seat.

"Yes, my Lady," I reply, gently. "I swore an oath which honours me to keep the confidentiality of my patients and anything that they say. Whatever you wish to tell me will not leave this room, I can assure you of that."

She's still looking at me as if she is unsure.

Annalise walks up to the other side of the bed and takes hold of her hand. I see her squeeze it gently and Sophia looks at me once more.

"The King …" she begins, before shaking her head, looking down at her hands.

"Nothing can happen to you in this room, Lady Sophia," I say, trying to encourage her. "All I wish to do is to help you."

"The King is not my Husband."

She says it suddenly, the words exploding from her, like she has wanted to say something for so long. I look at her in bafflement.

"I do not understand, my Lady?"

She's looking at me, her green eyes full of pain and fear and confusion.

"He brought me here against my will. He forced me to marry him. But I cannot be married to him for I am already wed."

I look across from her to Annalise, who seems as shocked as me at what she is hearing. I look back at Sophia, carefully.

"You are already married?" I ask, cautiously. "King Edmund said that you were living with a man?"

"Tom." She says, achingly.

"Tom Thornton. We married a year ago. Then one day when he was out at work, the King's men came and kidnapped me. They brought me back here and I was forced to marry the King. I didn't want to. I told him I couldn't and wouldn't as I was already married, but he forced me."

She thrusts out her injured arm towards me, her eyes blinded with tears.

"They held a burning candle to my arm until I said the vows. I didn't want to, but it hurt too much, I couldn't bear it."

She buries her head in her hands as she sobs. I look at her arm, the red, raw blisters covering one side and could see that it could have come from where she said.

Yet she is clearly sleep-deprived and hysterical. So maybe she just doesn't know what is real and what is not.

"The King said that this man was cruel to you."

"No." She shakes her head, strongly, cutting me off. "No, not Tom. He would never lay a finger on me. It is all lies. Lies to keep me here. Edmund doesn't love me. He just wants me. I am just a trophy to him. Something for him to keep to show that he has won."

She looks at me, tearfully.

"Tom won't know, he won't understand. When he got back from the woodlands, I would have just disappeared without a trace. He will be heartbroken. I need to get back to him, you have to help me, please!" She grasps for my hands but I don't know what I am supposed to do.

My head is spinning. It is all too much to take in. As she looks at me, I see her face fall.

"You don't believe me," she whispers, dropping my hands. "I told you all of this and you think I am lying."

"No, my Lady, not lying," I say, softly looking at her as I get up from my seat. "I just think that you are tired and unwell. And that you need to rest. I shall prepare a sleeping draught to help you."

"My wedding ring!" she cries out, stopping me in my tracks. "He took my wedding ring from me when he forced me to marry him. He will have kept it. I'm sure of it. Another trophy to prove that I am now his. A silver band studded with an emerald with our initials engraved on either side, T and S. If you find it, you will see, you will believe me!"

My blood runs cold as I look at her. She must see the look on my face as her expression changes from anguish to hope.

"You've seen it?" she whispers softly, a sob escaping her lips. "Then you must see that I am telling the truth, please!"

The ring in Edmund's study. The one he wouldn't tell me the story about, yet I recall the smile playing on his lips when I asked him. I go over to the table and grab the sleeping draught from my bag before making my way over to her again.

"Please ..." she begins again, but I hold up a gentle hand to stop her.

"I believe you," I say calmly, watching the relief spread across her face. "But I need to understand more, you are too tired and distressed to tell me properly. So please, take this draught and get some sleep. And I shall call on you again in the morning."

"You can't tell him any of this," she says, tearfully, grabbing hold of my hand again. "The King. He cannot know that you know."

I shake my head. "Your secret will not leave this room, Lady Sophia. I promise you."

I look her in the eyes, making sure she knows she can trust me as I hand her the bottle. She drinks it, the effect instantaneous as her eyes flicker shut and she falls into her first proper sleep, in what I can only assume a very long time.

SOPHIA

Cold dampness against my cheek woke me from a heavy slumber. As I blinked to clear my vision, I saw that I was in a dark, stone room, the only light coming from torches which flickered brightly on the walls. I caught sight of myself out of the corner of my eye, and as I looked down I saw that I was clothed in a long, white dress which I didn't recognise as my own, with lace at the sleeves and bodice and pearls which adorned the neck.

My head felt woozy and dreamlike as I raised my hand to rub my eyes, something didn't feel right. Then I looked down at my left hand and I felt sick as I saw that it was bare.

"Hello again Sophia."

A voice in my ear and a hand at my shoulder made me jump back. Edmund stood looking at me, a smile on his lips which didn't quite reach his eyes. I scrambled away from him, only stopping when I reached the wall.

"Please don't be scared," he said, his voice as smooth and calm as still water. "I have missed you so very much since you've been gone."

"Where is my wedding ring?" I replied, my voice shaking. "What have you done with it?"

He laughed. "You don't have a wedding ring my darling, not yet anyway. We are not married yet."

"I am already married, Edmund."

He looked at me in confusion and I wondered for a moment if he actually realised. Then one of the guards who captured me, appeared at his shoulder and whispered in his ear. As he listened he nodded in understanding.

"Ah, yes. The woodsman. Yes, Sophia, I am sure you have had a wonderful few years living this fantasy life of yours. But now the time has come to enter the real world."

I looked at him in anger, though despair was beginning to seep into my veins. "I am a married woman," I said, as strongly as I could manage as I rose to my feet. "I have paperwork to prove it!"

"Not here, Sophia." There was an air of impatience to his voice. "You have nothing to prove it here in my Kingdom. I do not recognise this so-called marriage. Therefore, you are free to marry me."

He raised his hand to stroke my cheek and I shrugged him off viciously. I turned away, making a run for the door at the end of the corridor. But as I reached it, two guardsman stepped out of the shadows, blocking my way.

"No …" I cried out tearfully, as they grabbed my arms and practically dragged me back to where the King stood, throwing me down at his feet, where I stayed.

"Why me?" I looked up at him, desperately.

"Because you were always mine, Sophia." His voice was now as dark as his eyes and I could feel the simmering anger he was trying to keep under control in his words.

"You were promised to me. You didn't have a choice in the matter. Yet you decided to make things difficult for us both, by disappearing into the night. That was a silly thing to do. I was always going to find you and bring you back here."

"I will not marry you. You cannot make me." I stared at him, begging myself not to show the fear I felt in my heart. My brain was foggy and I desperately tried to think of a way to get myself out of this hell. I looked around at the people in the room with me, looking for one single kind soul who may have taken pity on me and helped. But I knew that none of them would. Edmund grabbed hold of my hands, dragging me to my feet, keeping a tight hold of me.

I noticed the makeshift altar in front of us and choked back a sob, as a priest walked forward from the shadows.

I looked at him, shaking my head, pleading with him not to make me do this. But he looked as scared as I did, and I knew that he would have been threatened with his life should he not do this, even if he didn't want to.

"*You cannot make me!*" I screamed, turning to face Edmund. "*I will not speak the vows, I will not!*"

Edmund didn't reply. Instead he just smiled at me, which scared me more than anything. Turning to the priest, he nodded, instructing him to begin.

The priest swallowed, looking at me with pained eyes before looking down at the papers in his hands as he began to speak.

"Edmund Alastor Lawrence Rose, do you take this woman, Sophia Ellen Reynolds to be your lawfully wedded wife, to have and to hold, from this day forward, for better, for worse, for richer, for poorer, in sickness and in health, to love and to cherish for as long as you both shall live?"

The sound of my maiden name was alien to me. I hadn't been known by that name for such a long time and the bad memories that I ran away from all of those years ago came flooding back at the mention of it. Edmund smiled at me, the look in his eyes not of love but of lust and wanting. Of the achievement, at finally getting his prize.

"I do."

I felt sick at the sound of those two simple words. The priest turned to me, his eyes sympathetic and regretful as I silently mouthed my pleas for him not to do this once more.

"Sophia Ellen Reynolds …"

"That is not my name. My name is Sophia Ellen Thornton and I am already married to Thomas Oliver Thornton. He is my Husband and I will not betray my vows to h …" I gasped out in pain as Edmund grabbed hold of my wrist tightly, his fingernails digging into my skin.

"I will give you one chance to do this painlessly, Sophia," he hissed in my ear. "I do not want to hurt you but you are leaving me no choice if you continue to behave in this way."

He stared at me, his eyes cold and dark. I was scared of him. I always had been. But I couldn't and wouldn't break the vows I took with the man that I love, no matter how scared I was of what he may do to me. I shook my head.

"No."

Edmund's jaw clenched in rage as I said it. I felt my body trembling with fear as I waited for him to make his next move. He looked past me, towards a guard and silently nodded before turning me roughly back to face the priest.

"My apologies, Father." His voice was rueful. "Please continue."

Swallowing, the priest spoke once more.

"Sophia Ellen Reynolds ..."

As he started again, I felt someone grab hold of my arm, ripping at the sleeve of my dress until it tore, revealing my forearm. As I struggled, the priest looked to Edmund in confusion.

"Carry on!"

"D ... do you take this man, Edmund Alastor Lawrence Rose to be your lawfully wedded husband ..." As the priest stumbled over his words in panic, I saw the flame of a candle being brought closer to my arm and I tried desperately to pull away but to no avail.

"*To have and to hold, from this day forward, for better, for worse, for richer, for poorer …*"

As the flames licked my arm the searing pain began to take hold, my skin bubbling with the heat as the candle was pressed closer and closer. "*In sickness and in health, to love and to cherish for as long as you both shall live?*"

The tears were rolling down my cheeks now, and I could taste the blood from where I had bitten into my own lip to stop myself from screaming out.

"Say the words, Sophia," Edmund said calmly. "Say the words and it will stop."

The pain was agonising, the burning smell of my own flesh making me feel sick. I knew I couldn't stand it much longer.

I knew that he would never give in. As I closed my eyes, I saw Tom's face and I hated myself for what I was about to do. I just prayed that he would forgive me. I opened my eyes, blinking away the tears that clouded them. Then, looking down at the ground, I spoke the words that would seal my fate forever.

"I do."

It was as though I watched the rest of the ceremony from another place, as I took my mind as far away from the hell that I was being put through as I could. I felt him push the vulgar, thick ruby-studded band onto my ring finger as the priest confirmed us man and wife. I felt his rough kiss against my lips before he took my hand and walked us from the cold, dark room and through the corridors of the palace until we reached his opulent bedchamber.

He dragged me over until we stood in front of one of the large gold gilded mirrors that adorned his room.

"Just look at us," he said, as he pulled me in closer to him and the feeling of his body against mine made me want to vomit. "Don't we make the most beautiful couple in the whole Kingdom?"

I looked at us in the reflection. He was grinning widely, his dark hair pulled back into a perfect ponytail, his red velvet dress coat matching the ruby pendant resting against his chest. My face was pale and drawn, the tracks of my tears visible against my skin.

My heart ached as I remembered my wedding to Tom. How happy we looked.

That simple, blissful summer's day when I wore daisies in my hair and we danced in the meadow until the sun went down.

Then Edmund squeezed my injured arm, bringing me out of my dream and back into the nightmare of my present. I didn't even have the energy to cry out …

"I hate you," I whispered. My eyes glazed over with tears. He smirked at me before walking away.

"Escort Lady Sophia to her room to get some rest." I heard him instruct one of the guards. "Assign her one Lady-in-Waiting. No more. And I will not call on her until she comes to her senses and realises that she is mine now. No one else's."

"You'll be waiting a long time!" I spat at him.

With a grin he walked up to me, placing his hand at the back of my head so I couldn't move away. "As long as it takes, my darling. We've got our whole lives ahead of us."

He pulled me towards him, pressing his lips to mine, his touch rough and unfamiliar. As he broke away and walked out of the room I collapsed to the floor in tears, unable to hold them back any longer.

JAMES

The next day, I listened to Sophia's account of how she came to the Capital. I watched Annalise surreptitiously wipe the tears from her eyes as she listened to the horrific details that Sophia recounted, before excusing herself to get the poultice that we had prepared yesterday. As I reach into my bag, to take out the needles I require to drain the blisters on her arm, I watch Sophia carefully.

She seems calmer; more settled for finally unburdening her soul after so long. I see a spark of the younger Sophia back within her, though I fear this is because she feels I can solve her problems, when I know that I cannot.

"This will hurt a little, my Lady," I say, gently. "But it will feel much better once they are drained and the poultice is applied, I promise."

She nods in understanding, as I place the needle to the first blister and start to drain it. I see her face contort with the pain, but she doesn't cry out.

I slowly make my way along her arm, draining each blister which vary in size and severity.

As I reach the last one, Annalise walks back over with the cloth she applied the poultice to. Thanking her, I gently begin to wrap it around Sophia's arm, noting the instant relief in her face as it takes effect.

"Better?" I ask with a smile and she nods, gratefully. I turn to Annalise. "This needs to be changed every few hours. I can do it if you wish but I feel you are more than capable."

Annalise grins, her cheeks reddening. "I can do it, sir."

I smile and nod as she walks over to the table once more, beginning to prepare the various items she would need to redress the wounds. As I sit down next to Sophia's bedside once more, I see she is looking at me. And I fear I know why.

The physical pain has eased but the troubles in her mind and heart remain.

I sigh, softly. "I wish there was more that I could do, Lady Sophia. Really I do."

"It's fading …" As her eyes meet mine once more I see that they are brimming with tears. "His face. Every time I close my eyes I see him but he's fading away. And I'm scared that one day I won't see him at all."

I shake my head, sadly. "What is it you would have me do?"

She opens her mouth to speak before shaking her head and looking down at the bedsheets, "I can't live like this," she whispers. "I can't. I need to see him, even if it is just once. To explain. To say sorry."

"Please, think about what you are asking. Of me. Of him. You know the danger he would face even setting foot in the Capital. If they discovered who he was then …"

"I know!"

Her voice is wracked with sobs as she interrupts me.

"I know, and it scares me to death! But all I can think about is how he must have felt when he came home and found me gone. Found our dog dead in a pool of blood, me, vanished without a trace. I just ... I need him to know. To know that I want nothing more in the world than to come home to him. But I can't. And I'm sorry."

She breaks down in tears once more and I look at her, knowing that there is nothing I can do to fix the terrible things that have been done to her. I know that her life has been torn apart and there is no way of solving it. Annalise is looking at me and I know she is asking me silently to help. And isn't that what I'm meant to do?

"You know that for Tom to come here, it would put him in grave danger," I say eventually, my voice soft. "You know that. However ..." I stop, wondering if I'm really about to suggest this. Both women are looking at me closely. "Before I was summoned here by King Edmund, I was due to embark on a visiting tour of coastal medical schools. To meet the students and pass on advice. If you really want this, knowing the risks to both of you ... I could make a brief stop in your hometown. To see if he is still there." I watch Sophia's eyes widen in relief as I look at her seriously.

"In order for me to do this, however," I say, carefully. "In order for Edmund to allow me to leave and embark on this trip, I feel he will need to see that you have improved enough for me to leave you for a little while. And that means you being able to at least converse with him. Amicably."

Sophia swallows hard and I see her bottom jaw begin to shake again. "He scares me," she whispers. As Annalise takes hold of her hand, I smile softly.

"I understand that, My Lady, and I do not blame you after what has happened. I do believe, however, that Edmund does love you ... even if that love is unreturned," I say, quickly, seeing the look on her face. "All I mean is, if you can show him that you are not fighting against him anymore, even if it is only an act, he will not harm you again. I believe that."

She looks unsure. Annalise has the same wary look upon her face.

"This is the only way I will be allowed to leave you, Lady Sophia," I say again. "The only way I will be able to go and try to find Tom."

At the mention of his name it's as though she jolts back to life again. Taking a shaky breath she nods.

"I'll try."

SOPHIA

I didn't move from the moment the guards threw me to the ground of an unfamiliar room and left me there. The room was bigger than my entire farmhouse. It was plain, unlike the rest of Edmund's ruby and gold-gilded palace. It probably hadn't been used by anyone in a long time, if ever.

The walls were white and bare. The four-poster bed which sat over in the corner, looked too big and unwelcoming. Everything here was unfamiliar to me. And I felt more alone than I have ever felt in my life.

I heard the door click open and felt a jolt of panic in my chest as I scrambled hurriedly over to the wall wanting to protect myself from whoever it was. The cream-carpeted floor was so thick that I couldn't hear footsteps, so eventually I forced myself to look over and was surprised when I saw a young girl standing there looking as scared as me.

"Who are you?"

"A ... Annalise, my Lady," she stuttered as she dropped a messy curtsey towards me. "I'm y ... your lady-in-waiting."

I looked at her closely. She looked like a child. Big brown eyes full of fear, dark hair pulled up high onto her head and fixed with a grey bonnet and wearing a dress which looked too big for her.

"I don't want a Lady-in-Waiting." I turned away from her. "You can leave me. Please."

"P ... please ..." Her voice was panicked which made me look at her again. "They said I 'av to stay. If I don't do my job they said they'll p ... punish me."

Her eyes glistened with tears and I thought of everything that had been done to me; someone who Edmund said he loves. I dreaded to think what would be done to her. She was still looking at me, wide eyed and fearful as I nodded my head and I saw the relief wash over her as she walked over to me.

"There's a chair over there, my Lady." Her voice was still wary as she looked at me. "Would you like to sit there whilst I find a nightgown for you?"

I didn't have the energy to speak, so I just nodded and tried to smile. As she took hold of my arm to help me to my feet, I gasped in pain and she jumped back, panicked.

"M ... my Lady?"

I had forgotten the state of my arm and the pain they had inflicted upon me. It was all just part of a consuming nightmare that my life had become. I winced as I peeled back the ripped sleeve of my dress, exposing the burnt, blistered flesh of my wrist.

I glanced at Annalise and could see her looking at it in horror. As she caught my eye she composed herself, looking properly calm for the first time since we had met.

"I'll 'elp you dress for bed. Then we'll see if I can make you a little more comfortable."

She helped me up from the floor, taking my left arm this time and guided me to my feet. I remember being grateful for her support as I felt as though my legs would barely carry me. I let her guide me over to the soft, comfortable chair by the window before she left the room and I heard her opening drawers and cupboards, gathering various items.

As I looked out of the window at the Palace grounds, which were shrouded in the darkness of the evening, I began to wonder how much time had passed since I was taken from my home. It already felt like a lifetime. I remembered little of the journey here, other than how arduous it was; all of the days and nights blending into one. I cried until I could cry no more. Begged the guards to take me back until my throat was hoarse. I even offered them what little money I had. None of it made a difference. I was guarded constantly, so there was no chance of escape.

Then, when we finally arrived here, the last thing I remember before waking up in that room was being brought from the cart, the rough hands of the guards grasping tight onto my wrists as they dragged me towards a courtier who welcomed me home. It has been a month. One whole month since Tom walked out the door of our home and would have come back to find me gone.

To find Amos dead on the floor; his last moments spent trying to protect me. A sob caught in my throat as I imagined what horror must have awaited him as he got home. Would he have begun searching for me? Of-course he would. I already know that. I know he would have searched high and low; day and night trying to find me. But it would have been hopeless. Never in a million years would he have guessed that I was here, being held against my will, miles from home.

We never let our pasts define us. I never told him of mine, as I never wanted to. And yet now, I wished that I had. Because I knew he could have kept me safe. And maybe this would never have happened.

Instinctively, I grasped my wedding ring for comfort but it felt strange to touch and as I looked at it remembering that it was another thing which has been taken from me; replaced with a vulgar reminder that I was Edmund's possession now.

It was this that finally made the tears erupt from me, as Annalise walked back into the room carrying the various items she had gathered. At the sight of me she rushed over, placing the items on the floor as she crouched beside me and took hold of my hand.

Her gentle, unexpected touch was the first display of kindness I'd felt since arriving here, and I felt myself grasp her hand back tightly.

"Sounds like you've 'ad quite an emotional day, my Lady. Sleep will 'elp. Shall I 'elp you dress for bed?"

She closed the curtains and I got to my feet, letting her begin to unbutton and unlace the white dress that wasn't mine. I hadn't had anyone help me dress since I was a young girl, but as odd as it felt I knew I wouldn't have had the energy to do it myself and I just wanted to rid myself of the clothes which he had me dressed in.

I felt her slip a cool, cotton nightdress over my head and button it up. The simple garment was the closest thing to home and to myself that I had found here and it helped to calm me, even a little.

"Lavender water to soothe your arm, my Lady," Annalise said, as she guided me over to the bed where the bowl was steaming with the fragrant remedy.

I climbed into the unfamiliar bed which was so big I felt as though it would engulf me. But it was soft and the heavy blanket she placed across me cocooned me, making me feel safe. She dipped the cloth into the water before gently placing it against my wrist and I grimaced as the warm water stung my skin.

"Sorry, my Lady. It'll sting at first, but it should make it feel better."

It wasn't helping. I already knew that. But her face was so full of determination and pride that I couldn't bring myself to tell her otherwise. So, I gritted my teeth and let her continue to bathe it and gently dry it before rolling down my sleeve.

"I'll let you get some sleep now. But I'll stay in case you need me."

I didn't want to sleep. I was scared of what visions it would bring me. But my body was so tired that it eventually made the decision for me and I was dragged under.

Tom was the first thing my dreams brought me. I felt the relief wash over me as I saw him and I wanted to rush to him but I couldn't move. And I was calling his name and it was though he could hear me but could not see me. He started calling my name, searching for me with his eyes but he couldn't see me even though I was right in front of him. Then suddenly, Edmund appeared, flanked by two guards who grabbed Tom's arms and I screamed his name as Edmund turned to me, grinning, before plunging his dagger into Tom's chest.

I heard Annalise's voice shouting me and felt her gentle hands at my shoulders trying to calm me but my head was still within my nightmare and I was still trying to get to him, still screaming his name.

It took her a while to calm me down and even then it was as though I was seeing the world through a haze; unsure of what was real and what was in my mind. I didn't even realise Annalise had left the room and returned again until I felt her hand at my shoulder once more, as she placed something warm into my hands. "Warm milk and honey," she explained, gesturing to the teacup she had placed in my grasp. "I get nightmares, too."

I forced myself to rise and sit up in my bed, managing a small smile as she encouraged me to drink and I took a shaky sip of the sweet liquid. "Thank you."

I didn't want to sleep anymore. I didn't think it was possible but sleep brought me worse nightmares than the one I was living in already. "Is the fire still warm?" I asked, not wanting to talk or think any longer.

"It's just embers now, my Lady, but they are still giving off some heat."

"I'd like to sit by it for a while." I let her guide me over to the open fireplace. She settled me down on the floor beside it before taking a blanket and placing it across my knee. I asked her to sit with me, a request she looked wary at but did without question. Then we sat in silence, just listening to the crackling of the embers as they cooled, the orange glow the only thing left of the fire that once consumed them.

The fireside was where Tom and I would sit at home every evening when he returned from work.

He would bring home the odd pieces of wood that he had chopped which couldn't be sold and we would pile them up in the fireplace and light a fire. Then we would sit and talk late into the night, Amos occasionally getting up and moving to sit closer to me and then over to Tom whenever the mood took him.

Sitting there now was making the memories return so strongly and I didn't know whether I wanted to smile or cry.

All I knew is that somehow I had to find my way back to him. Whatever it took.

"Annalise?" I say her name and she jumps slightly. I can't blame her. I've barely muttered two words to her since the first day I arrived here. As she looks over at me I manage a small smile. "Will you sit with me for a while?"

She curtsies, which I don't think I will ever get used to, before coming to sit by my bedside.

I look at her. I've never asked her age but she looks so young, I'd hazard that she has barely reached her sixteenth year. Her deep brown eyes are wide, innocent and kind yet full of worry.

"Why were you chosen?" I ask her, curiously. "I know Edmund instructed his guards to find me just one Lady-in-Waiting. Why you?"

She looks down at the ground. "The guards came down to our servants quarters," she begins, still not looking at me. "None of 'em spoke. They just stood lookin' at us, mutterin' amongst themselves. I heard one of 'em say 'Her. She looks quiet.' I was told to go with 'em and then they said I'd be your Lady-in-Waitin'. I'd never been prepared for anythin' like this. I ain't from a rich family. I didn't know what was happenin'."

I feel guilt at her words, even though I know that none of this was my idea or choosing.

"I am sorry, Annalise," I say, unable to stop myself apologising to her. "That must have been very confusing for you."

She finally looks up, smiling shyly at me. "It was at first, my Lady." She nods. "But then I realised what an honour it is. To take care of you."

"An honour?" I shake my head in confusion. "Why would you think that? I am not special. I am just an ordinary woman."

She chuckles and the worry in her eyes disappears for a moment, replaced with a childlike wonder. "My Lady," she smiles, eventually. "You are the Queen."

"I'm not the Q ..." I stop myself. Partly because I don't want to admit the truth about what my life has now become. But also because I could hear the anger in my voice. And I had no right to be angry with her.

Closing my eyes, I sigh.

My bones are weary. Part of me just wants to stay here in this bed, forever. It has become my comfort blanket. My cocoon, protecting me from the evil that lies beyond the door. Yet I know that, if I am ever to stand a chance of seeing Tom again, then I need to find the strength from somewhere to fight.

I look at Annalise. The worry has returned to her eyes.

"M ... my Lady," she stutters. "I'm sorry, I didn't mean to offend you. This was before I knew what 'appened."

I raise a hand to reach for her cheek and she flinches away.

God knows what had been done to her in the past to make her so fearful.

"Annalise, I would never hurt you," I say, my voice gentle as I move my hand away, "please, don't be scared. I shouldn't have raised my voice, I'm sorry. It wasn't directed at you. It is myself and this situation that I am frustrated and angry about."

JEMMA ROBINSON

She is looking at me as I place my hand on top of hers and I am relieved when she doesn't flinch away this time. I smile at her and she gives me a small smile back.

"Would you please draw me a bath?" As I ask the question, her face lights up and I realise that she is just happy to be able to do something to help. With a curtsey, she makes her way into the bathroom. I take a shaky short inhale of breath and prepare to begin the act I know I must perform if I am ever to see Tom again.

As the warm, perfumed water gently laps against my skin I feel myself relax for the first time since I came here. Annalise sits at the side of the bath gently running a sponge across my arms, taking care not to touch the burns, which she has covered with a fresh poultice. I have always felt calm near water. Growing up in the Capital meant that I didn't get to fully appreciate the beauty and tranquillity of the sea of the coastal towns that surrounded us.

When I first settled in Lowshore, I was disappointed that I couldn't see the sea. The forests were beautiful and majestic but in my head I pictured sea and sand; seabirds and boats bobbing on the horizon. Then one day, after Tom finished work, he told me he wanted to take me somewhere. He was grinning cheekily, which he always did when he was planning something. He took my hand and led me through the forest, just as the sun was beginning to set.

41

And after a while, the pine smell of the forest began to fade, replaced with a smell I was unfamiliar with, one I couldn't place.

Then the earth under my feet began to feel softer and I looked down to see golden grains of what could only be sand. As I looked up at Tom again, he was still grinning as he nodded his head towards something in the distance and I squealed in delight, as I saw the sun setting over a calm, deep blue sea.

"I remember you talking about it," he said, as I grabbed his hand and pulled him forward towards the sea's edge. "How you wanted to visit the sea."

As we reached the edge of the water, the smell that I couldn't place became stronger. It smelled fresh and salty, unlike anything I'd ever smelled before and I loved it. The air was invigorating and cold, making me feel alive and I heard the whooshing noise as the tide washed in and I giggled as it touched my bare feet.

"I didn't even realise we were this close to it," I whispered, smiling up at him. He grinned back at me.

"This little place holds many surprises if you are willing to explore."

"My Lady?" Annalise's voice filters into my head and as I open my eyes I realise that I'm not by the seaside any longer. "Are you okay?"

She looks concerned and I manage a small smile. "I'm fine. I think I am ready to dress now."

Once I am dressed, we sit by the open fire, Annalise having helped me into a dark blue dress with a corset so tight it took me a while to figure out how to breathe again. I'm not used to wearing clothes like these. Tending to the farm means that I am far more used to wearing loose shirts and trousers or simple cotton dresses which allow me room to move.

"I never wanted any of this, you know," I say, looking into the deep red flames of the fire, as Annalise gently pulls a hairbrush through my curls. "All of the other girls my age would look up at this huge palace, which overlooked our houses and say 'wouldn't it be wonderful to live there.'"

I shake my head. "I could think of nothing worse. Edmund's father wanted him to grow up with the children of the Capital, so that he may understand a somewhat normal childhood. But he wasn't a normal child. He knew his standing. He knew his worth. And I hated the way he would bully the poorer children. Teasing them. Making fun of them. He used to try and talk to me whilst we played out in the courtyards but I would not entertain him. All of my friends thought I was crazy. But I knew he wasn't someone I wanted to like. And as he got older, he carried on trying to impress me, telling me about the hunts he had gone on. The poor defenceless animals he had killed, not for food but for sport. For pleasure. I still don't understand how anyone can find that impressive."

Annalise has stopped brushing my hair. It falls softly against my face in loose curls, part of it pinned back and secured with a navy-blue ribbon. I thank her, gesturing for her to come and sit beside me. "The marriage proposal came just days after my eighteenth birthday," I continue, as she sits next to me quietly. "It was brought to the door by a courtier, a sealed scroll bearing the wax stamp of King Alfred. My parents were thrilled. Prince Edmund had his choice of suitors. Noblewomen, princesses from far-away lands. They were so happy that he had chosen their little girl. But I felt sick. The moment I saw the words upon the scroll it felt like the world was crashing down around me. I couldn't breathe. I made the decision that evening to leave. I couldn't tell my parents. I knew they wouldn't understand. I took what little money I had and begged a ride on a carriage out of the Capital. I didn't care where it was going. I just needed to get out of here, get as far away as I possibly could. The carriage driver dropped me off in Lowshore. I had never visited before, but as soon as I stepped foot there, it felt right. Of course, I had no place to stay and barely any money so it was scary at first. But somehow, I knew I could make this my home. I befriended an elderly lady who I saw struggling to carry some items she had bought from the market. I offered her my help and she offered me a place to stay, in her little family farmhouse. It was only her left now, she told me. She had lost everyone else to illness, disease or war. Her name was Alice and she was as stubborn as the day is long. She needed the help but she was far too proud to ask for it. So I stayed. And eventually she became my family."

I smile sadly, thinking about her. "I lived with her for four years. I could see her starting to ail even if she refused to admit it herself. I nursed her, making sure she was as comfortable as she could be until she passed on into the next world, peacefully in the home she had always known."

Annalise is looking at me, not saying a word. The silence is comfortable though. It's as if she knows that I need to speak and she just wants to let me do it.

"The farmhouse became mine," I continue, with a small smile. "I wanted to make sure it would carry on. For Alice. So I worked hard. I tended to the land, began growing my own vegetables to sell, buying more animals from the market; a goat for milk, chickens to lay eggs. It was simple. Peaceful. And I lived alone, happily, until a few years later I met Tom…" At the thought of him, the words choke up inside of me.

I'm not ready to talk about him, about that part of my life. Not yet, not even with Annalise.

"Do you think I'm doing the right thing?" I ask suddenly. "Asking James to find him?"

She looks taken aback by this and takes a few moments to reply. "I'm not sure my opinion is worth anythin' my Lady."

"Sophia," I say, smiling. "Please call me Sophia. And your opinion is worth more than you realise. I trust you. You are the person I trust most in this whole place. Please."

She remains quiet for a few moments, thinking, before eventually she replies, "I can't say it ain't dangerous. The King …'e isn't the kindest of men. But seeing how happy the idea of seeing Tom again 'as made you. After seeing you so sad. I fink you deserve happiness."

The tears prick at my eyes at her words and I manage a small smile as I squeeze her hand. I glance out of the window as I do so. The sky is clear blue, the bare trees glisten with winter frost and for the first time in so long, I want to leave this room.

"Would you come for a walk with me, Annalise?" I ask, as I watch the smile spread across her face. "I think the fresh air would be good for us both."

She nods animatedly, curtseying before rushing off to find our cloaks. I take a deep breath, think of Tom and get to my feet, ready to start the next chapter in my life which will hopefully bring him back to me.

James

I requested to meet with Edmund later that day to advise him on my thoughts. As I was shown into his study, he welcomed me in with a broad smile, beckoning me over to his desk. I tried not to look at the ring which I now knew the story of. At least Sophia's side of the story of which I could find no reason for it not to be the truth.

"What are your findings, James?" He looks concerned, but for her or for himself it is hard to tell. "What has she told you?"

"Not a lot." I lie, convincingly enough, knowing that my oath prevents me from discussing details with him, "she is clearly distressed. Though her arm is what concerned me most."

I look for any flicker of guilt or regret in his face but see none. If anything, the only glimmer of emotion is one of sorrow. Working him out has always been problematic.

"It was like that when she arrived," he replies, quietly, shaking his head. "Though she kept it hidden at first. I only saw it properly when she became ill. God knows what he did to her."

His eyes flash with anger now as he looks at me. "Did she say how it happened?"

I shake my head. "No. She barely spoke two words. She was very withdrawn. Why wasn't her arm looked at the moment you realised?"

"Well I tried, James, of course I tried! She wouldn't let me near her … wouldn't let anyone near her. That useless maid of hers was supposed to be helping, she is the only one that Sophia will allow into her chambers."

"Young Annalise has been doing the best she can with limited knowledge," I say, calmly, trying to diffuse the situation. "Luckily, today Sophia let me attend to it. It appears to have been burnt but she could or would not tell me why."

"Burnt?" he says, his eyes still flashing with anger. "What kind of a man could do that? I'm just relieved I got her away from there before he could do anything worse. She is safe here now."

"Did you meet this man?"

"Gracious, no." He shakes his head. "If I had, I'm not sure I could have held my temper, James. The man is a vicious bully, by all accounts. And a drunk. A product of his standing in life, sadly." He reaches for the crystal decanter filled with port, pouring us each a glass. As he hands me mine he takes a seat opposite me. "What are your thoughts, James? Honestly."

I sip at my port as I look him in the eye, trying to find that boy I thought I knew so well in this man that I cannot work out.

"I think she is scared. And she needs to know that she is safe now. Hopefully, now that her arm has been treated a little, the pain will subside and that will help. I spoke with her a lot. Told her that she was safe here. She seemed calmer when I left. Perhaps she just needed to hear it from someone else. An outsider."

"She is safe now," he repeats, nodding his head. "Now that I have her back with me. Where she belongs."

"Yes, Edmund." I nod, carefully choosing my next words. "She needs to know that. She needs you to show her that."

"How?"

For the first time I see a flicker of anxiety across his features.

"Gently," I reply, honestly. "Lady Sophia is very fragile. Very scared of the world she finds herself in."

"How can she possibly be scared of this world?" He laughs. "My guards told me of the squalor she was living in before I had them rescue her! It was awful, James. A filthy, ramshackle hut not fit for a dog!"

"I understand that, Edmund. Of course I do, but going from that to living like this. Having her every need taken care of. You must understand how that might be difficult for her to comprehend?"

"Yes, of course." He smiles ruefully at me. "Gently, you say?"

"Start by just talking with her. Not about her past or the last few months. Just talking. Perhaps go for some walks, spend time with her. I appreciate this must be difficult. But, if you take things slowly, I feel it will really help Lady Sophia. Help you both."

He studies me carefully before heading over to the window, gazing out across the gardens.

"Well, James," he says eventually, turning to face me with a broad smile upon his face. "You always have been the master of your profession."

I look at him in confusion. "I don't …?"

He gestures towards me to join him at the window which I do, still confused by what he means. Then I see Sophia, clutching tight to Annalise's arm as they walk the frost covered gardens, wrapped up warm in cloaks, conversing with one another.

I am amazed by her resilience. And I realise at the sight of her, that I must at least try to do what she has asked of me. For I know how much bravery it must have taken to even find the strength to leave her bed.

"I wish to see her." Edmund's voice filters into my brain as I watch her and I turn to face him. "Will you ask her if she will meet with me?"

There is a sense of hope in his eyes which brings an uneasy feeling to my stomach as I tell him that I will speak with her and arrange a meeting for tomorrow.

Sophia

I knew it had to happen. But the moment James came to tell me that Edmund wished to meet, it sent a bolt of cold fear into my heart that I haven't been able to shake since. Annalise helped me to dress for the meeting. I chose a soft pink skirt and white blouse, not wanting to feel as though I couldn't breathe through a corset when breathing was already proving difficult. I sat as she twisted my hair up, securing it with pins, letting a few strands of it hang loose to frame my face. Then we waited. Waited for the moment I would see him again for the first time since he brought my whole world crashing down around me.

"Are you alright, my Lady?"

I turn to Annalise who is looking at me carefully. I shake my head. "No. I'm frightened ..."

I hate admitting it, but it's true. And as the tears begin burning up in me, my throat tight with them, I feel her hand take mine and squeeze it tightly. A gesture I was not expecting but one that is so welcome at this moment.

Then I hear a knock at the door and she suddenly drops my hand.

I can see the fear in her eyes which must mirror in my own, as I silently ask her to get the door. My hands are shaking. I didn't realise how much he scared me. And at this moment I honestly do not know if I can put up the pretence of civility towards him, let alone love.

As I hear footsteps entering the room, I take a shaky breath, relieved that it is James that I see first, knowing that I am safe with him here. Then I see Edmund walk in. The look on his face is one of relief, even of emotion. Yet it doesn't reach his eyes. They still remain dark, cold and menacing.

He told me that he would wait for me to love him. And here I am giving exactly what he wants, or so he thinks. To him he has won.

"Your Majesty." I curtsey to him. I haven't set eyes on him in over a month so formality seems the best option. He smiles at me as he walks forward and I ignore all of the impulses in my body to move away from him. He takes my hand in his, his skin cold to the touch as he brings it to his lips, placing a kiss upon it.

"There is no need for that, Sophia."

His voice is gentle, which sounds strange to my ear, and I know that this is all an act for James' sake but at least that means he isn't hurting me. I want to believe that now he thinks he is getting what he wants that the hurt will stop completely. But I am not a fool.

"Sorry. It is just all new to me. I'm still getting better, Edmund. It will take a little time."

"Of course." He nods in understanding. "James has explained everything to me. And I want to make sure that you feel comfortable here. And that in time, we may get to know each other once more. To begin again."

I'm forcing myself to smile, to nod in agreement.

His hand still holds onto mine, tightly, as if telling me silently that now he has me he is never letting me go and that frightens me more than anything.

"I've advised Edmund that he must take things very slowly with you." James' voice drifts over like a gentle breeze, calming me. "Taking things too quickly may cause you to become unwell again, and we do not want that."

"Absolutely not." Edmund shakes his head. "Not now that you look so well."

I look across at James, seeking reassurance which he gives me with a soft smile.

He knows how difficult this is for me.

Yet I know it is the only way I will be able to see Tom, even just one more time.

"James explained why I may have felt like I did," I begin, making myself look Edmund in the eyes, knowing that he will sense deception in an instant. "He told me that I was confusing my past and my present situations. Blaming you for what happened when you did nothing wrong." I feel sick with myself as I see him grinning at me, loving every moment of his victory. "He told me that I am safe here, with you. That nobody will hurt me anymore."

"It broke my heart to think that you blamed me for all of the things he did to you." He says it suddenly, looking at me with such despair that I can understand why to everyone else he is so well adored. He plays his part to perfection. I swallow down my revulsion, my sense of betrayal, knowing that this is all a part I must play too.

"I'm sorry, Edmund," I whisper, tears filling my eyes; tears which he need not know are not for him. "My mind was so confused because of what happened to me. What he did. Forgive me."

He edges closer to me. So close that I can feel his breath on my cheek as he wipes my tears away.

"I forgive you."

He looks at me for a moment as if he is going to kiss me, before thinking better of it. Instead he takes hold of my hands in his once more. "I do not want to dwell on the past any longer, Sophia. What is done is done. You are safe now. Let us start rebuilding a life together. The life you deserve."

I nod, my throat constricted with painful tears which will not allow me to speak. I don't even know what I would say if I could.

"I was wondering if you would like to accompany me on a walk of the gardens?" Edmund speaks again, realising that I am unable to. "I saw that you took a walk with your maid yesterday and wondered if that would be something you would enjoy?"

He's looking at me eagerly and I once again look to James for reassurance before I speak. A walk is a better option than most. And being around nature gives me some sense of home. Swallowing down my tears I manage a small smile as I turn back to Edmund and tell him that I would love to.

The next few days felt like a lifetime. Daily walks and dinners with Edmund who barely left my side when I was not in my chambers.

James accompanied us on some of the walks which was the only time I felt truly safe. The rest of the time when I was left alone with him I spent the full time frightened by what he might do or that my act was not enough to keep my true feelings at bay.

As the days had gone on, when James wasn't around, Edmund had begun his attempts to get closer to me. Slowly enough to keep his promise to James but enough to make my skin crawl every time he held my hand or kissed my cheek.

He had agreed for James to undertake his tour of the universities as planned, which wasn't a surprise to me. With James gone he would have nobody to keep up this act of chivalry to. And I would have no-one to make sure that he was sticking to his word. But I made a promise to myself to be brave, to carry on this charade knowing that James would eventually make his way to Lowshore and hopefully to find Tom.

Today has been particularly challenging. James left early this morning, leaving me to the mercy of Edmund without the protection of his presence.

And as much as I wanted him to go, the moment that he left it felt like my walls of defence had crumbled.

Edmund became more physical almost the moment that James left, his eyes leering over my body, his hand resting too long against my leg as we sat in the gardens, his breath hot against my cheek as he lingered with kisses, which I didn't want. Eventually, I managed to free myself from his grasp at the insistence that I felt tired and needed to rest. He walks me back into the Palace and I rush to my chamber the minute I leave his sight. As I burst through the door of my bedchamber, I am relieved to see that Annalise is here and the moment I see her I can hold my emotion back no longer.

"I can't do this." I shake my head tearfully as I walk into the room, Annalise hurriedly closing the door behind me before walking over to sit next to me on the bed. "He makes me feel sick every time he touches me," I whisper, as I look up at her.

"The sound of his voice makes my skin crawl. I can't keep up the pretence. I can't." As I break down again I feel Annalise grasp hold of my hand, squeezing it tightly.

"Tell me about Tom."

As she says his name I look up at her in confusion. "Tom?" I sniff, and she nods, smiling.

"I want to know about 'im," she says, softly. "Think of 'im. Tell me what he's like."

I swallow down the lump in my throat, closing my eyes, trying to remember the images of him that are fading fast. I remember the grin on his face when I would catch him looking at me, when he thought I wouldn't notice.

I remember the way he would sweep the hair back from my face when he kissed me, his delicate hands resting amongst the curls. I remember the smell of his skin, earthy and woody from his time spent in the forest. I remember his eyes most of all. The colour of woodland Forget-Me-Nots, eyes that were once so full of despair before love made them sparkle again.

"His mother died in childbirth," I say eventually, wanting to start from the very beginning. "He never knew her. And his father sold him to the workhouse at eight years old, to pay off his gambling debts. He's never had a proper home. That is what always amazed me about him. How someone who grew up with no love, no care, no support. Someone who suffered such cruelty at the hands of those who were supposed to love them. How someone like that could still be so kind. So gentle. So full of love. Whereas someone like Edmund, who had the life and childhood most people can only dream of, has always had such cruelty in his soul."

Annalise doesn't speak, she just sits still, watching me, waiting for me to continue.

"He's older than me. And I didn't fall in love with him the first time I met him. He's handsome, though he's the complete opposite of Edmund. The complete opposite of everything I was taught to believe I should fall in love with. But, the first time I met him, all I could see was how lost he looked. I had never seen anyone look so tired, so ready to give up. I wasn't afraid of him. I could tell instantly that there was no cruelty or evil in him. I knew he had a kind soul. I talked with him for a while. Found out that he had a trade but that he couldn't find employment with anyone, due to his past. I made the decision to ask him to come and do some jobs at the cottage."

I laugh, shaking my head. "If anyone would have told me that I would end up falling in love with him, I would have told them that they were ridiculous. But love is a funny thing, isn't it? I realised that he had saved me as much as I had saved him. He made me feel safe. He didn't expect me to be anyone other than I was. He loved me for who I was, not who he wanted me to be. And when he proposed under the stars one evening a few months later, I didn't think twice about saying yes."

As I look across at Annalise, I see she is smiling now. And I realise that I am smiling too. Talking about him is making me feel safe again. As though his arms are around me, cocooning me, shielding me from the world.

"Our village was only small," I continue. "And as people got to know Tom, they learned to trust him. We made friends, we were happy. And on our wedding day, we made our way down to the small church, just us and a few trusted friends, and we made our vows to one another. The sun was shining so brightly, the meadow was in full bloom and we ate and drank and danced until the sun came up. I had never felt happier. We didn't need anyone else. Just us, our little cottage and our animals. We made enough money to keep the roof over our heads. We lived simply. I imagined us growing old there. Raising our children there, watching them grow..."

Suddenly, the safe, warm feeling vanishes. Even if James manages to find Tom, there is no way we could ever escape

Edmund's clutches. No way we could ever go back to that simple, happy life.

"I miss him," I choke, as Annalise places a hand to my shoulder. "I miss home. I miss it so much."

As I fall into silent tears once more, I feel Annalise wrap her arms around me. A girl no older than sixteen sitting here comforting me, holding me like a mother would her child, soothing me as I cry into her shoulder, grieving for all that I have lost, the life I will never get back.

"I know it's tough, my Lady." I hear Annalise whisper into my hair. "But you need to try and be strong. You've already 'ad to be so strong, I know. But if you give up now then he has won. You might feel that he 'as already won, but if you give up then he 'as for sure. But if you keep fightin' ... there is always a chance. No matter how small a spark to hold onto."

I look up at her through clouded eyes. "How are you so wise?" I say, shaking my head, "Someone so young ..."

"I 'ad to grow up fast, my Lady," she replies, but doesn't expand any further and I do not wish to pry.

"I am glad you are here," I say, brushing the remaining tears from my eyes. "I feel like myself when I am around you."

She smiles at me, placing her hand on top of mine for a moment before getting to her feet. "I'll draw you a bath, my Lady."

I want to tell her again to please call me Sophia, but I know that she will not. So instead, I nod, grateful for her suggestion of something which she knows will calm my mind and settle me so that I start to feel like myself once more.

As the weeks go on, I begin a routine. A routine which helps me to cope with what I must do. For every moment that I must spend with Edmund, each time becoming more and more difficult, I tell myself that when it is over I can return to the safety of my chambers, where Annalise and I spend the time doing things that take my mind from where I am; make me feel like myself again.

"Where do you think James is now?" I ask, as we sit on the floor, looking at a map I took from Edmund's study when he wasn't looking. He has hundreds of them so I doubt he will miss one. Annalise has brought some food up from the kitchens for us both to share. Simple food which is served in the servants quarters. Peasant food Edmund would call it. But it's the best thing I've ever tasted because it tastes of home.

My hand traces the map, starting at the top of the Shorelands, at Highshore which was James' first point of call.

"He said he would visit Highshore first," I tell Annalise, pointing at the highest point of our land which juts out and meets the sea. "Then make his way down through Redshore, Clayshore and Evershore."

My finger is following the route which he told us, following the East coast of our land to visit the five main medical schools which are based here. People travel from far and wide to study medicine in the Shorelands, because it is known for having the best physicians; the best teachers; the best facilities. As my finger reaches the word Lowshore, I rest it there.

My town is the final stop on his tour. Meaning that though my wait is long and arduous, at least it means that if and when he finds Tom, his next step in his journey is back here to the Capital.

"It must be nice to visit other places." Annalise's voice drifts into my thoughts and as I look across at her I see she is focusing intently on the map. "I've never stepped foot out of the Capital."

"You were born here?" I'm intrigued.

She nods. "My mother was a servant 'ere at the palace for King Alfred."

"And your father?" The instant I see the look on her face, I regret my question. "I'm sorry Annalise, forgive me, I shouldn't pry."

"I'm told 'e was one of the King's courtiers," she says, quietly, not looking at me. "People tell me that 'e took a fancying to my mother, but she wasn't interested."

She stops, briefly, her gaze still focused intently on the map, as if breaking her gaze would mean that her composure would break too. "'E wouldn't take no for an answer. Got 'imself drunk one night and came down to the servants quarters."

I don't need her to tell me what happened next.

My heart is aching, both for Annalise and her mother, a woman I never knew but I am aware that a woman's fate is sealed far too easily.

"When they found out she was pregnant, they sent 'er away," she continues, still unable to look at me. "King Alfred was a kind man though. Made sure she was looked after at a convent. When I was born, he sent for me to be brought back 'ere. They couldn't risk an illegitimate child of a member of high society runnin' round. The King was furious with the courtier. Banished 'im from Court. I was brought up 'ere by the other maids, then given a job when I turned twelve."

"And your mother?" I ask, though I am not sure I want to hear the answer.

She smiles sadly at me. "Never saw her again. Don't even know what she looks like. Don't remember her at all. King Alfred said that she stayed at the convent. I don't even know if she's still alive …"

"Annalise, I'm sorry …" I don't know what else to say. Nothing would be enough. Annalise finally turns away from the map and faces me.

She's smiling sadly. "Nothin' to be sorry for, my Lady," she replies. "I've never known any different. When I was told the story it was as if they were tellin' me about someone else. This is the only life I've known."

She looks back down at the map and I take hold of her hand gently.

"Well, one day I'm going to take you away from here," I say, knowing that it is impossible but imagining it is the only thing that keeps me going. "I'll take you to the secret beach in Lowshore. It's the most beautiful place, Annalise. Soft white sand and blue seas for as far as the eye can see."

She's staring at me, her eyes wide with wonder and excitement. Even if it is just a dream, it is something to hold on to. I'm about to suggest that we put the map away, perhaps get out the playing cards for a while when there is a knock at the door.

My heart is beating fast in my chest with panic, as I tell Annalise to hide the map and get the door. I don't understand who it could be, yet I fear that I know. And the fact that he has come here, to my chambers, scares me more than anything. I see the look of fear on Annalise's face, as she returns to the room followed by Edmund who wears a broad smile upon his face. Seeing him here, in my sanctuary, the only place I feel completely safe, makes me feel sick.

"Edmund," I say, somehow managing to smile. "What are you doing here?"

He walks up to me, taking hold of my hand in his. "I wanted to see you, my darling."

"We took our walk this morning," I say, somehow managing to keep my voice sounding cheerful. "It was lovely."

"Yes, it was …" He squeezes my hand tighter and I have to force myself not to flinch, "but we have been meeting for weeks now. Building our relationship. Surely it is time that we started meeting more than once a day?" He laughs as he says it, as if it is the most obvious thing in the world.

I swallow. "Edmund, please," I say, warily. "I am still healing. James said we must take things slowly."

"How much slower can we take things Sophia?!" he bellows, making both me and Annalise jump, before he seems to jolt back into his perfect act, taking a breath and calming himself before speaking again. "Forgive me, Sophia, I should not have shouted, that was wrong of me. But I am your husband. I just want us to live a normal life."

"And we will. I promise you." I nod, wanting to calm the situation down. " We will."

He is silent for a few moments. His hand traces patterns against mine, his skin rough to touch making me feel sick. Then he turns to Annalise. "Would you leave us for a while, Miss?" he says, politely, smiling sweetly at her. "Perhaps go down to the servants' quarters, see if there are any jobs which you can help with?"

She looks at me in panic. I don't want her to go, but I do not want to displease Edmund any further so I nod my head, telling her that it is alright. She hesitates for a moment still, before curtseying to us both and leaving the room.

"Edmund…"

He places a finger to my lips, silencing me. My whole body is frozen in fear.

"I love you, Sophia," he whispers, his voice making my skin crawl. The way his eyes leer over my body, his hands that linger far too long. He moves in to kiss me and I force myself to let him, smelling the liquor on his breath, hoping that he will take this and leave me alone.

But the kisses continue and before I know it, his hands are unlacing the front of my dress.

"No, Edmund." I shake my head, trying to push him away from me, but he persists. His hands making their way up my skirts, his touch cold against my skin until I cannot bear it any longer and push him away from me. He stares at me, his eyes still dancing with the passion I stopped him from getting.

"Sophia, you need to trust me. I will not hurt you."

"I just … I don't think I'm ready yet, Edmund," I say, and I hear the shake in my voice. "Not for this. It's too soon."

"I have done as James asked, Sophia. I have been taking things slowly for weeks now."

"Yes." I nod, not wanting to displease him, not wanting to give him any reason to suspect anything. "Yes, you have. And I have loved spending more time with you. Getting to know you. I just don't think I'm ready for this …"

"You are just scared," he soothes. "But you need not be scared. You are my wife, Sophia. We must consummate our marriage. Make good our vows to one another."

He starts kissing me again and I am too scared to do anything to stop him. I cannot let him see through the act I am putting on in the hope that it will allow me just one more moment with Tom. To say sorry. To say goodbye. But I do not want this. And I have to bite down on my lip, to stop myself from screaming at him to stop.

Afterwards, I sit on the edge of the bed. Numb. Edmund finished and left with barely another word to me. I am just his possession and he needed to let me know that. There was no love there. I want to cry, but the tears will not come. As Annalise enters the room, I see the shock on her face as she takes in the sight of me with my dress still unlaced, grasped together by my hand to try and maintain some part of my dignity.

"My Lady?" She speaks warily, as she walks up to me and comes to stand beside me.

"I need to bathe." I whisper it, unable to look at her, and I see her curtsey before walking off into the next room to prepare a bath. When it was drawn, she came to get me but I asked her to leave me alone which she didn't want to, but agreed to in the end.

I walk into the bathroom, closing the door behind me before letting my dress fall to the ground. I step cautiously into the warm water, letting it immerse my body, washing away the sweat, the smell of him, the feeling of his skin against mine. And then the tears begin to fall.

For the first time, I feel as though I have betrayed the man I love. I fought like crazy not to marry Edmund, only giving in when he left me no other choice. But this? I didn't fight back. I let him take my body which is worse than him taking my name. A marriage on paper alone, isn't a marriage. But now that I have given myself to him, I belong to him.

And he knows that. For the first time, I find myself hoping that James will not find Tom. Because I do not think I can bear for him to know what I have done. What has been made of me. It would be better for us both.

JAMES

By the time I reached Lowshore, the tour was taking its toll on me. Weeks of travel from place to place, giving talks, taking classes, conversing with my university fellows means that my mind is as exhausted as my body; with my biggest test yet to come. I cannot help my thoughts from wandering back to the Capital and to Sophia; hoping that she is continuing to be strong enough to keep up this act with Edmund. The fact that I have not received a summons asking me to return, is giving me some sort of hope.

It is late now, the streetlamps are blazing orange, illuminating the dusty pathways of this quaint little farming village. I know that I should really locate my lodgings and retire for the evening. However, my attention is caught by the noise of a sign creaking in the cold wind and as I look up I see that it reads 'The Travellers Meet'; a painting of two men on horseback accompanying it.

Remembering what Edmund mentioned about this Tom's alleged drinking habits and the fact that I have little else to go on makes me decide that this would be as good a place as any to start.

And knowing how important this is to Sophia, means that I push my thoughts of going to bed to the back of my mind as I make my way through the swinging doors of the tavern.

The warmth from the open fire in the corner, which hits me as I walk in, is a welcome relief from the cold. The unfamiliar smell of ale and tobacco hits my nostrils as I take in the well-kept and clearly well used room, which houses dark wood tables at which groups of men sit and converse underneath the glow of the lamps upon the walls. The dark oak bar is set with stools all of which are taken by various men drinking alone in silent thought for the most part, aside from occasionally lifting their heads from their glasses to talk amiably with the barkeep when he speaks to them.

The barkeep is a thin man in his late sixties, dressed modestly in a loose-fitting shirt and waistcoat. His cropped steel grey hair matches his eyes and as I walk towards him, they fix onto me warily.

"I'm looking for Tom Thornton," I say quietly, as I reach the bar. "Would you know where I could find him?"

He studies me as he wipes down the bar, taking in my appearance which stands out a mile amongst the other men in here, drinking after a long day at work, their clothes covered in the dirt and sweat of their trade.

In comparison, my starched shirt and velvet frock coat give away my class and usual surroundings and the fact that I am very much an outsider here. Eventually he cocks his head to the left.

"He's over there," he says, carefully. "Though I'm not sure it's wise. He's been here since we opened. And as usual, he's had a bit too much to drink."

I look over in the direction which he indicated.

I see a man with fair hair slouched over the bar, clasping a glass full of an amber liquid with both hands, seemingly oblivious to anything and anyone around him.

"You're not here to cause trouble for him are you?" The barkeep asks, concern in his eyes. "He's been through a lot. He's not a bad lad. He just gets himself involved in things he shouldn't sometimes."

As if on cue, the man at the far end of the bar who I can now confirm is Tom Thornton bangs his empty glass down. "Jack," he says to the barkeep, his words slurred. "Get me another drink."

With a sigh, Jack walks over to where Tom sits. I follow, but keep at a distance, observing their conversation.

"You've had enough, Tom," he says, calmly but firmly. "Time you got off home."

Tom straightens up in his chair and looks straight at Jack. His blue eyes flash with annoyance. "I don't want to go home. I want another drink. You're the barkeep and I'm your customer. Give me a damn drink!"

"No …"

Tom jumps up from his seat with such ferocity that it flies across the bar, stopping people mid-conversation, as they turn to look at him. He grabs Jack by the collar with one arm, his other fist curled. Jack grabs hold of the arm almost holding him aloft and looks Tom in the eye.

"You don't want to do this, son," he says, gently. "Go on home. Sleep it off." He keeps looking at him, his eyes calm, his voice measured and I can tell that this isn't the first time he has had to do this.

After a few moments, Tom releases his grasp on Jack's collar and stumbles back, dragging his hands through his hair.

The other customers stay at a wary distance, watching it all unfold.

"Sorry," he mumbles to Jack. "I didn't mean …"

"I know, son," he says, softly. "It's alright. Get yourself home."

Tom pauses for a second as if to get his bearings, before grabbing his coat and walking out of the door. As it swings shut behind him, the customers start talking animatedly between themselves again and from snippets of conversation I hear, I add to my earlier reasoning that Tom's actions tonight were not a one-off. I look over at Jack, who has gone back to clearing the bar.

"I'll make sure he is alright." I take hold of my bag and he looks at me with the same wary expression as before. "I'm a doctor," I explain. "I'm not here to cause him any trouble, I promise you. I'm hoping I can help him."

He looks at me as though he is still not fully convinced of my intentions but nods and I make my way out of the tavern, following Tom down the dusty, lamp-lit streets towards an old farmhouse, where he stops.

I watch him struggle to get the key into the lock for a few moments before he manages it, stumbling through the door and slamming it shut behind him. Looking at the farmhouse, I can see that it was once a beautiful, well-kept home. Now it has fallen into deep disrepair. The thatched roof has numerous holes. The gate leading to the house lies broken off its hinges.

The only thing that looks remotely cared for is the farmland itself. The paddock and the chicken coop look perfectly intact as do the pigsty and the small barn from where I can hear the grunts, crows and bleats of various animals.

Taking a deep breath I make my way up to the farmhouse door still trying to figure out in my mind what I am going to say to him. Or, if I will even manage to say a word before he hits me. I knock at the door and hear a dog bark. After a few moments it opens. As I look at Tom's face in the firelight of the room, I see that his left eye is swollen and sporting a bruise which looks a few days old. Various other cuts and bruises adorn his face and hands. He looks at me, taking in my appearance from head to foot.

"Listen," he says, shaking his head, his voice slurred. "I don't know who you are but whatever it is, I'm not interested."

"My name is James Collins," I try, regardless. "I am a doctor. A medical doctor. I saw you in the tavern and I couldn't help but notice that you appear to have some injuries. I wanted to offer my help."

He scoffs, rolling his eyes. "Thank you for your concern, but I am fine. Now, if you'll excuse me." He goes to shut the door but I push my hand against it, standing firm much to my own amazement.

"That looks nasty." I observe, gesturing to a particularly deep wound on his cheek. "It would be against my moral principles not to help. I cannot just walk away, sir. Please ..."

He stares at me for a few moments. His face doesn't betray anything of what he is thinking. Finally, he sighs. "You professionals and your bloody moral principles," he mumbles. "Fine. But only so you will shut up and I can get out of this cold weather and back inside to my drink."

He walks back inside and I follow. A low growl sounds from the corner of the room and I look over to see a large dog with pale, wiry fur and orange eyes laying down near the open fire. I swallow nervously.

I have never been particularly confident around dogs, or animals in general. And this one does not sound particularly pleased to have a stranger in its home. But, as Tom goes over to sit down in the chair nearest to it, he strokes its head and it starts to calm.

"No, Amos," he says, softly. "Lie back down, boy. That's it."

The dog goes to lie down at his master's command, though it still eyes me warily. It slumps to the ground uncomfortably and I realise that this is the same dog which tried to protect Sophia when she was kidnapped.

Tom hasn't acknowledged me any further since allowing me inside. He just sits, staring into the fire, one hand still stroking Amos' fur, the other clasped around a glass of mead which he keeps bringing to his lips to take sips of.

I watch him, sadly. I very much doubt that the Tom I see here, drinking himself to sleep, getting himself into fights, is the Tom that Sophia fell in love with. The one she begged me to bring back to her. But a niggling part of my brain cannot help but think of how Edmund described the man that Sophia had found herself with. The cruel, drunken bully. Is this him? Is there a part of what Edmund is saying that is the truth?

I cannot fathom the man sitting in front of me at this moment, and it frustrates me.

"I see that look a lot." He speaks for the first time since our conversation at the doorway, taking me from my thoughts as he looks over at me, his blue eyes piercing even in the low light of the room. "That disappointed, disapproving look," he continues, bringing the glass to his lips again. "I drink because it stops me thinking. I think too much. My brain doesn't switch off. Drinking gives me oblivion. If only for a few hours." He rubs at his grazed knuckles as he stares into the fire.

"And the fighting?"

He looks over at me as I ask the question. "I fight because I like it."

I shake my head. "Really? That doesn't sound like the Tom some people have told me about."

73

"Then I don't know who you have been speaking to," he scoffs. "The whole damn village knows who I am and what I'm like." He stops, looking down at his hands again, then clasping them together in his lap.

I'm trying to work him out, trying to see beyond the facade I feel he is putting on.

"You want to know why I fight, really?" He looks up at me. He looks tired. I nod. "I fight because I like the pain. I like the ache in my hands after I've punched someone. I like the throbbing in my ribs with every kick I take and the stinging in my lip when someone splits it open. I like it because it takes over the pain that the thoughts in my head bring me. The pain that I cannot bear." He stops, suddenly, shaking his head. "Why the hell am I telling you all of this?" he says. "Why the hell are you even here? I've had enough sympathy for one night. I don't need your counsel. I just need you to leave me alone."

"Sophia," I say, softly, making my decision. "I'm here because of Sophia."

At the sound of her name, his face pales as though he's seen a ghost. "I don't understand."

"I'm here because Sophia asked me to come and find you," I begin, but break off as he laughs, shaking his head.

"You're lying." He growls. "Or is this some sort of sick joke? Did they put you up to it at the tavern? Trying to make a fool of me?"

I see the same flash of anger in his eyes that I saw in the tavern when he squared up to Jack.

As he stands up, I get to my feet as well, as does Amos, standing by his master's side, his teeth bared.

"Sophia Thornton," I say, gently, adopting the barkeep's technique. "Red hair. Green eyes. Silver wedding band studded with a single emerald and your initials engraved on either side."

He's looking at me in disbelief. His fingers are twisting at the ring I've only just noticed on his left hand. When he moves his hand away, I see the glint of an emerald he was keeping hidden.

"There is no way you could possibly know that," he says, shaking his head, his eyes still suspecting, "who are you?"

I see him glance at his bag which lays open on the floor, about eight axes glinting menacingly from within it.

"A friend," I say, calmly. "A friend of Sophia's and a friend of yours if you will let me."

"None of this makes any sense!" He turns and walks away from me, throwing his hands through his hair in frustration.

I try again, calmly. "How much did Sophia tell you about her past?"

As he turns back towards me he looks at me in confusion. "Her past? Nothing. I knew she had one. I knew she wasn't from these parts originally, but she never wanted to talk about it, so I didn't pry. We all have a past. Some of us want to keep it hidden. I get that more than most." He breaks off and looks at me, his eyes pained. "Please can you just tell me what this is about?"

I go to sit down again, gesturing for him to do the same. I think this is a conversation he should sit down for.

"Sophia was born in the Capital. She was an only child. She grew up in the shadow of finery and royalty, and endless possibilities to make her life better. But, she didn't want any of that. And she chose to run away, ten years ago. She ran away because the life she didn't want was about to be forced upon her. Her parents had promised her to someone and she had no choice in the matter."

His eyes narrow in confusion. "Promised? You mean like some sort of arranged marriage?"

I smile ruefully. "It's a bit more complicated than that. Sophia was promised to King Edmund."

He's staring at me. I don't know what I can say so I stay silent and let him take it in.

Then suddenly he starts to laugh, taking me by complete surprise. The laughter explodes from him, his face creasing with it, his breaths gasping until he calms himself down.

"You know, I thought maybe it was a bad childhood," he says eventually, wiping his eyes, "an abusive relationship perhaps. Only Sophia could go and get herself noticed by the bloody King!" He shakes his head, still laughing to himself, until the reality of what I am saying seems to hit him like a ton of bricks, and he looks at me with haunted eyes. "Are you saying what I think you are?" he says, his voice hollow, "you are telling me that he has taken her?"

He knows the answer without me having to say or do anything. Swallowing, he turns back towards the fire, his eyes focusing intently on the flames.

"She was so happy that day," he says, his voice choked, as Amos limps back over to his side and collapses down next to him. He strokes him as he carries on talking. "I remember her face, like it was yesterday. She was laughing and her eyes would come alive whenever she laughed. They were vivid that morning. I kissed her goodbye and walked outside. The sun was shining, there were no clouds in the sky. Everything was so perfect. I had ridden for about ten minutes before I realised I had left my good axe at home."

He reaches down into his bag and pulls out the smallest axe of the lot. The silver blade glints in the firelight as he holds it up. "Doesn't look like much but it's the best axe I've ever owned. I was going to head back, but I thought that by the time I rode back, got teased mercilessly by Sophia then set off again, I would have lost a good forty minutes. And it was such a nice day that I thought if I could get finished quicker, we would be able to enjoy more of the evening together." He stops, burying his head in his hands. "I should have gone back. Maybe I could have stopped them, stopped any of this from happening. The axe was on the floor when I got back. She must have tried to defend herself."

He hunches over, fists clenched, his knuckles turning white with the effort. The dog whines as if he knows and Tom looks up at him. "When I saw Amos, I knew something bad must've happened. Something he had tried to protect her from. He was lying in a pool of blood and Sophia was nowhere to be seen. I went to the police. I told them what had happened. I begged them to search for her but they barely searched the village before giving up. They didn't believe me. They told me to give it up. They said that women leave their husbands all the time and I just had to accept it."

I'm looking at him as he comes to the same realisation as me.

"Of course," he laughs, "It makes sense now. They are all in his pocket."

I look down, sadly. "I'm sorry Tom."

"What for? It's not your fault. You're just the messenger."

We sit in silence for a few moments. Tom's hand rests atop of Amos' head. As I look at him, I see that he couldn't be more different from Edmund. A product of his upbringing, Edmund was every inch the polished prince, dark haired and handsome, with eyes so brown they almost look black in a certain light. All of the girls of the kingdom were determined to be noticed by him. Tom was older than both Sophia and Edmund, by a few years for sure. Unkempt and unshaven right now but by no means any less handsome than Edmund, his light brown hair and blue eyes put him in stark contrast to the King.

If Edmund were a polished ruby like the ones adorning his crest, Tom was a diamond in the rough.

And I can instantly see why Sophia, always so different to all of the other girls her age, would fall in love with this man and this lifestyle.

I could see that they would have been happy here. I could imagine that happy girl again, the one whose eyes had since lost all of the life and sparkle which Tom talked about. And I curse Edmund for still being that same spoilt, stubborn child that I tried to tame all of those years ago. For taking away her happiness and ruining the lives of two people who had never done anything to deserve it.

"I need to sort some things," he says, suddenly, and I look at him. "I'll talk to Jack first thing tomorrow. See if he'll take care of Amos and look after the farm ... that's if he's still talking to me."

"Tom ..."

"I need to apologise anyway. I just hope he'll help or else I don't know."

"Tom." As I interrupt him again he finally looks at me. I feel the guilt eating away at me as I work out how I am going to say what I need to tell him. "You cannot come back with me." He looks at me curiously, a bemused grin appearing on his face.

"What?"

"It's not as simple as travelling to the Capital and taking her back. I know King Edmund. He is a dangerous man."

"He's taken my wife prisoner! Did you really just expect me to sit here and ..." He stops, taking in the look on my face.

"There's something you're not telling me."

"Tom ..."

"Tell me!"

"He married her." I don't know how else to say it so I just come out with it. Tom looks baffled.

"What? What are you talking about? He can't. She's already married. We have papers, the church has records."

"I do not know for certain but I would guess that he has already had any official records destroyed. Your papers would mean nothing if that is the case. He would dismiss them as forgery."

"He can't do that." He shakes his head and I smile, sadly.

"He's the leader of the Kingdom. He sees it that he can do exactly as he wishes."

He's staring at me, and I can see the hope draining from his eyes by the second.

"She wouldn't," he says, suddenly, his voice ringing with conviction. "She wouldn't do it. I know she wouldn't."

I swallow, closing my eyes as I remember the state of Sophia's arm and how she told me it happened.

"I don't think he gave her much choice."

As he looks at me I see the shake in his jaw, the pain in his eyes, his fists clenched by his sides. "I'll kill him."

"And this is exactly why you cannot come to the Capital!" I shake my head, my voice raised for the first time, "this isn't some drunken thug in the street that you can brawl with and win. This is the King! He won't fight you, you wouldn't get the chance. He would arrest you and torture you and kill you without a second thought."

"So why are you here?" he roars back, taking me by surprise. "Why are you here putting me through this fresh hell if there is nothing I can do? She is my wife. She is the only person I have ever loved and you are here telling me that I've lost her? That she's scared and hurting and there is nothing I can do about it?"

"I ..." I stumble over my own thoughts. I don't know what to say. The truth is that I didn't know what I would do if I found him. Maybe deep down I was wishing I wouldn't find him at all. "She begged me to come and find you," I manage, eventually. "And she was hurting so much and all I wanted to do was make her better. That's what I'm supposed to do. I'm supposed to make people feel better. So I agreed. But I suppose I was hoping that I wouldn't find you. Hoping that you had moved on so that I could try to help her to close this chapter of her life, no matter how tough, and find a way to survive. Because he won't let her go, Tom. He won't. And I'm sorry. I wish there was more I could do."

"Please ..." His voice is breaking with tears and as I look up at him I see he is struggling to hold himself together. "I'd rather die trying to get her back then live like this," he chokes. "I can't do this anymore. Not now. Not now that I know."

I curse myself as I watch this grown man break down in tears. All I have done is managed to make things worse. I see the whiskey bottle on the side dresser. Pouring us two glasses, I tip the contents of a sleeping draught into one of them before walking over and taking the seat opposite him.

"I'll go to the church." He sniffs, attempting to get himself up from the chair, Amos watching him carefully. "I need to see the records. They must be there. I need to see them."

I place a hand to his shoulder, easily managing to guide him back down into the seat. "It's late, Tom," I say, gently. "And you've had a lot to drink. Sleep it off. We can go to the church tomorrow."

"I can't sleep." He shakes his head, "I can't."

I hand him one of the glasses. "Have this. A nightcap. As a doctor, I probably shouldn't be advising alcohol but after the amount you've already drunk I cannot see how one more will do any harm."

I look at him closely as I down mine and he does the same. The effect of the sleeping draught is almost instantaneous and I watch his head loll forwards as he falls into sleep. I hear Amos whine and I'm momentarily panicked at the fact he might attack me for hurting his master but he seems to understand that it's help, not harm that I am bringing him.

As he settles again by Tom's feet, I find a blanket and lay it across him before deciding what I am going to do until morning. I sit for a while, listening to the crackling of the fire as it starts to die down until my curiosity starts to get the better of me and I decide to take a look around. Amos opens an eye and looks at me as I stand but he doesn't move from Tom's side as he continues to sleep soundly.

The farmhouse is small and homely but as I venture into the bedroom I see that it is a room that has been left untouched for a long time. The bed is perfectly made and I note, with sadness, a women's nightdress folded neatly on top of one of the pillows. The nightstand holds a few items and I move closer to inspect them. The thing that stands out amongst everything else is a black and white photograph in a silver oval frame. The sight of it cements the thing in my mind that I knew deep down all along, as on closer inspection the photograph is from their wedding day.

They stand in front of a cornflower field and I recognise the happy, carefree Sophia that I used to know as she stands staring up at Tom, her eyes alive with joy, her arms wrapped around his waist. Tom doesn't look like the man I met moments ago. His eyes aren't full of pain and hopelessness. He is peaceful, content and happy as he looks at his new wife like she is the only person in the world, his hands resting protectively against her back.

I place it back down on the nightstand with a sigh.

The other items resting upon it are all tiny wooden carvings, beautifully whittled into birds and flowers and woodland creatures. I don't need to be told that it was Tom who made these for Sophia. And it's obvious to me now that Edmund did indeed travel down that dangerous road that I feared he would when he was a young boy. And that everything he had told me since my arrival in the Capital has been a lie.

TOM

As I wake from my sleep which I don't remember falling into, the embers of the fire are giving off the last of their heat. Amos lays at my feet and there is a blanket across my lap which I don't recall putting there. My cheek which was split open in a fight a couple of days ago feels odd, tight and stinging but not with the same pain I've felt up until now. In curiosity, I place a hand to it, noting that it is no longer crusted with dried blood. Now it feels clean, and smaller somehow.

"I treated it whilst you were sleeping."

I jump as I hear a voice from the stove and look to see a man standing there. Vague recollections start swirling around in my mind as he walks over to me carrying two cups of tea which he sets down on the table. As he takes a seat opposite me, the memories of yesterday come flooding back. Part of me wished it were a nightmare. At least then I could wake up from it. But it isn't. After all of these months I finally have my answer. And it is worse than anything I could have imagined.

"I told you that it looked deep," James continues, looking at me carefully. "I cleaned it and treated it with some ointment. It should clear up in a few days."

I nod, unable to get my mouth to work just yet. I look at him properly for the first time with sober eyes. He's in his mid-fifties, with short brown hair and hazel eyes. He's kind-looking, you see him and know you can trust him, which I suppose for a doctor is a good thing. He's wearing the finery of court, yet it doesn't look right on him, as though he feels uncomfortable and would much rather be wearing something else.

I stifle a yawn as I reach for the cup of tea, clasping my hands around it. "I'm sorry," I say, quietly. "About yesterday. I know what I'm like when I drink. I never wanted or needed to when I was with Sophia. The darkness that only oblivion could take away wasn't there when I was with her. I thought it had left me for good until …"

"You don't have to apologise." James shakes his head. "It was my choice to come and find you. To tell you. I'm sorry I have caused you more pain."

I look away from him, down at the cup in my hands, watching the steam swirl upwards from it into the air, desperately trying to keep my mind from thinking about everything I learned last night, even though I'm fighting a losing battle. "I must have drunk more than usual," I reply, eventually, meeting his eyes once more. "I can't remember the last time I slept a full night without waking."

He gives me a rueful look. "I'm afraid that was me as well," he admits and I look at him in confusion. "You were determined to go to the church. I didn't think it was a good idea due to the lateness of the evening and ..." He stops, looking for the right word to describe my drunken stupor of last night which I know he is referring to. I let him know with a nod of my head that he doesn't need to explain. "I gave you a sleeping draught," he continues. "I'm sorry for the deception. I just didn't want you to do something foolish whilst you were not quite yourself."

"Thank you," I reply, genuinely. "It felt good to sleep without my usual nightmares for a change."

He nods but says no more. We sit in silence for a while until the words which I need to speak will not stay silent within me any longer.

"I do want to go to church, though. I need to see for myself."

James sighs, as I knew he would. "Are you sure? Whatever you find, it will only bring you more pain."

I smile sadly. "I don't think I can feel any more pain than what I'm feeling now. At least if I see it for myself, then I know that the pain has a reason for being. That it's not just due to the unanswered questions of months gone by."

I can see from his face that he knows he's fighting a losing battle and eventually he agrees to come with me to the little village church in which me and Sophia married, what seems like so long ago now. The ground glistens with frost as we make our way down the stone path which leads to the old church doors.

For a moment, I can picture her so vividly, standing at the doorway smiling at me and the halo of daisies at her head. The image is so strong that I stop in my tracks, staring at the doorway until James's voice breaks the spell.

"Are you sure you want to do this?" He asks looking at me in concern and I focus myself, knowing that I need to do this whatever the answer is that I find.

Nodding my head I carry on walking, pushing open the heavy oak doors that lead inside. I see Father Aiden standing by the altar, and the knot in my stomach begins to ease a little. Father Aiden conducted our wedding. He knows us. Surely he will be able to put my mind at rest. As we walk towards him I see him glance at us before busying himself with his papers.

"May I help you?"

I feel a twinge of panic at his tone but shrug it off.

"Father, I wish to see the marriage records," I begin, before breaking off as I see him shaking his head.

"I'm afraid that is not possible," he replies, acting as though he barely knows me which scares me even more. "You are not permitted to see the records."

I scoff, shaking my head. "I wish to see the record of my marriage, Father." I press on. "My marriage to Sophia Reynolds. Which you conducted."

I see a flicker of something in his face before the vague, disinterested look appears once more.

"I'm afraid I cannot help you."

"Father ..."

It is James that speaks this time. I turn to him as he looks at Father Aiden. "It is of vital importance that Mr Thornton sees these records," he says, his voice calm. "As his doctor, I implore you to see reason and allow him access to them. For the sake of his health."

I swallow heavily as Father Aiden finally turns to me and I recognise the sadness that flickers across his face this time. Without a word, he disappears into another room before returning with the large, red leather-bound book which I recognise from my wedding day.

"I shall leave you for a few moments." Father Aiden speaks hurriedly before making his way back through to the Vestry, closing the door behind him.

My hands are shaking as I open the heavy book and begin searching through the pages. Part of me believes this is all one big mistake. That you cannot destroy a document which belongs to the house of God. Yet if that is so, then where does it leave me? Back not knowing where she is or why she left. Either way I turn, I am living in a nightmare.

I check the records from cover to cover. But it isn't there. There is no mention of our names, of our witnesses names, anything. Frustration building up inside of me I slam the book shut before starting to read from the beginning again.

"Tom ..."

James's voice is calm in my ear but I don't stop. I can't stop. I must have missed it somehow.

"Tom, it's not there."

"No ..." I shake my head, refusing to believe him, my hands frantically skimming the pages until I feel his hands take hold of the book and shut it. I feel sick.

My hands are shaking, my mind spinning with nauseating realisation and hopelessness.

"Tom, I'm sorry..."

I barely hear him as I brush past him, out of the door and into the fresh air before the panic consumes me.

JAMES

I knew this was a bad idea. I should have stood my ground and told him no from the start. Or better still, never come to find him at all. I curse my own feeble heart and the fact that my need to help people gets me into situations like this. I rush out of the church after him and see him striding towards the tavern.

"Tom!" I call after him but when he doesn't stop I quicken my pace, getting to the door before he has a chance to open it, blocking his way. "You don't want this."

"Don't tell me what I want, James." His voice is weary as he once again tries to push past me but I stand my ground and he sighs. "Are you like this with everyone? Or just the poor fools like me who you think you can save?"

"Let's just get you home," I say, calmly, still trying to diffuse the situation. "You need rest. Not liquor."

"Home." He scoffs, shaking his head. "What's that? I don't have a home. I have an empty shell filled with memories that torture me day after day. I don't belong there without her."

"You have Amos," I say, gently. "He's a part of her. She would want you to take care of him, surely?"

His eyes focus intently on mine. I can see that he still wants to run away and I know that if I stood aside right now, then that is exactly what he would do. So I don't. And eventually, to my relief, he turns walking back dejectedly across the frost covered ground towards home.

When we reach it, Amos comes to the door as soon as we enter, and I see Tom place a gentle hand to his fur. He tells me to sit down as he busies himself making us tea and I know he is trying to keep his mind occupied. Trying to stop himself from reaching for the alcohol on which he has come to depend upon. As he comes to sit down opposite me he speaks, before I get a chance to.

"Thank you. For stopping me."

"You made the choice to come home yourself, Tom."

"Yes. But only because you were standing there. Forcing my hand." He looks down at his teacup before speaking again. "This place. It's all her."

His voice is quiet. I don't interrupt. I wait for him to speak again knowing that he needs to.

"The past six months, waking up here every day I am reminded of her. And I don't know what visions my mind is going to conjure up as each day begins. Sometimes, I'm convinced that I can see her in the paddock, tending to the chickens. She's so happy and I just want to go to her, to hold her but as soon as I get there she's gone."

His eyes are closed and I wonder if he's trying to conjure up those memories again. Then with a shuddering breath he opens his eyes once more, his gaze settled on mine. "Other days I see Amos, bleeding out on the floor, Sophia screaming over his body before masked men come and drag her away and there is nothing I can do to stop it." He lifts the teacup to his mouth, taking a drink and I notice that his hands are shaking. "I look after the farm and Amos because it's what I know she would want. Then I go to the tavern and drink until I forget who I am and what my life has become. I get into fights, come back here, patch myself up if I have the energy to, then sit here by the fire until sleep comes for me. Bringing me nothing but nightmares. I haven't slept in our bed since she was taken. I can't. I can't even make myself walk in there. I'm not living, James. I'm surviving." He swallows heavily.

I sigh sadly. All I wanted to do was help. Yet all I seem to have done is cause more pain. "I truly am sorry, Tom," I say, honestly. "I only wish there was more that I could do."

He stays silent, his hand reaching for Amos who has come to sit beside him, as he drains the last of his tea from the teacup.

"What will you do now?" I want to know. I've brought this man nothing but confirmation of his worst nightmares and my own conscience needs to know that he will be alright. He looks at me, his blue eyes rimmed red with tears, shaded with fatigue.

"I will ask you one more time," he replies, his voice strong. "Take me with you. Back to the Capital. I would rather risk my life there, for the chance to see her again than live here in this hell with only her ghost for company. Please, James. I beg of you."

I shake my head. "I cannot do that. This isn't just about you, or Sophia. Bringing you back would put my life in danger too."

"I wouldn't let anything happen."

"You cannot know that! If you were to be discovered, tortured ... do not tell me that you would be able to hold your tongue. I've witnessed torture, Tom. I've seen the strongest of men confess to anything just to stop the pain. You would be no different."

"It wouldn't come to that."

"I'm sorry," I shake my head. "I can't."

"And what will you tell her?" He carries on determinedly. "Will you tell her that you found me but forbid me to come back with you? Or will you lie and say that I wasn't here. That I had moved on? Could you really do that to her?"

"Sophia doesn't know what she wants." I sigh. "She thinks she wants to see you again because she thinks you can save her."

"I can ..." He's staring at me defiantly, his eyes bearing into mine and I don't think I have ever met anyone more determined. Or foolhardy. "She's my wife, James." His voice is quiet now, the determination almost vanished from it. "He can burn records, force her to speak some vows but it's not real. It can't be real. This is real ..."

He holds up his left hand, the emerald in his wedding ring glinting in the sunlight and my mind casts itself back to seeing Sophia's identical ring displayed amongst the trophies in Edmund's study. "And I won't rest until I can bring her back home to me. Whatever it takes."

TOM

The next few days felt like an age, as I waited for James to complete his duties at the Medical School of Lowshore. I didn't give him much choice but to let me accompany him back to the Capital. I said I would just go myself, that there was no way that I could stay in Lowshore anymore, not knowing what I know now. And that I meant what I said. That I would protect him if I were discovered.

But I'm not planning on letting that happen.

The carriage ride back to the Capital has been long and arduous. I don't understand why people see this as a preferred mode of transport to horse riding. At least then you can feel the wind in your hair as you ride; appreciate the nature which is mostly shut out of the carriage by heavy curtains. As we reach our destination, James outstretches a hand to the curtain and looks out towards the palace.

My stomach is knotted with nerves, making me feel sick as I realise how close I am to her once more.

"It's his birthday ..." James' face is a picture of realisation, his voice raised in shock and I finally force myself to look out of the window to see carriage after carriage pulling up to the palace gates.

Men in fine dress coats leading ladies wearing ball gowns of jewelled colours down towards the drawbridge entrance. "I had completely forgotten I was due back on his birthday." James shakes his head. "Of all the days ..."

"Surely this is a good thing?" I shrug. "The palace milling with people? Gives him less time to suspect anything untoward." I reach into my jacket pocket and bring out a sheet of paper, turning it over in my hands.

"I still cannot believe you did that." James is watching me carefully, shaking his head.

"I needed papers, James," I reply, as I look at the document in my hands, reading the writing upon it. "It's not like I could use mine."

"So you stole his?"

"Not stole." I correct him. "The gentleman dropped them. I just picked them up."

"And chose not to return them to him."

"I'm merely borrowing them," I reply. "Once all of this is sorted, I promise I will put them back where I found them, and someone can return them to ... Mr Benjamin Redfield." I look at the name of the man that I am pretending to be. The man whose work James looked at when he had asked the professor which students showed an aptitude of learning the afflictions of the mind.

I didn't get a good look when I bumped into him outside the school as I waited for James. I apologised profusely as I helped him to gather up his books and papers.

The snide remarks coming out of his mouth as I did so, making me feel unconcerned in the slightest at the fact that his identity papers never made their way back into his hands. I know that James isn't impressed. And I'm not proud of it. But I do what I have to do. Like I always have done.

Our carriage stops just outside the entrance of the palace. As I get out I see that as well as the fine clothing which guests are wearing they are also wearing masks. I laugh to myself, shaking my head. Of course he would throw a masquerade ball to celebrate his birthday. I would have expected nothing less.

Still, despite the fact that I am pretty sure nobody here has ever seen my face, it lessens my panic a little that I am able to disguise it in some way. I pick one from the basket offered to me. It's black and decorated with ornate birds across the top. As I fasten it with the gold ribbon, I look over at James to see that he is putting one on too. He looks as nervous as I feel. The good news for him is that I'm used to making up stories to get into places. I've been doing it for pretty much my whole life just to survive.

"We'll be fine," I mumble, my voice giving off more confidence than I actually feel. "We know the story. Just stick to it. And I'm good at thinking on my feet, so I'll dodge any difficult questions, if he asks them."

"You sound like you've done this before." He mutters under his breath. As he looks at me I raise an eyebrow and he rolls his eyes. "Of course you have. I should have known."

I follow him into the palace. As we are shown through to the grand ballroom, my heart is thumping in my chest. Someone offers us drinks from a silver platter and I take one, grateful for the rush of alcohol which hits my veins, as I knock it back and reach for another. I'm looking around, trying to catch a glimpse of her but the room is full of masked people and it is impossible to make one person out from another in the melee.

"James?"

A smooth, well-spoken voice calls out to James, and I turn to see the King walking over to us. I only recognise him from the portraits, which I must admit are a good likeness. They've even captured the smirk on his face to a tee. I feel the muscle twitch in my jaw as I try to maintain the air of composure, which I must, if I am to keep up the pretence which will help me find her again.

"I thought you weren't going to make it," King Edmund says, clapping James on the shoulder, "it is wonderful to see you here."

"And you, Edmund," James replies warmly, shaking his hand. "May I wish you many happy returns on your birthday."

He smiles his thanks, then his eyes turn to me.

I swallow down my nerves, praying that the composure remains on my face and James clears his throat.

"Edmund. May I introduce …"

"Benjamin Redfield," I say politely. "It is an honour to meet you, Your Majesty." I extend a bow, which I assume is the right thing to do in front of a King. He looks at me, his eyes taking me in from behind his elaborate gold mask. I am thankful to James for suggesting I change my clothes before arriving here. In a royal blue dress coat, cravat, dark breeches and boots I look far more likely to be someone who James may be acquainted with than in my usual attire. He doesn't speak, so I open my mouth to begin speaking again when James cuts in.

"Benjamin is a medical student at Lowshore University, in his final year of studies," he explains and I'm surprised to see that he is just as good at lying as I am. "He asked if he may work as my assistant for a while, to allow him to further his skills. After seeing his work, I was impressed and agreed that he could shadow me for one year."

The King is still staring at me, which is starting to rattle me slightly. I am about to try to speak once more when finally he utters something.

"You're a little old to be a medical student aren't you?"

I glance over at James, who is telling me silently with his eyes to keep my cool. I cough to rid myself of the anger which was no doubt going to appear in my voice and plaster a smile on my face.

"I had to fund my own education," I say and I am surprised at the calmness of my own voice. "My parents were not of money, so I had to work a trade straight from school in order for me to train as a physician."

He nods, with faint interest.

"Benjamin's studies are a specialism in affliction of the mind," James interrupts. "I thought it might be useful to have him alongside me. To help Lady Sophia."

I'm grateful for the mask covering half of my face because for a brief moment, at the mention of her name I falter before regaining my composure.

"How is she?" James inquires, and the King looks over his shoulder before grinning.

"See for yourself."

My breath catches in my throat, as I see her walking towards us. Her emerald green ball gown makes her hair glow like flames and it skims the floor behind her as she walks.

Her mask matches the green of the dress, adorned with red peacock feathers at the corners which mingle with the red of her hair. As she reaches Edmund, he pulls her in towards him and I don't know if it's me just seeing what I want to see, but I see her body stiffen as he does so.

"My darling," he says, which makes my skin crawl and my fist clench in anger. "You remember James, don't you?"

"Of course." Her voice is as soft as I ever remember, and my heart aches at the sound of it. "It is good to see you, Doctor."

"And you." James smiles, taking her hand and kissing it. "You are looking better than the last time I saw you, my Lady."

"And this is Benjamin Redfield," the King says, holding out his arm in introduction. "James' assistant."

As her eyes meet mine, I know that she has realised I'm no Benjamin Redfield. She knows my eyes as well as I know hers. I see the flash of recognition, of shock, surprise and relief. But also fear which scares me more than anything else.

"Mr Redfield." She composes herself enough to hold out her hand to me. As I take it in my own, the feeling is electric. All of the memories seeping back into my head of our perfect life together before this hell happened.

I try to disguise the shake in my hand as I bring hers to my lips, placing a gentle kiss against it.

"My Lady."

I never want to let her go, but I already feel as though I have been holding her hand for far too long, and any longer may raise suspicion. She must feel the same as she pulls her hand away before bringing the fan to her face to cool herself whilst holding my gaze.

"My darling? Are you alright?" Edmund is looking at her in concern.

"I am fine. A little flushed is all."

He shakes his head. "Darling, this is your first engagement since getting back on your feet. I should have known it may have been too much for you."

"Edmund, really, I'm fine."

"Go, get some rest. I shall see you in the morning," Edmund interrupts her, blatantly ignoring her wishes. I see her glance at me again, before averting her gaze.

"Yes, Edmund." Her voice is full of the same fear that I see in her eyes and it breaks my heart. As Edmund leans in to kiss her, I have to turn away. Thankfully, James turns to me as well and begins talking to me about the latest developments in the medical world. I am barely listening, but I am grateful for the distraction and by the time we turn back, Sophia is nowhere to be seen.

"Well gentlemen." Edmund smiles with his hands held exuberantly at each side of his body. "If you will excuse me, I must go and make conversation with some of the other guests. The work of a King is never done, even on his birthday! You will join me later on for drinks in my study though, yes? I must hear all about your tour, James."

We both nod our thanks, though I can think of nothing worse and watch as he makes his way over to some people who are dressed in such finery, that they can only be of royal blood.

I follow James over to the corner of the room; the quietest, least populated area. We stand, watching the crowd for a while, some people are dancing, others stood conversing with glasses in hand.

"Are you alright?" James asks suddenly, watching me closely and I nod, though I do not feel alright at all. "She looks well," he says, genuinely. "Compared to how she looked when ..."

"She's petrified, James." My voice is harsher than I intend it to be but I cannot shake the look of fear on her face from my mind. "Can't you see that?" I ask. "Can't you hear it in her voice?"

"I know this is difficult, Tom." His voice is so quiet I can barely hear it above the chatter and music within the room. "But you know that you must stay strong. Not just for her but for yourself. You are in the middle of a dangerous trap here. One wrong move and you do not need me to tell you what will happen. Edmund is not his father. Alfred was a kind man who believed in mercy. Edmund would show you no such thing. Believe me when I say that Sophia does look better than when I first met her. And that has taken such bravery. More than you can believe. You must show that same strength and bravery if you are going to survive being here."

He is right of course. Knowing what I know now, knowing what James has told me; to see her standing there in a room full of people, brave enough to put on this act even if I am able to see through it - that must have taken a strength I do not even know that I possess.

"Sorry, James." I say, eventually. "You are right. It's just seeing her again after so long … "

"It will have been a shock." James nods. "But you mustn't let it cloud your mind. It is vital you remain focused at all times. For all of our sakes."

As his words filter into my mind a niggling sense of panic starts creeping in at just how dangerous this really is. But then, I see Sophia in my mind's eye and I'm reminded of what Edmund has done to her, the pain he has caused and I know that the danger is worth it.

"Gentlemen!" Edmund appears from nowhere, striding over to us with a grin upon his face, "will you join me in my study for a drink? I have had enough of festivities for one evening. I would prefer some good conversation and a decent glass of port."

James accepts the invitation on both of our behalf, as I manage an appreciative smile and follow them both onwards to his study.

Edmund's study is as expected, full of all of the pomp and splendour one would expect from a man of his vanity. His portrait hangs upon the wall, the first thing you see as you enter the room which is furnished with dark wood, gold and drapes of ruby red velvet.

As he shows us over to the comfortable chairs beside the fire, I catch sight of something which makes my heart ache and almost breaks my act.

It's Sophia's wedding ring, the emerald glinting at me from beneath the crystal cloche which imprisons it. I can feel my heart thumping in my chest as I stare, the anger building in me as the realisation of who this man is and what he has done becomes ever clearer in my mind.

"Benjamin?" James' voice is strong, forcing me out of the swirling thoughts in my mind as I turn to him. "I see you have found Edmund's trophies," he says calmly, his face urging me silently to remain calm too. "I'm sure he will tell you about them at some point, but for now I would like to discuss the tour and my findings. Would you care to join us?"

"Yes, James." Edmund nods enthusiastically. "Three months is a long time, we have much to catch up on. Please Mr Redfield, do sit down, join us. I am interested in how you came to impress James so much for him to agree to you joining him here."

I swallow before plastering a smile on my face and walking over to join them.

I've done this so many times before yet not on such a huge scale. With such huge risk. James is right, I must remain focused for us all. As I take my seat, Edmund hands me a glass of port which I force myself to sip at, knowing that the more I drink the more prone I will be to say something I shouldn't.

"Tell me about the tour, James," Edmund asks, as he takes his seat and lifts his own glass to his mouth. "I must confess that I have not visited the coastal towns of this land in a long while, though I suspect not much has changed."

"The coast is beautiful, Edmund," James replies, pleasantly. "You should try and visit sometime. The sea air is marvellous for your health, I feel most refreshed from my visit."

"Perhaps." Edmund nods with mild interest. "Though from what I have heard about Lowshore and the state which my darling wife was living in before she was rescued would make me think twice. Apologies, Benjamin, I know that is your hometown."

"No apology necessary, your Majesty." I am impressed by the sincerity of my own voice and my ability to look him directly in the eye as I lie to his face. "Though you must forgive my ignorance as I never realised that Lady Sophia hailed from Lowshore. I assumed that she lived here, in the Capital."

"She found herself living there for a time in unfortunate circumstances," Edmund replies, barely missing a beat. "I cannot go into the story in detail as it angers me too much. All I will say is that she is now safe and well."

"Well, I am pleased to hear that," I reply, somehow managing to smile pleasantly. "There are parts of Lowshore which are indeed rundown and unfit for someone as important and gracious as Lady Sophia to live. She deserves the beauty and comfort which only the Capital and this fine palace can offer."

I see him raise an eyebrow as he brings his glass to his lips again and takes a drink. I catch sight of James but his face betrays nothing of what he is thinking.

"I must say, James, that I am impressed with your choice of assistant," Edmund says, finally. "How did you find him?"

"Benjamin had written a paper on afflictions of the mind which was shown to me by his professor, to ask my opinion." James isn't looking at me, his gaze is focused entirely on Edmund as he weaves his own impressive tale. "I was most excited by it. I asked to meet with him and as I explained earlier, decided that I would agree to him shadowing me for a year, to develop his skills."

"Well Benjamin, I daresay you will learn a lot from James," Edmund says with a smile. "This man taught me everything I know about philosophy, languages and the arts. I'm sure he will guide you well in your medical studies."

"I am sure of that as well, your Majesty. I had heard great things about Doctor Collins and so was eager to seek him out and ask for this opportunity. I am just grateful he accepted."

"And how have you been, Edmund?" James asks. "Lady Sophia looked a lot better than the last time I saw her."

I feel my heart beginning to race again at the sound of her name. Keeping up this act is far simpler when I am talking of my non-existent education and fake medical apprenticeship. Yet I know that I must master this part too, if I am to remain undiscovered.

"I am well, James, as is she." He smiles. "Of course we have been taking things slowly, getting to know one another again after so long apart. But, it seems that my beloved Sophia is coming back to me once more."

I feel the flicker of anger at my jaw and take a drink to disguise it.

"I am glad to hear it." James smiles politely. "I was worried that perhaps she would struggle a little at first."

"I worried the same." Edmund nods. "As I said, we took things slowly but even I was surprised at how eager she was to see me and to spend time together."

I see James glance in my direction and I realise that I am grasping my glass so tightly in my hand that it may shatter. Taking a deep breath, I drain the rest of my port and force myself to smile and listen as they converse about life, the tour and how my wife is settling better into life as a Queen, as the days go on.

Eventually, Edmund appeared to grow tired of our company and James thankfully suggested that we retire to our rooms for the evening. Edmund insisted that a steward show us to our chambers before shaking both our hands and bidding us goodnight.

"I need to see her James." My voice is low as I walk with him to the rooms which have been made up for us, a steward leading the way. James glances at the steward slowing his pace so the gap between us and him widens.

"I don't think it would be a good idea. Not tonight at least."

"I've just walked back into her life unexpectedly," I say, my tone hushed but urgent. "She looked like she was going to faint earlier, not that I could blame her. I just want to see that she is alright."

I'm so engrossed in trying to get him to agree with me that we don't realise that the steward has stopped and we almost bump into him as we stop abruptly. The steward opens the door to James' chamber and he walks in, closing the door behind him.

Frustrated, I try my best to smile and thank the steward as he does the same when we arrive at my chamber.

I walk in and close my door too, not caring in the slightest about the opulence of the room, even if it is the most expensive looking place I will ever have stayed in. I place an ear to the door, listening for the footsteps of the steward making his way down the corridor. I wait until I cannot hear him any longer before opening the door again and knocking lightly on James' door.

I'm starting to worry that he is ignoring me, as it takes so long for the door to open. When it does he looks at me, exasperated.

"Tom ..."

"Just five minutes," I interrupt him. "I just want to see her for five minutes, as myself. Not pretending to be someone else. I need to see my wife, James. Please."

Eventually he sighs, shaking his head.

"Fine. Five minutes. But if there is anyone anywhere near her bedchamber then we leave this until another day. There is no way we can come up with any reason for going to see her at this time of night. Even as physicians."

I nod, praying to God that it is late enough for no-one else to be around. I need to see her. Seeing her in the ballroom took my breath away and it took everything I had in me to hold it together and keep up the act that was to keep me safe. I wanted to take her in my arms there and then and never let her go. Tell her how sorry I am, that I wasn't there to keep her safe when she needed me most. How I gave up on her, leaving her here to live through months of hell whilst I drank myself into oblivion.

"Tom?"

I shake myself out of my thoughts to see James looking at me, concern etched across his features.

"Are you sure you want to do this?" he says, carefully. "It's been a long night, you've had a drink. Maybe it would be best to get some rest and ..."

"No. No, I'm fine. I just need to see her."

He nods, grasping my arm before leading the way down the corridors. I follow him, not paying much attention to where we are going. My thoughts are just filled with Sophia. How I can get her out of this place. Away from him. Away from all of the horrible memories to try and make some better ones. I notice that James is slowing and I can feel my heart thumping in my chest as he stops in front of a door.

There is nobody around.

He looks at me as if to check once more that this is definitely what I want and as I nod he knocks lightly at the door. I can feel my hands shaking and I can't believe how nervous I feel. The door opens and for a moment I'm confused as I am expecting Sophia to be standing there but it isn't.

I look at James in mild panic but he shakes his head.

"This is Annalise," he explains. "She is Sophia's lady-in-waiting. She knows about everything. It's okay."

Annalise looks at me with a smile and curtseys. I'm not sure what I should do in response and I eventually manage a small smile and incline my head slightly. She looks from me back to James, before checking that there is no one else around and invites us in.

"She told me what 'appened," she says, in hushed tones as she closes the door behind us. "She kept sayin' that she saw Tom, but I didn't know if she was just imaginin' fings again. But she weren't, you really are 'ere."

She's looking at me with some kind of awe which I don't know that I deserve.

"Where is she?" I ask her, trying to keep my voice steady. "Please ..."

She smiles gently at me. "Through there."

Annalise points towards a closed door. She nods, encouraging me over to it. Taking a deep breath, I reach for the handle and as I open it I see her, pacing the floor. Her ivory nightdress, a stark contrast to the green dress of earlier, clings to the curves of her body as she walks. At the sound of the door opening, she turns and I meet her eyes.

She is pale and thinner than I remember, the tracks of tears still visible on her face as she looks at me. We stand just staring at each other, wondering if this is real, if it is really happening after all this time. Then suddenly, we are rushing over to one another and she is in my arms and I am holding her so tightly, breathing her in as she clings to my shoulder.

"I'm sorry." I whisper it into her hair, over and over as she sobs into my shoulder, my own tears flowing down my face. Her cries grow louder and I pull her in tighter to my body, my hand gently stroking through her hair, desperately trying to soothe her.

"Shhhh. Sophia, shhhh, it's alright. I'm here. We can sort this now. I'm not leaving you again."

"It's too late ... it's too late!" She pulls away from me, shaking her head, trying to release herself from my grasp but I hold firm, looking at her in confusion.

"No," I say, shaking my head. "No, I'm here, Sophia. We can sort this, I can bring you home, I ..."

She grabs hold of my hand, placing it to her stomach. She's so slight that it isn't visible yet, but I can feel the curve of her stomach under her nightdress and I realise with a sickening jolt what she means. She's looking at me, still shaking her

THE STARS THAT GUIDE YOU HOME

head, the tears falling free and fast down her cheeks. Once again she tries to break away, but I pull her in close to me again.

"I'm sorry!" she chokes, her voice muffled against my shoulder. "I couldn't stop h ... him. I wanted to. I didn't want him anywhere n ... near me but ..." She lifts her head from my shoulder, looking over at James who must have entered the room with Annalise after hearing the commotion.

"I did what you said," she whispers, directing her words at James. "I didn't think he would do that, but I couldn't stop him or he would have known ... I ..."

I don't understand what she means but as I feel her go floppy in my arms, I lift her up.

She's as light as a feather and I have to try and stop myself from crying, as she cradles herself into me like a child and I carry her over to the bed.

"Forgive me, please, Tom, I never meant for this to happen."

I swallow down the tightness in my throat as I look at her.

"Don't ask me to forgive you when there is nothing to forgive." I place her down gently on the bed, stroking back the hair from her tear-stained face.

"You can't stay here," she whispers, shaking her head. "Not now. You have to go. Forget me. Move on."

I laugh through my own tears which have started to spill down my cheeks. "Like it is that simple, Sophia." I shake my head as I grab hold of her hand. "I love you. And I am never leaving you again." I'm so focused on her that I barely notice James at my side holding a vial of liquid out to me.

"It's a sleeping draught," he says, calmly. "It's perfectly safe for Sophia and the ..." He stops himself from speaking the word that none of us want to hear. I don't want unwilling sleep to take her from me, nor do I want to leave her here at all, but I can see she is exhausted and forcing herself to stay awake. I take it from him, uncorking the top as I place it to her lips.

"No." She shakes her head, closing her mouth. I place a hand to her cheek making her look at me.

"You need to rest," I say, gently but firmly. "We will fix this. Somehow. But you need to rest and look after yourself. For me. Please."

She's looking at me, her green eyes as deep and rich as the forest trees. I never thought I would see those eyes again. And it is taking every ounce of strength that I have not to walk out of here, find that bastard and squeeze the life from him. For taking her away from me. For what he has done to her. And for making sure that I will likely never get her back again. The only thing stopping me from doing that is Sophia. Once again I lift the bottle filled with the sleeping draught to her lips and this time she drinks it. It works quickly, her eyes flickering shut as she grasps for my hand and I take hold of it tightly.

"I'm here," I say, softly, as she is pulled into sleep. "I love you, Sophia. I love you so much."

As sleep finally overcomes her, I sit on the edge of her bed, stroking back her hair, watching her chest rise and fall with gentle breaths. Annalise and James are still in the room but all that matters at this moment is me and her. Sat in this strange place miles away from home.

"Tom." James eventually speaks, his voice is soft and I know he is trying to keep me calm. It is taking everything I have to keep myself steady, to stop that anger from taking over. "Tom, we need to go. I don't trust Edmund not to send someone to check in on her. And to find us both here at this time of night would be bad news for us all. Please."

I look at her, sleeping peacefully at last, preparing myself to leave her again. I get up, her hand still grasped in my own as I lean forward and press my lips to her forehead. Brushing the tears roughly from my face with my free hand, I finally let go of hers with my other.

"I need a drink." I say, as I storm past James and Annalise towards the door.

Sophia

I sit at my windowsill, having finally got up to try and face another day. I changed with Annalise's help, into a dress of pink and gold, one of the simplest of all of the dresses he filled my room with after bringing me here.

'*Clothes to show you off,*' he said. Like I am his property. Movement from the window brings my attention outside, as

I see Edmund striding off on his horse, followed by five of his most trusted guards. He's going on a hunt. I know this because it is the same routine for him every day. And every day I pray to the gods that he will be mauled by one of the poor boars he sets out to chase through the forest and kill.

He turns as he rides away and looks up towards me at the window. I see him smile and raise his hand in farewell and I respond in kind, though the smile on my face is forced. Doing what I have to do.

Part of me still cannot believe that last night was real. That Tom is really here. It took Annalise grasping me by the hands and looking me in the eyes with a smile to get me to believe that it actually happened.

But, I don't think I will fully accept it until I see him again, in daylight. Not under the haze of exhaustion and upset, as I was last night.

James is expected to call on me this morning. And if last night's events were true, then he should be with him. My heart flutters at the thought of it, yet at the same time it aches. This shouldn't be happening, this isn't how our lives were meant to end up. Me, here, trapped by this tiny living thing growing in my womb. This child, which is not his when it should be.

A light knock at the door brings me to my senses and I wipe the tears that I didn't realise I had shed from my face, as I tell them they can come in. The door opens and as I see him.

"Where is …?" I begin, wondering where James is.

Tom looks at me, his face unreadable. "He's in the next room," he replies, his voice soft. "He wanted to give us the chance to speak, first. Properly."

I rise from the windowsill, brushing the skirts of my dress until they lie straight. He stands stock still, just looking at me, as if he is unsure of what to do. I have never seen him look like this before. Dressed in the finery of the men at court, as opposed to his usual loose shirt and trousers he would wear for his work. He looks different and yet, calmingly familiar.

I walk towards him, wanting, needing to touch him, to feel his skin against mine. As I reach him, I place a hand to his cheek, tracing the line of his jaw as he closes his eyes.

"I've dreamt of this," I whisper, not wanting to move away. "I thought I was dreaming last night."

His lips suddenly find mine, silencing me, his taste familiar and addictive as our mouths explore one another's, our hands at each other's hair, wanting, needing that piece of us back that was torn apart all those months ago. Eventually, we break away and I stand just looking at him, tears creeping into my eyes again.

"Don't," he says, shaking his head as he pulls me into his body, his arms wrapped tight around me, "don't cry, Sophia, please."

We stand there for what seems like forever, just us, in this little bubble where nothing can hurt us. But, reality starts to seep in like water through cracks and I find myself needing to say things, to explain. To grieve.

"That day they took me," I begin, but as I look up at him I see the wobble in his jaw as he turns away from me, shaking his head.

"Please don't talk about it."

"I thought it was you," I whisper, and as he turns back towards me I see the tears in his eyes and I feel my heart break, "your axe. You forgot it. I thought you would come back for it."

"I should have," he sniffs, his eyes pained. "I was going to, but I didn't. And I'll never forgive myself for that. If I'd have been there ..."

"They would likely have killed you," I say strongly, taking hold of his hand. "Or brought you back here so that he could have you killed in front of me. That is the type of person he is. He's a monster!"

"I made a vow to protect you!" he cries, his voice crumbling. "And I wasn't there to keep it."

It's my turn to hold him as he breaks down. The man I love, who has always been so strong, now standing here broken and I cannot bear it.

"I wish we could go home," I whisper into his ear.

He pulls away, his blue eyes searching my face. "Why can't we?" he whispers. "I can take you, right now. We can get away from here, far away where he will never find you."

"I cannot leave this room, Tom," I say sadly, watching the hope in his eyes fade once again to despair. "I am his trophy. His prisoner. This room is my only sense of freedom, where I am not watched or followed by his spies and guards at every turn. If we were to leave this room and even try to escape, he would have us captured and brought back here before we reached the gates. I won't risk your life, I won't!"

The sting of tears reaches my eyes once again and I try to pull away from him but he doesn't let me, enveloping me into his body once again.

"Shhhh," he soothes, gently, stroking a hand through my hair. "We will figure this out. I won't let him hurt either of us, I promise you."

I place a hand to his chest, to feel the rhythmic beat of his heart against my palm, trying to soothe myself. His hand finds mine, his thumb tracing the vulgar rubies of my wedding band. I look at his face and see that he is looking at it, biting his lip, trying to stop his tears once more.

Glancing down at his left hand I feel a dull thud in my heart as I see his ring finger bare. Looking back at him I see that he is watching me. Slowly he reaches into the neck of his shirt before pulling out a piece of rope tied around his neck. Attached to it is his wedding ring, the emerald glinting in the light of the room.

"I didn't think that having it on display would be the wisest idea." He's grinning at me through tear-filled eyes and I can't help but smile back. I reach for it, my fingers tracing the engraved initials of our names. Solid, real proof of us.

"He took mine."

"I know." Tom nods, and I see his jaw clench. "I saw it in his study. Along with his other prizes."

I'm still holding onto Tom's ring as my mind flashes back to that day and I feel all of the pain and fear rushing back into my veins. "I didn't want to marry him, Tom, I swear."

He shakes his head, taking hold of my hand that holds the ring and enveloping it in his. "You don't need to tell me that. I know."

"I told him I was married," I carry on, unable to stop myself. "I told him that I had papers, but he just laughed."

"I went to the church." Tom's voice is hollow and as I look up at him, I see that he has closed his eyes. "I saw Father Aiden," he says, quietly. "He acted as though he barely knew me." He's shaking his head in disbelief as he opens his eyes and looks at me. "At first, he wouldn't let me see the records. But I persisted until he did." He swallows. "They weren't there. I looked from cover to cover three times to make sure, but there was no mention of our marriage. How can that be possible?"

"Edmund doesn't care what is right or wrong, even in law," I respond, eventually. "He sees it that he is the King. His word is law. And people are too scared to go against him. The priest he forced to marry us was as scared as I was." I blink vicious tears from my eyes. "I told him I would never marry him. I told him that he couldn't make me."

Tom opens his mouth to speak, but I pull up my right sleeve and I see his eyes widen at the state of my arm. James did his best and he stopped the pain but the real damage was already done. Raised scars of dark pink and purple cover the underside of it, where the candle was held against my flesh.

"I had to do what he said just so they would stop."

I daren't look at Tom. I have just about managed to stop the tears from falling and I know that one look at his face would break me again. I feel him wrap his arms around me, pulling me into him and I cling to him tightly, feeling safe again for the first time in so long. He places a kiss against my hair, as I whisper into his chest how sorry I am.

"Stop it, Sophia," he says, softly. "Stop saying sorry. You have nothing to be sorry for."

"I should have fought harder." I whisper it, my throat tight with tears. "I fought so hard to not go through with the marriage. But when he ..." I stop, unable to speak the words, unable to admit what he did to me out loud. "I should have fought him off then. But I was too scared. So I just lay there, and let him. It's my fault."

"Sophia, listen to me." His voice is strong, though I hear the pain in it. And I cling to him tighter as he continues to speak. "What he did. That was not your fault and you couldn't have stopped him. I've spent time with him now and I know the kind of man that he is. He is cruel and arrogant and believes that the world and everything in it is his to own. But it isn't. You aren't. He had no right to do that to you. But the blame lies with him, not you. I will not let you punish yourself over this."

My tears soak into his shirt, as I feel his arms pull me in tighter. I let myself take the comfort which he is offering without question, still unable to look at him for fear of breaking down completely. "I love you," I whisper, finally making myself look at him then wishing that I hadn't.

For just as I thought I would never get to say those words again, he likely never thought he would hear them. His eyes are sparkling with tears, his chin wobbling as he tries to hold them back. And all that does is make the tears that I had managed to quell burst from me once more, as I reach my hands to his face, stroking back his hair, taking in every part of him; every precious detail of the man that I love so deeply, and who loves me so deeply in return.

"I love you." I say it again as I kiss him, tasting salty tears against my lips, mine or his I don't know. Our first kiss after I saw him again was impulsive, instinctive. Raw. This one is gentle and quiet.

Healing us both, giving us a tiny piece of ourselves back what was lost so many months ago.

After giving us much needed time to talk, there was a knock on the door and James' voice asking if he could come in. Hearing his voice brought reality crashing down on me once more, as I remembered that he would have to confirm my worst fears and then relay that news to my worst enemy.

"My Lady," James begins, his normally calm and reassuring voice tight with nerves. "King Edmund has asked me to check on your health, to make sure you have been well in my absence."

I nod, wishing that were all it was, yet the niggling feeling within me which has been there for weeks is rising up. The niggling feeling that perhaps he already suspects. Tom says nothing, though his face betrays everything he is feeling without words, and he keeps a tight hold of my hand as he helps me over to my bed and I settle myself down upon it.

As James comes over and places his bag on the table, I feel Tom leave my side and watch as he goes to stand over near Annalise, his eyes never leaving me. I stay quiet as James places his hands to the curve of my stomach, which is all but hidden under the skirts of my dress. He too stays silent as he works, his eyes closed as his gentle hands press lightly against my bump. He asks me questions about my health which I answer easily enough. Then he goes quiet and as I look at him I realise he is trying to find a way to ask me the thing neither of us want to talk about.

"How many times did Edmund ...?" he finally asks, stopping before he reaches the end of the sentence, either unwilling or unable to say the word.

"I lost count," I whisper my reply, unable to even look in Tom's direction for fear of seeing the look on his face. "It happened so many times." My voice is choked. I feel sick even thinking about it. I can still feel his touch against my skin, his eyes leering at my body, the feeling of utter helplessness coursing through my veins, as I was forced to let him take me.

"I implored him to take things slowly." James looks rattled. He has grasped his hands together as he looks at me. I think deep down maybe he knew that Edmund wouldn't listen to him. Yet he hoped he would as only a good-hearted person would hope.

"And he did," I reply. "Whilst you were here. Once you had gone, he became more forceful. Unwilling to listen even when I said no. Then eventually he came to my room." My tears cloud my eyes as I look at James whose usually unreadable face looks stricken with guilt and pain. "I didn't want him here. This is my sanctuary away from him. But I couldn't stop him. I was scared and I kept saying no."

As the tears begin to fall from my eyes I feel a warm hand take hold of mine, squeezing it tightly and I look up to see Tom at my side. I can tell by the set of his jaw how angry he is and from the look in his eyes the guilt he feels at something which he could do nothing about. "Then a few weeks ago, he stopped," I continue, having found the strength to stop my tears. "I didn't understand why, but perhaps he had an inkling." I swallow, shaking my head as I look at James. "I don't want this. I do not want this child."

"My Lady." James sighs, as I feel Tom grasp my hand tighter. "Edmund expects me to inform him of how you are. It is my medical opinion, as far as I can tell, that you have been with child for at least two months. Perhaps three. If he suspects as you think ..."

"I don't know," I reply, panicked. "I just assumed. Perhaps he doesn't suspect at all. You could give me something. Something to ..."

"Sophia, no." It's Tom's voice I hear now, drowning out everything else, the fear and the panic as he crouches by my side and looks at me. "You cannot." He shakes his head, his own voice tight with emotion. "You have always wanted to be a mother."

"Not like this," I reply. "Not like this."

"You have suffered loss before." He carries on, and I can see the tears shining in his eyes making the blue of his irises even brighter. "I saw what that did to you. You cannot willingly put yourself through that again, do not tell me that you can."

The pain of our own loss still haunts me. The child which we longed for that left us before we ever got the chance to meet them. And I know that he is right.

I couldn't bear another loss like that. Or place the fate of this child in my own hands.

"This isn't how it was supposed to be." I shake my head as I see him swallow down his tears. Tom places a hand to my cheek as the tears begin to fall down his. His voice is choked and I cannot bear it. For all the pain I am feeling, I know that the pain he is going through is just as bad and just as valid.

"I know. And I wish to God I could turn back the clock and stop all of this from happening. Or wake up and realise this is all some horrible dream and we are back home, together and safe. But I can't. So all I can do is stay here loving and protecting you from a distance. Making sure you are safe."

He pulls me in close to him and I cling to him tightly as he presses a kiss against my hair.

"I will never let him hurt you again, Sophia. I swear it on my life."

TOM

James eventually left to tell Edmund his findings. He suggested it may be best if I didn't accompany him and for once I had to agree. I couldn't promise that I could keep my temper so soon after listening to what he had done. James also suggested that I return to my quarters, but that I refused. I needed to make sure that Sophia was alright, I didn't just want to leave her, again. James agreed to this, though he felt as though he probably had little choice.

As Annalise makes us tea, I sit at the table by the window with Sophia. She's quiet, her gaze focused on the grounds outside beyond the window of her room. Even as Annalise brings the tea and cakes and sits it down upon the table, she doesn't stir.

"Thank you." I smile at the young girl and she curtseys before moving away. "Annalise?" I call to her, and she turns around. "It is Annalise, isn't it?"

"Yes, sir,"

"I never got the chance to properly thank you," I say, and she looks at me in confusion. "For taking care of Sophia."

"It's my job, sir."

"Even so," I say, with a smile. "Thank you. I know how much you have helped her. How much you continue to help." My smile falters a little, as I look at Sophia and see she hasn't stirred, her gaze still intent on the world beyond these four walls. "Will you take tea with us?" I say, regaining my composure, as I turn to face Annalise again.

She looks shocked, her cheeks flushing red as she shakes her head. "I c ... couldn't, sir," she stutters. "It wouldn't be right. I'm not ..."

"What?" I chuckle, shaking my head. "Not what?"

"N ... noble," she stutters again. "A l ... lady. I'm just a servin' girl. I can't sit and take tea with you."

I cannot help but laugh. "I am a woodsman in fancy clothes, Annalise." I smile, looking down at my unfamiliar attire. "And Sophia and I lived on a farm back home. We are no more noble than you. Please ..." I gesture to the seat again. She's blushing redder now, unable to meet my eyes but she curtseys before awkwardly taking a seat. As I begin to pour the tea into the teacups, I once again try to rouse Sophia.

"Sophia ..." I venture, as I place a cup down in front of her and spoon sugar into it before pouring in milk. "Here, sweetheart."

"Hmm?"

"Tea," I say gently, gesturing to the cup. "And you should try to eat something." I offer her one of the dainty little cakes filled with currants, but she shakes her head.

"They are nice, my Lady." Annalise's quiet voice pipes up suddenly, as she takes one herself. "I helped Cook make 'em this morning."

Sophia watches her take a bite, smiling softly at her, before warily taking the cake I had offered and breaking off a piece, bringing it to her lips. I smile my thanks at Annalise once more as I sip at my tea, feeling at a loss as to what I can do to help. I watch as Sophia lifts the teacup to her lips but her hands are shaking and I am not quick enough to take it away from her before it spills and she gasps in pain as the hot tea scalds her wrist.

Annalise is up in an instant, rushing over to the basin as I get up and go to her, moving the teacup away as I crouch down beside her. Her eyes are clouded with tears and she is still so distant, it is though I am looking at a ghost.

"Tell me what I can do?" I say, my hand at her cheek making her look at me. As Annalise returns with a cloth soaked in water which she places against Sophia's wrist, I urge her with my eyes to speak to me, to let me help her. She's looking into my eyes and I've never seen her look so hopeless.

"I don't want this," she chokes and I close my eyes, shaking my head.

"I know, Sophia, I know. And I wish things were different but …"

"I don't mean the baby," she whispers, looking straight at me. "I couldn't … I know I couldn't purposely do that to a living thing."

"Then what?"

I cannot bear the pain in her eyes and the fact that I have no idea what I can even do to make it better. She takes deep shaking breaths as she looks at me, trying to regain some composure.

"I don't want to be here. This child …" She places a hand to her stomach and my heart aches. "Edmund will see it only as another prize, another victory. He will mould the child into his own image, make sure he or she is brought up the way he sees fit. I cannot bear that. It was meant to be so different. Our children were meant to grow up on the farm, surrounded by nature and love, not wealth and duty."

I wipe the stray tear which has fallen down her cheek.

"I don't understand what it is you want me to do, Sophia."

"Take me home." She answers so suddenly, it takes me by surprise. "I want to go home, Tom."

I glance at Annalise who looks warily at me from where she sits, still holding the cloth against her wrist.

"The more I realise what this life will mean for this child, the more I know I cannot stay here. Please. Please find a way to get us home."

I swallow. There is hope in her eyes for the first time. I know I should dissuade her. I know it is just the fear and the situation making her act so rashly. Yet the draw of home is too strong for me, too. And it is the reason I came here in the first place. To bring her home.

"Okay," I nod. "I'll find a way."

She smiles at my words and I finally feel her come back to me before suddenly her face drops once more.

"Edmund …"

I see the fear in her eyes as she says his name. I can hear his voice now, and James' as he tries and fails to dissuade him from his visit. Sophia turns to me in panic and I know why. I shouldn't be here. I cannot explain my presence here without James, and no doubt he has given Edmund some story as to where I supposedly am right now. As their voices grow louder, I suddenly feel a hand at my arm.

"This way, sir."

Annalise guides me hurriedly towards a door at the rear of the room. I do not even have time to look at Sophia before I am pulled away, yet I know it is for the best. I open the door and am faced with a staircase leading downwards into darkness, the only light coming from various lamps on the walls.

"Stay quiet, sir," Annalise says, gently. "'E won't come near this door, trust me. But you must stay quiet."

I nod, and she smiles softly before closing the door, leaving me in semi-darkness just as I hear Edmund's voice booming from the next room.

"Sophia, my darling, James has just told me the good news!" His voice grows louder as he comes closer to the table where Sophia sits.

"Yes Edmund." I hear her reply, though her voice doesn't sound like her own. "Isn't it wonderful?"

"My son and heir."

"We do not know it is a boy, Edmund."

"Ah yes, but I feel it, my love. You are carrying my son in your womb. And when he is born, he will learn what it is to be a King, to carry on my legacy."

I feel the twitch of my jaw with barely contained anger and I try to breathe through it. I realise now that it was more than fear which made Sophia ask what she did. And that I need to find a way to get her far away from here. I'm not even sure where this staircase leads but I cannot bear to listen any longer, so I turn and begin walking downwards until I can no longer hear their voices.

I wait until nightfall, when the palace is still and the grounds are lit only by the moonlit sky. There are guards scattered around but I am used to making my way through the night unnoticed, and I manage to get into the grounds with relative ease. Stopping for a moment in an alcove I think of what it is I am doing, the risk I am taking and whether it is worth it.

Then in my mind's eye, I see the look of utter hopelessness on Sophia's face and I already know my answer. Surveying my surroundings, I know that the main gates would be our obvious escape. Yet, obvious means easy and easy means that it would be far too heavily guarded to even consider. Instead, I make my way into the gardens, stopping every few moments to check I am not being watched or followed. I have only seen the gardens from the palace windows so the route I am navigating is new to me.

Dark green hedges create maze-like walkways to either side of me and though they would no doubt provide more cover from being spotted, I do not know my bearings here well enough to trust in my sense of direction. Instead, I follow the main paved pathway which leads towards an ornate fountain that is gilded in gold. It shoots bursts of water out rhythmically and I am momentarily halted in my journey as I find myself standing and watching it, feeling the spray of water against my face as it hits the light breeze of the evening.

A noise suddenly breaks me from my gaze, making me jump as I turn in the direction from which it came and sigh as I see a young fox staring at me, its amber eyes glinting in the moonlight as it stands there.

"You shouldn't creep up on people like that," I say to it, smiling ruefully. "Especially when they are not supposed to be out here and are trying not to get caught." I chuckle lightly. "Away now. Before you get us both into trouble."

I watch as it turns and runs past the fountain and into semi-darkness. Something makes me follow its lead and I find that the path leads further on, until I see a wall in the distance.

It is built of pale stone and is covered in dark green ivy which creeps upwards and over it. I run a hand over the cool stone before grasping hold of a part of the ivy and tugging it experimentally to see if it could hold my weight. Which it does. Grinning, I brace myself to begin climbing it and see what lies beyond it.

"STOP!" A stern voice right behind me stops me in my tracks. "What are you doing out in the grounds at this time, sir?"

I raise my hands as I turn. There are three guards all standing watching me closely, their hands resting on the swords at their belts. I plaster a confident smile onto my face.

"My sincere apologies," I begin. "I couldn't sleep and so decided to take a walk. But, it is only my first few days here and I am not yet familiar with my surroundings. I appear to have gotten lost."

"And you thought that climbing this wall would get you back into the palace?"

I laugh, shaking my head. "Climbing? No, you are mistaken. I was merely looking at it. I have an interest in architecture you see." I stop as I see the guard reach for the handcuffs at his belt. "This is all a misunderstanding," I say, calmly, as he walks forward and clamps the cuffs around my wrists. "Speak with Doctor Collins. He will vouch for me, I assure you."

"We will let King Edmund decide what to do with you, and what he chooses to believe," the guard replies, and I wince as I feel the tip of a sword press into my back. "Now move."

I'm given no choice but to do as he says, my heart thumping in my chest as I try to keep my panic at bay. I curse myself for being foolish enough to let my guard down and get caught so easily. So early.

It is not myself that I fear for, though I know how cruel Edmund is capable of being. It is Sophia, and the fact that I would no longer be able to protect her. And James, who I promised I would let no harm come to if he brought me here. As we reach the front steps of the Palace, a young courtier comes rushing forward to greet us.

"Get the King here." The head guard orders, sternly, keeping a tight grip on my arm. "Now."

The courtier looks nervously from me and back to the guards. "It is rather late ... the King has retired for the evening."

"He's right," I reply, pressing my luck. "Honestly, this is all just a misunderstanding, there is no need to disturb the ..." The guard to my right jabs the butt of his sword against my ribs painfully and I stop talking, admitting defeat.

"It wasn't a request." The head guard's tone is menacing and this time the courtier doesn't even think of answering back. We stand silently as we wait, my arms aching from the weight of the cuffs at my wrists. I hear Edmund before I see him, his voice sharp with irritability drifting down the corridors until I see him emerge at the top of the stairs, swathed in a ruby red housecoat, his hair hastily swept back into its ponytail.

"What on earth is this all about?" he roars as he descends the stairs. Out of the corner of my eye I see James appear from the direction of our quarters and though I cannot see his face, I can hazard a guess at what he is thinking.

"Your Majesty." The head guard bows as Edmund approaches us. "We found him in the gardens. It appeared he was trying to climb the Palace walls."

"Benjamin?"

The King looks at me as if realising for the first time that it is me. He takes in the chains at my wrists, the guard holding tight to my arm before his gaze reaches mine, and I force myself to look him in the eye and steady my nerve.

"What are they talking about?"

"Your Majesty." I bow my head respectfully. "This is all a misunderstanding, I assure you."

"Edmund?" As I hear her voice drift from the top of the stairs, I bow my head, turning my gaze to the floor.

"Darling, go back to your chambers," Edmund says, a dismissive tone to his voice. "I am dealing with this. It is nothing for you to worry about."

I cannot help but raise my head to glance at her, but as I see the panic in her eyes I wish that I hadn't. James has made his way down the stairs now and is standing beside Edmund, looking at me with an expression I cannot quite work out.

"What is all of this about, Benjamin?" It's James's voice I hear now, breaking my gaze away from Sophia, as I turn to look at him.

"I couldn't sleep. I decided to take a walk and I got lost. That's all."

"Then what is all this about climbing the palace walls?"

"He said he was looking at the architecture." The head guard scoffs, shaking his head. I open my mouth to speak but James gets there first.

"He does have an interest in architecture," he says to Edmund, his voice calm and measured as always, no hint of deceit. "He told me of it on our journey here. It was your grandfather who started your interest, was it not?"

As he looks at me, I nod. I dare not speak for fear of revealing the truth.

Edmund is now conversing with James so quietly that I cannot hear what is being said. I can hear the blood pumping in my ears, as I realise just how scared I actually am of what might happen. Then finally they turn to face me. Edmund's dark eyes fix with mine and it feels like he is silent for an age before he speaks.

"Release him." He orders the guard, as I let out a shaky sigh of relief. "I am sure this was just a misunderstanding. I appreciate your dedication to protecting me and these grounds but I do believe Mr Redfield is telling the truth."

The guard says nothing, yet his jaw is set with anger, as he takes the key and roughly releases my hands. I rub at my wrists as I bow to Edmund once more.

"Thank you, your Majesty. It was a mistake. I will not make it again, you have my word."

He nods, dismissing us all with a wave of his hand and I begin walking towards the stairs, James following on behind me. Sophia is still standing stock still halfway down the staircase, her wide eyes bearing into mine as I reach her and stop.

"My sincerest apologies, my Lady," I say gently. "For disturbing your evening."

I bow to her before walking on towards my chambers, hating the fact that I let her down. Hating the way things are and the fact that this is the way they will now have to be.

The belief I had within me that I could take her away from all of this is now fading.

And neither of our lives can ever go back to how they once were, no matter how badly we would like them to.

As I reach the door to my room, I don't bother to close it as I know that James is right behind me and, sure enough, as I go over to the table and pour myself a drink, I hear the door click shut as James' surprisingly calm voice fills the air.

"What was that really about, Tom?"

I ignore his question, swallowing the glass of liquor in one before reaching for another.

"You know, most of the time I believe you are most intelligent," he continues, as I walk over to the window. "Then other times it appears plain stupidity takes over you."

"I'm sorry," I say without turning back to him, my gaze focused on the gardens. Usually a comment like that would rile me into arguing back, which I think is what he wants. But I don't even have the energy.

"Why?" he replies eventually with a sigh, and I finally turn back to face him. "I thought we'd agreed. I thought you understood."

"You didn't see her." My voice is hollow as I make my way over to the table and reach for the liquor bottle again before thinking better of it. "After you left to tell Edmund about the baby." He's watching me carefully as he takes a seat opposite me. "It was like talking to a ghost," I continue. "She was there, but she wasn't. She wouldn't speak, wouldn't even look at me. It was as if she had shut down and I couldn't bear it. And when I finally got through to her, she asked me to take her home."

I see the look on his face as he opens his mouth to speak and I shake my head.

"I know, James. I know. Please do not say it. I should have said no there and then. I shouldn't have got her hopes up. But you didn't see her. And the minute I told her I would try it was as if she came back to me."

He doesn't speak, he just sits studying me until a gentle smile appears on his lips.

"And you really thought that climbing a wall was the best way out?"

I can't help but laugh at the incredulous look on his face.

"Not climbing, James." I grin. "Exploring my interest in architecture, remember."

The next morning, I received a note from the King, requesting my presence in his study. I spent around ten minutes just pacing the floor of my room after James departed for his rounds, preparing myself for what might be about to happen, until I eventually pulled myself together and headed out of the door.

I shrugged off the note with a veil of confidence as I read it, even though I could see from the look on James' face when he handed it over that he was as concerned as I. Edmund had every opportunity to arrest me last night, publicly. Surely someone of his arrogance would choose to do that rather than send me off quietly? My panic is eased a little by this, yet still the niggle of doubt remains in my heart as I reach the door to the study and knock on the door.

As he beckons me in I swallow down my nerves and enter. I see him straight away, standing by the fireside, a courtier helping him into his ruby red cloak. He turns as I enter the room, a broad smile on his face.

"Ah, Benjamin. I am grateful to you for accepting my invitation. I thought we could take a walk in the gardens whilst we speak. So you can familiarise yourself with them, after last night." He's still grinning at me but I pale at his words.

"Your Majesty, as I said last night, I assure you …"

He shakes his head, walking over and placing a hand to my shoulder to stop my stuttered response.

"I'm jesting, Benjamin! My guards are very good at their jobs. But they can be, let's say, a little overzealous? I reminded them of that after last night. I trust you and I told them as much. You have no need to apologise. It is forgotten. Now, shall we?"

As he gestures to the door for me to lead on, I'm still reeling from his words. James had told me previously how difficult it is to read Edmund, yet this is the first time I've seen it properly for myself.

I know that I cannot trust him and that I cannot afford to lower my guard around him. As we reach the front steps, I take in a deep breath of fresh air. The chill of winter is beginning to give way to the brightness of spring. Pale blue skies are emerging from the clouds and the floor underfoot is wet with dew rather than the crisp frost of the last few months.

I can hear birdsong coming from the tall oak trees, and as I take my first proper look at the gardens in daylight, I cannot help but think how beautiful they are. The hedgerows are deep green and bordered with flower beds which bloom with red, winter pansies.

The only things which spoil the surroundings, are the gold-gilded statues of cherubs which match the ones displayed on the Palace front.

"How much has James told you of Sophia's past?" Edmund asks suddenly, breaking the silence as we walk the stone gravelled path towards the fountain.

I shake my head. "Not much. I was of the impression that he wanted me to make my own interpretation upon speaking with her. And I haven't yet had the chance, what with the wonderful news about her being with child."

I'm amazed at the calmness of my tone.

It's as though I'm taking myself away from the situation. I'm just playing a part in some wicked play.

Edmund smiles widely at the mention of his unborn child and I feel my jaw twitch in anger, which I pray he doesn't notice.

"It is the most wonderful news." He nods. "Sophia was born to be a mother. Of course, I am anxious that the safety of both her and my unborn son are made the highest priority of James and yourself."

"Well, of course, Your Majesty. It is our duty to ensure her continued wellbeing and now that of your unborn child as well."

He smiles at me, yet it doesn't meet his eyes.

He stops walking as we reach the fountain, turning to me with a thoughtful look on his face.

"When I found Sophia again she was in a most terrible state," he begins. "Living in squalor with a man who beat her. Who expected her to do all of the work, whilst he drank himself into a stupor. Truly it broke my heart to know how she had been forced to live for so long. Benjamin? Are you alright?" He stops and looks at me and I realise that I am clenching my fists tight by my side, and I can feel the set of my jaw with the anger I am barely managing to contain.

"My apologies, Your Majesty." I bow my head, forcing myself to relax. "I just never realised that Lady Sophia had been through such horror." I reposition myself to not look so uncomfortable.

"James never told you anything?"

"No details, Your Majesty. Only that she was suffering an affliction of the mind and that it was not his specialism."

"It is yours, I gather?"

"I …" I open my mouth to speak but the words won't come.

"Don't be modest, Benjamin." Edmund smiles with a shake of his head. "James has told me of the work you showed him. It takes a lot to impress him."

"I am still a student, Your Majesty," I reply. "I am deeply grateful for Doctor Collins' praise, yet I do not wish you to believe that I can perform miracles."

Edmund laughs, clapping me on the shoulder and I take a moment to swallow down the nerves which have reappeared from nowhere.

"I do not expect miracles, Benjamin. Besides, James has already done a fine job in helping the Sophia I know and love come back to me. All I ask of you, is that you carry on helping her see that this life, with me, is where she is safe now."

"Surely she knows this, Your Majesty?" I reply graciously, having finally managed to regain the confidence of my act. "She could not be safer than she is right now, here with you."

"I would hope that is the case," he says, a woeful look appearing on his face. "Yet this affliction of the mind from which she suffers sometimes makes her believe that this man actually loved her. That she would be better off with him. That it is actually I who is causing her pain." He breaks off, shaking his head before turning his gaze to mine once more. "You must make her see, Benjamin." His dark eyes are filled with menace again. "It was Thomas Thornton who did those things to her, not I. She must understand this. You must help her so that she can truly come back to me once and for all."

We continued our walk for a little while longer, Edmund suddenly changing tact, the darkness in his eyes replaced by pride as he spoke of his home, pointing out different parts of the palace and the gardens, and telling me of their history. As I made my way back to the Palace afterwards, my mind was reeling. How I managed to maintain my emotions and my cover is a mystery to me. Hearing him talk like that about Sophia, about us, made my blood boil and all I want to do is take her away from him, but I cannot, that much is obvious now.

As I reach the Palace doors, my mind flashes instantly to her and I have to force myself to turn right rather than left at the top of the ruby carpeted staircase and make my way back to my own chambers. Unsure as to whether or not James is back from his rounds, I knock on his door and am grateful when he opens it, happy to have someone to talk with as myself. He looks at me and then beyond me, as if expecting someone else.

"The King?"

"It was time for his morning hunt," I say, as he invites me in and closes the door behind me. "He invited me along but I politely declined. Didn't fancy ending up with a stray arrow in my back."

"You think he suspects?"

I'm grinning but James's voice is serious now, his eyes searching my face for clues. I shake my head, trying to rid myself of my own niggling worries. "No. No, he cannot suspect. It is as you say, if that were the case then he would've had me locked up and tortured last night. I doubt he is a man who wastes time."

James nods but adds no further comment which doesn't ease the niggle in my mind. He takes a seat at his desk upon which sits some open bottles, I must have interrupted him from working when I came to the door.

"May I ask you something, James?"

He finishes pouring drops from each bottle into one smaller one and corking it before looking over at me and nodding.

"Do you honestly like that man? I cannot understand why. You are the complete opposite of him. The things he does ... surely it goes against everything you stand for?" I see James watching me carefully, and I hold up my hands. "My apologies, I am speaking out of turn."

"No, no." he replies. "You are entitled to ask and your observations are correct. We are very much different people. With opposing opinions about the world. Yet when I taught Edmund as a young boy, I saw a glimmer of something in him. Something that I thought would make him a wonderful King when his time came. Sadly, it appears he chose to act upon the more selfish aspects of his nature, and that saddens me. The truth is, I admired the boy that I taught all of those years ago. And I still hope that he is in there somewhere. Yet I fear with each passing day that this is not the case. But for my own safety, and for yours and Sophia's, it is vital that I remain his loyal servant."

As I listen to him, I realise that he is right. He is having to put on an act as we all are. In order to stay safe. Though I cannot imagine Edmund as the boy James says he knew, it must be even more difficult for him coming to the realisation that he isn't the person he thought he was.

"Forgive me," I say, quietly. "You are right, of course. As you always are."

He gives me a small smile as he stands up and walks over to me. "Would you like to accompany me to visit Sophia?"

I look at him in confusion. "I assumed you had already completed your visits?"

He nods as he hands me the small bottle I watched him make up earlier.

"I have. Sophia was anxious when you didn't accompany me. I assured her that everything was fine and that I would make her up a tonic for her nerves, which we would bring her once you got back from your meeting with Edmund. We had better go now, as to not cause her any further distress."

I look from the small bottle in my hand before looking back at him.

"Thank you."

"There is no need to thank me." He shakes his head. "I am just doing my job. Making sure she is alright."

SOPHIA

As Edmund heads off on his daily hunt, I smile and wave from the window as I normally do. Except the smile on my face isn't forced this time. He may think I'm smiling at him. Which is fine, let him think that. I'll let him live in the fantasy world inside his head where I am hopelessly and madly in love with him. He must and will never know the real reason for my smile.

As the weeks have gone on, Tom and I have settled into a routine of sorts. I see him almost every day when he accompanies James on his visits. Even though this is nothing like what we wanted or needed it to be, just being able to see each other; to hold each other, to talk, to smile, to laugh after so long; somehow it is enough.

Deep down I know that it cannot last. I know that I have to send him away before someone discovers us. But sometimes I feel like I want to be selfish. Because having him here is bringing me back a little of the old me that I lost. I feel happiness when I am with him and I don't want that to end.

A noise behind me makes me jump and I spin around in panic before I see Tom standing there, a grin on his face.

"What are you doing here?" I shake my head in confusion as he places the bag he is holding down on the floor.

"James was called away. Someone in the town required a physician and he was the closest. That meant that he couldn't attend on you like he was supposed to. Which technically means that I couldn't either. But I needed to see you. Then I remembered about the servant's staircase."

I can't help but giggle as I run over, melting into him as his kiss touches my lips. I never want him to stop but eventually I break away, placing my arms tight around his waist as he kisses the top of my head.

"What's in the bag?" I ask curiously, and he grins at me like a child. I release him from my grasp so that he can pick the bag up and open it.

"Bread, cheese, ham." He lists as he takes each item from it. "Chicken, which I'm excited about. Lemonade, apple pie ... not as good as yours obviously. And ..." He pulls out a red and white checked blanket, and I look at him in wonder. I watch him as he places it down on the thick white carpet before placing all of the beautiful food he had brought down on it.

"I know you love a picnic," he says, looking up at me with a small smile. "And I know this isn't the same as being outside in the sun. But, I just wanted to bring you something to make you smile."

I'm smiling now. The smile coming naturally, the fact that he decided to do this for me is making my heart sing for the first time in forever.

"Where did you get all the food?"

"Annalise helped me," he replies, with a chuckle. "She said there is always so much left to waste, nobody would notice."

"You two are as bad as each other!" I chastise jokingly as he gestures to the space next to him and I sit down.

"Are you hungry or what?"

I grin, nodding my head and he laughs as he begins to share out the spoils. I find myself enjoying food for the first time in so long. Edmund has plied me with the rich, decadent meals which he considers normal since my arrival here. But most of it I've refused and the other I've only eaten begrudgingly so that I wouldn't starve. The simpleness of bread, cheese and meat, sitting down to eat it with the man I love, this feels like a luxury to me. And if I close my eyes I can almost imagine that I'm back home, in the paddock, feeling the sun on my skin. I look over at Tom, a smile still lingering on my lips, wanting to thank him for doing this. I watch him as he breaks slices of bread and meat into smaller pieces, placing some in his mouth but putting the other to a side on the blanket. I cock my head to a side curiously.

"What on earth are you doing?" I laugh, as he looks at me and I gesture to the small pile of bread and meat he is building.

As he looks at it, he shakes his head. "Force of habit. I'd always share some of my food with Amos, remember? It used to drive you crazy so I just did it more! I just wish he could be here to share it now."

The mention of Amos' name makes my eyes prick with tears and I feel the wobble of my chin as I try to hold them back. Tom notices instantly and shuffles over to me, his eyes full of worry, as he places a hand to my cheek.

"Sophia, what is it?"

"He looked after me so many times," I reply, quietly. "From the moment I found him, when he was weak and scared himself, he still had this natural instinct to protect me. And it broke my heart watching him try and defend me against men with swords, doing what he knew he had to do. The last image I have of Amos is him watching me get dragged out of there as the blood pooled out of him." I brush the tears from my eyes. I feel bad for spoiling something so nice. I know Tom wouldn't have meant to upset me.

Then I feel his hand at my cheek again, his thumb gently brushing away the rest of my tears, a small smile on his lips.

"He's alive, Sophia," he says softly. "He had a deep wound to his leg, but I fixed him up."

I look at him in amazement. "He's alive?" I repeat his words and he nods. "He yelped out in so much pain, I thought..."

"That dog is too stubborn to die," Tom replies, and I find myself chuckling despite my tears. "He's a fighter, that one. You knew that from the minute you found him."

"Where is he?"

"With Jack and Mary, at the tavern."

"But I thought Mary ...?"

Tom smiles. "She made an exception for him."

I feel like a small weight has been lifted. On top of all of the hurt and guilt I feel, knowing that Amos didn't die trying to save me, brings me a little peace. I gesture to Tom to lay down, which he does, and I fold myself into him, feeling the movement of his chest with gentle breaths as I reach for the rope holding his wedding ring and grasp it in my hand.

"Tell me about home," I whisper, closing my eyes. I feel his body shudder as he takes a shaky breath and it feels like an age before he speaks.

"I'm afraid I haven't been looking after it as best I could." His voice is wobbly and I feel for his hand with my other one, taking hold of it and squeezing it tight. "There are a few holes in the roof. And the gate is broken. But, I made sure to look after the farm and the animals, as I knew you would kill me if I didn't."

I manage a laugh and look up at him to see his eyes are swimming with tears. "Tom ..."

"Jack and Mary looked after me," he continues. "They made sure I was okay. As okay as I could be. They encouraged me to work, which I did most days. But some days I just couldn't face it. Some days it just felt like the whole world was crashing down around me, and all I could feel was pity from the people who cared. Accusations from those who didn't. On those days, I went to the beach, it was where I felt closest to you. I'd sit there from sunrise to sunset with Amos, just watching the waves crash against the shore. Watching the sun as it moved across the sky. Imagining you were sitting there next to me."

I look up at him and see that he has closed his eyes, likely taking himself back to that hidden beach we loved so much. I pull myself in tighter to him as I rest my head against his chest once more and close my eyes too.

"I'm here now," I say, and I feel him take hold of me tighter as I speak. "We can at least pretend like we are there."

With my eyes closed and in the quietness of my room, I can just about take myself back there, back to that beach. And for a moment, I can even imagine the sound of the waves crashing against the sand.

When Edmund requested that I call on him in his study later that day, I was still riding high from spending the morning with Tom in my room. We lay in each other's arms for what felt like an age, before he finally forced himself to leave, knowing that he would need to be back transcribing papers in James' office before he returned from his visit.

As I reach Edmund's study, I wonder what he could possibly be presenting me with now; more jewellery, more ball gowns. Some precious stone from some far away land that he had acquired because of his highly stature. I don't want any of it. I long for the simple pleasures of picking fruit to bake into pies or finding beautiful seashells that have been washed up on the shore.

Knocking on the door, I enter and I see him in the corner of the room, talking with two people who have their backs to me. As Edmund acknowledges me, they turn and my breath catches in my throat as I see my parents.

"Mama? Papa?" I don't understand what is happening but the overwhelming feeling of seeing my parents again after so long takes over and before I know what I'm doing, I find myself rushing over to them, enveloping myself in their embrace, breathing in their familiar, homely smell.

"Sophia," my mother whispers into my hair, as they squeeze me tighter. "We thought we'd never see you again."

As I pull back from them I shake my head, looking at them as the tears cloud my eyes. They look the same. I was always told I looked like my mother. With her red hair and delicate features she forever looked younger than her years. But I have my father's eyes and his shine with tears as he looks at me.

There are a few more greys scattered in his dark brown hair but aside from that, it is as if I only saw him yesterday, watching him go out to work and earn a decent living which allowed us to live comfortably in the Capital, surrounded by those born into money.

"What are you doing here?"

"I invited them, my love." Edmund answers my question as he walks towards us. I feel myself instinctively grasp hold of my father's arm tighter. "With you being so unwell until recently, I didn't think it was right to let your parents know until I knew if you could or would get well again."

"King Edmund told us what happened to you," my mother says, her voice harsh with anger. "I'm so sorry, my darling. I wish we'd have known."

"She's safe now, Mrs Reynolds," Edmund replies, his voice soft. "That's what matters, isn't it, Sophia?"

He's smiling at me. He's saying this to cement the idea in his head that I belong to him. That's all he cares about. And bringing my parents here is just another move in his chess game because he knows that I could never admit anything to them.

"I'm forever grateful to Edmund for rescuing me," I say, plastering a thankful smile upon my face. "I was a fool to leave and to refuse his proposal. I know that now."

I don't sound like me. I wonder if my parents can tell. My mother just looks relieved. My father too, but I can see in his eyes a flicker of uncertainty. Just a flicker and then it goes. For the best, I think. This fantasy of Edmund's is the only way I have of keeping everyone safe. Edmund holds out a hand to me and I try not to flinch as I take it.

"I wanted to wait until you got here before I told your parents our wonderful news." He smiles broadly, my mother is looking expectantly from Edmund then back to me. My father's focus remains entirely on me. "You are to be Grandparents," Edmund continues, joyfully. "My darling Sophia is with child. She is carrying my son and Heir."

I place a protective hand instinctively to my stomach. Though I am showing now, underneath the cut of my skirts it is still not noticeable to those who do not know.

My mother throws her arms around me again, whispering in my ear what wonderful news this is, as I try to keep the smile on my face. I can see my father watching me from over her shoulder and as I break away from her I walk over to him, placing my arms tightly around him, craving the protection of my youth. I'm waiting for him to speak, but he doesn't.

I do not know if this is due to shock, or something else. My father has always been the one to calm me when I have felt lost. Yet right now, without his words to guide me, I feel more adrift than ever.

Eventually, I tear myself away from him, as Edmund announces a dinner will be held this evening in my parents honour, and I feel a jolt of panic as he says that James and Benjamin will be invited, too. Not knowing how much longer I can keep up the pretence, I excuse myself to get ready, walking from the room as naturally as I can before rushing back to the safety of my chambers as soon as I am out of their sight.

As Annalise helped me into my evening dress of lilac silk and did my hair, I could barely speak. Earlier on in the day, I had been so excited to see her. To innocently chastise her for helping Tom create his stolen picnic. To tell her how wonderful it had been just to have some time alone with him. How it felt so calm.

Instead all I could tell her was that my parents were back and that Edmund had arranged a dinner for this evening. I couldn't go into details. I still feel numb. My mother was so full of joy at seeing me again, at the news of my pregnancy. Yet my father who always protected me, who had always understood me ... understood my heart, stayed quiet. And I knew deep down that it was because he could sense something was wrong.

As Annalise finishes tying a pale gold ribbon around my hair, there is a knock at the door and I ask her to get it. I look at myself in the mirror of my dressing table. My happy glow of earlier has disappeared. It feels like a lifetime ago since Tom held me in his arms in this very room.

"My Lady ..." Annalise's voice shakes me from my thoughts and as I look across I see she is standing nervously next to my father.

"Papa."

I get up from the table and rush over to him, throwing my arms around his neck as he pulls me into a protective embrace. "I needed to see you," he says quietly into my ear, his voice gentle. "Alone. Without the King or your mother there."

There are tears of relief in my eyes as I look over at Annalise and ask if she will leave us. As she closes the door, I pull my father in close to me again.

"My little lamb," he says softly, and I feel his arms embrace me tighter. "What on earth has happened to you?"

I take his hand and guide him over to the table. He takes a seat opposite me, looking straight into my eyes with his identical ones and I know that he can see right through me.

"I'm fine, Papa. I am."

"You aren't, Sophia. I know you aren't."

I swallow down my tears, plastering a smile on my face. "Isn't this what you wanted for me?" I whisper. "To know that I am comfortable and want for nothing? I know how hard you worked bringing in the money to give us the life we had. You did that to give me opportunities like this."

"Not if they make you unhappy." He looks at me closely. "Be honest with me lamb," he says gently. "Tell me what is happening."

"I can't," I choke up. "Please don't make me."

"Sophia, you are scaring me."

"I'm fine, Papa. I promise. As long as I do what he says then I am fine."

His eyes narrow as I say this. "Edmund told us that he rescued you from an abusive situation. But it sounds to me like this is exactly what this is."

The tears are beginning to roll down my cheeks and he wipes them away with a gentle thumb.

"I just want to protect you," I whisper. "The more you know …"

"I'm your father, Sophia." He shakes his head, interrupting me. "I'm meant to be the one protecting you."

As a child, I would tell my father everything. I couldn't keep a secret from him and I never wanted to. He was my best friend. But how can I tell him this? How can I admit that I am living a life of hell? It would kill him. And I know that he would want to confront Edmund and I cannot let that happen. It's taking enough of my energy protecting Tom.

"Where did you go?" He breaks the silence with a question. "When you left home?"

"Lowshore."

He smiles at me. "My family originated from there."

"They did?" I say in surprise, and he nods. "I never knew."

"My great-grandparents owned farmland there for many years."

"I had a farm." I whisper it wistfully, knowing full well that as always, keeping secrets from my father is impossible for me.

He smiles again. "I could see you doing something like that. Living off the land like they did."

I give him a tearful smile and he grasps for my hand again.

"You were happy there, weren't you?" I nod and he squeezes my hand. "Then why...?"

"I can't tell you that, Papa," I say, honestly. "Please. Not just for yours and Mama's sake. There are other people I am protecting by keeping up this pretence too."

He closes his eyes, turning away from me. "That day we received word from the palace that Edmund wanted your hand in marriage, we were so happy for you. You were our only child. Our beautiful daughter. You weren't of money or social standing. Edmund had his choice of so many rich, society girls, yet he chose you. You grew up surrounded by wealth and privilege but we taught you to work hard and be kind to others. And that made you different. We thought that is what he loved about you."

"He doesn't love me, Papa." I shake my head. "He likes beautiful things that he can show off and admire. He just wanted to own me. And now he does. I am a bird in a gilded cage. And there is nothing anyone can do about it."

"I won't let this go on," he says, getting to his feet. "This isn't right."

"Papa, please!" I rush from the table and grab hold of his arm. "Please! Edmund is dangerous. You don't know how dangerous he is. The only reason that any of us are safe right now is because he believes that I love him. Take that away, and the whole thing starts to unravel putting everyone that I truly love in danger. Please."

He looks at me again and I can tell he is still in two minds as of what to do.

"Please, Papa. If not for me ... then for your grandchild." His eyes soften as I say this, his sad gaze reaching my stomach. "You see I cannot leave him or this place. Now or ever. I am carrying his child. If it is a boy, he will be heir to the throne. His legacy. He will never let me go, never. So you have to trust me. Trust that I can find some happiness by which to live this life as best I can."

He walks back over to me and I rest my head against his shoulder, letting my tears soak into his jacket.

"Oh Sophia," he whispers into my hair. "I wish you could have told me. I could have protected you. Stopped any of this from happening." I can hear the pain in his voice. Pain that stops me from telling him that even the man I love couldn't stop this from happening. Nobody could.

"I am as happy as I can be here, Papa," I say, truthfully, still grasping onto the warm, comforting thoughts of this morning. "Please believe me."

He sits quietly, searching my face with his eyes before finally lifting his hand and wiping the remnants of my tears gently from my face. "I've missed you so much little lamb."

"I've missed you, too."

I manage a smile as I throw my arms around him again and stay there until I feel myself begin to calm. Then when I am ready, he helps me up from my chair and takes my arm, accompanying me to the banqueting room where Edmund's grand dinner is about to begin.

The doors are opened by courtiers as we reach it. Edmund is at the head of the long table and stands as we enter the room. My mother, dressed in a beautiful gown of green silk, stands to his right, next to James and at the opposite side of the table is Tom, wearing the same navy blue coat he wore when I saw him again for the first time. My breath catches in my throat as he smiles at me and I feel my cheeks beginning to flush, so I force myself to look away towards Edmund and I curtsey to him before my father helps me to my seat and takes his own.

Edmund keeps on telling me that I need not curtsey. Yet it gives me some sort of strength. He may think I am his wife. But to me he is just my King and I will treat him as such.

As we begin to be served course after course of decadent food, Edmund converses charmingly with my parents whilst I force myself to keep smiling.

I can see why people would fall for his charm.

He is handsome and a great conversationalist. But it is all a front. One big act, to disguise the true darkness in his soul. I can tell my mother is taken with him. I know my father isn't. He keeps glancing at me and I know it is taking all of his patience to keep his tongue.

"Sophia! Your arm." My mother's horrified voice rings out suddenly, as I reach for my glass and she catches sight of the twisted scars which cover it.

I place my glass back down and take hold of her hand. "It's nothing, Mama," I say softly, trying to calm her. "I got hurt but it is better now. Doctor Collins looked after me very well."

"Now, now, Sophia." It is Edmund who speaks now. "You mustn't hide from the past, my darling." I can hear the smirk in his voice as I look at him. "You must face up to it in order to help you to remember that you are safe here. This is something Benjamin has been helping you with, am I correct, Benjamin?"

Tom's eyes flash from me to Edmund as he swallows down his mouthful of wine. "Yes, your Majesty," he replies, his voice steady. "We are taking it slowly, for Lady Sophia's sake."

"But surely it is best for her to come to terms with it? And here, surrounded by her family and the people she trusts most, surely this is a safe space?" Edmund smiles.

"Yes, Your Majesty, but ..."

"Sophia, my darling." Edmund cuts Tom off before he can protest. "You are safe here. You can tell them what he did to you."

"Who?" My mother looks at him curiously. My father is now watching him too, his eyes giving nothing away.

"The drunkard she was living with before I rescued her. A thug named Thomas Thornton," he replies, darkly. I daren't look at Tom. My eyes instead find James, who is watching all of this unfold quietly, his face betraying nothing of his thoughts.

"What did he do to you, Sophia?" My mother's eyes are full of worry as she keeps a tight hold of my hand. My gaze flashes around the table.

Edmund still watches me, his eyes intent on mine, his face full of anger yet I see the smirk behind his eyes at what he is forcing me to do. I don't think my father wants to know. Because he knows that whatever I will say is not the truth, just another part of this tale I must weave to keep us all safe. Tom will not meet my eyes, his gaze focused intently on his plate, and James is watching everything unfold quietly, yet I know that of everyone here he is the one with the most influence to stop this.

"I ... I don't want to think about it," I stutter, shaking my head, as I try desperately to catch James' eye. "It is in the past now."

"Your parents need to know, Sophia," Edmund says. "I need to know."

I cannot bear to make up some horrific story of what Tom is meant to have put me through, as he sits there across from the man who actually did it. But Edmund is being persistent. I feel the tears welling up in my eyes, as I open my mouth to speak before I hear James' voice first and relief floods into my veins.

"Lady Sophia seems distressed, Your Majesty. Perhaps this can wait for another time."

I look at him with grateful eyes before turning my gaze to Edmund. He stays silent, his own gaze now directed at James and I wonder if he is going to pursue it.

"You are right, James," he says, eventually and I breathe a sigh of relief. "This is supposed to be a celebration! There will be a time to dwell on the past and come to terms with what happened."

"Indeed, Your Majesty." Tom's voice suddenly rings out and I look over at him in surprise but he is focusing on Edmund. "I just hope this hasn't set her recovery back. The mind is a delicate thing."

The tension in his voice is clear. I watch as Edmund stares him down, opening his mouth to speak before seemingly thinking better of it.

"I'd like to make an announcement." Edmund suddenly gets to his feet, chiming his fork against his glass to alert our attention. He smiles widely at me, and I instantly feel a stab of panic in my heart. "As I explained to your parents earlier, my darling, we married quietly soon after your arrival here. We wanted to commit to one another but you weren't well enough to cope with a full ceremony. And of course, to protect you from the dangerous man you were living with. But now that you are in much better health and enough time has passed, I am thinking it is only right that we have a celebration, a ceremony that your parents can experience. Being that you are their only child it feels right."

"I ..."

He walks over to me, taking hold of my hand as I look at him in confusion.

"I've spoken to the priest," he says, softly. "We can have a blessing. Cementing our union in front of all of our family and friends. Letting the people see what a beautiful bride I have chosen."

My mother is joyous. My father is putting on a brave face and James is ever the faithful servant. As they dissolve into happy conversation, I snatch a glance at Tom. Outwardly his face betrays nothing. Yet his eyes are full of pain that only I can see. It was hellish enough for him finding out that Edmund had married me. Now he has to sit and watch it happen all over again.

"Joyous news, my Lady." James walks over to me, placing a kiss against my hand before taking Edmund's and shaking it.

"Thank you, James," he replies, as he takes hold of my hand once more. "I just felt that it was time the whole of the land knew and could celebrate our love with us. And of course, yourself and Benjamin are invited as our special guests. A thank you for all of your hard work in helping my darling Sophia back to health."

I don't know how Tom is managing to keep his cool. It must be taking every ounce of strength he has.

I turn to him again, watching as he gets up from his seat and walks over to us. He bows to Edmund before reaching for my hand, placing a kiss against it just as he did the first time I saw him again.

My skin tingles at his touch and I beg myself not to show it.

"It is an honour to have been asked, Your Majesty. My Lady," he says, my heart aching at his words. "Just as it is an honour helping you back to health again."

"You are both doing an exceptional job." Edmund nods in approval at both Tom and James. "You shall both be sorely missed when the time comes for you to leave us." I see Tom's eyes widen until Edmund speaks again. "Of course, that will not be any time yet. There is no-one I would trust more to bring my son and heir into the world than you, James."

As James bows graciously, I snatch a look at Tom and see his composure falter slightly for a brief moment before he smiles again.

"If you would all excuse me, I am feeling a little fatigued. The festivities of the evening appear to have taken their toll on me. It has been a long day." He turns to say his goodbyes to my parents and James, before once again bowing respectfully to Edmund and myself.

"Your Majesty. My Lady."

I watch him walk away from us, out of the hall and towards his quarters as Edmund takes hold of my hand once more, bringing my attention back into the room as he makes a toast to our happy union.

I thought he would come and find me. I half expected him to be sitting in my room when I returned. But there was only Annalise, waiting to help me dress for bed. The news was a sickening shock to me, so god only knows how it made Tom feel.

"We should get you ready for bed, my Lady." Annalise's voice filters into my thoughts. "It's gettin' late."

"I need to see Tom, Annalise." I look at her. "Can you get a message to him?"

I reach for a quill and dip it in the ink pot on my desk, scrawling a quick message onto a scrap of paper before letting it dry and folding it. As I walk over to her, she looks at me in concern. "My Lady …"

"Please," I fold the piece of paper into her hand. "Take the servants' staircase. Get it to him any way that you can."

"I need to 'elp you dress for bed, my Lady."

"I can dress myself. This is more important. Please?"

Eventually, giving me a small smile, she nods.

"Thank you. Please be careful."

As Annalise leaves, I go to wash my face and change into my nightgown before sitting down at my dressing table to brush my hair. Glancing down at my stomach, seeing the rounded curve of it beneath the white satin, I feel conflicted.

A child is all I have wanted for so long, a child that would complete our little family. And knowing that there is a little baby growing safe inside of me, makes my heart want to burst with happiness. But it's not Toms. As much as I wish it could be, it's not. And that must be killing him. I know that there is no way I can make him stay and watch not just my wedding ceremony, but the birth of someone else's child. As much as it hurts me, I need to say goodbye.

The door clicks behind me and I turn to see him standing there, still wearing his earlier attire, minus his jacket; his white shirt now open at the neck just enough so that I can see the rope that holds his wedding ring.

"I got your message." His voice is quiet, as I get to my feet and walk over to him.

"I needed to see you."

"About the big wedding news? That was a surprise."

"I swear I knew nothing of it until he announced it at dinner," I say, taking hold of his hands, relieved that he doesn't pull away. "I didn't even know my parents were here until he summoned me to his study and he was standing there with them. You must know I don't want this."

"I know, Sophia," he replies, a small smile playing on his lips. "Of course I know. This whole thing has Edmund's name written all over it. Bringing your parents in was a master stroke. How could you possibly refuse then?"

I remember my conversation with my father and I squeeze Tom's hands tighter.

"My father knows something is wrong," I say and I see his eyes widen in panic. "No ... no I haven't told him anything. He just ... he knows. He knows I am unhappy. But I've told him I have to do this. To keep everyone safe."

My voice breaks on the last word and Tom pulls me in close. "It's just a play on a big stage, Sophia," he whispers into my hair. "That's all it is."

"You don't have to watch. You shouldn't have to."

"Refuse a direct invitation from the King?" he replies. "Not sure that would be the wisest idea, or how I could possibly explain it."

I pull back from him looking at the smile on his face but seeing the sadness behind his eyes. And I know that as hard as it will be, I need to tell him the truth.

"You have to go soon."

"I know. It's late."

"No. I mean ..." He's looking at me in confusion and I swallow back my tears. "Leave here, go back home."

His lips twitch into a smile as he shakes his head. "No. No, we've talked about this. I'm not lea ..."

"I should have told you to go the first day I spoke to you properly," I whisper, unable to look at him. "Looking back, I shouldn't have even asked James to find you. It was a stupid, stupid idea. I was being selfish."

"Don't say that."

"I was!" I cry out, tears blurring my eyes. "Maybe at that point there was some small chance that I could find a way out of here. But when you arrived when I told you that I was ..." I subconsciously place a hand to my stomach. "I should have insisted that you leave then. Because what good is this doing either of us? In the end it's just going to cause us more pain."

"We've worked it out so far," he says, the conviction in his voice unmistakable. "It won't be easy but we love each other. We can make this w ..."

"No. No, Tom, we can't." I shake my head, interrupting him. "Deep down, you know that this can't go on."

"What are you trying to say?" He looks at me, his brow furrowed in confusion. "You don't love me enough?"

His words hit me like a slap in the face and I can't bear the pain. "Don't you dare!" I hiss viciously. "Don't you dare say that Thomas, not after everything!" I turn and walk away from him but he grabs hold of my arm, pulling me into him tightly and I don't try to pull back.

"I'm sorry. I'm sorry, Sophia, I shouldn't have said that. Forgive me." He pulls his arms around me tighter and I can't stop myself from relaxing against him, forever drawn to him, no matter how much I want to pull away for both our sakes.

"I love you more than anything in this world," I choke up and I feel him place a kiss against my hair. "Don't you understand? That's why I have to let you go. How can I possibly expect you to stay and watch as I get married, have another man's child, live this existence that I cannot ever escape from? It would break you. Don't try and tell me that it wouldn't."

"But what is the alternative?" he asks, quietly. "Go back home to a town that part pities and part despises me? Pretend to live a normal life knowing that you are here being forced to live this one? You don't think that would kill me? At least if I'm here I can see you; have moments together, no matter how fleeting."

"You heard what Edmund said." I sigh. "He will have no reason for James to stay once his child is safely delivered into this world. He will free you both of your duties and will expect you to leave."

"I'll ask him for a job," he replies, strongly. "Spin him some story, make him feel sorry for me. Allow me to stay."

"As what? A doctor? You came here with false papers, Tom. They will only get you so far. Without James beside you, you would have no idea what you were doing. They would discover you in no time and then what?"

I see the hope beginning to drain from his face and I wonder if I have been too harsh. I don't want to talk or think about this anymore. I just want to enjoy however many moments I have left with him. Taking his hand, I lead him over to the bed and we both lie down on top of the covers facing one another. He's searching my eyes with his, trying to read me, asking me silently if this is what I really want. Which he knows it isn't. But we both know neither of us have a choice. Then his hand finds my stomach, resting gently against my bump and my heart aches at the simple gesture.

"I'm sorry I couldn't …" His voice is choked, as he looks at me and I see his eyes are filled with tears.

"No, Tom, don't." I place a hand to his cheek, feeling the wetness of his tears against my palm. "It wasn't our time." I soothe, feeling my own tears begin to prick at my eyes. "It was nobody's fault you know that."

"I always wanted a girl," he says, quietly, his hand still resting on my small bump. "A beautiful baby girl who would be the image of her mother. Watching her grow up on the farm surrounded by nature and all of those animals. She would have been so loved."

My throat is tight with emotion making it impossible to speak.

As I try to compose myself, I start stroking one hand through his hair, the other finding the one he still rests upon my stomach until finally I manage to reply.

"Yes. She would …"

TOM

The sound of birdsong begins to wake me from my sleep. As I open my eyes, the early morning sun is streaming in through the window, casting the room in an ethereal, warm glow.

I look over and see Sophia still sleeping peacefully and I smile. Let her sleep a while, I think to myself. I'll sort out the animals before I head to work. I sit up and it's only then that I realise where we are. This isn't home. Her opulent, palace room is quiet but I hear the murmurings of movement outside and I panic, realising that I must have fallen asleep here last night.

Sophia still hasn't stirred and I don't want to worry her so I get up quietly, finding a blanket and resting it over her before placing the lightest of kisses against her hair and making my way down the servants' staircase to the next floor. I quickly re-tie the fastening on my shirt and attempt to make myself look more presentable before walking the long, ruby red carpeted halls towards my quarters. And as I reach them, I see James waiting outside, the look on his face telling me that he isn't impressed.

"I've been knocking on your door for the past twenty minutes," he whispers harshly. "I was about to call the guards to open it, thinking you had been taken ill! It's a good job I didn't. How on earth would I have explained you not even being there?"

"I'm sorry..."

"Where were you anyway?" he asks, before seeing the look on my face and shaking his head. "Oh no. Please tell me you weren't."

"Nothing happened," I say, honestly. "We fell asleep. That's all. She wanted to see me, to explain about the ceremony. We talked. Then we must have fallen asleep."

James shakes his head as he walks closer to me, looking around to check that we aren't being overheard before speaking again. "You are playing a dangerous game, Tom. Your visits with me are just about explainable. But this."

"It was one mistake," I reply. "You know I'm always careful. Last night was difficult. It won't happen again, I swear it."

He looks at me in disbelief, but I am serious. My time with Sophia is the only thing I am living for right now. To be discovered would break us both. James studies me closely before sighing. "We're staying in my study today. No arguments. I've got papers that need transcribing. You can do that whilst I do my research."

By the tenth page, my arm is starting to ache. Having never been properly schooled, my writing is scruffy to say the least. I'm guessing James doesn't really need these transcripts and he's just given them to me for something to do. At least I hope.

A knock on the door draws both our attention and brings a few moments of welcome relief.

I put down the quill and stretch my hand out as a steward walks over to James, handing him a piece of paper. Nodding his thanks as the steward leaves, James begins to read the paper.

"Lady Sophia's mother has been taken ill," he says, his eyes scrolling the note. "I've been requested to call on her." I get to my feet but he shakes his head. "I don't think that would be a good idea."

"Why? I'm supposed to be your assistant. Surely, it would seem even more strange for me not to accompany you?"

James is easy to convince, I've noticed that over the months. He doesn't reply, but nor does he attempt to stop me, as I follow him out of the room.

It becomes clear when we arrive at their chambers, that we were called at the request of Sophia's father. Her mother sits at her dressing table shaking her head and brushing her husband's concerns away.

"I just felt a little faint, George. That's all. You make too much fuss."

"You turned as white as a ghost, Rebecca. And after everything that happened yesterday I wouldn't blame you. I just wanted to make sure you were okay. I'm sure the good doctor and his assistant don't mind."

"Not at all," James says warmly, as I shake my head in response. "Lady Sophia is a wonderful woman. To assist her parents in any way is an honour."

As James checks on Mrs Reynolds, asking me periodically to hand him different items from his bag, Sophia's father turns to me.

"How long have you worked with James then …?"

"Benjamin," I say, holding out my hand to shake his. "And not long. I'm in my final year of studies. I was bold enough to ask Doctor Collins if I could work with him to further my learning, and happily he accepted."

As James smiles over at me, Sophia's father speaks again. "Which school are you training at?"

"Lowshore, sir."

"Oh you'll be popular with my husband," Rebecca calls, from where she sits at her dresser as George raises an eyebrow. "George's family are from Lowshore. Though when I met him, I told him there was no way I was living there and being a farmer's wife. I was a Capital girl through and through. I had standards. And it wasn't easy but we managed it, didn't we, George?"

"It took many, many hours of hard graft," he replies, with a wry smile. "But, there is nothing wrong with a farmer's life, Rebecca. It's a good, honest living."

"I was relieved when we got the news from Edmund that Sophia had finally come to her senses," Rebecca continues, ignoring George's statement. "She deserves a life of luxury like the one he can provide for her."

George catches my eye for a brief moment before turning his gaze to the ground. "Yes. Yes she does, my dear."

"I do wish we could have been here for the wedding." Rebecca sighs whimsically. "But the blessing will be just as magical, I am sure. And of course, the Spring Ball this weekend will be a wonderful way to spread the news!"

"Spring Ball?" Her words pique my interest and I turn to James.

"The King announced it last night after you left," he explains. "It is an annual event. Every year important people from across the different kingdoms are invited. I was wondering if he would cancel it, what with the blessing due to happen, but he appears he wants the chance to spread the news as far and wide as possible, before the blessing itself."

"I love a Ball," Rebecca says, happily. "It has been so long since I last attended one. It must have been before Sophia was even born!"

"The King puts on a spectacular party." James smiles, as he begins to mix together liquids from the bottles I handed him. "You will enjoy yourself, I have no doubt."

As Rebecca asks James if we will be attending too and I hear him tell her that we shall, I manage a smile but I can tell it looks forced. As George looks at me, I turn back to the table, placing items back into James' medical bag, hoping that my true thoughts weren't completely obvious and now understanding why James suggested I didn't come.

"Is she happy here?" George's voice is so quiet I barely hear it. I look up in the direction it came from and see him standing, watching me closely.

"I don't know what you mean, sir."

"Edmund told us that Sophia was unwell when she arrived here. And that James and yourself have been trying to get her back to health. So I feel you are the best people to ask the question to."

I swallow, busying myself sorting through bottles that don't need sorting, as I try to work out what I can say. Sophia told me that her father suspected something. And he doesn't look like an idiotic man to me. I don't think I can fool him with lies. But I don't want to cause trouble.

"On occasion, she is happy, sir," I reply, eventually, remembering how happy we were just the other day when we picnicked together in her room. "And she is well cared for. You have my word."

"Benjamin?" James calls to me and I turn, thankful for the distraction before I say something I might regret. "Pass me the blue bottle from my bag," he continues. "Mrs Reynolds is a little overwrought. A tincture to calm the nerves and some rest, and she should be just fine."

I reach for the bottle, ignoring George's gaze as I walk over and hand it to James, just about managing to smile as I listen to Rebecca recall tales of Sophia's childhood and how she was always destined to be a Queen.

"So," I say to James, on the way back to his study. "The Spring Ball. And we are both invited."

"As I said, he made the announcement after you had left, and then asked if we would attend. I could hardly refuse."

"I know that. Of course you couldn't. Besides, it might be fun, getting to spend time with Sophia in actual society rather than trapped in her room."

"Tom …" James' voice is low, his tone serious as we get back to his study and he closes the door behind us. "You must be careful! I know how difficult this is. Believe me, I do. But please, do not let your emotions cloud your judgement."

"I'm fine, James," I reply, sharply. "I know what I am doing."

"Challenging the King last night? Falling asleep in Sophia's room?"

"Falling asleep there was a mistake," I say, genuinely. "It won't happen again, I swear it."

"And last night? At dinner?"

"Didn't you see what he was doing to her? The smirk on his face as he was trying to make her blame something he had done on me, in front of her parents?"

"There's something else as well." James sighs, as he looks at me.

"Honestly, James? Just come out with it. I'm pretty sure things can't get much worse than me having to watch my wife walk down the aisle and marry someone else, whilst carrying his child."

"That's just it," he says, and I look up at him in confusion.

"The Spring Ball. It wasn't meant to … like I say, it is an annual event which was due to take place anyway. But Edmund has decided …"

"Decided what?"

"The Ball is on Friday. He is inviting people from across the Kingdom to be here, to celebrate the news of his marriage. And, because they will already be here ..." He stops again and I look at him, baffled.

"James?"

"The blessing will take place the very next day. All the guests will stay at the palace over the weekend, in order to allow them to be here for it. For Edmund to show off his bride to the Kingdom, and beyond."

SOPHIA

As the evening of the Spring Ball arrives, I feel sick with nerves. I know that Edmund will make a display of me. To prove once and for all that I am his and his alone, before cementing that before God once again; making me go through the hell of saying those words, which almost killed me the first time; and this time in front of Tom.

I know he tells me that it is just a play, that none of it is real. But the pain, and guilt I felt being forced to say the words the first time, felt real to me and I already know it will shatter his heart to hear me betray the vows I made to him, act or not.

"My lady?" Annalise's voice pulls me out of my thoughts and into the present, as she laces me into the red dress which Edmund has chosen for me. Full-skirted and threaded with delicate gold silk, the cut of the skirts disguising my stomach which has begun to grow more and more with each passing day. I cannot deny that it is beautiful. But it is not me. It is just another way of Edmund moulding me into who he wants me to be.

As Annalise finishes lacing up the dress, she fastens a choker of gold satin around my neck from which hangs a ruby, matching the one on Edmund's pendant. My hair is piled high upon my head, my cheeks are flush with rouge and I feel like a fraud.

'It's just a play.' Tom's words float into my mind once more, as I stare at my reflection. 'It's just a play on a big stage, Sophia. That's all it is.'

There is a knock at the door and Annalise hurries off to open it as I get to my feet, surveying my reflection once more, Tom's words still so strong in my mind.

"Sophia? Darling?" As Edmund strides into the room, I brush down my skirts and turn to face him, the besotted smile of his faithful, loving wife fixed upon my face.

"Edmund." I curtsey to him and as I straighten up, I see him staring at me, his dark eyes sparkling.

"You are beautiful."

He cannot stop staring at me, his possession. Dressed in his colour, so that everybody knows that I am his. I thank him, making myself appear meek and obedient, as he would want. He holds out his arm and I take it, as he guides me from the room, down corridor after corridor until finally we reach the top of the golden staircase.

"Ladies and Gentlemen, may I have your attention please?"

At the sound of Edmund's voice, the throngs of guests turn to face us where we stand. People who Edmund has invited from across the land, noblemen and women who appeal to his sense of importance, his need for recognition.

I scan the room, looking for Tom but there are too many people for me to make anyone out. Perhaps he decided not to attend. Maybe that is for the best.

Though I doubt he can escape the invitation to the blessing tomorrow, making him live through this as well feels too cruel.

"I would like to introduce you all, formally, to my beautiful wife, the Lady Sophia."

My jaw aches from the smile that I have forced upon my face. Murmurings from the crowd grow louder as guests turn to face one another, shocked and intrigued by this unexpected news. I turn to Edmund and see that he is grinning. This is clearly the reaction which he had hoped for, allowing him to be the centre of attention, the talking point of the crowd.

"Yes, yes I know this has come as a shock to you all." He is still grinning as he addresses the crowd once more. "We married quietly a few months past. Lady Sophia's ill health at the time denied us the chance of a proper celebration. And so, I am afraid that your invitation to the Spring Ball this year has come under false pretences."

He holds the crowd in the palm of his hand, letting the confused murmurings amongst the guests continue until he is ready to make his big announcement.

"Tonight is a celebration. For tomorrow, you are all invited to the blessing of our marriage. A chance for you all to celebrate our joyous union now that Sophia is well again. And our guests of honour will be the two gentlemen who nursed her back to health. Who I shall be eternally indebted to;

THE STARS THAT GUIDE YOU HOME

Doctor James Collins and his assistant, Mr Benjamin Redfield."

He raises a hand, gesturing across the room and I finally see him standing at the back of the room with James, both of them awkwardly accepting the mumblings of praise from the crowd at Edmund's words. He's too far away for me to gauge the look on his face, but I already know without having to see it. And I wish I could spare him the pain of both this and what is to come.

"So!" Edmund's voice rings out bringing the attention back to him. "Without further ado, let us all enjoy the evening's festivities and celebrate the blessings to come tomorrow."

He places a kiss against my lips unexpectedly, and the guests erupt into cheers and applause. Then before I know what is happening, Edmund is shepherding me from group to group, introducing me to well-dressed dignitaries and royals, who I neither know nor care to.

My eyes scan the room, looking for Tom, but all of the men are dressed the same, in black dress coats with white shirts and cravats of different colours, making it impossible to make one person out from another in the throng.

Edmund is the only one dressed differently, allowing people to instantly recognise him in the room. He wears his favoured red velvet dress coat and matching cravat and his most treasured, vulgar ruby pendant sitting proudly against his chest.

As he begins talking animatedly to the Prince of Moniatenia, I excuse myself politely, taking a drink from a silver platter carried by a passing waiter as I turn my attention to the dancing; watching in awe as the fine dressed gentlemen spin beautiful ladies dressed in jewel-coloured gowns, around the floor to the sound of joyful music.

"Are you going to dance, my Lady?"

Tom's gentle voice in my ear takes me by surprise and I jump slightly, as I see him looking at me.

The cravat at his neck is light gold which makes his blue eyes shine even more vividly. He's as handsome as I've ever seen him, and I have to force myself to stop gazing at him. I have to take a moment to find composure to reply.

"I would love to. But sadly, Edmund is not fond of dancing." Edmund glances over at me at the mention of his name. He has a glass of port in his hand and is smiling at me. It is still early enough in the evening for him to be enjoying himself.

"It is not befitting of a King to join in the festivities of his own gathering, my darling," he replies. "He should observe and take pleasure in the joy of others."

This is a lie. The only reason he refuses to dance is because he doesn't want to make a fool of himself. But I smile back sweetly in reply, as I turn once more to watch as the dance comes to an end. The musicians are beginning to play a waltz now and I am starting to watch the couples take to the floor, when I hear Tom speak once more.

"Your Majesty, with your permission may I ask Lady Sophia to dance? It would be an honour."

I feel the colour drain from my face at his words. He's looking at Edmund. My hands are shaking so much that I hastily place my glass down upon the table beside me. What on earth is he thinking? There is no way Edmund would agree to such a thing. I glance at James and though his face betrays nothing, I can see from the set of his jaw that he is as shocked as I.

Edmund is studying him closely, and I am so tense that I am barely remembering to breathe. Then his face relaxes and he gives a slight incline of his head in agreement.

"My wife certainly seems eager to dance this evening, Mr Redfield," he replies. "And I would not want to disappoint her. You have my permission."

I cannot believe what I am hearing. Glancing over at James again, I can see he feels the same.

Perhaps Edmund has had more to drink than I realise. There is no anger or suspicion in his face. And though the nerves continue to course through me, as Tom comes to stand in front of me extending his hand to mine I know that I am not going to refuse.

"May I have this dance, my Lady?"

I take hold of his hand without a second thought. It feels strong and warm in mine and I feel safe for the first time in so long. I let him lead me towards the dance floor, as the musicians begin playing their waltz.

Resting his right hand gently against my back he takes hold of my hand with the other, as I place my hand against his shoulder. Then he's leading me in perfect time to the music, our bodies moving in sync with one another and I realise how happy I am. In this moment. With him.

It's as if the rest of the room has faded away and it is just the two of us. He's looking at me as we continue to dance, his eyes alive with joy. He's holding on to my hand so tight as if trying to convince himself this is real. The music is beautifully soft and melodic, rising and falling with us as we spin around the room. I feel safe in his arms and I never want this moment to end but almost as soon as it has started, the dance finishes. The men are bowing to the ladies, starting to leave the floor. Tom takes hold of my hand once more, kissing it as he bows.

"I never knew you could dance," I whisper, though the conversation around us is so loud I doubt anyone would hear us. He raises an eyebrow as he straightens up.

"We danced on our wedding day."

"Swinging me around in a field does not count as dancing." He's grinning at me and I cannot help but smile back.

The more I stand here, the more the world around me starts to fade, leaving just the two of us, here in this bubble.

I'm looking at him, fighting the urge to reach up and kiss him, to place my hand to the curve of his jaw, to take in every piece of him, wishing this moment could last forever.

"Well Benjamin, I dare say if you are as good at your medical studies as you are at dancing, you will make a fine physician." James has walked over to us and I can tell he is putting a stop to something before it starts.

"Very true, James." Edmund's voice drifts over as he walks to stand beside James. His eyes are focused on Tom and I feel a hint of panic. "Where did you learn to dance, Mr Redfield?"

"My mother was a dancer," Tom replies, without a flicker. "She wanted to pass the gift down to her children."

Edmund nods. He even looks mildly impressed. Yet I don't trust him, and suddenly I feel foolish for letting myself get caught up in the moment like that.

"Thank you, Mr Redfield," I say, hastily, unable to look at him properly. "You are indeed a good dancer. I am honoured to have been asked."

Tom opens his mouth to speak but I turn to Edmund before he can. "Darling, you were going to introduce me to Lady Valentina, I would very much like to meet her. I hear she is most skilled in flower arrangement. I would love to ask her opinion on the flowers for the blessing."

"Absolutely." Edmund smiles, turning to James and Tom and I force myself to turn too. "Goodnight, gentlemen."

They both bow to Edmund before each taking my hand and placing a kiss upon it, Tom's kiss still lingering as I take Edmund's arm and walk away.

TOM

We have been seated front and centre of the grand ballroom for the blessing. The best seats in the house to watch this nightmare unfold. As I turn to James, he gestures to my hand and I realise that I am tapping my finger manically against my leg. I clasp my hands together in my lap to try and stop my nerves from showing.

"I'm sorry you have to go through this." His low voice cannot be heard by anyone other than me, over the din of noise coming from the expectant crowd, giving us a chance to speak even if I don't want to.

"I'm fine." I smile, but he knows me too well and is not fooled.

"No you aren't. And I wouldn't expect you to be. I wish we didn't have to be here, but I could hardly say no."

"I know, James. Please stop trying to apologise. It is what it is." A play, I tell myself. Just as I told Sophia. Just a big play on a big stage. But, as much as I try to tell myself this, the knot of sickening pain in my heart tells me to stop being a fool.

That watching this is going to hurt more than anything I have already been through. Because with every word she is forced to speak to Edmund, it will begin to take over the happy memories of our own day.

The happiest day of my life.

"Tom ..." Jack's voice filtered into my brain as I waited nervously at the altar. "Tom, will you stop fidgeting, you'll wear the floor out!"

As I finally focused on him fully, I saw that he was standing chuckling at me. "Sorry." I shook my head, "nerves." I smiled ruefully at him and he placed a hand on my shoulder.

"It's a big day. I'm not surprised. Everyone feels nervous on their wedding day. I drank so much whiskey the night before mine to quell my nerves, that I almost didn't make it! Luckily, my wife-to-be saw the funny side."

He winked over at Mary who shook her head in despair. I tried to smile but the niggling demons that I was desperately trying to keep at bay were finally winning their war.

"What if she doesn't show?" I said to him, the panic that had plagued me all night creeping into my voice. "What if this was all too quick and she's changed her mind?"

"Why on earth would you think that, son?" he said, with a shake of his head, "that girl of yours adores you. It's clear for anyone to see."

"I had only known her a few months, when I asked her to marry me." I continued, unable to stop the thoughts from swirling around in my mind, "maybe I should have waited. Given her a chance to get to know me better. I shouldn't have come on so strong ... oh God, I'm a fool!"

As I ran a stressed hand through my hair I saw Jack shake his head once more, rolling his eyes at my words, which didn't help. This wasn't a baseless fear: I had been shunned and abandoned my whole life, even by those who were supposed to love me. I was about to open my mouth to retort at him, when he placed a hand on my shoulder nodding his head towards the back of the church and I turned.

The sun filtered through the open doorway where she stood in a beautiful long white dress which skimmed the floor as she walked. She was clutching a bouquet of daisies in her hands which matched the crown of them upon her head. She looked like an angel, more beautiful than I had ever seen her which I never thought possible. Her red hair glowed like flames, as it fell in waves across her shoulders.

And, as her gaze reached mine, she smiled - a smile so big and so bright it lit up her whole face. I couldn't take my eyes off her, as she walked down the aisle towards me, her own gaze fixed upon mine.

As she came to stand beside me, handing her bouquet to her bridesmaid, I opened my mouth to say something but the words wouldn't come. She studied my face curiously before placing a hand to my cheek.

"Why do you look so worried?" she asked, softly. "Please tell me you didn't think I was going to abandon you at the altar?" I gave her a sheepish grin and she laughed, shaking her head. "I've been dreaming of this day ever since that night under the stars when you asked me to be your wife," she said with a smile. "I know you are scared because of what has happened in the past. But I would never abandon you. You don't need to be afraid anymore. I'm yours, forever. You're safe now."

I swallowed, managing a wobbly smile. She could read me like a book. She always seemed to know what was going on in my head. And though I doubted that I'd ever fully be able to shake the feeling that this was all too good to be true, her words had started to melt away at the lifelong fears that had been my demons since childhood. And I knew then that she was right. I felt safe.

She stood looking at me, taking in my new clothes which I had saved money for. I didn't want to marry her dressed in the same old stuff I wore every day for work. The cravat at my neck felt odd but the navy-blue jacket and breeches were soft against my skin. I looked at her, embarrassment creeping into my cheeks as I tried to work out what she was thinking when she finally spoke.

"You scrub up pretty well, Thomas Thornton." She said with a shy smile and I grinned back at her.

"You don't look too bad yourself, soon-to-be Mrs Thomas Thornton."

As she laughed, I couldn't help but lean forwards and kiss her, and it appeared she felt the same as she melted into me and the rest of the world melted away. Until the sound of someone clearing their throat brought us back into the present, and I saw Father Aiden standing in front of us, his eyebrow raised. "I do believe the vows come before I say you can kiss your bride, Thomas."

As Sophia and Jack tried to hold back sniggers of laughter, I at least had the decency to appear apologetic as I took Sophia's hand and asked him to begin.

The sound of music draws my attention from the past back to the present and I realise that it is about to happen.

I now see Edmund standing by an alter at the front of the room, dressed in his red velvet dress coat, a red cravat at his neck, his dark hair pulled back into a ponytail and fixed with a red velvet ribbon.

He looks joyful and to everyone else in the room, no doubt he looks the picture of happiness at being able to celebrate his love with the world. But, I see past that. I see nothing but a hunter who has caught his prey, showing it off to the world, proving himself to be the best.

I begin to hear murmurs from the crowd, gasps and sighs of wonder, as they get to their feet and turn to look at the back of the room as the sound of a choir singing begins to drift around the room. I brace myself knowing how odd it will look if I do not turn as well, no matter how much I do not want to bring myself to. Then I do it before I can talk myself out of it.

I cannot say she does not look beautiful. She will always be the most beautiful thing on this earth to me. But I can barely stand to look at her. The white dress she is wearing is nothing like the simple gown she wore on our wedding day. This one has layered skirts of white silk and ivory lace which disguise her stomach.

The train is long, held by six young flower girls who each wear the same red roses in their hair that Sophia holds in her hands. Her red hair is piled up on her head and fixed with a tiara of rubies. She looks just like the Queen she is expected to be. And though I know that this is not what she wants, seeing her like this has pricked at the part of my conscience that has always thought she deserved more than what I could give her.

She's smiling at Edmund as she walks down the aisle, but I can tell that it is forced. As she passes me, I catch her eye but she turns away.

I know why she did it, but still it makes the ache in my heart grow even stronger. I look across at the other side of the room. Rebecca is gazing at her daughter as she reaches the front and stops beside Edmund.

George isn't looking at her. He has caught my eye. I try to smile but he doesn't return it. He looks pale and tired and slightly unsteady on his feet. I continue looking across at him, trying to figure out what's wrong until the sound of the choir fades and the priest begins to speak, drawing my attention back to Sophia.

"Dearly beloved, we are gathered here today to bless the union of our King, Edmund Rose and his bride, Sophia Reynolds in front of their family, trusted friends and honoured guests. It is a union that took many years to happen and now they want to celebrate and cement their love and their union here, with you all today."

Sophia is looking at Edmund, her gaze soft and loving. I know it is all an act, but it is a good one. One that is convincing even myself, feeding my insecurities, forcing me to keep on reminding myself that this is all just one big performance.

The priest continues his speech, talking about the joy of love and reminding us all of the sanctity of marriage. It is at this point that I realise I am digging my nails into the palm of my hand so hard that I've drawn blood. I glance across at George and Rebecca again, and the difference in them is startling. Rebecca is beaming with pride at Sophia, hung on every word which the priest speaks. George looks at a loss. As if he'd rather be anywhere else than here. A feeling which I share but for all of our sakes I am keeping hidden. The look of disapproval on his face is clear for anyone to see.

Luckily, the rest of the room is far too taken with this charade to notice, and I hope it stays that way.

"Edmund Alastor Rose, you have taken Sophia Ellen Reynolds to be your wife. Do you promise to love her, comfort her, honour and keep her, in sickness and in health; and, forsaking all others, to be faithful to her as long as you both shall live?"

I force myself to watch as the priest asks Edmund the question. He is grinning widely, his dark eyes dancing with delight as he looks at Sophia.

"I do."

The words stab at my heart like a knife, and it is taking every ounce of control that I have not to get up and stop this, before the next blow that will surely break it.

"Sophia Ellen Reynolds, you have taken Edmund Alastor Rose to be your husband. Do you promise to love him, comfort him, honour and keep him, in sickness and in health; and, forsaking all others, to be faithful to him as long as you both shall live?"

I'm watching Sophia. To everyone else in the room she is still nothing but the beautiful bride, besotted with her new husband. But I know her too well.

In the glassy look of her eyes, which to everyone else belong to a woman overcome with love and emotion, I can see the pain and the fear she is trying so desperately to hide. And as she says the words, I hear the break in her voice which pierces my heart with the force of a thousand more knives.

My eyes are damp as they kiss and the room erupts into applause. I force myself to join in, managing somehow to smile as she and Edmund look over in our direction. She's telling me silently with her gaze how sorry she is.

And I'm telling her silently with mine that it isn't her fault. That there is only one person to blame. And that is the man holding tight onto her arm as he whisks her past me and down the aisle, bathing in the adulation of his victory.

A dinner held in their honour is the next step in this seemingly never-ending nightmare. Myself and Rebecca are seated nearest to Edmund, at the head of a long table adorned with candles and arrangements of red roses which all of the guests from the wedding are sitting around. I am as far away from Sophia as possible. She sits at the opposite end, closest to James and her father. I don't know if this is a good thing or a bad thing. Edmund keeps offering Rebecca wine which she politely declines.

I, on the other hand, have already drank more than I perhaps should have. The speeches have been made, the toasts have been given and platter after platter of food has been served. Asparagus soup, oysters then roast pheasant followed by jellies and cakes. Now tea is being served in china cups, as the guests begin to talk animatedly amongst themselves. I sip at my tea, trying to ignore the crystal decanter full of port which is calling to me, as I listen to Edmund charmingly conversing with Rebecca.

If it wasn't already obvious from the ceremony, it is now totally clear that she is besotted with her new son-in-law. As he regales her with tales of his kingship, she gasps and chuckles and congratulates him on his accomplishments, occasionally placing a companionable hand against his arm.

"What did you think of the ceremony, Mr Redfield?"

I look over at the mention of my alias and see that Rebecca is now smiling over at me, as is Edmund.

"It was a beautiful ceremony," I reply, smiling. "Lady Sophia looked every inch the Queen she was destined to be."

"And that is in part thanks to you, Benjamin." There is an edge to Edmund's voice. Or maybe I'm just imagining it, the alcohol feeding my paranoid brain.

"I don't …?"

"You and James, of course! Without both of you, I very much doubt my darling Sophia would have been in any fit state to allow this celebration to happen. I shall be eternally grateful to you both for what you have done, in helping her back to health."

His voice is warm and jovial now, making me wonder if it really was just my mind playing tricks on me. I incline my head in gratitude as I take another sip of tea. Then from the other end of the table, I hear the tinkling of a fork against glass and I look over to see George getting unsteadily to his feet.

"I would like to make an announcement." His voice is slurred. He had clearly been drinking since before the ceremony. I glance at Edmund and see that he looks surprised at this sudden interruption to the festivities.

"George, sit down you silly fool!" Rebecca's genial voice is tinged with embarrassment. "We have already had the toasts. Sit down, darling."

"This isn't a toast, Rebecca." He shakes his head, and I see Sophia reach for his arm as James glances at me.

"Papa, please. Sit down."

"My daughter, Sophia is my pride and my joy," he continues, ignoring Sophia's pleas. The guests have all turned to face him now, smiles upon their faces as they listen to a father on the most wondrous day of his daughter's life. But, I can feel my heart thumping with panic in my chest. I can see James watching George closely, his face unreadable, though I know he will be feeling the same panic as me. "All I have ever wanted is for her to be happy and cared for. To love and be loved in return. And seeing her today on her wedding day, I know that this is not the case."

It takes the guests a few moments to realise what he has said. Then the murmurings of confusion begin to rise, as they turn to one another, whispering in hushed tones. I glance at Edmund who sits watching, his face betraying nothing, his hand clasped together against pursed lips.

"Papa ..." Sophia tries again, the panic rising in her voice. "Papa, I do not know what you are talking about. I am blissfully happy here with Edmund. Perhaps you need to retire to your room, you look fatigued."

"No, Sophia. Let me say my piece." George looks at his daughter and even though he is intoxicated, I know that what he is saying is coming from truth, which is what scares me most. "I know my daughter," he continues, strongly. "I know when she is truly happy and when she is putting on an act of happiness, in order to do what she thinks is right by us. I don't want you to be unhappy just to make us happy, little lamb."

"Papa ..." Sophia's eyes are filled with tears now and it is taking everything I have to hold my tongue and my nerve.

"This is most unexpected, George." Edmund's voice finally rings out, as he gets to his feet and the crowd turn to look. "I was under the impression that you were most relieved to see your daughter happy and settled, after what had happened to her?"

As George turns to face Edmund, I catch Sophia's eye for a brief moment. She looks terrified and at a loss of what to do. Part of me wishes I had done something earlier when I spotted the signs at the ceremony. Maybe I could have persuaded him not to attend the dinner. Told them he was unwell.

"Your Majesty." George continues, "you are obviously a very intelligent man. A man who knows how to mould situations to his advantage. Charm audiences to his reasoning. But I can see the fear in my daughter's eyes whenever she is with you. And I wonder just how unhappy she supposedly was before she came here. How fearful. Because to me, she has never looked as scared as she does now."

"George!" Rebecca's voice rings out. "Enough of this nonsense! Your Majesty, I apologise for my husband's behaviour, it is most unlike him."

"I am speaking the truth, Rebecca, as difficult as it may be to hear. You have been utterly convinced by this charade and it is easy to see why."

"Mr Reynolds." Edmund's voice is still calm and measured yet I can see the glint of annoyance in his eye. "Your daughter was living with a drunk. A drunk who beat her and made her life a living hell. Tell him, my darling."

"It's true, Papa." Sophia is grasping desperately to her father's arm now, trying to force his gaze back to her, yet his eyes remain fixed on Edmund. "Edmund saved me. I am happy here, I do not know why you think otherwise."

I watch him turn to Sophia as she says this, placing a gentle hand against her cheek. "You know why, little lamb. I'm sorry."

He is walking over to Edmund now, ignoring the screams and protestations of his wife and daughter and before I know what I am doing, I am on my feet and rushing over to him.

"Mr Reynolds, please." I place a calming hand to his shoulder. "It has been a long and emotional day for everyone, especially your daughter. And I think perhaps you have had a little too much liquor. Lady Sophia is right, a lie down may help."

He's looking right at me and I am urging him with my gaze to see sense. After a while, the tension in his body seems to relax under my grasp for a moment and I take my arm away. There is silence in the room, nobody knowing what to say, some of us praying that this is an end to it.

Then suddenly, I see George raise his fist and I get between him and Edmund taking the full force of his punch to my jaw. The next few moments are a blur, as I hear the rush of feet towards us. Edmund furiously ordering his guards to arrest him, Sophia screaming, pleading with him not to.

As James appears at my side, placing a hand on my cheek and trying to get me to focus on him, I hear the crash of crockery hitting the floor and Edmund screaming for everyone to leave. By the time the room has stopped spinning enough for me to sit up, I see that James and I are the only ones who remain, surrounded by a stark reminder of a moment which may have brought our dangerous deception ever closer to being discovered.

JAMES

"What on earth possessed him to do that?" I shake my head as I sit in my study with Tom, whose jaw is swollen and beginning to bruise.

"Liquor can make us do regrettable things." Tom's voice is muffled and he winces as he says it. I shake my head.

"No. It was more than that. The excessive consumption of alcohol certainly played a role, but he clearly knew something."

"Like he said, he knows his daughter." He shrugs as he reaches for the whiskey bottle and pours himself a glass before I can protest. But he won't meet my eye and he looks sheepish.

"Thomas …"

"Alright, so he may have had more of an idea than you realise." He sighs as he swallows the whiskey down in one before reaching for the bottle again. "And before you say anything, it's medicinal."

"What do you mean more of an idea?"

He finally looks at me as he sips at his drink. "Sophia told me that he had worked out she wasn't happy here. He figured it out on the day he arrived. And she didn't tell him ... but nor did she dissuade him from the idea. He doesn't know details. He doesn't know about me and her. He just knows that she isn't happy here. Add that to drinking too much and having to sit through that charade, well, it's no surprise that he snapped."

I sit in silence as I take in the news. "You should have told me." I say eventually, shaking my head.

"Come on, James. How was I supposed to know he would do something like this? I keep thinking that maybe if I had spoken to him straight after the ceremony, maybe I could have prevented it from happening somehow."

"And maybe it would have made the truth a little more obvious." I sigh. "George is an intelligent man. I doubt it would have taken much for him to work it out."

"What do you think will happen to him?" Tom's voice is sombre as he looks over at me, nursing the glass of liquor in his hands.

George was carted off to the dungeons within seconds of him hitting Tom. I watched in horror as Edmund proceeded to wreck the dining room, nobody able to stop the burning rage within him from escaping.

"I do not know," I answer, honestly. "He tried to strike the King. And if you hadn't got in the way, he would have succeeded. He will not take that lightly."

The next morning, my heart is heavy with regret as I make my way to Sophia's chamber with the unenviable task of informing her of her father's fate.

"Transportation?" Her voice is horror struck as she repeats the word I just said. I didn't manage to see Edmund himself, though that is not a surprise. I got word of the sentence he has passed upon George from a courtier.

"Yes, my Lady. There is a ship in Highshore bound for the Veragales. It leaves in five days. It is my understanding that your father will be transported to Highshore by prison cart tomorrow, in order to board the ship."

"The Veragales? But that is the other side of the world."

"There is a penal colony there," I continue, hating myself as I see the look on her face. "It is a colony for ... dangerous prisoners. The main work involves ..."

"Dangerous?" Sophia's voice interrupts me again. "My father is not a dangerous man! This is not fair. James, please."

"Sophia, your father tried to strike the King."

Rebecca finally speaks up, getting up from a chair in the corner. "And if Mr Redfield hadn't stepped forward he would have succeeded."

I see Sophia's eyes flash over to where Tom stands near the door, nursing his bruised jaw. He hasn't spoken, perhaps because he doesn't agree with the sentence either. Neither of us do, but what can we do?

"Mama ... You are saying you accept this?" Sophia is staring at her mother in disbelief, as Rebecca turns to meet her eye.

"Of course not, Sophia! But would you rather see him dead? King Edmund has shown your father leniency, and for that I will be forever grateful. If it is a choice between him losing his head and this then ..." She breaks off, turning away towards the window once more.

"Why must it be a choice between death and this though?" Sophia asks, directing her question at me. "Surely there is another way?"

"My Lady." I shake my head. "Your mother is right. Given King Edmund's temper in situations like this, the fact that he has passed the sentence of transportation, rather than death must be seen as an act of leniency."

"Sending him to the other side of the world? To a place meant for dangerous criminals? He won't survive! He's not a dangerous man. Mr Redfield, please, I know he struck you ... I know he meant to strike Edmund, but surely you do not think that he is deserving of such a severe sentence?"

She's staring at Tom now. Begging him with her gaze to help her. I watch with trepidation as he walks forward into the room, unable to judge what he might say.

"I know he isn't a dangerous man, my Lady." Tom's voice is gentle and calm and I see Sophia instantly relax a little as he speaks. "I know he never meant to strike me. And although at the time it was clear he intended to strike the King, I feel that the emotion of the day and the consumption of too much liquor played a major part in his unfortunate decision." He turns to me, his face serious. "James, are you sure you cannot speak with the King, on behalf of Lady Sophia? For I fear that sending her father to the other side of the world would have a detrimental effect on her mind, just when we have begun to make progress."

"Benjamin, I ..."

"Surely, there is a punishment which is suitable and just yet easier for Lady Sophia to accept and deal with?" His eyes bore into mine, once again pushing me into a corner that I will struggle to get out of.

"I can speak with King Edmund, my Lady," I respond, eventually. "Though I do not know what good it will do. I fear his mind is already made up. But I can argue the case for your health and what this may do to it, especially as you are with child."

As I walk back with Tom towards our quarters following the discussion with Sophia and her mother, I am silent. Tom seems to sense my annoyance as he doesn't try to speak until we reach my room, but as he opens his mouth I shut him down.

"Why did you do that?"

"James ..."

"You know what Edmund is like! You saw his reaction to what George did. He is not a forgiving man." I regret my tone as I see the look on his face. I know he is only thinking about Sophia and I am, too. The fury I saw in Edmund made me expect the worst. And although his sentence is severe, it could easily have been death. At least this way he is still here.

"She's only just found him again."

"Isn't this preferable to death?" I shake my head. "I genuinely believed that Edmund would pass that sentence. I fully expected that she would be forced to stand and watch her father get executed."

"But sending him to a penal colony on the other side of the world, for a punch which never actually reached the King? Sentenced to hard labour, day in, day out for the rest of his life? There are kinder sentences, James. More fitting ones. Especially for the father of the woman he claims to love."

He's watching me closely, his gaze strong. But as I shake my head he sighs and turns away.

"This is Edmund's way," I say gently, placing a hand to his shoulder. "He is not his father. I have no doubt that King Alfred would have pardoned George. But Edmund is a proud man. He will not let this stand. He sees this as a kindness and we must accept it as one." I wait, expecting another argument but it does not come. Instead, I see him nod his head.

"I understand. And I'm sorry for putting you in that position. I was only thinking of Sophia."

"I know." I nod, and he smiles back.

"I shall retire to my room," he says, eventually. "I want to make sure I am well-rested. Sophia will need us both to be strong for her tomorrow."

He bids me goodnight and I watch him walk from the room with a sigh, truly wishing that there was something more I could do.

TOM

A few hours after bidding goodnight to James and I am now making my way down to the dungeons, grasping onto a tray of food with shaking hands. I don't know if it is my mind playing tricks on me but the air feels colder down here; thicker somehow. I've talked my way in and out of most situations my entire life, but this feels more serious. Because I know that if I fail, Sophia will lose her father and I will likely end up losing my head beside him.

The tray I am carrying consists of bread and cheese along with a bottle of mead and as I reach the dungeons I see two of Edmund's guards sitting in front of one of the cells which I deduce must hold Sophia's father. Straightening up, I clear my throat as I walk toward them and they clock the tray instantly.

"What's this?"

"Doctor Collins sent me." I lie. "To check on the prisoner and bring him some food."

One of the guards gets to his feet, inspecting the tray. "Mead?"

"Yes." I nod. "The prisoner is Lady Sophia's father. We ... well, I thought that because of this, he was entitled to..."

"No." The guard snatches the bottle from the tray, passing it to his companion before turning to open the cell door. "Ten minutes."

I nod my understanding before walking in, as I hear the guard open the bottle of mead. The door slams shut behind me and in the low light of the room I see George sitting against the wall. He smiles as he sees me and begins to get to his feet.

"No, don't get up." I shake my head before sitting down next to him on the floor instead. I can see straight away that his eye is swollen, the remnants of blood at his nose.

"They've beaten you?"

He shrugs. "It doesn't matter. You cannot stop them. And by tomorrow it will mean nothing."

I glance at the door, listening for the sound of the guards but I hear nothing.

"Mead?" George says, raising an eyebrow in amusement, as I turn back towards him. "Surely you didn't think they would let you bring me mead."

I smile. "It wasn't for you."

Hearing silence at the door was what I had hoped for. I wanted them to take it and drink it. The sleeping draught I tipped into it is enough to keep them sleeping for a few hours. Enough to allow me to somehow smuggle George out of the palace and to safety.

"Benjamin, what have you done?"

He's looking at me sternly but I stand my ground. "You don't deserve the sentence he passed," I say, strongly. "You've done nothing wrong."

"You cannot take the law into your own hands! I made a mistake. I broke my promise to Sophia, now I must face the consequences."

"She is broken! She thinks this is all her fault. You told the truth and because of Edmund's thirst for power, his determination to show her that she belongs to him, she is going to lose you. She's only just found you again. It's not fair."

"She is going to lose me whatever happens. And I hate that. But, there is nothing I can do. I did a foolish thing, I am lucky to be leaving here with my life."

"Mr Reynolds ..."

"And she's got you." His words take me by surprise and I look at him in confusion.

"I don't ..."

"You aren't a doctor's assistant. It's obvious." He smiles, then he must see the look on my face as he shakes his head. "You don't need to worry. I don't believe anyone else has realised that you are not who you say you are. It is only because I know my daughter so well. I see the way she looks at you. The way you look at her." He's smiling at me.

There is no anger in his eyes, no accusation. I never realised that it would be so obvious. We always tried so hard to hide it in public. "You are him, aren't you?" he says, and I look him in the eye. "Thomas Thornton."

I swallow. "I'm not the person he says I am," I say strongly. "I'm not a drunk. And I would never hurt her. It is him who hurts her. I love your daughter, Mr Reynolds, I just want to protect her."

"I know, son," he says gently, the word unusual to my ears, "I know my Sophia. She never wanted this life and I see the fear in her eyes every time he is near her. I just wish there was more I could do."

I don't know what to say so I say nothing, sitting beside him in silence until he speaks again.

"Sophia said that she lived in Lowshore for a while when she left here. She told me that she was happy there."

I nod. "We were." He's watching me closely.

"What happened?" he asks gently. "How did she end up back here?"

I close my eyes, conjuring up memories that both make me smile and make my heart ache. "We shared a farmhouse together. We were happy. She never told me about her past, I guess she never wanted it to become a part of this new life she had made. But, it meant that we weren't prepared. Edmund abducted her whilst I was working. Well, he had her abducted. Of course he would never do the deed himself. I knew she would never leave, I tried for months to get anybody to listen to me, to help, but they wouldn't. I knew something wasn't right but I didn't understand until James ..." I stop, panicked by my slip of the tongue, but George shakes his head.

"Your secret is safe with me. I would never betray you. Or the good doctor. And besides, I have hours left here and two sleeping guards for company so who could I tell?"

I can't help but grin at this. And part of me feels relief that someone else can see the truth. Someone else can see that this is real. Being here, playing this role ... sometimes it makes me wonder what is real and what is in my head.

"I'm sorry for hitting you." He looks at me apologetically. I shake my head and smile.

"You're not the first to have punched me. You've got a decent aim on you, I'll give you that."

He smiles ruefully. "Would you believe that you are the first person I have ever punched? It's just unfortunate that you ended up in the way, when I chose to strike the King of all people!" He laughs at this and I cannot help but join him.

"Please, let me help you." I implore again as our laughter fades. "The guards will be sleeping for at least a couple of hours. It's enough time."

"No. Tom." He shakes his head. "If you do this, they will work it out. They will work out that you helped me. Did you even think past this point? How you would get me out of here, without being caught?" As he looks at me, I know that he knows the truth. He smiles softly. "I appreciate you trying to help me. I do. But I cannot let you. I am a lost cause. There is nothing that can be done to save me from my fate. But she needs you."

"I can't help her." I shake my head. "I thought I could come here and find her and bring her home. In my head it was that simple …" I scoff, shaking my head. "She is carrying his child. All I want to do is take her away from all of this but I can't. And I don't …" I stop, shaking my head as George looks at me. "I don't think I'm strong enough to stay here and watch her live this life, knowing there is nothing I can do to help."

"You were strong enough to come here," he replies. "Strong enough to leave your home to come here and find my daughter. Then stay, even though you knew you couldn't bring her home. Even though you knew the danger you would face. You are stronger than you realise and so is she."

I swallow back my tears once more as I listen to him.

"I should tell you to go," he continues. "I should tell you to do the safe, sensible thing. But, I think we both know that you won't. You can't."

I nod in agreement, realising that he is right. "I'll look after her," I say, strongly. "However I can."

"I know you will." He smiles as he places a hand to my shoulder. "Now you must go. Before someone finds you."

I don't want to leave. I want him to change his mind and come with me. But, I know that his mind is made up. With a heavy heart I get to my feet.

"Eat," I say, gesturing to the tray. "And try to sleep. I'll pray for you."

He nods his thanks and as he reaches for the bread and begins to eat, I make my way from the cell, past the still sleeping guards and back up to my chambers.

SOPHIA

The next morning I can barely find the energy to dress. My body feels heavy with the grief of the impending injustice set to take my father away from me over to the other side of the world, where he will forever be known and treated as a criminal.

As Annalise finally manages to make me presentable in an ink blue dress - the closest colour to black which I can choose - there is a knock at the door and suddenly Tom is there.

"Sophia …"

Annalise leaves the room, giving us a moment together. A moment which I desperately need, as I walk over to him and wrap my arms around him.

"Where is James?"

"I don't know. I thought he might be here."

"Do you think he's gone to speak with Edmund?" I finally release myself from his grasp, looking up at him with the last remaining ounce of hope in my eyes.

But it fades, the moment I see his face.

"He was adamant that he wouldn't, Sophia. It's not that he didn't want to, believe me. He just didn't want to make things worse. He knows Edmund better than any of us. He told me that this is him showing your father a kindness, I know …" He shakes his head as I open my mouth to speak. "I know this is no kindness. A kindness would have been to pardon him, understanding that it was a moment of madness caused by liquor. But, we are talking about the man who had you kidnapped from your home. The man who told his guards to hold a burning candle to your wrist." He breaks off, his voice breaking as he turns away for a moment to compose himself. "So we must accept this. As hard as it is. And be grateful that he isn't taking his head."

"I don't want to say goodbye …"

"You must." He places a hand to my cheek, his touch warm and soothing as I manage to look at him through blurred eyes. "If you don't, then you will regret it for the rest of your life. He will be strong for you. You must be strong for him too."

The walk to the courtyard where they will bring my father out to say his goodbyes, feels like I'm wading through mud. My mother walks beside me, as does Tom. Mother hasn't spoken a word to either of us. She looks pale and drawn and I want to reach out and take her hand, to offer us both some comfort yet something deep down is stopping me.

I still haven't seen James. We were expecting him to make the walk here with us, but he did not show. But, as we reach the courtyard which is already filling up with people, I see him rushing towards us looking flustered, which is a sight I am not used to seeing.

"My Lady, Mrs Reynolds." He bows to us quickly, his eyes flashing towards Tom before reaching mine once more. "There has been a change to your father's sentence."

Ice cold fear claws at my chest at his words. "A change? What do you mean?"

"I went to speak with the King this morning," he continues and I feel the panic in me ebb away slightly. "I wanted to at least try and explain how you are feeling and the fact that this sentence passed against your father may indeed set your recovery back, which would be dangerous, especially now that you are with child."

"And?" I can barely draw breath, as I wait what seems like an age for him to reply.

"King Edmund has agreed to reduce his sentence. He is to be banished from the Capital. He will never be allowed to return here again."

"Banishment?" I echo. "Not imprisonment?" I look over at my mother. She is staring at James and as ever I cannot tell what she is thinking.

"No, my Lady," James replies. "Not imprisonment. He is to leave here with nothing and never return."

I let his words sink in. I do not know how I feel about this.

In the space of a few moments, my heart has been heavy with grief, before being given a brief moment of relief and now it just feels empty. "How will he survive?"

I turn to my mother, wanting her to say something and finally she looks at me. "You wanted this, Sophia. King Edmund had already been most gracious in sentencing your father. I told you that the penalty for what he did should have been death. Simply banishing him is more than we could ever have wished for. You should be grateful."

"Grateful?" I shake my head in horror. "I didn't want any of this. I just want my father alive and safe. He doesn't deserve this!"

"My Lady ..." It's Tom's voice that I hear now. As I turn to him, I see that he is watching me closely. He has his hands clasped behind his back and I wonder if it is to stop himself from reaching out to me. "Your father strikes me as an intelligent man," he says kindly. "I believe that he will be able to find work and shelter. Begin again away from here. He is alive, not imprisoned and not being sent to the other side of the world. It is the best outcome you can hope for."

I know that he is right. My heart just doesn't want to believe it right now.

"I must tell you both that there is something else." James' voice is sombre once more, which draws my attention away from Tom, as I look into the doctor's eyes. "Edmund made it clear that for this to be the case, he wanted George to be punished publicly before he is banished. He sees it that he was humiliated during the wedding banquet by George. And now he wants justice to be served. Fifty lashes. Here, in the courtyard, in a few moments."

I feel sick at his words. Even my mother looks horrified for a moment, before seemingly composing herself. James places a gentle hand to my shoulder.

"I could not dissuade him from this, my Lady. He was adamant that this punishment would stand."

With gentle encouragement, he guides me over to the makeshift stage where some seats have been placed, as if this is some sort of theatrical performance rather than a brutal punishment. I take a seat next to my mother and to my surprise Tom takes the seat next to me at the other side.

It is a small gesture which I am grateful for, as I turn to see a huge crowd of people now standing in the courtyard. I never recall ever seeing a public punishment or execution when I lived here. I doubt King Alfred made use of them much. His reign was fair and just. If they ever did happen, I assume that my parents kept me away. Not like the people in this crowd. Women with babes-in-arms, men carrying their sons upon their shoulders so they can see the show. I see the whipping post which has been placed in the centre of the stage, a hooded man dressed in black stood beside it silently; in his hand a thick leather whip.

I swallow down my revulsion at the sight of it as movement and noise from the crowd draws my attention over to them and suddenly, I see my father being brought out by two guards. It has only been a few days since I last saw him, but the sight of him brings tears to my eyes. He looks dishevelled, still wearing the clothes he wore at the blessing; his shirt now open at the neck, his feet bare.

His nose is bloody, his face bruised and I choke back a sob as he catches my eye and tries to smile. Subconsciously, I find myself grasping for my mother's arm and am relieved when she doesn't pull away.

"We want the King!"

A chant goes up from the crowd, the words being said over and over again, until a cheer goes up as Edmund appears on the stage.

He lifts his hand in recognition of the cheers, soaking up all of the adulation. His eyes find mine and he smiles before lowering his hand to ask for quiet, a sudden solemn look appearing on his face.

"My loyal subjects. This is something which I wish did not have to happen. As you all should know by now, I have wed my darling Sophia, your Queen, who carries my son and heir to the throne in her womb."

I can barely listen to him speak the lies coming out of his mouth. He wants this. If he didn't, he could have stopped it. He raises his hand towards my father as he continues.

"This man is her father. And two nights ago, on the evening of the blessing of my marriage to his daughter, for reasons unbeknownst to myself, he attempted to strike me. Which he would have succeeded to do had it not have been for the bravery of Mr Redfield here, stepping in and taking the blow himself."

Tom doesn't look at the crowd as the gasps and murmurings begin to rise at this news, the bruise from where my father struck him clearly visible against his jaw.

He inclines his head respectfully to Edmund, before turning to James and whispering something in his ear that I cannot make out.

"I have sentenced him to be banished from the Capital indefinitely," Edmund continues, a smirk upon his face. "As the father of my beloved Sophia, I have chosen this sentence as a kindness. Many others would have lost their life for such an act. I hope that he is grateful of the leniency which his King has shown him."

My eyes flash to my father who bows his head submissively before raising his gaze to meet mine. Telling me that he is sorry without words. I want to tell him that he has no need to be sorry. I should have been stronger. Should have kept all of this a secret from him and protected him from the horrible truth which brought us to this point.

"I felt it appropriate however, that he face some sort of public punishment for his crime. Which is why you are all here today. As is my darling wife, who understands and accepts why this should happen. The prisoner will receive fifty lashes, to begin imminently."

A sickening feeling rises up in me, as Edmund instructs his guards to rid my father of his shirt and bind him to the post. The hooded man walks forward to take his position.

And at Edmund's signal, he begins. The whip whistles as it flies through the air, and as it is brought down against my father's back, it cracks like thunder. My father makes a grunting sound as it hits which pains my heart. His skin is already reddening after the first three blows, which is enough to make me dread what a state he will be in by the time he reaches the fiftieth.

I turn to my mother, taking hold of her hand in my own, instinctively wanting to comfort her whilst receiving comfort of my own. But she doesn't return my grasp.

Her hands remain clenched in her lap, her focus completely fixed on the horror unfolding in front of us. With each blow, the crowd becomes more animated, jeering at my father, revelling in his pain, urging the hooded man to hit him harder. I glance at Tom and see he has his eyes closed, his head bowed and I watch him tense up at the sound of each lash.

I know why. I know it must be conjuring up memories in his mind of his own suffering. I've seen the scars across his back. Traced them gently with my fingers as he slept. Though he's never talked about it, it's obvious where they came from. And now my father will bear the same scars and carry the same pain. As the whip cracks down against his skin again and I hear the gasps of glee from the crowd, I close my eyes, unable to bear it any longer.

"I can't watch." I whisper, folding my body into Tom's before I realise what I am doing. I feel his body stiffen but he doesn't shrug me off.

I remove myself from his grasp and my panicked eyes flash to where Edmund stands at the side of the stage but his gaze is fixed on my father, a sickening grin on his face as he watches his punishment continue. My father has always been a proud man. A brave man. And I've watched him stoically taking every blow, watching the blood begin to pour from the crisscross of scars across his back, until I finally hear him cry out with the pain of the latest blow and I'm rushing over to Edmund before I even realise what I'm doing.

"Edmund, please! Surely he's suffered enough?"

I know that I cannot be heard over the cheers of the crowd every time the whip is brought down against my father's back. But Edmund keeps the joyful smile on his face as he takes hold of my arm tighter than is comfortable, and whispers in my ear. "I wanted him killed. But, I felt that would look too severe a sentence for the father of my wife. So I decided upon transportation. Even that was denied me because it was felt that it would set your recovery back. So I will have this, Sophia."

I open my mouth to speak but I'm halted by another groan of pain from my father and I close my eyes, turning away.

"I do not know what you said to him to make him act in such a way," Edmund continues. "He was acting oddly the entire day of the blessing." He looks at me in suspicion and I shake my head adamantly.

"Nothing. I said nothing, I swear it. I do not know why he did what he did. I can only ask that you show him mercy, please!"

"This is mercy, my darling." He spits through gritted teeth.

"So you will stand here beside your husband as a loyal wife should, and see this punishment to the end."

I do as he says, unable to do anything else, standing by his side watching as my father grows weaker and weaker, barely able to keep standing as his feet slide on the blood which pours from his back. It feels like it goes on forever. The sound of the whip, the groans of pain escaping my father's lips, the cheers of the crowd every time the lash is brought down against his back.

I am beginning to wonder if it will ever end, if Edmund will just keep on watching it happen until it kills him. Then finally, he raises his hand and the torture stops. James and Tom are called on to check him over and I turn away, wanting to give him some dignity. I walk back over to my mother, taking hold of her hand once more, as I try to catch her eye but she will not meet my gaze. She is staring at my father, a mix of horror and pain upon her face. But also embarrassment.

"My loyal subjects." Edmund's voice brings my attention back to him and I see that my father has been helped back into his shirt and is managing to stand with the help of Tom and James. As he looks at me, I see the tears of pain in his eyes, the flush of exertion on his cheeks and all I want to do is rush over to him but I daren't. "The prisoner's punishment is concluded," Edmund continues. "He will now be banished from this place for the rest of his days. Should he ever set foot here again, he will be executed. I now ask that you leave us, so that his family can say their goodbyes in private."

I feel sick as the crowd chants "God save the King!" before beginning to disperse, many of them still gleefully discussing today's entertainment. Eventually, it is just us. James and Tom finally leave my father's side after making sure he is able to stand by himself. Then Edmund invites my mother to say her farewell and I watch as she makes her way towards him.

As she reaches him she places her arms around him. I'm too far away to know what she is saying. My head is woozy with panic, guilt and heartache. The only noise I can hear is the sound of my own blood thumping in my ears, as I wait my turn.

I glance at Edmund standing by my side but his face betrays nothing. Part of me was hoping that he may change his mind. Pardon him completely. But, I should have known that would never happen. He wanted justice and he was already cheated out of his preferred choice thanks to James appealing on my behalf. He and Tom are talking with one another at the opposite side of the stage to me, their brows furrowed, their faces serious.

Tom is talking animatedly, his hands moving fast and expressively. James is replying, calmly and measured as ever and I wonder what they are discussing. My mother is walking back towards me now. I cannot tell what she is thinking. But, as she comes to stand beside Edmund, I see her smile as he places an arm against her shoulder.

It's my turn now. I look to Edmund for permission and he gives it with a nod of his head. My legs are shaking as I begin walking towards my father, my heart breaking with every step. I look up as I get closer and see that he is managing to smile at me. I cannot bear it.

"Papa!" I run to him, throwing my arms around him but I jump back as he gasps in pain and I curse my stupidity, as the tears begin to fall down my cheeks.

"Don't cry, little lamb." He shakes his head. "I'm sorry this had to happen. And I'm sorry I went against your wishes. But, I couldn't just stand there and let this happen to you. We should have stopped this right at the start, all those years ago. Told him no. Maybe things would have been different."

I try to speak but the words won't come. I just stand there holding him, gently this time, breathing in his warm, familiar scent that reminds me of home.

"You picked a good man." As he whispers it into my ear suddenly, I look at him, shaking my head in confusion.

"How do you …?

"I know you, little lamb," he whispers, softly. "You would choose a good, honest man like him."

"I'm scared for him, Papa," I reply. "Edmund is dangerous. I don't want him to …"

"End up like me?" He smiles again, and I feel the tears prick my eyes once more as he shakes his head. "He's sensible. He wouldn't do anything that would put either of you in danger. He will look after you."

"He can't."

"He can, if you'll let him," he replies, quickly, sensing his time is short. "Trust him."

"It's not fair on him, Papa."

"Sometimes life isn't fair, lamb. But, we must do what we can in the hope that the way in which we deal with our struggles is repaid to us in kind one day."

"Time's up." One of the guards calls as he walks over and drags my father back.

"No!" I run to him again, throwing my arms around him once more. I feel him press a kiss against my cheek.

"Let me go, little lamb. I will never ever stop loving you, no matter where I am. But it's time to let me go."

As I watch the guards march him down towards the city gates, I know that I will never see him again.

My hands are sticky with his blood and as I stare at it I feel the world start to spin and I find myself falling. But I don't hit the ground. Strong arms catch me, lifting me up. Not Edmund's.

"We'll get her back to the palace, Your Majesty." Tom's voice floats into my mind as I grow weightless in his arms. "Let her rest."

I hear Edmund respond but I cannot make out what he says. As my eyes flicker open, I find myself looking straight into Tom's for a brief moment before the world goes black.

The next thing I remember is the noise of conversation at my bedside waking me from my sleep.

"She got herself too worked up. I told her that she shouldn't have gone."

"With all due respect, Mrs Reynolds, it was her father. She needed the chance to say goodbye."

"Of course, I understand that. But the stress of it all, it isn't good for her or the child. And I doubt she has eaten today, she is skin and bone. She needs feeding up."

"She needs rest first of all. She is well cared for, you have my word."

I feel something cool against my forehead and look up to see Tom holding a damp cloth against my skin. I open my mouth to speak his name, which is on the tip of my tongue, before he interrupts me.

"Steady, my Lady," he says, his voice gentle, but firm, reminding me where we are and who he is meant to be. "You were taken unwell and we are back at the palace now. Doctor Collins has checked, and your baby is well. You just need to rest." He nods his head encouragingly and I have to resist the urge to grab for his hand.

"My father?"

Tom turns away, busying himself at the table, tidying things away as I feel my mother take hold of my hand from the other side of the bed.

"He had already left the gates, sweetheart." She soothes. "He was not allowed to return. Edmund was most upset by it but it is the law, there was nothing he could do."

"He's the King," I say, unable to keep the venom from my voice, which draws Tom's attention back to me. "The leader of the Kingdom. He's changed rules to suit himself before so why not for my father?"

I see my mother stiffen. She isn't one for showing emotion, never has been. Everything is as it is. Just so. No need for fuss or drama. She would agree to anything just to keep her life as uncomplicated as possible. As she regains composure, her face relaxes once more and she squeezes my hand.

"It's for the best, love."

"For the best?" I shake my head. "He's your husband!"

"And he went against the King, Sophia," she says, solemnly. "He chose to act as he did and the King was right to punish him."

"If you love someone you are supposed to fight for them," I reply, desperately trying to stop my gaze from reaching Tom. "All he was doing was trying to protect me!"

"How on earth was he protecting you, Sophia?" she asks. "Getting drunk and coming out with all sorts of nonsense about Edmund not treating you right. Then trying to strike him ... I don't know what possessed him. But, he only has himself to blame."

"Mrs. Reynolds." Tom's voice floats across from the other side of the room and I finally look at him, angry tears clouding my eyes. "Your daughter needs to rest," he says. "It has been a long day for you both."

"Yes. Yes of course," my mother replies, getting to her feet. "Some rest will do us both good I'm sure."

She leans forward to embrace me but I turn away, blinking the tears from my eyes as she places a kiss against my cheek. I don't look at her as she walks from the room, only relaxing once I hear the door click shut and I know that I am alone and safe with him once more.

"Sophia."

"How could she be so cruel?" I whisper, as he comes to sit on the edge of my bed. "How could she just watch as they sent him away? Then defend Edmund?"

"I don't think she had much of a choice."

"There's always a choice." My voice is vicious which I regret instantly, knowing I am directing my anger at the wrong person. He places his hand against my cheek and I kiss his palm as I look at him. "I would have done anything if that were you." As I say it, he gives me that small half smile, the one he only uses for me as he reaches for my hand.

"We aren't going to let it come to that."

"I'm never going to see him again, am I?"

The realisation hits me properly for the first time, and all I feel is pain. I grieved for him once before, when I left this place in the middle of the night all those years ago, to start a new life in Lowshore. I never thought I would see him again after that, and the joy of having him back in my life was overwhelming. Though he isn't being sent to the other side of the world I know that as long as I am here, trapped in this place as Edmund's prisoner, I will never get the chance to try and find him again.

The tears prick at my eyes and I don't try to stop them. I look up at Tom, remembering what Papa said to me.

"He knew," I whisper. "About us."

He smiles at me softly. "I know."

"How …?"

He turns away from me as he continues to speak. "Last night. I went down to the cells to see him. It was before Edmund changed his mind about the sentence. I was going to try and break him out, but he refused. He'd worked it out pretty much straight away. And he knew that if they linked anything back to me, then I would be discovered and he couldn't have that on his conscience. He's a good man, Sophia."

I swallow down my tears, managing a watery smile as I look at him. "I think you and him would have been friends," I whisper. "I think he would have really liked to get to know you." I look at him, and I realise that he is the only thing keeping me strong. The only person I want near me right now. "Tom …" I squeeze his hand tighter and his brow furrows. "I don't want you to go." I shake my head. "I said that I did, but I don't. I won't cope here without you."

He places a kiss against my forehead, his touch soothing me. "I'm not going anywhere. I swear it. I'm going to look after you. I'm going to keep you safe whilst I figure out a way to get you home." He must see the look on my face as he smiles sadly. "I know. I know that's all but impossible. But that's the only thing keeping me strong so I have to believe." He kisses me again before getting up from the bed. "You need to rest. James just thinks that it was a combination of everything that happened today, making you feel faint. But you need to look after yourself. And the baby."

"Can't you stay?"

"You know I can't," he replies. "As much as I want to. I cannot. I will find Annalise. She can sit with you, make sure you are alright."

He gives me a small smile and I watch him as he walks out of the door. I close my eyes and try to force sleep upon myself, but all I can see in my mind's eye is the horror that my father just went through; and the fear that the same or worse could befall Tom at any moment. I cannot live without him, yet I am putting him in danger every moment that I ask him to stay.

I want to scream, but I do not have the energy. Instead, I let the tears fall silently down my face as I wait for sleep and the nightmares it will bring.

I do not know how I survived the weeks that followed. Watching my father's punishment left me with nightmares, that made me scared to go to sleep; even though my body craved it. His banishment and my grief at losing him all over again caused me to retreat back to the safety of my bed, cocooned in blankets, gazing at the same four walls day in, day out.

My mother stayed on as Edmund's guest but I refused to have her anywhere near me. The sight of her causing me nothing but anger at the way she had just seemingly let my father go without a fight. My only saving grace was him. And, the fact that I had retreated so severely back towards the state which I was in, when James was first asked to attend on me, meant that Tom was called on more to try and help me, at Edmund's insistence.

In the first few days I didn't even want to speak and he would just sit upon the edge of my bed stroking a gentle hand through my hair, the repetitive nature of it soothing me and calming my racing thoughts.

Then, as I began to feel more like myself I would ask him to tell me stories from our life before all of this. Of our trips to the beach, which made me feel calm. Of the simple days, just spent tending to the farm and the animals. Of the day that he tried and failed miserably to bake a cake for my birthday and I woke up to a kitchen, a husband and a dog completely covered in flour and a flat cake which was burnt on the edges but still raw in the middle. The images of this day were so vivid that I laughed and Tom grinned, telling me it was the first time he had heard me laugh in so long and supposed he was glad it was at his expense.

And finally, with Annalise's help, I once again began to enjoy the things that I had started to enjoy in the months since Tom's arrival here. Picnics in my room and walks around the grounds. Which is where we are going today.

Edmund is out of the country on royal business, my mother has taken a trip into town to buy silk for dresses. Meaning that with Annalise and James for company, Tom and I can be allowed some sense of who we really are. I am getting further and further along in my pregnancy and as the freshness of spring gave way to the warmth of summer, the child in my womb began letting me know more and more that it is growing; moving and kicking with vigour and despite everything, each time I feel it I cannot help but smile.

As we begin our walk through the grounds today, I converse comfortably with Annalise, linking her arm with mine. James and Tom walk in step beside us, discussing Edmund's current trip to Fallean where he has gone to continue to try and build bridges between our two nations after years of unrest. I care little about this, however, I know that we must appear to be conversing normally whilst in earshot of the grounds and anyone who may be listening. But, as we travel deeper into the gardens and much farther away from the palace, Annalise lets go of my arm, allowing me to spend a while with Tom. And though we must remain at a respectable, unassuming distance, the fact that I am able to spend even a little time with him outside helps to bring even more happiness back to my soul.

We have been walking for a while when suddenly my eyes catch sight of a hidden alcove, covered in ivy, just like the ones which would lead to a secret garden in a fairy story. Annalise and James are walking ever so slightly ahead of me and Tom, and I slow my pace a little to make the space between us even wider. As I glance in Tom's direction, I see that he is looking at me curiously and I grin before taking a final glance in the direction of James and Annalise to check they are not looking then quickly make my way over and into the alcove.

"What are you doing?"

I'm not surprised when I hear his voice behind me and as I turn to face him I see that he is stood watching me, arms folded and eyebrow raised.

"Hiding!" I giggle, and he shakes his head.

"I can see that." He grins, as I grab hold of his hands and pull him closer to me. "Did you know about this place?" he asks me, as he looks around at the idyllic, quiet space we find ourselves in.

"No." I shake my head. "I just spotted it now. Isn't it beautiful?"

I glance around at the secret place, the ivy dark green, the flowerbeds alive with so many vivid, beautiful summer blooms; bright pink peonies, delicate white sweet peas and primroses as blue as the sky above. The calming smell of lavender wafts through the gentle breeze too, and I finally feel free and more alive than I have in months.

With Edmund hundreds of miles away in a different country, his grasp on me feels less somehow. And though I know that this place is still dangerous for us, in this moment I cannot help but take some precious joy for ourselves.

"Lady Sophia?" I hear James call my name and I giggle as Tom turns to look at me. "Benjamin?"

I pull Tom in towards me, letting his lips find mine and letting myself sink into him, letting the world melt away until it is just us in this magical secret place together.

"I love you." He whispers it between kisses and I pull myself in closer to him, letting him know silently that I feel the same way.

"Lady Sophia?" James' calls are becoming more urgent, Annalise's voice joining his, as they call for us both.

"We should go," I whisper breathlessly, before my lips are drawn to his once more and I ignore my own words; the pull of him, of us, too strong in this moment. I hear James call again and I finally break away from Tom, both of us grinning like school children playing hide-and-seek.

"You go first," he whispers at my ear, his breath tickling my cheek. "Make up some story. I'll follow on."

As I unwillingly turn to leave, he suddenly grasps for my arm once more, pulling me back for a final kiss before reaching for a beautiful blue primrose and plucking it before placing it in my hair.

Flustered, I manage to make my way out of the alcove and as soon as James spots me he makes his way over followed closely by Annalise.

"My Lady, we were worried ..."

"I'm sorry," I say, trying to make myself sound rueful. "I saw a rabbit. It looked injured. I couldn't leave it."

"It was a thorn in its paw, Sophia. I got it out. It's fine now." Tom appears suddenly, continuing the story I have just created with ease, though I very much doubt that James is convinced by it. As he passes me, I feel his hand trace the bottom of my back sending shivers through my body which I struggle to hide. James sees this, I can tell. The normally measured and unreadable doctor is struggling to hold back a wry smile of exasperation.

"Well then," he says eventually, I can even see Annalise trying to hold back a giggle. "After that very commendable act of kindness and chivalry, Benjamin, perhaps it is time that we head back towards the palace and take some tea? We could even sit outside and enjoy this beautiful weather a while longer."

When we reach the palace, Annalise rushes off to prepare tea, cakes and sandwiches for us to enjoy out near the fountains, where a table has been laid at James' request.

When she returns she tries to refuse as I asked her to sit with us but eventually she concedes to the pressure from us all, taking a seat shyly beside me as Tom pours the tea.

"Have you spoken to your mother recently?" As James innocently asks the question I stiffen and I see Tom glance in my direction warily.

"No," I reply honestly, sipping at my tea to compose myself. "And nor do I wish to. I cannot forgive her for what she did to my father."

"She speaks about you, a lot," he presses on, watching me closely. "Perhaps you should try and talk to her?"

"Are you saying that you agree with how she has acted, James?" I shake my head. "She placed the blame entirely on my father. She didn't try to stop his punishment and then said goodbye as though he were just going out to work for the day, not like she would never see him again!"

I break off, turning my head to the sky as I watch a swallow gracefully soar through the blue, cloudless space above. I know that I am taking my anger out on the wrong person and James does not deserve it. As I look at him again to try and apologise I see that he is glancing around, waiting for a steward who is passing close by our table to head out of earshot, before turning back to the table and talking again, his voice low.

"I understand how you must feel, my Lady, believe me, I do. But I do not feel your mother had much of a choice. Seeing how Edmund punished your father for even questioning your relationship; you can hardly blame her for not wanting to be handed a similar fate by even appearing to side with him."

I turn to Tom, wanting him to agree with me but I can see by the look on his face that he has taken the doctor's point of view.

"James is right, Sophia," he says, confirming my suspicions. "Your mother was placed in an impossible situation. And your father wouldn't have wanted either of you to suffer anymore because of him. I agree she could have handled it better, but with the emotions of the day running so high perhaps we should allow her some leniency."

As he gives me a sad smile, I sigh. I suppose they are both right. Looking at it now, weeks on from that horrific day, I can see it from their point of view. And although the idea of it makes me feel sick, I agree to my mother calling on me later on today when she returns from town.

When I hear the knock at my door later on that day, I brace myself as I ask Annalise to let my mother in and then leave us. I sit at my table near to the window, gazing out over the grounds which bask in the haze of the slowly setting summer sun.

Having not set eyes on her in over a month, I do not know how I will feel upon seeing her again. But, I know that what James and Tom have said is true. And deep down, do I really want to lose both of my parents so soon after finding them again? My mother is my one remaining link to my father.

The memories we share are all that I have left of him. Perhaps we can help heal one another.

"Sophia?"

I turn my gaze from the window as I hear my mother's voice. She is standing in the middle of the room, dressed in a light-blue summer dress, a matching thin, silk shawl draped across her shoulders and in her hands she carries a parcel wrapped in brown paper.

"Mama."

"I was surprised that you had asked to see me," she says. "I have been requesting to call on you for weeks now and have been refused each time."

"James suggested it," I reply as I invite her to take the seat opposite me, which she does. "He told me that you had been asking after me and suggested it may be good for us to talk."

"I think he is right. This distance between us is not good for either of us."

"I need to understand something," I begin, and I see her eyes narrow in confusion.

"Is this about your father?" She's looking at me closely and I nod.

"What did Papa say to you? When you said your goodbyes?" I see a flicker of emotion behind her steady eyes and she composes herself before answering me.

"He told me that he was sorry," she says. "That he was only looking out for you. I told him that I didn't understand why he did what he did. And he told me that he was just worried for you. But you had told him yourself at the dinner that there was nothing for him to worry about. I cannot understand why he continued down that path."

"Maybe he saw something even you or I could not see," I say, watching her closely, begging her silently with my gaze to see my true heart and soul the way my father always could. But she shakes her head.

"Your father is a sensitive soul. Always worrying that he had somehow disappointed me, even though I told him over and over that this was nonsense. Perhaps it was just all too much for him. Finding you again after so long, seeing how much your life has changed. You were his little girl when you left us. Now you are a grown woman."

I swallow back my tears. I desperately want to unburden my soul to my mother. Want to feel that protection which a mother's love should bring. Yet something stops me. She isn't my father. Sensitive or not, he knew me better than I know myself. And I know that my mother would not understand my situation as he did.

"I miss him, Mama," I whisper eventually, my voice choked. "I cannot bear the thought that I will never see him again. And you just seemed so calm about it, so matter of fact. It felt like you didn't care."

I watch as she gets up and walks over to me, crouching down as she places a cool hand to my cheek.

"You are so like your father," she says, softly. "That same gentle soul that feels so deeply. Of course I miss him. He has been by my side for almost thirty years. After you left, it was just him and I."

"Then how could you let him go without a fight?" I ask her, shaking my head in confusion. "You never even tried to stop his punishment, even when he could barely stand, his back cut to pieces!"

"It wasn't my place, Sophia." She sighs. "I had no right to beg the King for leniency, especially after he had already lessened your father's sentence. And as much as watching him go through that broke me, I tried to take comfort in the fact that at least he was still alive."

She takes hold of my hand, a gesture which I was not expecting, and one that feels unusual to me but I do not pull away. "I am so happy for you, Sophia." She smiles at me, her eyes bright with tears, something I've never seen in her before. "I didn't want to cause any more trouble for you. Edmund has been most gracious, both in his clemency towards George and in letting me stay here for a while to be with you and welcome my grandchild into the world." She gazes down at my ever expanding stomach lovingly. "It cannot be long now until he is ready to make his arrival?"

"About a month."

The mixed emotions I feel about the new life that I carry in my womb, threaten to overcome me once again.

I glance at my mother, wondering if she can see. Surely she can see the fear in my eyes; the worry and uncertainty. But her face shows nothing but pride and joy.

"When is Edmund due back?" she asks, as she walks back over to her chair.

"He's due back within the next week or so. Building bridges with Fallean is very important to him, Mama, I doubt anything would have stopped him from going."

"Yes, I suppose so," she says nonchalantly. "The work of a King is never done."

She reaches for the brown paper package which she was carrying when she entered the room. "I saw this at the market the other day and wanted to buy it for you. I wasn't sure if I would get a chance to give you it, what with us not talking. I am glad that we have made amends, sweetheart. Perhaps this can be an olive branch of sorts?"

She gestures to me to open the parcel. I untie the string and unfold the brown paper to reveal swathes of beautiful peach silk, threaded with iridescent strands of silver. I take hold of it in my hands, feeling the cool softness of it against my skin.

"It is beautiful, Mama."

"I thought we could get your seamstress to create you a dress from it." She beams. "To wear once your child is born. The colour will suit you beautifully."

"I would like that very much." I give her a small smile and she reaches out to take my hand once more.

"I love and miss your father so much," she says as she squeezes my hand. "And despite everything that has happened, we only ever wanted the best for you. You will understand that when you bring your child into the world. You are so lucky to live this life, Sophia. Your child will want for nothing. And I know that your father would be proud of you. And he'll always be with us both in our hearts and minds."

My earlier smile is frozen on my face as I manage to nod my head at her words. When I agreed to see my mother again, I had hoped that perhaps I could get her to understand.

Or at least hope she would see how I really feel. Now I know that she never would.

As the days move closer towards my child's arrival into this world, Tom and I have been taking as many opportunities as possible to see one another knowing that as much as we want to pretend that it isn't, our time together is growing ever shorter.

The usual visits to my chambers have continued on each morning when Edmund goes on his daily hunt. The routine always the same. Tom accompanying James then staying a while as the doctor completes his rounds. Nobody ever questioned it, but if they did, James would just tell them that Benjamin was talking with me, preparing me for this next chapter in my life, making sure that the affliction of the mind with which I am cursed with, stays under control.

Today is different though. Edmund has travelled to Greyshore, a couple of hours' ride north of the Capital, to take part in a hunting competition and my mother has gone to meet with friends in the town square. Meaning that Tom and I have the chance of spending a proper amount of time together, rather than the snatched moments we are used to.

Annalise has gone to eat in the servants' quarters but not before handing Tom a bag of various foods which we have sat and eaten together in a comfortable silence; wanting to savour and hold onto each precious moment we still have left.

"Oooh." I wince suddenly, as the baby kicks violently, taking me by surprise.

I rub my stomach gently.

Tom is looking at me, concern spread across his features. I smile at him.

"I'm alright. She's just kicking. A little too hard today. Just letting me know she's here."

"She?" he says, "You think it's a girl?"

"I hope it's a girl," I reply, sadly staring down at my ever-expanding stomach, my hand resting gently upon it. "At least she may be granted a little more freedom to live her life. A boy would have his whole life mapped out in front of him. Heir to the throne. Edmund would begin teaching him his ways and the laws of the land from the moment he could walk and there would be nothing I could do to stop it happening."

I force my mind away from the idea of it and look over at Tom. He's staring intently at his hands.

I curse my stupidity.

We tried for a year to have children of our own. It never happened. We came so close and it was snatched away from us, breaking both our hearts. I know how much he longed for children, we both did. And I know how much it frustrated and upset him that he couldn't give me the thing that would make our family complete.

Now here I am, pregnant with another man's child, worrying about what the future holds for it, whilst he has to sit and watch.

"Oh Tom, I should never have unburdened all of this onto you. It's not fair. I'm sorry."

"No …" He shakes his head as he reaches for my hand, his delicate fingers interlocking with my own. "Don't. You have nothing to apologise for. I should be the one apologising to you. For being selfish. For thinking of myself when you are going through this…"

We sit in silence for a few moments, his hand never leaving mine, his grasp comforting, reassuring and familiar.

"What a mess," I say eventually, looking over at him. He matches my gaze, his mouth curling into a little half smile as a laugh escapes his lips.

"A fine mess." He nods in agreement. "Though I'd expect no less from us two."

I manage a smile myself, as I carry on looking at him, the face I know so well, the face I dream of every night as I fall into fitful sleep. I know the curve of his jaw, the softness of his lips, his eyes full of innocent hope one minute then full of mischief the next. I realise I miss him even though he is right here next to me. I miss us. And right here, right now, alone and as hidden as the safety of my chambers allows, part of me can't help but wonder if I could steal back just one precious moment of how we used to be.

I'm sitting trying to talk myself out of the idea when he answers the question for me. His lips find mine, his teeth gently graze my bottom lip as his hands caress my face. He doesn't close his eyes and nor do I, we are connected as his hands travel down my body, pushing their way underneath my skirts, the touch of his fingers electric against my skin as he reaches my thighs. I let out a gasp as I'm touched in a way I haven't been for so long. I had forgotten how it felt to be this loved, this close with another person, so in-sync.

I don't want him to stop. I'm grasping hold of his hair tightly as I kiss him, his taste transporting me back home, to happier times, making me forget everyone and everything, but him. Us.

I'm looking at him, begging him silently with my gaze to carry on until I can take it no more and he doesn't, staying with me until I feel my body shudder and he finally leaves me, peppering my lips with kisses as my heart rate slows.

"I love you." I manage to say it in a breathless whisper. His eyes are glassy, like he's not sure what just happened, the euphoria of the moment overtaking us both. Then I feel the tears start to well up inside of me like a storm and as I let out a sob, he looks at me in horror.

"Hey." His hand is at my cheek, his eyes focused on mine. "What is it Sophia? Did I hurt you? I …"

"No." I shake my head. "No it's just … how can I expect you to stand by and watch whilst I'm forced to live this life? You deserve to be happy again, you deserve to find someone who can love you completely, normally. Not like this. I want you to be happy."

"Sophia." He says my name so gently, and as I look at him, I see that he is smiling, like he always manages to do despite this hell that has happened to him.

"There is no one else in this world that can ever be to me what you are. And besides, there is no one but you who would put up with me!"

I laugh, wiping my eyes as he grins at me.

"I love you," he says, his voice suddenly serious, his hand finding mine again and grasping it tightly, "it was my choice to come here. I want you in my life anyway that I can, even if it is just watching from afar, protecting you like I vowed to do. So I'm staying. I am staying as long as I can. And you need feel no guilt. Okay?"

The tears are still pooling in my eyes as I nod and he kisses me again, pulling me in close, his steady heartbeat making me feel safe.

"Sophia?" As I hear my mother's voice, my heart drops like a stone. Tom's face is inches from mine, his eyes mirroring the fear in my own. I never even heard the door open. Normally Annalise is nearby, in the next room, able to hear the door and dissuade any visitors with white lies that I am resting because of the pregnancy.

"What on earth is going on?" Her voice comes out like a hiss as she walks over and we break away from one other, Tom getting to his feet. "You've been crying." She places a hand to my cheek, wiping away my tears. "Did he hurt you? What have you done to her?" She turns to Tom viciously, as he opens his mouth to speak but I get there first.

"Mama, no, please, you don't understand!"

"Get out."

"Mama, please!"

I watch as she walks up to Tom who stands stock still, almost regimental as she approaches him. His eyes are fixed on her and for the first time in so long I am terrified for him.

"You are in a position of trust," she spits. "How dare you take advantage of her like this?"

"Mrs. Reynolds, I ..."

"No! I do not want to hear anything you have to say. I want you to get away from my daughter right now. The King will know about this."

"No!" I scream, walking towards them. "I can explain, Mama, please, I can explain."

I stare at Tom, wanting nothing more than to rush over to him, tell my mother everything there and then but I'm too scared.

My mother isn't one to make false threats. I am in no doubt that she will find a way to tell Edmund everything, especially when she is as angry as she is now. I need to try and calm the situation down, somehow. For both our sakes.

"Mama," I try again, attempting to keep my voice steady. "Please. Let him go and let me try and explain everything. I can explain, I swear."

She looks at me, the anger still flashing in her eyes. I keep my eyes fixed on her, desperately trying to make her calm down. We face each other in this standoff until eventually she looks away, turning to Tom once again who is watching us both, and I can see the panic in his eyes.

"Get out," she tells him again. "I do not want to see you anywhere near this room again. Stay away from my daughter."

I see the pain in his eyes as he looks at her, his gaze unable to meet mine. He bows respectfully to her before walking from the room and leaving us alone.

My mother stands staring at the door he walked out of for a few moments before turning back to face me.

"Mama …"

"Sophia be honest with me." Her voice is serious, her eyes pained. "Did that man force himself on you?"

"No!" I shake my head, horrified. "No, Mama! I wanted him to be here, he never did anything I did not want nor ask him to."

"Why, Sophia?" She shakes her head. "Why on earth would you risk your marriage, your life here? For some doctor's assistant?"

I stare at her open-mouthed, unable to find the words I want to speak. My mother isn't like my father. He understood. But I have to try.

"You do not know Edmund," I say, eventually. "Not really. He doesn't love me, Mama."

"Don't be ridiculous." She shakes her head and I feel my heart sink. "It's clear for anyone to see that he adores you, darling. I've seen the way he looks at you, the way he speaks about you."

"It's all an act." I sigh. I'm tired. Tired and scared and I feel completely lost once again. My pillars of strength are being taken from me one by one, leaving me completely vulnerable. "He doesn't love me. He just wants me. I'm there at his parties and banquets for him to parade around, with me on his arm. I'm there to give him a son so that his legacy can continue. But he doesn't love me, Mama." I close my eyes. "He barely spends any time with me, unless it benefits him. I can go weeks without even seeing him. But T ... Benjamin has been there for me. He makes me feel like I am worth something again. I've needed that, Mama. Don't you understand?"

She smiles softly at me, grasping my hands. "Darling girl. All marriages take work. You have to make the effort. Both of you. Men can be ... difficult sometimes, I know."

"Papa wasn't."

"Your papa was difficult in his own way," she replies, and I feel a pang of hurt in my heart at her use of the past tense. "I told you, he was too needy. Always wanting to please. Sometimes I felt so suffocated by him."

"Are you saying you do not love him?"

"Of course not, Sophia! How could you say that?"

"I just cannot understand why you are talking in this way about him? And why you will not listen to me, when I am telling you that I am not happy here."

"You married him, Sophia!" She lets out an exasperated sigh. "It has been mere months. None of what you are saying makes any sense. Edmund has loved you for years. You were blissfully happy at the blessing. Lord knows what your father was thinking to do what he did that day. Perhaps Mr Redfield had clouded his judgement too, telling him the same tales which he has poisoned your mind with. When the reality is that he has taken advantage of you when you are at your most vulnerable. And Edmund needs to know about that. He needs to deal with that man once and for all."

"No!"

As she turns to walk out of the door again I scream, grasping hold of her dress as I fall to the floor in tears. She looks at me in horror, cradling me to her chest and soothing me as I cannot help but blurt out the truth I have been so desperately trying to hide.

"Please Mama," I whisper into her skirts, as she strokes my hair. "You cannot tell Edmund. He will have him killed and I couldn't bear it. He is my whole world. Please …"

"Hush, darling," she soothes. "Is this what your father knew? Is this the reason he did what he did?"

I nod my head, the tears still streaming down my face.

"He guessed, Mama. I never told him. He just knew. Papa knows me, he knows my heart. He realised that I am unhappy here. Please, Mama, I beg you. Edmund expects Tom and James to leave here once the baby is born. Please just let him leave with James when the time comes. Let him go safe from here, please."

She doesn't speak and I am about to plead my case once more when suddenly her voice pipes up.

"Does Doctor Collins know who this man really is?"

I feel icy fear clutch at my chest at her words.

I never even thought of the repercussions for James. I am so preoccupied with protecting Tom that I had forgotten that James holds our secret too.

"No," I say, strongly. "Doctor Collins believes that he is Benjamin Redfield, a student from the medical school of Lowshore. Tom stole his papers and convinced him of this during his trip there. He realised who Doctor Collins was and knew it was his best chance of getting back here to me. We have both been deceiving him. He would be horrified to learn the truth."

There is silence as she holds me in her arms, like a child. My heart is pounding, aching with pain and fear as I wait for her to make her decision.

"I will not betray your secret, Sophia," she says eventually, her voice soft. "You have my word. There isn't long until the child arrives. Then he will leave and you can begin again. Forget this whole thing ever happened and live your life the way that is expected of you."

As her hand continues to stroke through my hair, I try to settle. I know she does not understand but she is my mother. And I have poured my heart out to her. Surely she will keep her promise. For if not, I have just placed Tom in even more danger than he already was.

TOM

The first thing I did when I got back to my room was pour myself a drink. As I knocked it back the alcohol burned into my system, dulling the thud of panic in my heart. I curse myself for letting us get caught.

James was right, I needed to be more careful. And now … who knows? All I know is that it cannot be good. I'm pouring my fourth drink when there is a knock at my door and I swallow down my fear. Is this it? Is this the moment I am led away by Edmund's guards to face my death? I drain the glass of whiskey before straightening up and walking over to the door in an effort to face my fate with honour.

But, as I open the door I am shocked to find Sophia's mother standing there.

"Mrs. Reynolds …"

"May I come in?" She smiles politely and I bow my head respectfully, as I stand aside. I see her gaze fall upon the open whiskey bottle and glass at my table as I turn to close the door.

I stand for a moment, trying to calm my nerves before turning and speaking.

"Mrs. Reynolds, if you would let me exp …"

"I don't need you to explain anything, Mr. Thornton," she replies, and my heart thumps in panic at her use of my real name. "Sophia has told me everything." She gestures to the table that holds the whiskey bottle and she smiles once again. "Shall we take a seat?"

I watch as she sits down, my mind racing. I cannot work her out. I do not feel the same friendly demeanour from her that I did with Sophia's father. Though she is smiling, I cannot help but feel as though I should remain guarded with her. As I take a seat, she looks at the bottle again.

"Would you like a drink, Ma'am?" I ask, but she shakes her head.

"Oh no, thank you. But please, do not let me stop you if you need one."

I feel my jaw tighten with annoyance. I know what she is trying to do. I place the stopper back in the bottle, wishing I hadn't already had four.

"Mrs. Reynolds," I begin. "If Sophia has told you everything then surely you see that this is all wrong? That she is unhappy here. That she had a life and he stole her away from it."

I already know by the look on her face that she doesn't agree. "I understand that. I do. But regardless of all of that, Sophia made a mistake running away all of those years ago. Had she just stayed and made the most of it, she would never have met you or created this life."

"We are married." The ache in my voice is unmistakable as I look at her. "Whether or not you wanted her to have that life ... our life, you cannot change it. We have a home. A farm. People who care for and miss her."

I can see by her facial expression that I am losing this battle.

She shakes her head. "Edmund is the King. He can provide her with a life most young women can only dream of. You are just a woodsman. What can you possibly give her that he cannot?"

"Love." I say it with conviction, looking her straight in the eye. Money has never mattered to me. I've never had enough of it for it to matter. I never knew love before Sophia. And it's because of her that I know that as long as you have that, you can do anything, you can feel happy. Safe. And I know Sophia feels the same. I know Sophia. Her mother watches me for a few moments before smiling at me as she places a hand to my arm, her touch cold.

"Love can only get you so far. George loved me dearly and I him. But he could never give me what I truly wanted. I grew up here. My family is wealthy, I wanted for nothing my entire childhood. I didn't know George wasn't from the Capital when I met him. And when I found out he was in fact from Lowshore, it didn't bother me. I loved him too much for that to make a difference. I told my parents that I would marry him regardless of what they said. They disowned me. And at first I was so blissfully happy that I didn't care. George said that he would move to the Capital, find work there. Give me the life I deserved. But all that meant was hours of hard work just to keep the roof over our heads. It didn't give me back the privileges I had lost when I decided to marry him. And I began to resent him for it. Sophia would have too. She isn't meant to live the life of a woodsman's wife. Tending to a farm, baking. She was born to be a Queen. And she will learn to love this life and in time, love Edmund too."

"No…" I shake my head. "You don't know her. She ran away in the middle of the night because she never wanted this life. We were married for a year before he took her. We had difficult times but never did it stop us loving one another. Never did she even think of coming back here. Your daughter was a shell of the woman I love when I first found her again. She was scared and broken and so alone. I'm the only one that is keeping her strong. Just as she is me."

"And that is why you need to leave," she replies, her voice harsh. "How will she ever learn to move on when she has this reminder of the past watching over her?"

"I won't leave her."

The tears are stinging my eyes now and I blink them away furiously, unwilling to let her see me cry.

"You will," she says, and I shake my head again. "Sophia told me. She told me that Edmund will expect you to leave along with Doctor Collins once the baby is born, which won't be long now. I have promised her that I will not say a word to Edmund. And I will keep that promise. As long as you stay away from my daughter for the remainder of your time here. And once Doctor Collins delivers her baby into the world, you leave here for good."

I open my mouth to speak, but she continues. "I know that you have deceived that good man just as you have deceived the King and everyone else here. No doubt it was you who set my husband on the path to his own unfortunate fate as well."

"Mr Reynolds could see that his daughter was unhappy here." My voice is shaking but I push on. "I never told him anything. He just knew his daughter better than you clearly do. And I wish to God that he could have stayed quiet, for his own sake, not for mine. But, he wanted to protect her, just like I do. The King is selfish and cruel, Mrs Reynolds. He doesn't love Sophia. Is that the life you want for her?"

"There are sacrifices we all must make for the greater good, Mr Thornton," she presses on and I shake my head in disbelief. "Sophia was promised to Edmund and she cannot run away from that. This is the sacrifice that she must make. And yours must be to let her go." She gets to her feet, her eyes still fixed on mine. "I mean it. Stay away from her. If I see you anywhere near her then I will tell the King everything. And God help you if that happens."

I feel sick. I want to scream at her but I can't even find the strength to speak.

"I'll see myself out."

She smiles at me as she leaves the room. As soon as the door closes behind her I grab the whiskey bottle, pouring myself a large glass and downing it in one before reaching for the bottle again.

JAMES

It is the most beautiful day. This year's summer has blessed us with such glorious warmth and the longest of days which do not see the sun setting until late into the evening.

The palace gardens are alive with nature; vivid with colour and strong with the scent of all of the different flowers and herbs. Sophia is nearing the end of her pregnancy and although I would advocate rest, I feel like she would really benefit from the fresh air.

Of course, I have an ulterior motive for suggesting this as well. A walk around the grounds means a chance for Tom and Sophia to spend some time together outside of the confines of her room. With Annalise and I with them, there is never any reason why anyone would suspect anything untoward. I pack my bag before leaving my room and walk a few meters down the hall towards Tom's.

I knock on the door and at first he doesn't show. I curse him inwardly. We had this conversation mere months ago about being careful.

He promised me that he would and I cannot see him going back on his word. I knock again and this time I breathe a sigh of relief as I hear footsteps approaching the door.

But, when I see him the relief turns to concern. He's dishevelled, his eyes red and bloodshot. I note the empty bottle of whiskey on the table as I walk in and come to the likely conclusion.

"What has happened?" I ask, placing my bag down on the table as I look at him. He sits down heavily on the bed.

"Nothing."

"It doesn't look like nothing."

As he meets my eyes, I see that same defeated look that I saw when I first met him back in Lowshore. I am so confused. When I saw him yesterday he was happy, as happy as he could be.

"You've been drinking."

He shrugs. "That's what I do."

"No." I shake my head. "Not like this. Not since you found Sophia again."

He turns away from me as I say her name.

"Tom ..."

"Please, James. I'm fine." His voice is harsh, bitter. I haven't heard him speak like this in a long time. I take a seat next to him, watching him closely.

"I'm about to go and see Sophia," I say, gently. "I thought we could take a walk around the gardens. Get some fresh air. It might make you feel better."

I watch him take a shaky breath. And as he turns back towards me a sad smile is playing on his lips.

"Thank you for the offer. But I do not feel well enough."

My natural instincts are turning to worry amidst the confusion. Something is wrong. And if he won't tell me then I know it must be something serious.

"Tom," I try again. "You know me. You know that you can trust me. Whatever has happened, if you tell me we can try and sort it together."

He's watching me, carefully. I can feel that whatever it is, he is so close to telling me. I keep my focus on him, urging him silently to unburden himself of whatever is making him feel this way. But as he turns away once more I know that the chance has left us.

"Please give my apologies," he says, as he gets up from the bed, unable to look at me anymore. "To Lady Sophia."

I sit, continuing to watch him for a few moments as he makes his way over to the window, staring out at the grounds. Any hope that I had that he would change his mind vanishes quickly. He refuses to acknowledge me until I eventually take my leave and make my way to Sophia's room. And as Annalise opens the door she has the same concerned, confused look on her face that must show on mine.

"Is Lady Sophia alright, child?" I ask, and she opens her mouth to reply but just as she does Sophia's mother arrives at the door.

"Mrs. Reynolds" I bow to her and she smiles.

"Doctor Collins, how nice to see you."

"I wasn't expecting to see you here, Ma'am."

"Well with my daughter being so close to expecting her child, I felt it best that I begin to spend more time with her. To help her."

I glance at Annalise who looks perturbed. I manage to maintain my pleasant smile as I nod my head.

"And how is Lady Sophia today? I called to check on her, and to see if she needs anything."

"How kind of you, Doctor. Follow me, I am sure that she will be happy to see you." Still feeling confused by the situation, my head trying to work out how all of the pieces of today fit together, I follow Mrs. Reynolds through to Sophia's room.

I see that she is up and dressed, sitting at her dressing table with a piece of needlework resting upon her stomach. She looks up and smiles when she sees me but I see her face fall when she realises that I am alone. There seems to be somewhat of a spark missing in her look this morning.

"My Lady," I say, bowing my head. "I have come to see how you are feeling and if you need anything at all?"

Annalise walks in behind me, closing the door as Mrs Reynolds goes to stand beside her daughter.

"She is looking well, don't you think, Doctor?" She smiles, placing a kiss against Sophia's hair. "Being with child is clearly good for her."

Sophia is smiling but I can tell that it is forced. I am completely at a loss as to what is going on but everything about today just feels wrong.

"I am well, thank you, James," Sophia says, finally. "A little tired but apart from that I am fine."

"Tiredness is to be expected, my Lady," I reply, with a smile. "Being so close to the end of your pregnancy. I can prepare a tonic which might help a little, if you like?"

Sophia nods gratefully and I smile, setting down my bag and asking Annalise if she would help me to prepare it.

"I was also going to suggest a walk, my Lady." I say, as I start mixing the ingredients. "Just a small stroll around the gardens. It is a beautiful day and the fresh air might help with the tiredness too?"

"That would be lovely, wouldn't it darling?" Mrs Reynolds replies. "I think we could both do with some fresh air and a look at the flowers."

"That sounds wonderful, James," Sophia adds, looking at me closely. "Will ... Mr. Redfield not be joining you today?"

Her eyes are searching mine, looking for answers but I see her mother stiffen at the sound of his name. Brain whirring, I shake my head.

"Mr Redfield sends his apologies, my Lady. He is a little unwell today."

"Oh ..." Sophia's eyes widen but her mother visibly relaxes at my words. "Nothing serious, I hope?"

I smile softly at her, trying to ease her worry.

"A chill, my Lady, nothing more. A few days rest and he will be fine."

She nods but I see the sadness in her eyes.

"I shall go and find you a shawl, Sophia," Mrs. Reynolds says. "It may be warm but best not to take any chances. And then after our walk, we can choose a dress for your dinner with Edmund."

"You are dining with the King?" I say, unable to keep the surprise from my voice.

Her mother smiles at me.

"Yes. I know Edmund is a very busy man but I have told him that he must start making more time for Sophia. He has been neglecting her of late and that that will not do. So I have arranged with his advisors for him to set aside some time each day now, just for the two of them. Which is nice, isn't it darling?"

"Yes, Mama." Her smile is still forced. As her mother leaves the room, I hurriedly grab the tonic and walk over to Sophia, crouching down beside her as I place the glass in her hand.

"My Lady, what is happening?" I whisper, grasping her hand. "Dinners with Edmund? I don't understand …"

She squeezes my hand tight, desperation in her eyes.

"It's my mother," she whispers back. "She …"

"Here we are, darling."

Sophia drops my hand as her mother walks back into the room clutching a thin gold silk shawl. As she drinks the tonic, her mother places the shawl around her shoulders and reaches for her hand, helping her to her feet.

"Shall we?" Mrs. Reynolds looks over at me. "We should try to be back before the midday sun arrives. Too much heat would not be good for Sophia, I'm sure you would agree, Doctor?"

I incline my head in agreement. "Absolutely, Mrs Reynolds. I shall just pack away my things and then we can leave."

I glance at Sophia once more but her mother is already fussing around her, instructing Annalise to take away the glass and bring the parasols. Things are starting to come together in my mind a little now and although I do not have the full picture, I am already concerned by what I know.

As Sophia walks ahead, her mother linking arms tightly with her as she points out the various plants and flowers, I walk with Annalise, keeping a distance between us and them so I can try to speak with her.

"I don't understand, Annalise," I say in hushed tones. "Sophia's mother being around like this. I know that they have made amends after what happened to her father. But they've never been this close. This isn't normal."

"She was 'ere last night, sir. When I came to help Lady Sophia dress for bed," Annalise replies. "My Lady 'ad been cryin'. Her mother was soothin' her. Then she got up and left the room. I asked My Lady what had 'appened but she wouldn't tell me. Then this mornin' her mother was back again."

I shake my head in confusion. This whole situation is becoming more and more concerning to me.

"Tom is the same," I reply, quietly. "Unwilling to tell me what is wrong when something clearly is. I need to get to the bottom of this."

"You don't fink ..." Annalise begins, looking at me with concern. "You don't fink that she knows somethin'?"

I swallow. It's the idea I didn't want to think of, yet I know deep down that it is the only likely explanation. For Tom's distress. For Sophia's forced smiles. For her mother's increased presence in her life. I need to understand what is going on.

As we walk back towards the fountains I hastily take my notebook and pencil from my pocket, scrawling something down on the page before ripping it out and folding it. I hand it to Annalise along with the pencil.

"Go and sit with Sophia. Give her this. I will talk with Mrs Reynolds whilst you do."

Annalise nods and as we reach the fountain I call to Mrs Reynolds, beckoning her over, commenting on the various flowers and their healing properties of which ones are good during pregnancy. Out of the corner of my eye, I see Annalise press the note and the pencil into Sophia's hand. She looks confused for a moment until she unfolds the note and I see her face relax.

I keep talking with her mother as I give her the chance to write something back to me, and finally as Mrs Reynolds turns back towards her daughter I breathe a relieved sigh as I see no evidence of my secret message.

"Sophia, darling, we must be heading back. Thank you, Doctor. This walk has been most pleasant."

I bow to her, smiling as Annalise walks with Sophia back towards us.

"Thank you James," she says with a small smile. "You were right, as ever. The fresh air has done me the world of good." As she holds out her hands to take mine I feel her press the pencil and note tightly into my hand as she squeezes them.

"I am glad to hear it, my Lady," I reply, softly. "Making sure you are well and cared for is my greatest concern whilst I am here."

I see that her eyes shine bright with tears as she nods, smiling at me. Then her mother takes her arm again and leads her on, as Annalise comes to my side and we begin walking back. I wait a few moments, making sure that they are far enough ahead before I unfurl my hand and take the note from it, opening it up, my worst fears realised as I read.

She knows. She barely lets me out of her sight now.
I'm trapped. Tell Tom I'm sorry.

I can tell that Tom has been drinking the moment he opens the door when I call on him following my walk with Sophia.

Shaking my head as I walk in and he closes the door behind me, I place my bag down on the table before turning to him.

"You really must stop drinking."

He scoffs. He's unsteady on his feet as he makes his way over to the bed and sits down heavily upon it.

"I'll drink if I want to, James."

"And what do you think Sophia would say?"

I see the briefest flicker of remorse upon his features but he doesn't reply. I walk over to him, pulling up a chair and sitting opposite him as I take the note from my pocket and hand it to him.

"I know, Tom." I watch his face crease with emotion as he reads Sophia's words upon the page. I don't say a word, letting him take it in, hoping he will now find the strength to tell me what happened.

"We were careful. I swear." His voice is quiet as he looks at me with pained eyes. "It was the same as any other day. I went to see her in her room. Annalise had returned to the servants' quarters to eat, so it was just the two of us. We sat. We talked. We just tried to enjoy the time together. As I was about to leave, I kissed her. And that was when her mother walked in." He sighs. "She was angry. Really angry. She threatened to tell Edmund. Sophia was screaming, begging her not to. I couldn't say a word … I daren't say a word. She kept saying how I had abused my position of trust. This was before she knew …"

I look at him, my concern heightened at his words.

"Are you saying she knows who you really are?"

As he nods I sigh, closing my eyes and shaking my head.

"Sophia must have told her. I don't know why," he continues. "Her mother came here, to my room later on that evening. Told me that she knew everything. She knew that Edmund would expect us to leave after the child is born. And she told me that if I didn't leave or if I tried to see Sophia before then, that she would tell Edmund everything."

As he puts his head in his hands I just sit watching him. Surely, deep down I knew it would end like this. I was a fool to ever think otherwise. The only thing I can try and do now is keep him safe until the time comes that we are asked to leave. Then help him to find some way to move forward.

"I told her I would always be here, no matter what." His voice is quiet still and as I turn to him, I see he is now looking at me. He looks drained - physically and emotionally, and I know that is not just the alcohol.

I open my mouth to speak but he carries on. "I said that I would stay and look after her in whatever way I could. But I can't…" His eyes shine with tears as he looks at me. "This is killing me. Knowing she is minutes away but not being able to see her. And you know what? I'm not scared of Edmund. I'm not scared of what he could do to me. And deep down I think … maybe it would be better if her mother does tell him. Because I can't live like this. I can't live without her. So maybe I would be better off dead."

"Tom, no." I shake my head, horrified by his words. "You cannot think like that. Think what that would do to Sophia. Are you saying you could really put her through the pain of seeing you arrested? Tortured? Executed? You couldn't do that to her. I know you couldn't."

He turns away from me, brushing the tears from his eyes as he grasps the note in his hand. "Tell Sophia that I love her."

"Tom …"

"Please …" He looks back at me again and all of my natural instincts are turning to panic as I see the complete lack of hope in his face. Worried about what he might do if left to his own devices, I look in my bag and find a sleeping draught in the hope that I can get him to drink it. And at least be content, that I can leave him alone until the morning without fear of him doing something foolish.

"I want you to drink this," I instruct, holding out the bottle to him but he pushes it away.

"I don't want it, James," he says, tiredly. "I have whiskey. That's all I need."

"Whiskey will not do you any good," I reply, my voice stern. "I'm saying this as a doctor, Tom. Not as a friend. You need to drink this and get some rest."

I see him open his mouth to protest again but he must see the look on my face and decide against it. He takes the bottle from me and drinks the liquid within it. As his eyes begin to droop I guide him down onto the bed, relieved when I see sleep finally wash over him.

The guilt I feel grows stronger as I think of everything that has happened today. I cannot help but wonder if things would have been better for them both had I not have found him at all.

SOPHIA

My mother chose me a deep pink dress for dinner with Edmund. She did my hair, piling it up tightly upon my head and fixing it with a tiara that made it ache. She did my make-up, placing rouge upon my cheeks to make me look healthy. *'He is making the effort for you,'* she said as she applied it, *'it's only right you do the same for him.'*

I am so tired. The child in my womb doesn't seem to want to settle anymore, constantly moving around as if telling me that they are ready to arrive. The thought of it makes me feel sick. The arrival of my child just means another chapter to the nightmare I am living. Another pawn for Edmund to use against me and the thing that will take Tom from my life for good. As I reach the dining room and the steward opens the door, I find that Edmund is not yet there.

The banquet table is already set with two seats at either side and the steward guides me to my chair, helping me into it before bowing and leaving the room.

Candles line the middle of the table and crystal glasses stand ready to be filled with port to drink.

Edmund finally appears, his arrival announced by a steward who bows as he enters the room. He's dressed in his finest ruby red dress coat and breeches, his long dark hair tied back and fixed with a red velvet ribbon. His eyes light up as he sees me, like a hunter who has spotted his prey and as he sweeps towards me I find myself struggling to maintain the forced smile upon my lips.

"My darling wife," he says, as I shudder inwardly. "You look a picture of beauty."

His lips meet mine and I have to force myself not to pull back. His kisses are forceful, for his pleasure alone, and they linger for far too long. When he eventually releases me I manage a smile, as he walks to the far end of the table and takes his seat. He instructs the steward to fill our glasses and when he does I sip at mine, grateful that it takes the edge off my nerves.

"I have had something wonderful prepared for dinner, my love," Edmund says, with a grin. "Shot by myself during yesterday's competition. The winning beast!" He claps his hands and the doors open.

In walks the chef followed by stewards carrying a large platter and I feel my stomach turn as I see it is a young boar, its mouth stuffed with an apple, its skin dark and crisp, the smell of it making me feel sick. As they place it down in the middle of the table and the chef begins to carve, I see Edmund beaming at me from his chair.

"What do you think, Sophia?"

"Impressive, my darling," I reply. "You are a most skilled huntsman."

The chef plates our meals before departing and Edmund tucks in with gusto as I push my food around my plate.

"It was the most thrilling competition, Sophia." He grins as he shovels his food into his mouth. "I wish you could have been there to see my victory. I dedicated it to you, of course."

I smile at him as I manage to eat a little more of the poor beast killed in my name, so not to displease him. "I am honoured. And I too, wish that I could have been there to see it."

"I gather from your mother though, that you had some time together in my absence? I hear you had a rather interesting conversation."

His words jolt me from my own thoughts back into the room. He's smirking at me and I feel my heart begin to thud with panic.

"I don't ..." My mouth is so dry that I can barely speak. I take a gulp of water to steady my nerves.

"She tells me that you would like even more children once we welcome this one into the world." He grins and I feel my panic start to ebb away. "Of course, I only require one heir, my darling but I am willing to give you whatever you desire."

His lustful eyes travel down my body and I have to force myself not to show the revulsion on my face, which I feel in my bones.

"My mother is most excited to welcome her first grandchild into the world." I manage to reply. "I feel she is getting a little carried away by the idea."

We fall into silence once more as Edmund carries on eating, continuing to tell me of his recent hunting victories and his successful trip to Fallean. I smile and try to show as much interest as I can muster. Eventually though, I hear him clear his throat and as I look up at him, I see that he is looking at me in annoyance.

"Sophia. You have barely spoken two words to me. I promised your mother that I would try to make more time for you. But I wonder what is the point if you just sit there morosely, not speaking and barely eating the beast that I caught especially for you."

"Edmund, I am very tired," I say, honestly. "Your child is most unsettled at the moment and is not allowing me much time for rest. I apologise if I am not the best company."

He smiles as he gets up from his seat and walks over to me. I feel my skin begin to prickle with unease at his presence so close to me.

"My son and heir must almost be ready to make his entrance into the world," he says, softly, gazing at my stomach. "And I am most looking forward to teaching him how to rule a Kingdom."

I feel my heart sink, as he places a kiss against my cheek.

"You do look tired, my love," he says, as he stands, studying me. "Perhaps you should retire for the evening. Tomorrow we can dine a little earlier. Or take a walk."

"Thank you, Edmund." I get to my feet hurriedly before he changes his mind. I am already dreading what tomorrow has planned. "That would be lovely."

"Would you like me to accompany you back to your room?" he asks, and I feel horror at his words. "To make sure that you are alright?"

"No … thank you, my darling," I say, forcing the smile back onto my lips. "I will be just fine, it isn't too far away. You stay, enjoy the spoils of your labour."

He kisses me deeply again before clapping his hands and the doors open. I thank the steward and as the doors close behind me, I breathe a sigh of relief.

There is nobody around, not even my mother. For the first time since everything happened I feel a small sense of freedom. I begin walking back to my room when I see the corridor which leads to the wing of the palace where James and Tom stay.

My heart aches at the thought of being so close to him and before I realise it I am walking in that direction. I am meters from his door and I start to feel safe and comforted by the mere thought of him.

"Sophia?" As my mother's voice sounds across the hall I feel that safety net fall. The tears prick my eyes as I turn to her.

"Mama …"

"What are you doing here, Sophia?" Her voice is light but I sense the darkness beneath her jovial tone.

"I came to call on Doctor Collins." I lie. "The child is keeping me awake at night. I wanted to see if there was anything he could prescribe to help me sleep."

I cannot tell if I have convinced her. But eventually she smiles, taking hold of my arm.

"It is late, my darling. I am sure Doctor Collins would not wish to be disturbed. Let's get you back to your room. I shall have your maid place some lavender oil against your pillow. That will help you to sleep."

I have no choice but to follow her, my heart aching with every step. When we arrive back at my room, Annalise is there, ready to help me dress for bed.

As my mother lists off instructions to her, I sit at my dressing table wishing her to leave. I barely register her telling me goodnight as she places a kiss against my hair and finally leaves. I can't even bring myself to talk to Annalise who dutifully takes the pins from my hair, ridding it of the tiara before beginning to brush it.

The rhythm of it is relaxing and I close my eyes just letting myself become soothed by the simple act. When she finishes, she helps me dress for bed before placing a few drops of lavender oil against my pillow at my mother's request. She helps me under the covers, settling me in before curtseying and turning to leave.

"Annalise ..."

As I say her name she turns back to face me and the tears start to swim into my eyes once more. "Stay with me awhile. Please?"

She curtsies again before taking a seat at the side of my bed, as I take hold of her hand tightly.

"I'm trapped, Annalise," I whisper, tearfully. "My mother is watching everything that I do. Forcing me to spend time with Edmund in the hope that I will somehow start to love him. But I will never." I shake my head, vicious tears falling down my cheeks. "My heart belongs to Tom. I will never stop loving him. I don't care what my mother thinks. But I cannot even see him. And he will not call on me. Not even of a night when I can finally escape her clutches. I don't understand."

Her hand goes to my hair, stroking it back; once again this young girl soothing me, which feels wrong but the comfort is so strong and so needed that I let her continue without question. "Every day that passes is a day closer to my child coming into the world and I am so scared of what the future holds when that happens." The tears stream down my cheeks now, Annalise hushing me like a mother would her child as she continues to stroke a hand through my hair. "I don't want this child, Annalise," I choke up. "I don't want to lose him. I'm so scared."

As the realisation of my impending future crashes down on me, I sob into her shoulder as she clings to me, trying to tell me that everything will be alright when I know that it can never be.

JAMES

The next few days passed without incident. If anything, Tom seemed calmer, more settled. He still wouldn't go to Sophia, not even when I informed him that he could go later on in the evening; something I had implicitly advised against since our arrival here. However, he had stopped drinking and was wanting to help me in any small way he could.

So, I would leave him papers to transcribe in my office, relieved that he appeared to be feeling better in some way. Maybe this was for the best. Knowing that, with Sophia due to give birth any day and our time here growing increasingly shorter, perhaps he was beginning to prepare himself to leave her.

I leave my room early and begin my rounds. Though my main concern and focus is Sophia's wellbeing, Edmund felt that I could make myself useful in other ways during my time here, using my skills and knowledge to help others in the palace who were suffering from ailments and illness.

From chefs burned by the heat of the stoves to courtiers suffering with gout, there was always something that I could help with in some way.

"Doctor Collins!"

As I am walking the hall towards my next patient I hear an urgent voice calling mine and I turn to see Annalise rushing up to me, her face panicked.

"What is it, child?"

"It's Lady Sophia, sir," she says, catching her breath as she stops beside me. "You need to come quick … I fink the baby is comin'."

I follow her back towards Sophia's bedchamber in haste and I hear her screams coming through the closed door even as I approach. As I walk in, the curtains are drawn around the bed. I can hear her mother's voice attempting to calm her.

"You need to try to breathe, Sophia," she says, her voice harsh. "Screaming will not do you or the child any good."

I take off my jacket, rolling up my sleeves as I pull back the curtains. Sophia's eyes find mine instantly. She is in her nightgown, her face puce with exertion, her hair falling loose down her shoulders, strands of it clinging to the sheen of sweat against her brow. I see her hold out her hand to mine and I take it, grasping it tightly.

"Please make it stop," she whispers, making my heart ache. "I don't want this."

"You are being hysterical, Sophia," her mother says, exasperated. "Doctor Collins, please. Please make her see sense."

"She is scared, Ma'am," I reply, trying to keep my voice calm and pleasant. "She needs reassurance, not scolding."

I look at Sophia, my hand still clasped tight in hers. "I cannot stop this, my Lady," I say gently, as a sob escapes her lips. "You must bring this child into the world, there is no other way. But I know you can do this."

"I want …"

I see her eyes flicker towards her mother fearfully before she screams out again as the pain takes hold. Her mother stays by her side as the minutes draw on. I keep gently encouraging her, trying to offset the unhelpful words of Mrs Reynolds, whose comments are beginning to rile me.

"This is the King's child you are bringing into the world, Sophia. If it is a boy it will be his son and heir. You need to make sure that you deliver him safely."

"Mrs Reynolds." My voice is sharp and I see that she notices. "Childbirth can be a frightening, painful experience, especially the first time. Your daughter needs support, not further pressure upon her shoulders. Please try to understand that."

She appears taken aback by my comment, her mouth open like she wants to speak but the words are unforthcoming. Which is a relief.

But my worries grow for Sophia who seems unwilling or unable to make the effort to deliver her child. And that not only means danger for the baby but for herself as well. In between her screams when the pain takes hold she lies motionless, the tears falling down her cheeks, mingling with the sweat of her exertion.

I'm wrestling with my own mind, trying to work out if the one thing that might get her through this is worth the risk to take. Sophia's breathing begins to get shallower, her eyes closed, murmurings of discomfort escaping her lips. And I make my decision.

"Mrs Reynolds, your daughter is in danger, not only of losing the child but her own life as well. I need you to leave the room and give me the space to work and concentrate on saving them both."

I see her open her mouth to protest and I stop her.

"Please, Mrs Reynolds I promise you that I will do everything in my power to save both mother and child. But I need to be able to work with Sophia, have her concentrate on what I am telling her."

For once I see a glimmer of worry and care in her mother's eyes as she nods, placing a kiss against Sophia's hair before departing the room. I turn to Annalise who has been watching everything happening, tears in her eyes at the fear of losing her mistress.

"Go and find Tom," I say in hushed tones, even though we are the only ones apart from Sophia now in the room. "Tell him he needs to come here now."

She shakes her head. "What if he won't, sir?" she replies, worriedly. "He hasn't called on her in days."

"I know." I nod. "He has his reasons, believe me, it isn't because he doesn't want to."

"But what shall I say to him, sir?"

I swallow, looking across at Sophia who is failing by the minute.

"Tell him that Sophia needs him. Tell him that the baby is coming but she is giving up. She needs hope. Or she may well not survive this."

TOM

My darling Sophia,

I'm writing this because I need you to know how much I love you. That I never knew love before you and I'll never know love like yours again. You complete me. You make me whole. And without you I feel like a ship lost at sea.

I don't even know how to begin to think of my life without you. And so I hope you will forgive me for what I am about to do. I do not want to leave you. I never want to leave you. But I realise now that I have no choice.

I thought when I came here that I could bring you home. Carry on our beautiful little quiet life and find happiness again. Then when I realised that I couldn't, I made the decision to stay. To love you and protect you the best I could. And now I cannot even do that. If your mother tells Edmund about us then I know my life is over. But the truth is that it is over anyway.

And I don't want to cause you the pain of watching me get executed. I couldn't have that on my conscience. So this is a kinder way.

Please forgive me. And know that I went to the next world loving you with all of my heart.

Until we meet again.

Tom.

I place the quill back in the ink pot as I look at the bottle of laudanum which I stole from James' bag. I'm hoping that if I drink it I will just fall into a sleep from which I will never wake up.

It's not the worst way to go. And it has to be kinder than what Edmund might have planned for me and what that would put Sophia through.

The ink now dry, I fold the note in half and get to my feet, planning on placing it under James' door, so that he finds it when he gets back from his rounds.

Then a loud and frantic knock at my door stops me in my tracks.

Placing the note back on the table I walk to the door, my heart thumping. I haven't been anywhere near Sophia. Surely her mother won't have gone back on her word?

"Who is it?"

"It's Annalise, sir."

As Annalise's voice replies to my question I feel myself relax a little and I open the door. But as I see her standing there staring at me, her brown eyes full of tears, I feel the panic begin to prick at my heart once more.

"What's wrong?" I place a hand to her arm as she carries on looking at me.

"It's … it's Lady Sophia," she replies, and my panic begins to intensify. "The baby is comin'."

My heart aches as I think of Sophia, of what she must be going through. And selfishly I wish that I could have ended my life before I knew this.

"Thank you, Annalise, for letting me know," I reply, unsure of what else I can say. I go to see her out when she grasps hold of my hand.

"No, sir … I need you to come with me. Doctor Collins …"

"Annalise, please." My voice breaks, as I shake my head. "I can't. I can't go there. I'm sorry."

"Please, sir." There is desperation in her eyes which scares me more than anything. "Doctor Collins said she needs you. 'e said …" She stops, looking at me her mouth open like she wants to tell me something else but she is scared to.

"What? What is it? Tell me, please."

"Doctor Collins says that she is givin' up. That she needs hope. 'E said that she might not survive."

"No." I shake my head. "No, she can't give up."

"Please, sir," Annalise tries again. She's squeezing my arm, her eyes never leaving mine. "If she sees you then she might find that strength."

"What can I do?" I say, desperately. "How can I possibly help her through this? I don't know how."

"She loves you. And you love her. Sometimes that's all you need."

I swallow down my tears as I listen to her. Sophia always talked about how this young girl always seemed older than her years but this is the first time I have ever experienced her wisdom.

"I want to," I say, quietly, realising just how much my heart aches to see her. "But I can't. Her mother …"

"James … Doctor Collins." She corrects herself hurriedly. "'E sent her out of the room. She was makin' things worse. And that's when 'e told me to come and get you."

Her face is full of such faith, such belief that I can make a difference. My head is telling me to say no. To stay here and do what I was going to do. Stop the pain. But my heart is pulling me back towards her and before I know what I am doing I find myself nodding, following Annalise out of the door and towards the servants' staircase which has become so familiar to me now.

My secret pathway to her. As we get closer, I begin to hear her tearful screams and my heart feels like it is going to break in two. Annalise opens the door and walks in but I cannot seem to make myself move. She turns back towards me urging me in but when I don't follow she goes behind the drawn curtains of the bed, and a few seconds later James appears.

"Tom," he begins, but as she screams out again I feel the colour drain from my face as I look at him.

"I can't …"

"Tom, she needs you," he implores. "If she doesn't deliver this child soon then we will lose them both, do you understand?"

"How can I tell her that everything will be alright when we both know that it won't?"

He grasps my arm. "If she dies, then any hope dies with her. With life comes hope, Tom. Hope and possibility, no matter how small."

"But her mother."

"I refuse to let that woman inadvertently cause the death of her own daughter because she is too blind to see what it is that she needs!"

I am shocked by his outburst.

The normally calm and measured doctor looks angry, his eyes flashing with annoyance. And I realise that he is right. That I would never forgive myself if she died without me trying to help her.

Nodding at him, I take a shaky breath before pulling back the curtain, my breath catching in my throat as I see her. I can tell she is exhausted, on the verge of giving up. The sweat is soaking into her nightdress, her red hair damp with it. Her eyes are red with tears and I have to force myself to keep it together as she looks at me.

"Tom?" She smiles at me, the biggest smile despite her pain and I somehow manage a watery one in return. "You wouldn't ... see me. I didn't ... understand, I ..."

"Shhh." I rush to her side, grasping hold of her hand as I sweep the hair back from her face with the other. "I'm sorry. I didn't mean to hurt you. I'm here now."

"I can't do this," she whispers, her green eyes swimming with tears as she looks at me. "I can't."

"You can, Sophia," I say strongly. "You have carried this child safely for nine months. Now it is time to bring them into the world."

"I don't want to lose you." She chokes up and I place a kiss against her hair, desperately trying to quell my own tears.

"You won't. I promise. We will figure something out. Me and James. Find some way to stay here. Somehow. I swear."

"But my mother …"

"Listen to me." I take her head in my hands, resting them gently against her cheeks, making her focus on me. "Whatever happens. As long as we are both still here, still fighting. There is always hope."

I don't know if I believe it but right now I have to try, because she needs to believe it. And as she screams again I let her squeeze my hand tighter, whispering words of encouragement into her hair, telling her how much I love her.

James keeps gently calling instruction and encouragement to her but I'm not listening to him. I'm focused on her and her alone until a piercing cry fills the room and I feel Sophia relax back into my arms, her own tears falling silently, soaking into my shirt. I watch as James rushes over to the table, holding the screaming bundle in his arms, Annalise by his side. Sophia is clinging to my arm as we both watch, waiting for James to turn. And when he finally does, he is smiling softly, carrying a now quiet bundle wrapped in a deep red blanket in his arms.

"You have a daughter, my Lady."

As he places her into Sophia's arms, we both look down at the tiny, sleepy baby in silence.

I watch as Sophia lifts a gentle hand to stroke her cheek and I pull her in tight to me, resisting the urge to reach a hand out to the child as well. Because in this moment it would be easy to forget everything and everyone else and focus on the only thing me and Sophia had longed for. The two of us and a child in our arms. The world seems to stand still for a while, everything else melting away as I watch Sophia gaze lovingly at the beautiful baby girl in her arms. She is a natural mother, just as I knew she would be. I place a kiss to her hair as she raises her eyes towards me.

"She's beautiful, Sophia," I whisper, softly. "The image of you."

Her eyes are full of tears. I see the joy on her face at the new life she has brought into the world, mingled with the pain of the fact that this isn't how either of us know it should be.

"Sophia?"

As I hear Rebecca's voice, I jump up from Sophia's side. I do not have enough time to make my way back down the servants' staircase before she arrives so I come to stand respectfully by James's side, noting the brief flicker of panic across his features. She doesn't notice me at first as she rushes to Sophia's side, placing a kiss against her hair as she coos over her granddaughter.

"You did it, darling," she says, joyfully, gazing down at the child. "I knew that you could. Doctor Collins, thank..." As she turns to James she spots me, her eyes first full of shock, then anger as she fixes her gaze with mine. "Mr Redfield," she says, sharply, regaining her composure a little. "I didn't realise ..."

"I called upon Mr Redfield for his assistance, ma'am," James responds. "I didn't want to, as I know he has felt unwell recently. However, I was deeply concerned for Sophia's welfare and I needed some support. Without him I do not know if I could have safely delivered the child."

I glance at Sophia and can see the fear upon her face. The same fear that must show on my own. As Rebecca opens her mouth to reply she is stopped by the sight of Edmund rushing into the room. We bow, hurriedly, but his focus is entirely on Sophia as he rushes to her side.

"Sophia?" He places a hand to her hair, stroking it back from her tear stained face. "I heard there were complications. I didn't know what to do with myself, I have been so worried."

He looks every inch the concerned, loving husband as Sophia takes hold of the hand he rests against her cheek, letting him know she is alright.

"You have a daughter, Edmund."

Her voice is so strong, so brave. But seeing him sitting at her bedside as she hands him his daughter makes my heart ache so badly that I cannot stand to watch any longer. And with the whole room's focus now completely on the King and Queen and their new baby Princess, I quietly make my exit through the servants' staircase before it breaks entirely.

I've made my decision by the time I reach my chambers. I have to leave. Not through fear of what is likely to happen to me now that our secret is about to be exposed. But of what it would do to Sophia.

And the danger in which James could find himself if I am unable to hold my tongue. I do not even have time to leave a note. I just hope that Sophia will understand and can forgive me. I know that James will look after her, and that brings me comfort. Perhaps he will even be allowed to stay here, to help look after her and the child as she grows.

And of course, she has Annalise too. I know that I am just trying to ease my own guilt at abandoning her at her most vulnerable. But I couldn't bear for her to watch him break me. Watch him kill me and leave her with nightmares for the rest of her days.

I reach for my bag, grabbing spare clothes and some fruit from the crystal bowl which sits in the middle of the table. I do not know how long I will have to travel without shelter or sustenance so I had better prepare.

My eyes glance at the open bottle of whiskey next to the fruit bowl and I take hold of it without a second thought, replacing the stopper before placing it into the bag.

"Going somewhere, Mr Redfield?"

As I hear a voice behind me, I freeze.

The King's head guard is standing at the door, arms folded, a smirk playing on his lips. "It would be a shame to leave before the King has a chance to speak with you."

I swallow, placing the bag down on the bed as I turn to face him properly.

"Unusually quiet for a change. No witty remarks this time?" He continues to try and rile me, as I walk towards him. "No ridiculous excuses?"

I glance at the cuffs at his belt as I come to stand in front of him. "I think you and I both know that I have run out of luck," I reply, as I hold out my wrists in surrender.

"Oh no." The guard chuckles, shaking his head. "No, the King doesn't want anyone to be alerted to this right now. Least of all his beloved wife. And you are not going to do anything foolish now, are you?"

I shake my head and he scoffs, gesturing to me to leave the room before following on, keeping a firm but inconspicuous hold on my arm. We make our way down the stairs, straight past Edmund's study and it's then that I know for certain that he knows.

The Palace is quietly milling with servants and courtiers going about their daily business. As we pass by them, he lets go of my arm as he responds to their greetings and I try to make myself smile naturally as well, despite the panic thumping in my veins.

Edmund may not want Sophia to know what has happened yet and neither do I. If she finds out, I know that she will try and find me, try to stop the inevitable from happening. But she will not be able to. And I cannot bear for her to see what he will do to me. I saw what he did to George for even suggesting that their relationship was a fraud.

I saw what that did to her. And I know that my fate will be worse. I need to spare her the pain for as long as I possibly can. The guard carries on leading me further through the palace until we reach the door that I know leads to the cells and the dungeons below.

I was last here only months ago when I tried to rescue George from his fate. Now I am being led to mine.

The damp stone walls are lit with torches, the flames glowing red, making the light dance down the dark corridor as they flicker. When we finally reach the dungeon, I am expecting to find Edmund waiting there but there are only two other guards standing beside a makeshift platform in the middle of the room. This place is brighter than the corridor which led to it, in part due to the large fire pits situated in each corner which burn brightly, giving off such fierce heat that I feel like I am in hell.

The head guard pushes me towards the two men who grab my wrists and wrench them behind my back, tying them so tightly with a piece of rope that I can feel it breaking my skin.

As I look around I catch sight of numerous, ominous looking metal implements glinting menacingly from hooks on the wall to my left, and force myself to look away. The two guards now stand to either side of me, clad in black, staring silently at the door and I cannot stop my stubborn head from thinking of a way to escape.

I pull at my bound wrists experimentally but the rope holds annoyingly firm, and the effort serves only to get me a baton to the stomach from the brute to my right, which renders me breathless for a few moments. I'm still trying to catch my breath when the heavy iron door opens and Edmund appears flanked by two more guards.

He walks forward and stops right in front of me where he stands staring at me, the torchlight flickering.

"You don't have to torture me to get me to speak," I say, resolutely, "I'll tell you anything you want to know."

He laughs. "Oh, I know that. Besides, I don't need you to tell me anything. I already know everything I need to know. I'm not an idiotic man, contrary to what you may believe. And I know that you are not either. I was starting to wonder about a few things. The amount of time you were spending with my wife seemed extreme, even for her physician. So, I took it upon myself to look into your background and it turns out that Master Benjamin Redfield is still studying at Lowshore University, as we speak. And having seemingly lost his papers, he had to request new ones. So you see, I had already figured out who you were before Sophia's mother requested to see me, Thomas Thornton."

I swallow, realising finally that I have little or no way out of this.

"I see fear in your eyes." Edmund grins, interrupting my thoughts, "Fear of the axe perhaps? That's understandable, but I don't think it's that. No, I think it's a fear of Sophia being left with a constant reminder of just how pathetic you are. And how she may finally realise just how lucky she is to be with someone like me."

"Kidnapping someone and forcing them to marry you, does not equal love," I say calmly as I can muster. "Sophia has never loved you. And she never will. Killing me will not change that."

"She's an impressive woman, isn't she?" He grins as he backs away from me, pacing the floor. My eyes follow him as he confidently glides around the room. "I always knew she was from the moment I saw her. Beautiful, caring, intelligent. I knew she would make the most wonderful Queen."

I shake my head, unable to stop the ironic smile appearing on my lips at just how deluded he actually is.

"You've done nothing but frighten her and cause her pain," I reply eventually, my voice bitter. "You've broken her. Taken everything away from her that made her the woman you say you love. But carry on living in this fantasy world inside your head, if it makes you feel good."

He walks back up to me and I force myself to keep looking him straight in the eye. He reaches a hand to my neck and pulls out the rope that holds my wedding ring. He grabs hold of it tightly, yanking it forwards making the rope cut into the back of my neck. He looks at it closely, a smile appearing on his lips.

"I wondered where you had been hiding it," he says, smugly. "I knew you must have been pathetic enough to bring it with you. Maybe you thought in some delusional way that you could get her back. Go back to that ramshackle hut you call home and live happily ever after."

I feel my jaw starting to twitch as I try my hardest to maintain my composure knowing that he is only doing this to force a reaction.

"Well you might as well take it now," I say eventually, my voice strong. "A matching trophy for the one you took from Sophia."

He smirks at me, his finger tracing the small emerald in the centre of the ring. "I don't need this cheap piece of metal." He scoffs, before dropping it, "I've got the main prize."

I bow my head and close my eyes, ignoring him, refusing to rise to his baiting.

"How did you manage it?" Edmund speaks again, clearly rattled by my refusal to fight back. "You managed to make Sophia take pity on you, take you in from the streets and give you a home. You preyed on her good nature and somehow managed to convince her to love you."

"No." I shake my head, forcing myself to look at him again. "I know what I am. I've never tried to be anything else and maybe she did pity me. You're right. But I never asked her to, I never forced her to. She loves me for who I am, just as I love her. And our home and our life far away from this place that she tried to escape because she never wanted you. Or this hell you call a life."

"Yet, you couldn't give her a child." He mocks. "You had her for over a year yet couldn't put a child in her womb. Whereas now she lies upstairs with our daughter against her breast."

The smug, triumphant gloat which leaves his lips is the thing that tips me over the edge and I crack my head into his, watching him stumble back as the blood begins to pour from his nose. I try to reach him again but the guards have a tight hold of me now. Edmund's dark eyes are full of rage as he draws the ruby hilted dagger from his belt and storms towards me, placing it against my neck.

"I would dearly love to kill you right here and now!" he hisses, twisting the dagger against my skin until I feel the blood begin to trickle down my neck. "But why should I deny you the humiliation of a public execution? I might even make sure Sophia is there to see it."

This makes my composure falter, making me feel sick at the thought of Sophia having to watch me die. My thoughts are still overcome with this horror, as Edmund nods to the guards.

They grab hold of me, lifting me onto the platform that is so flimsy I know it won't be there for long, before wrenching my bound arms backwards and attaching them to a hook against the wall behind me, twisting them painfully out of position.

Edmund stares up at me, a cruel smile playing on his lips and I know he knows that he has won. Then without warning, he kicks the platform away and I drop like a stone.

The pain is instantaneous and vicious, so intense that I can't help but cry out. I feel it burning through my joints as they are forced into the unnatural position, taking the full weight of my body with nothing I can do to stop it. I'm not sure how much I can take and part of me hopes that this finishes me off, so that I spare Sophia the anguish of what he has planned for me.

As the pain becomes almost too much to bear, I feel myself giving into unconsciousness, my mind drifting to happier times far, far away from here.

"*Tom, hurry!*" *Sophia giggles , as she drags me closer to the edge of the sea.*

"*What's the hurry? It's not going anywhere.*"

"*Oh very funny, Thomas Thornton.*" *She rolls her eyes.* "*I don't know why I put up with you sometimes.*"

"*Because you love me.*" *I grin at her, dragging her back towards me and pulling her in for a kiss. I feel her relax into me and it seems like an age before we both come up for air.*

"*Love is a strong word.*" *She teases, grinning at me as she places one more quick kiss against my lips before grabbing my arm and dragging me towards the sea once again.* "*Come on, I want to find some seashells before the tide comes in!*"

As we reach the edge, I watch as she kneels down on the damp sand, her hands reaching for different shells and pebbles. As she finds the ones she likes, she hands them to me, my pockets full by the time she has finished. Then before I can say no, she grasps hold of my arm again pulling me into the sea.

"*Sophia!*" *I gasp at the sudden shock of the cold water and she laughs at me, her face lighting up with joy.*

"*It isn't that cold, you big baby.*"

"*What did you call me?*"

I raise an eyebrow, grinning at her and she shakes her head, squealing as I pick her up over my shoulder and dunk her in. Her face is a picture as she emerges from the water, her hair falling down her back where it has come undone from its braid.

"You are going to regret that, Thomas," she says, her eyes alive with fire.

"Sophia, don't you dare."

Giggling, she dives forward, grabbing hold of me and pulling us both down into the cold blue water with a splash.

I gasp as ice cold water hits me. As I blink it out of my eyes and see a guard holding a now empty bucket, I remember where I am. They have replaced the platform beneath my feet, allowing my arms a brief respite from the agonising pain burning through them.

Edmund stands in front of me, grinning as he watches me spluttering, trying to catch my breath.

"You were calling her name." He smirks, as he looks up at me.

I swallow, not willing to engage in his mockery.

"Did she come to you in your dreams?" He simpers, looking over at the guards who snigger gleefully. "Did you think she had come to save you? Because she can't. Nobody can. And you should make the most of your visions. Because it is the only way you will ever see my wife again."

With a nod of his head, the platform is kicked away once more and I hear my own screams of pain echoing off the damp stone walls.

Edmund

As I watch him hanging there helplessly, his screams echoing all around me, I feel a sense of satisfaction. All of these months here under my nose. Daily visits to my wife.

Of course, I had begun to have my suspicions. When he was caught in the gardens. When they danced together at the Spring Ball. The way she looked at him. The way she smiled. Never has she looked at me that way. I wondered how he could possibly have fooled James. A man of high intelligence such as him. But then again he fooled me well enough.

Sophia's mother coming to me with her news, was the final piece in the puzzle. She told me that she had found out a week or so ago but Sophia had begged her to keep her secret.

I understand this. The bond between mother and daughter is a special one. My mind is still trying to decide when to tell Sophia. Straight after this, so she can see just how pathetic her perfect man is after all? No. Better to wait until the day of his execution.

Give her a nice surprise to remember him by. I feel my mouth twitch with barely contained happiness at the idea as I instruct the guards to replace the platform and steady him.

He coughs as they do, gasping to try and catch his breath, the sweat dripping from his hair.

"How many times have you lay with my wife since your arrival here?"

As I ask the question, he raises his head so that his eyes meet mine. And a small part of me cannot help but feel slightly impressed by his tenacity.

"I haven't …"

"You've kissed her though?" I see him smirk at me and I feel my blood begin to boil.

"Yes. I've kissed her and she has kissed me. And it made her happy. You can't stand that, can you? Knowing that I can give her the one thing you never can."

I shake my head, chuckling to myself as I reach into my jacket and retrieve the note which my guards found in his room. I scoffed as I read it. A pitiful plea for forgiveness for what he was about to do, knowing that he had lost. A farewell to the only person he believed had ever loved him. I hold it up to him and watch with joy as he lowers his head in shame.

"You really think that Sophia could love someone as pathetic as this?" I taunt. "Someone who knew that he had lost so would rather kill himself than face his fate with honour? I will show her what it is like to love a real man. A strong man who can look after her. Give her the life she deserves."

"She will never love you."

He's still looking at the ground, too scared to look me in the eye. "Oh, she will. But you will not be here to see it."

"She hates you."

He finally looks at me, fixing his eyes with mine and I feel my jaw twitch with anger. "You make her feel sick. You can shower her with as many jewels and gowns as you want, but it will not matter. She cannot stand you. And killing me will just make her hate you even more."

I nod to the guards who kick the platform away again and I watch as he drops and the screams start over. My anger begins to cool knowing that I am once again in control and able to put him through hell. His words are meaningless. I have my prize and she will love me.

"This type of torture is used to elicit a confession from its victims," I say, raising my voice so it is heard above his screams. "But as I told you, I do not need a confession. I do have questions though."

Instructing the guards to steady him once again, I watch him as he regains his composure. It's taking longer each time. I see the tears of pain in his eyes this time as he splutters, his breathing shallow.

"How did you work out where she was?" I ask, curiously. "I'm guessing my darling wife never informed you of the arrangement of her marriage to me."

"I knew ... she was from ... the Capital." He gasps, his eyes fixed on mine. "When your men took her. A button came away from their ... uniform. I'm not stupid. I made ... the connection."

"And James?" I ask. "I've known James since I were a child. He isn't a fool. How did you manage to convince him?"

He laughs, shaking his head having finally caught his breath. "I heard people at the tavern, saying that the King's physician was in town for a tour of the country's medical schools. I decided he was my best chance of finding her again. I've done this since my childhood. Making up stories, tricking people. Doing what I had to in order to survive. I waited near the school, listened to the students talking. I stole the papers of a student whose work he had been impressed by. I made out to him like I was looking to develop my skills by working alongside someone like him. He had no reason to doubt me, he is too kind, too eager to help. I could see that and I took advantage of it."

"You took advantage of Sophia too."

"No!" His voice is harsh as he spits the word at me. "I love her and she loves me. You just cannot accept that, can you? She is the love of my life and you took her from me!" He breaks off, taking his eyes off me for the first time and I can see his resolve beginning to crumble, just as I want it to.

"You never had her," I hiss, glaring at him. "She wasn't yours to have."

"You cannot own someone," he snarls back, wrenching at his arms to try and get free for the first time since I walked in here. "She's not a possession. Not a trophy, that's all you see her as!"

I glance to my right, smirking as I catch sight of something. I look to one of the guards who nods, understanding my silent instruction.

"You can own a person. Slave masters have owned slaves for years. My ancestors owned slaves. It was the mark of wealth and power. Of course, I do not mean that Sophia is my slave, goodness, no. She is my wife. We are bound together by God. But you …" I see his eyes widen as the guard walks over with the white hot branding iron he has just removed from the flames of the fire.

I watch as he surreptitiously tries to once again free himself from his bonds without success.

"Did you know that they would brand them?" I continue. "To let everyone know what they were."

The guard hands me the iron as he walks over to Thornton, ripping open his shirt. The iron feels strange in my hands. Heavier than I expected. Never have I carried out my own punishment or torture. But this one. This one is special.

"We might as well let my wife, and all of the people of this city know exactly what you are before you die."

I watch him swallow. His eyes are fixed on mine once more and I cannot help but once again feel mildly impressed by his nerve. I walk towards him, the iron now glowing red and I steady myself.

"An X to mark you for death. Seems appropriate, don't you think?"

Before he has a chance to speak, I thrust the iron against his chest. His gargled scream assaults my ears as the smell of burning flesh hits my nostrils. I don't want to stop. I could kill him, right here and now if I wanted to. And I do want to. But this isn't public enough. I want him humiliated, I wrench the iron away, throwing it to the floor and kicking the platform away once more before he has a chance to compose himself.

He screams at me to stop, his breathless pleas coming thick and fast as I stumble backwards, breathing heavily as I try to control my rage.

The same pathetic words escape his lips over and over, and I feel a sense of victory as I call for a quill and some parchment and with shaking hands, begin scrawling a note. Folding it I hand it to a guard.

"Get this to Doctor Collins immediately," I say, as he nods. "I need his expert opinion."

As the guard leaves, I stand watching the man I despise hanging there defeated, broken. I win.

JAMES

Watching Sophia bond with her baby brought me such joy, especially after how scared she was earlier. I never saw Tom leave the room, my mind preoccupied by Edmund proudly holding his daughter in his arms, proclaiming to all of us how proud his wife had made him.

Eventually, I began to see fatigue taking over from joy in Sophia's eyes and I asked everyone to leave the room barring Annalise, to allow her some rest. It was at this moment she realised that Tom was no longer here and began to panic; until I assured her that he had likely just returned to his chambers, to escape hearing Edmund's joy at a moment which cannot have been easy for him. I told her that I would make sure that he called on her a little later on, when I would make my evening visit to check on mother and child.

And it was this that finally soothed her, enough to allow her mind to let her body rest for a while after the exertion it had just been through.

Both mother and child are sleeping peacefully when a guard enters the room, handing me a folded note addressed to myself in Edmund's hand.

James,

I require your assistance presently.

Please meet me in the dungeons below the palace.
My guard will escort you.

Edmund.

The guard is watching me closely and I try to keep the panic thumping in my chest from showing on my face. I pray to God this is not what I think it is about, but deep down I fear I already know.

Folding the note back up I get to my feet, making sure not to disturb Sophia or the child who are still fast asleep. Annalise is quietly folding clothes over by the window and turns to me as I get up.

"The King requires my assistance for a short while," I explain, trying to keep my voice steady. "I shall be back a little later on to check on Lady Sophia and the child."

She drops a curtsey before turning back to carry on her task as I follow the guard from the room.

"What is this about?" I ask the guard, fighting to keep my voice light and jovial.

"The King will explain."

He says nothing more to me, as we walk further through the palace. The opulence of the rooms seen by the public giving way to the cold, dark stone corridors that only the most unfortunate souls get to see. As we reach the dungeon, I see Edmund standing waiting by the doors and he looks up as I come to stand in front of him, extending a bow. I can hear moans of pain coming from behind the closed door and I swallow down the sickening feeling in my throat as Edmund looks at me, carefully.

"I need your opinion, James," he says, and I cannot work out the tone of his voice. "Your medical opinion."

Finally getting my mouth to work I incline my head respectfully. "You know that I am always available to give advice, Edmund. Both professionally and personally."

He smiles, before instructing the guards to open the doors and I have to stop myself from giving away my allegiance at the sight of Tom. His face is pouring with blood, and dripping down onto his shirt which is ripped open revealing more wounds, and I dread to think how he got them.

"Benjamin?"

I turn back to Edmund, hoping that he takes the look of shock on my face as confusion, rather than sickening guilt. I do not know if or what Tom has told him; and whether or not I will find myself up there beside him soon.

"I do not understand …"

Edmund smirks, as he comes to stand beside me, looking up at Tom. "Are you going to tell him, or am I?"

I watch Tom shake his head, closing his eyes. I do not know if he will not or cannot bring himself to speak.

Edmund sighs. "I'm afraid you have been lied to, James," he says, as he turns to me. "This man is not who you think he is."

I laugh, shaking my head, begging myself to keep up the pretence. "I do not know what you mean, Edmund. This is Benjamin Redfield, a student from the medical school of Lowshore. I've seen his papers."

"Were you introduced by his professor?"

"No." I shake my head. "Benjamin was not in school the day that I was shown his work. He came to me the day after, telling me that he had heard from his classmates that I had been most impressed by his work."

"Then I am afraid you have been taken for a fool, my dear friend." He shakes his head, looking up at Tom. "Tell him who you really are."

Again, Tom doesn't speak. He keeps his head bowed and his eyes closed. I can see Edmund getting more and more frustrated by his lack of compliance.

"Tell him!" he bellows eventually, kicking the platform away in a fit of frustration. I feel sick as Tom screams out in pain, as Edmund carries on shouting at him to reveal who he really is.

"Thomas!" His breathless voice eventually cries out. "Thomas ... Thornton. Please! Please stop, please ..."

I cannot bear to listen to his pained pleas. He told me when we met that he would never give me away, even under duress. I never believed him, knowing that nobody could hold their tongue under such pressure. But it seems as though he has. He's protecting me, protecting Sophia, even now.

"I do not understand." My voice comes out in a stutter. "Please will somebody explain this?"

"Tell him how you tricked him," Edmund presses on at Tom, instructing the guards to replace the platform below him. I watch him desperately trying to catch his breath, the sweat dripping from his face as he looks at me.

"I stole … Benjamin's papers." He gasps. "I heard … you talking about him. I needed a way … here. I needed to save her … this was the perfect … opportunity."

"This is him, James." Edmund hisses. "The drunkard. The one who took my Sophia from me. He tricked you. Tricked us all."

Tom's agonising pleading is becoming quieter and more muffled as his body begins to fail him.

"The prisoner is asking for us to stop." Edmund's voice brings my focus back and I turn away from Tom's near lifeless body to look at him. "I need to know if you believe, as a medical professional, that we should."

As I once again turn to Tom, I look up at him and he meets my eyes with his weary ones. He shakes his head. And I know him well enough now, to know that he isn't doing that because he's begging me to get them to stop. He's telling me not to give myself away by ending it.

Swallowing heavily, I gesture for the guards to bring me some steps to allow me to reach him. Climbing up onto the platform I see that he has closed his eyes, relief spreading across his features as his body is given time to relax, even for a little while. I catch sight of something on his chest which concerns me and as I peel back his shirt I see him wince.

I am grateful that I have my back to Edmund as I fear the look on my face would have given me away.

"Don't." His muffled voice is so weak that I barely hear him. As I look up from the branded mark on his chest I see that he is looking straight at me, his blue eyes vivid against his face which has drained of all colour.

"She needs you," he mumbles again. "I can cope."

You can't, I want to reply. But I know that I mustn't. I know that he has been through too much already and I should tell Edmund as much. And as a doctor, it is my job to heal people. Not bring them more pain, yet I know that Edmund is still likely trying to work out who he can trust, and I know that Tom needs someone to protect Sophia.

Hating myself, I close my eyes and begin to speak, hoping God will forgive me.

"You lied to me," I say, my voice harsh. "You took advantage of my kindness. I feel humiliated, betrayed."

"I'm sorry." He raises his head, his eyes connecting with mine. "I needed … to see her again. You were my best shot. My only chance … forgive me, please."

"You wanted to come here and take her away from this? King Edmund has told me what you did to her. How you treated her so badly that she came here broken. And I let you close to her again because I believed you could help her."

"Please …"

"I trusted you." I hiss. "You took me for a fool. Why should I help you now?"

I carry on looking at him, hoping he can see how sorry I am for doing this before I turn away.

"In normal circumstances, I would say that the prisoner has had enough," I say, desperately trying to keep my voice solemn and serious, as I make my way down from the platform and walk over to Edmund once more. "However, seeing as this prisoner tricked me into bringing him here under false pretences, putting many people's lives in danger, including your own." I glance at Tom one last time before turning to face Edmund. "I'd say that whilst he is still conscious, then there is no need to stop."

I see Tom bracing himself and I wonder what on earth must be going through his mind right now. I know he is trying to protect me by telling me that he can cope, but he wouldn't be human if he wasn't scared of the pain they were continuing to put him through. Edmund is grinning wildly, I force myself to watch as the guards kick the platform away once more. The howl that pierces the air makes my blood run cold and I close my eyes instinctively. He lets out an almighty scream, before suddenly the room grows eerily silent and I force myself to turn back towards him.

His eyes are closed now, his body limp and swaying from the hook he is bound to. I instruct the guards to once again place the platform near him so I can check on him.

As I climb up onto it, I place a hand to his neck to feel for a pulse. Warm blood drips from his nose and mouth onto my wrist as I do.

His pulse is strong though, which gives me hope as I turn to Edmund.

"I think now, he's had enough."

Edmund nods at me as I step down from the platform before signalling to the guards to cut Tom down. As they slice the rope from his wrists, I watch him crash down to the ground and stay there.

I notice his right arm lies at an odd angle and I can tell instantly that something is seriously wrong.

"His arm." I gesture to Edmund but he shakes his head, placing a companionable hand upon my shoulder.

"James. I know it is your natural instinct to help people. I understand that. But you must remember that this man betrayed your trust, you owe him nothing. And besides, he will be dead in a few days when the executioner arrives. He deserves to spend his last days on this earth in pain." He looks to the guards again. "Throw him in the end cell," he instructs them. "I don't want to hear him screaming when he wakes up."

As I watch the guards drag Tom's lifeless body past me out of the room, I feel Edmund once again clap his hand against my shoulder.

"I'm sorry you had to witness that, James. But you appreciate that I value your opinion above any other. Come and join me in my study. A stiff drink will help with the shock."

I force myself to smile; knowing Tom didn't go through all of that for me to give myself up now, as I follow Edmund back towards his study.

I must have drunk three large glasses of port as I listened to Edmund, feigning interest at the delight he was clearly taking at Tom's arrest and subsequent torture. Eventually I excused myself telling him that I must call on Lady Sophia and the baby before retiring for the evening.

The guilt in my heart made every step that I took towards her chamber feel as heavy as if I were bound in chains. What on earth could I tell her? I knock on the door and Annalise answers. She's smiling widely at me.

"She's doin' so well, sir," she says, glancing over her shoulder into Sophia's room. "And the baby is beautiful."

I manage a small smile as she beckons me in. My heart is thumping as I walk in and see Sophia at the window, her daughter in her arms.

She hasn't seen me, her focus is completely on her child and I can already tell she is a natural mother. She's rocking her gently as she looks out over the gardens, whispering words to her that I cannot make out. Then suddenly, she notices my presence and she looks across at me, her face beaming with a smile that breaks my heart.

"I was so scared of bringing her into the world," she says, her voice soft. "I didn't know what it would mean or how I would feel. But she's perfect."

I walk over to her, placing a hand against her arm as I look down at the child. She sleeps peacefully in her mother's arms and the sight of it brings tears to my eyes.

"I couldn't have done it without you," she whispers. "Or Tom."

"Sophia." I never call her by her name. She must notice this as she looks up at me for the first time, and as she sees my face her eyes widen.

"James, what is it?" she says, urgently. "Where is he?"

I shake my head, unable to stop the images from swirling around my mind. Unable to speak the words I know that she both needs and cannot bear to hear.

"James, please."

Her voice is shaking. The baby begins to stir, shifting in her arms and she rocks her but she won't settle. Placing her back in her crib she runs back over to me.

"Where is he, James? Please!"

"Edmund ..."

It's the only word that will come out of my mouth but it is the only one she needs to hear.

"No!" She screams it, collapsing to the floor, as Annalise comes rushing into the room at the commotion. She looks at me in confusion before rushing to Sophia's side. "Is he dead?" she gasps, as Annalise holds her close. "Has he killed him?"

"No. No he's in the cells below the palace. Sophia, wait!" As she gets to her feet and makes to run for the door I take hold of her arm.

"I have to see him."

"You can't. You do not want to, trust me. You do not …"

"What do you mean?" She shakes her head, her eyes glistening with tears. "You've seen him?"

I close my eyes, swallowing heavily. "I received a note from Edmund. It was to ask me to meet him at the dungeons." A choking sob escapes her lips and she clasps a hand to her mouth to try and stop it. "I don't want you to see him as I did. I don't want you to have those memories."

"What has he done to him?"

I open my mouth to speak, but once again the words won't come.

"I'm going to see him," she snaps, the tears falling down her cheeks. "I need to see him."

"Take my cloak, my Lady." Annalise's voice springs up from nowhere, surprising us both as she rushes to the coat stand and reaches for her cloak. Walking back over to Sophia she presses it into her hands. "Take the servants' staircase."

"Sophia, please." I implore her, trying one more time to get her to change her mind. She ties the cloak around her neck before grasping my arm once more.

"I'm sorry," she whispers before turning to Annalise. "Stay here and look after the baby."

As Annalise nods, Sophia turns without looking at me, pulling the hood over her head as she retreats out of the room.

Tom

The walls drip with water which falls to the floor in a constant dull thud; the only noise I can hear and one which I fear will begin to drive me mad the longer I am in here.

To my left is a low bunk, housing a pillow and a thin blanket which doesn't look in any way comfortable, but it has to be better than the floor they threw me to. Bracing myself, I manage with some difficulty to crawl over to it and drag myself onto it; realising my right arm is seriously hurt. Collapsing down, I try to catch my breath, my energy wiped as I look up at the dark stone ceiling.

"Guess this is it then," I say to myself, with a sigh. Maybe it was always going to come to this. I was stupid to think otherwise. Did I really believe I could come here, deceive the King and bring Sophia back home? I should have known it was hopeless from the start. I am a fool and perhaps I deserve this. But she doesn't.

"Tom?"

The sound of her voice suddenly reaches my ears like a beacon of light in this hellish darkness and I wonder if I'm hearing things.

"Sophia?"

I can barely make her out through the darkness, as I struggle to my feet and stumble over to the cell door. But as soon as I get there, I see her and I reach my good arm through the bars to grab hers. My hands feel like ice compared to the warmth of her touch and I savour it. Her face is white and tear-stained and my heart aches at the sight of it.

"What are you doing here?"

"I had to see you."

"Does he know you are here?" She shakes her head and I sigh.

"Sophia, you must go back before he finds you. Where is the baby? Is she safe?"

"She's sleeping," she whispers. "I left her with Annalise".

"You should be resting." I shake my head, "how did you even get down here? What about the guards?"

Her voice is quiet as she replies, "I paid them …"

She looks so horrified with herself that part of me cannot help but laugh. And once I start, I cannot seem to stop, the tears streaming from my eyes as I try and fail to compose myself. Even she raises a smile as I eventually manage to stop myself.

"I think you've spent way too much time with me," I say. "Clearly I've been a bad influence."

She's looking at me, her eyes full of different tears. I'm trying and failing to stop the chatter of my teeth and she reaches a gentle hand to my forehead.

"You are burning up," she says, her voice full of concern. "You shouldn't be down here. You need to be in bed. I will have James call on you."

"Sophia, leave it. Please."

She tries to reach for my other arm and I gasp in pain, my head spinning as I pull myself away. She's staring at me, taking in the mess they have made of my face before her eyes look down towards my shirt and I instinctively cover the mark he branded me with. I hoped she wouldn't notice, but of course she has and reaches a gentle hand through the bars and pulls back my shirt. I wince, as the fabric pulls away from the wound and I cannot make myself look at her.

"What has he done to you?" Her tearful voice is full of horror. I reach for her hand again, squeezing it tightly as I close my eyes.

"I'm sorry," I say and I feel her hand at my jaw gently lifting my head until my eyes meet hers.

"Don't say that." She shakes her head. "What on earth are you apologising for?"

"I tried so hard to be strong for you. All I wanted to do was protect you. I didn't want to let him break me. But he did."

My voice is struggling and I want to look away as the tears prick my eyes but her hand remains resting against my jaw making it impossible.

"He's a monster," she says, viciously, her eyes never leaving my face. "Do not apologise for the things that he has done. I'm going to fix this. I'll get you out of here."

"Sophia." I shake my head. "There is no time. I have days, if that. And I won't let you risk your safety for me. It's a lost cause and I'm not worth it."

I look at her blank expression and realise with a jolt that she doesn't know.

"He hasn't told you, has he?" I squeeze her hand again and try to steady my voice. "I'm to be executed next week," I begin, and the wobble in my voice remains, despite my best efforts. "The King has summoned his best executioner from Midshore, apparently. Lucky old me, eh?"

She looks horrified. "No … no! He cannot kill you, I won't let him."

I shake my head and open my mouth to reply but she carries on. "It was my mother, wasn't it?" she cries. "She told him. She promised me she would keep our secret, I should never have trusted her."

I shake my head as I squeeze her hands. "He already knew, Sophia. He had known for a while. Most likely since that first time I tried to find us a way to escape. He isn't stupid." I can see her eyes twitching as her mind runs wild with where she went wrong or what we could have done differently.

I try to ease her thoughts. "Remember the first day we met?" I say softly, and she nods. "I was in the forest with Arthur. I hadn't eaten in days, I looked in a complete state. I was sat by a tree, plucking up the courage to sell my only friend in the world in order to survive. And you came up and spoke to me." I smile thinking about it. "You were the first person in so long to talk to me like another human being. You listened and you cared. And it made me feel like I was worth something. I think I fell in love with you there and then."

She doesn't speak, but I feel her hand grasp mine tighter and I continue. "You said you had a problem with the roof of your cottage and did I know anything about how to fix them."

She smiles at this and I wonder if she is taking herself back to that moment, the moment I remember so vividly in my own mind. I manage to smile at her as I squeeze her hand, the memory warming my heart.

"There was nothing wrong with the bloody roof when I got there." I laugh. "But of course you knew that. Everything in that cottage was pristine. Yet you insisted I stay and help out. I constantly had to tell myself that you didn't just feel sorry for me."

She shakes her head. "I just knew that you were worth more than what people thought of you," she replies, "What you thought of yourself. I wanted to show you. I never expected to fall in lo …" Her voice falters and I squeeze her hand.

"Bet you're regretting that decision now." I'm grinning, but I see her face fall.

"Never," she whispers. "You were the best thing that ever happened to me. He can't take you from me. I'll kill myself if he does."

"Don't say that." I shake my head, horrified. "You are my world. He's taken you from me. And there is nothing I can do about it. I have nothing else to live for if I don't have you, but you have her. Don't let her grow up without a mother, Sophia. I never had a mother to guide me or shield me or love me growing up. Don't you dare take it away from that little girl for me, I won't let you."

She's looking at me, her green eyes brighter because of the tears in them. That kindness in them always there, never waning, even after everything that has happened. I can't help but smile at her, though I can feel my heart breaking.

"I always thought you'd be a wonderful mother."

"Don't Tom, please."

"That little girl needs you to show her that in this world; which can be so cruel and scary, there are people who are kind and gentle and full of love, who will always look after them."

I reach for her face and wipe the tears away. "And if she turns out to be even one tiny bit like her mother, then the world will already be a more beautiful place."

I should take my hand away but I just can't force myself to. Her lips brush my palm and I curse the cold metal bars that separate us.

"You changed my life, Sophia. You made me happy for the first time in my life. And I can die a better man because of it."

I want so much to just hold her properly in my arms. All I can do is hold her hand and hope that she knows how much I love her. The fingers of her other hand grasp the rope at my neck which holds my wedding ring. A part of us that he hasn't been able to take away or pretend never existed. It's here, it's real. It's us.

"Take it."

She looks up at me, shaking her head. "No, I can't."

"What use will it be to me, after I'm gone?" I say. "It'll be thrown in the river with what's left of me." I grin, but as her face falls I realise I've gone too far. I close my eyes. "I shouldn't have said that. I'm sorry. I don't like to admit it," I start, forcing myself to open my eyes and look at her. "Especially not to you because I know it is the last thing you need to hear. But I'm actually petrified. The thought of being brought out in front of a crowd of people waiting for a masked man with an axe to take my head from my shoulders."

I swallow hard. "Making a joke of things is the only thing that keeps me sane sometimes. But it doesn't mean I don't care. I just need to laugh or I'd probably cry." My voice breaks again and I curse myself as the tears sting my eyes once more.

"Tom," she whispers, and I can't bear the pity in her voice, as I feel her hand grasp mine tighter.

I sniff, composing myself as best I can before looking up at her again, attempting a smile. "Bet you are wondering why you ever married such a pathetic man?"

"He cannot do this. I won't let it happen."

"He is and it will," I reply, gently. "And I need you to promise me something."

"What?"

"Don't come to the execution," I say, remembering Edmund's words to me in the dungeon. "I don't want your last memory of me to be watching from a crowd of strangers as my head leaves my body. Let this be our goodbye. The two of us together. Where I am still able to hold your hand."

Our foreheads are touching through the bars. I feel the wetness of her cheeks against mine, just as she can feel mine against hers. Her lips meet mine and with my eyes closed I can almost take myself back to the first time I ever kissed her. Knowing that this is goodbye, I pull the rope from my neck, letting the ring fall into my hand as it breaks, before pressing it into her hand, closing her fingers around it.

"Go now," I whisper, unable to stop myself from touching her face one last time.

"I can't leave you."

"Sophia, go now. Please. Just go."

My voice is harsher than I intend it to be, but I can feel the tears welling up inside of me and I can't bear for her to see me break down. She grasps my hand tightly once more before turning to leave, disappearing from sight as quickly as she appeared, taking the warmth with her.

As the chill quickly returns to the air, I collapse down against the door in wrenching sobs, unable to keep up the pretence of confidence any longer.

SOPHIA

I cannot stop the tears from falling as I walk away from his cell. From him. The choking sobs explode from me as I rush past the guard I had paid to let me see him. I'm clutching his wedding ring in my hand tightly, as I make my way to Edmund's study. I don't knock. I walk straight in and see him sat by the fire, glass of port in hand. He turns as I walk in and smiles.

"My darling. What on earth are you doing here? You should be in your chambers with our daughter."

"How could you?" I hiss, and I see his expression change, the darkness returning to his eyes.

"You've been to see him?"

He stands up and I see that he is unsteady on his feet. Edmund never drinks to excess, so this is a new and worrying addition to his personality. "How the hell did you find out?" he snarls, walking up to me. "Who told you?"

"I heard servants talking." I lie. "They must have overheard the guards. News travels fast in this place."

He scoffs, shaking his head. "I wanted to be the one to tell you. I wanted to surprise you on the day of his execution."

"Why?" I scream. "Why would you do that to him?"

"He lied his way into this palace. He made a fool of me, he thought he could just take you back. I wanted him to know that you are mine now and you always will be!"

"You branded him." I can hardly bear to say it. Edmund chuckles which makes me feel sick. He reaches out a hand to brush my cheek and I push him away.

"He said that you cannot own a person. I wanted to show him that you can, so I now own him. For the next few days at least. Before I take his head."

"I won't let you."

"My dear," he says, his voice sickeningly sweet. "You cannot stop me. And what is more, I am going to make sure you get to watch. You will stand on that stage and watch his head leave his body knowing that I won. And you are mine forever."

"None of this is his fault. You brought me here. You took me from my home. From our life which I loved with all of my heart. You stole me away. Tom is right, you think you own me. Are you going to brand me too?"

His hand thunders across my face and I cry out, clutching my own hands to it to stop the stinging pain. He grabs my hair, wrenching me forward until I'm close enough that I can smell the liquor on his breath.

"I don't need to brand you, my darling. Everyone knows that you are mine now. Our blessing means that the whole country knows. And once your beloved is sent to the next world, there will be no other peasants thinking they can take what is mine." He rubs my tears away with his thumb before placing his hand against the cheek he just smacked. "And then of course there is our daughter."

Icy fear clutches at my heart, at the cunning tone to his voice.

"She is my child. She will be under my roof and my guard until she comes of age. As will all of our other children."

I am frozen in fear and pain as he places a kiss against my lips. As he breaks away, I find myself trying to appeal to any last shred of humanity he may have.

"He's ill," I choke out. "He has a fever. At least let Doctor Collins attend to him, make him comfortable, please!"

"Why? He'll be dead in a few days. And James has far more important things to do. Like caring for my wife and daughter." His expression changes from a smirk to the darkness I know so well. "Now, go back to our child before I have the guards drag you back there and lock you in."

He pushes me away, turning back towards the fire as I stumble from the room in tears, my heart broken as I feel my world shatter into a million pieces. I somehow manage to find my way back to my chamber, barely noticing where I am going until I arrive at the door and wrench it open. Annalise and James are still there waiting and at the sight of them I collapse to the ground, my legs unable to carry me any longer.

"Sophia …" I feel James and Annalise get to the floor beside me, Annalise grasping my arm as I lift my head to look at James.

"You have to help him," I cry, as his eyes study my face carefully. "Please!"

"Sophia. there is nothing I can do."

He's looking at me with such pity I can hardly bear it. Unclasping my hand, I stare at Tom's wedding ring, choking back tears.

"Try..." I whisper. "I beg you."

JAMES

Edmund refused all visitors the next day. And the day after, which worried me slightly. Ever since he was a child, if ever he were angry or frustrated he would lock himself away, the anger building higher and higher in him until finally he would snap.

Yet the longer it takes for me to see him, the less time I have to check on Tom. Sophia is growing more anxious by the day and it is becoming more and more difficult to settle her. After she burst back into the room, her cheek red from where Edmund's hand had scolded her, I promised her I would try to talk him into seeing some sense. With Annalise's help, I have managed to keep her as focused as possible on caring for her child.

Finally today, Edmund has agreed to visitors. And as I am called into his study I see him standing at the fire with his back to me, a glass of port in his hand.

"Your Majesty," I say, bowing to him though he still has not turned to face me.

"He is delayed, James." His voice is sharp, bitter. And as he turns to face me I see the glint of anger in his eyes.

"The executioner. He was meant to be here this week. But he is currently in Evershore. More than two weeks away by road. Maybe more." He slams his glass down on the table as he strides over to me. "I want Thornton dealt with, James. I want to see his head on a spike. I want her to watch as it leaves his body and she knows that I have won. That she is mine."

His eyes are manic and I wonder just how little sleep and how much liquor these past two days have been filled with. I choose my next words and my tone carefully.

"That is most unfortunate, Edmund. However, you must try not to let this setback frustrate you. You will get the justice you deserve. As shall he. A few more days gives you time to prepare. Make sure that as many of your loyal subjects can be there to watch as justice is served."

Though his eyes are still alive with fire, I see that my words are beginning to calm him and as he picks up his glass again and takes a sip, he nods. "Thank you, James. You are and always have been a voice of reason."

I incline my head as he pours himself another glass and does the same for me.

"Perhaps you should call on him," he muses carefully and I feel some relief in my chest. "My guards tell me that he is unwell. And though I care little for his health, I am determined he should face a public execution. Fix him up enough so that he will not die down there, James. But do not waste all of your energies on him. He does not deserve it."

As I reach the cells after being dismissed by Edmund, I swallow heavily. All I could hear as I made my way down here were his moans of pain; which echoed down the corridors, from where he is being held in the very depths of the palace.

I instruct the guard at his door to leave us. All patients are entitled to the privacy which my oath allows them and this means that I will be able to talk with him as a friend, not the person that I was forced to be in the dungeons.

As the cell door slams shut behind me and I hear the guard walking away, I look over to where Tom is huddled in a blanket on the small bed in the corner of the cell. The air is stale with the smell of sweat and damp. The only light comes from a solitary torch upon the wall. He's tossing and turning, unable to get comfortable. I do not know if he is even aware of my presence but as he turns towards me he sees me and speaks.

"It's a little c … cold down here, J … James. I think I should lodge a c … complaint." He's grinning at me and I manage a smile back as I walk up to him and place a hand to his forehead where I feel, as I suspected, that he is burning up with fever.

"It is." I nod in agreement. "Let's try to make you a little more comfortable."

His hair is damp with sweat as is the thin pillow he rests his head upon. Worryingly, I see fresh cuts and bruises upon his face, too fresh to be the ones which had been inflicted upon him the last time I saw him in the dungeons.

He shifts slightly as I begin to lift his shirt away from his chest, murmurings of discomfort escaping his lips.

The putrid smell of infection hits my nostrils as I uncover the wound which the branding iron left behind, confirming my suspicions.

There is dirt in the wound too, left by the unmistakable shape of a footprint against it. I swallow heavily as I place my hand to his forehead once again.

"Tom? The King will not allow me to fix your arm. But the wound on your chest is infected. I need to treat it and make you more comfortable."

"No." He mumbles it, shaking his head as he opens his weary eyes to look at me and I sigh.

"Tom, you need medicine to treat the infection. It will make you feel better."

"What's the point?" he asks, tiredly. "I'll be dead soon. Save yourself the bother."

"You cannot think like that."

"I'm tired, James," he replies, quietly. "I don't want to fight this anymore."

He always had a spark of belief. Even when everything seemed lost. Even through all of these months he had to watch his wife carry someone else's child. But looking in his eyes now, I can see that the spark looks as though it has burned out.

"It's the fever talking, Tom," I try, again. "You'll feel better if I treat it, I promise you."

"Is he here yet? The executioner?"

I sigh, shaking my head. "The King advises that he's been delayed. Perhaps by another two weeks."

"Then please. Just let me die here."

"Tom."

"I don't want you to make me better just so I can lose my head in front of the whole C … Capital." He's begging me silently, but I just cannot do it.

"Tom. You are sick already and this infection has only just started. This will kill you slowly and painfully and I will not let that happen."

"Because an axe is quicker?"

I do not know what I am supposed to say to him. "I'm sorry, Tom. I shouldn't have come to find you. If I hadn't, then none of this would have happened."

"No." He shakes his head. "I wouldn't change anything. Except maybe the getting caught bit." He laughs and I try to smile in order to help him, even though I don't feel like it. Eventually though, the laughter fades from his eyes and he looks at me wearily again. "He's going to make her watch." His voice is quiet. "I don't want that."

"Is that why you won't let me treat you?"

He swallows and I see his jaw wobble. "I can't put her through t …that. Not after everything else."

He closes his eyes, turning away from me on the small bed and drawing the thin blanket across himself once again. He's shivering constantly and I know that if I don't treat him soon, then it will be too late.

"If I make sure she isn't there, somehow," I say, not knowing how on earth I would even manage it. "Will you let me treat you?"

He turns back towards me, his eyes now full of tears.

"You'll keep her away?"

His voice is quiet. He looks like a child. I know I'm lying to him but I won't let him die here. As hideous as the idea is; execution would be quicker.

I nod. He shifts himself back so that I can treat him. I soak a cloth in iodine before placing it against the wound. He cries out in pain and I apologise telling him that it will help to draw out the infection and make him better. The bottle of medicine I take from my bag is a strong opiate which I hope will make him sleep. That will help, too. He drinks the dose and the relief in his face is instant.

As he falls asleep, I clean and dress the wound then tend to the ones on his face before tidying up my things and walking over to the door, banging on it to instruct the guard that I am finished.

Tonight's guard is one of Edmund's longest serving, loyal to a fault. Meaning his feelings towards Tom are cold at best and that he is likely the cause of his more recent suffering.

"Any change in his condition and I am to be informed immediately," I tell him, as he walks up to the door and unlocks it.

When he fails to respond I speak again. "The King expects him to be fit enough for his execution. And I'm sure you wouldn't want to disappoint the King."

His face pales at this and he shakes his head. "No, sir."

"Then, any changes and I will expect you to notify me. He should sleep for a while now. I shall be back to check on him in the morning but if I am needed before, then I shall expect to be informed."

He nods, though I don't know if I believe him. And I already know that I'll be coming back down here to check for myself before the night is out.

TOM

Pain is the first thing I feel upon waking. Though not the torturous, agonising pain of the last few days. Now it feels duller, more manageable. Blinking to clear my vision, I see James sitting on the edge of my bunk, sorting through the bottles in his bag. I try to sit up but have no strength in my right arm and my movement attracts James' attention.

"Don't try to move," he says, shaking his head. "You've been unwell for a few days. Barely conscious. I'm glad to see you looking better."

Looking down, I see that my chest is covered with bandages where the iron branded my skin. And my arm no longer sits at a strange angle, though I have no strength in it and can barely move it.

"You fixed my arm?" I venture cautiously and he smiles as he nods his head. "I thought you weren't allowed to?"

"I couldn't leave you like that," he replies, his voice dark. "It went against every principle I hold as a physician. I told Edmund that the injury to your arm was adding to your condition. And that it may kill you. Luckily, the King isn't trained in such matters so it was easy enough to convince him."

He's smiling again now and I manage a small grin in return.

"He's still insistent on taking my head then?" I try to make my voice light but James can see right through me, the sad smile on his lips confirming what I already knew before I asked the question. Reaching for a flask of water he brings it to my lips, and I realise how thirsty I am as I drink it.

"The executioner is closer to the Capital than first thought," he replies. "He is now due here in four days."

He takes the flask away. He isn't trying to avoid the point or trying to make me feel better about it. Which I'm grateful for.

"Well I am obliged to you," I say, honestly. "Though I'm not sure how much use I will have for it, I'm glad at least not to have to spend my final days on this earth in such pain."

"I'm sorry, Tom." James isn't looking at me, instead he's focusing intently on his medical bag. "I should have stopped this before it started. I wish I had never answered Edmund's summons."

"No." As I say the word he finally looks at me. His face is full of regret, regret which he need not feel. "Please don't think like that. If I had my time over again I would make the same choice. Every time. You brought a tiny spark of the Sophia that I love back. You nursed her back to health. You gave us a few more precious moments together when I thought I would never see her again. Without you, I don't know if she would still be here now. I think she would have given up the fight long ago. And now she has a baby girl who needs her. And they need you to help guide them."

"You would make the same decision?" he says, looking at me closely. "Knowing what you know now?"

I swallow. "I don't want to die, James. But I meant what I said when I first met you that night in Lowshore. I would rather die trying to get her back than live the rest of my life knowing where she was and how unhappy it was making her. And if you keep your promise to me, then I hope that I can at least spare her the worst of it."

"You remember that?" He looks at me in surprise and I chuckle.

"Fever or not, my request would have remained the same. I don't want her to have to watch. Because then everything that was good in our lives will be tainted by my last moments, leaving her with nothing but nightmares when she deserves only happiness."

He's watching me silently and I cannot tell what he is thinking. "It is the least I can do for you." His reply is gentle, so quiet, that I barely hear it as he turns to face me. "I'll keep her away. Somehow."

"Thank you."

My eyes grow heavy as sleep begins calling to me once more. He must notice, as he gets up from the bunk and adjusts the thin pillows at my head. I think I mumble my thanks and he may say something in return but exhaustion wins and I'm asleep before I even see him leave my cell.

As the days grow ever closer to my fate, I begin to reflect on my life - trying to make sense of everything that has happened to bring me to this point. My arm has regained some of its strength and so I requested a quill and paper in order to write down some of the thoughts swirling around my head. I addressed each one to Sophia, even though I knew it was highly unlikely they would ever reach her hands.

No doubt Edmund will keep them, probably placing them under one of his crystal cloches, another trophy to signal his victory. I am just finishing my most recent musings when I hear commotion from outside my cell, a woman's tearful pleas, the guards' harsh tones. I get to my feet in confusion as the door opens and Annalise is pushed to her knees on the cold, damp floor.

"Two traitors together." The guard sneers as choking sobs begin to escape Annalise's mouth, "you'll have some time to catch up before our guest arrives to send you both into the next world."

The guards snigger as they slam the cell door shut and I rush over to where Annalise hasn't moved from the floor.

"Annalise? What's happened?" I place an arm around her to help her up, but as I do this she cries out in pain, and I stop. Looking properly, I see the back of her dress is ripped open and her back is covered in vicious red welts and bleeding, open wounds.

"They k … kept sayin' I 'ad to confess," she chokes out, as I lead her over to my bunk. "Confess to bringin' you 'ere. I kept tellin' 'em that I didn't. But they just kept hurtin' me. I confessed just so they would s … stop."

My throat constricts with emotion as I listen to her. I pull her in tight to me with my good arm and I feel her relax against me as she breaks down.

"Listen to me." I say strongly, "anyone would confess to anything to get them to stop the pain. It's why they do it. They don't care about what's right or wrong. They choose what they want to believe and make the facts fit."

"Did you?" She sniffs, looking up at me with red-rimmed eyes and I smile, sadly.

"They didn't torture me to get me to confess," I say, gently. "I told them before they even started that I'd answer any questions they had. Edmund just wanted to hurt me. For his own benefit, knowing it would hurt Sophia just as much."

"S … so there was nothin' you could do to get 'em to stop?"

"They stopped when I lost consciousness and couldn't feel it any longer," I reply. "It wasn't entertaining for them after that."

"I'm scared," she whispers, tearfully. "I don't want to die."
I shake my head and pull her in close once more.

"You aren't going to die here. I won't let that happen. I need you to look after Sophia when I'm gone. She doesn't have many people she can trust."

"G … gone?"

I look at her knowingly and she shakes her head, breaking down in tears once more. I let her fold herself into me again, holding onto her as tight as I can.

"Get some sleep, Annalise. Nobody will hurt you now, I promise. You're safe with me."

I wait until she is sleeping before gently removing her from the crook of my arm. Taking off my jacket, I place it under her head and cover her with the thin blanket which provides the only source of warmth in this cell. I watch as she stirs slightly before settling back down into sleep.

"I request an audience with the King." I direct my request at the guard standing watch outside my cell. He ignores me so I speak again. "Tell him I wish to discuss Sophia," I continue. "And I'm sure his arrogance won't allow him to ignore such a request."

This gets the guard's attention. "You need to watch your tongue."

"Why?" I scoff. "You've tortured me and I'm going to be executed this week. How else could you possibly punish me?"

"There are ways."

I swallow nervously, his tone unsettling me somewhat.

"Surely I am entitled to a last request?" I push on. "Surely we are all entitled to that?"

The guard turns away from me once more. Frustrated, I try one last time.

"I have a confession to make. A confession of guilt that I wish for the King to hear."

"He knows everything he needs to know."

"No." I say it strongly, and this makes the guard turn back. "He doesn't."

It must be an hour or so before the door to my cell opens and the guards gesture for me to get to my feet. The noise disturbs Annalise who begins to stir, blinking up at me sleepily. "Tom?"

"It's alright. Nothing to worry about, I promise, I'll be back soon. Try to sleep some more." She looks at me uncertainly but settles herself back down as I am marched from the room.

"You shouldn't give her hope like that." The guard spits, as he walks me down the dark, stone corridor, "she will die, just like you, when the executioner arrives."

"Not if I can help it," I reply, under my breath, as we reach a room and he pushes me inside. He gestures to a chair and I sit, as he grabs my arms and wrenches them behind me before securing them with rope. I gasp as the pain from my damaged right arm burns into me, and the guard sneers.

I ignore him, unwilling to give him any more satisfaction than he's already had. The King, clearly, is not a man to rush and it feels like forever before he sweeps through the door, looking as picture perfect as any fairy tale prince should be; so long as you don't look close enough to see the darkness behind his eyes. He takes a seat opposite before addressing the guards who stand either side of me.

"You may leave us now." At his instruction they bow, before leaving the room, the door closing with a heavy clang behind them.

He sits, silently for a while, studying me. "What is this all about?" he asks eventually.

With a deep breath, I speak. "Annalise."

"Who?"

"Sophia's lady-in-waiting. The seventeen-year-old girl you had tortured and flogged before throwing her in a cell with me."

"Ah yes, your little helper. What of her?"

I shake my head, unable to understand the mentality of a man like him. "She had nothing to do with any of this."

"You expect me to believe that you managed all of this?" He laughs, rolling his eyes. "Thought all of this up by yourself? Without help from anyone? No. No, you had help. Someone of lowly stature, like yourself. And a servant girl would be perfectly placed. To help fool James, to fool me, to facilitate your passage into my palace, my kingdom, my world. No doubt she was the one who told Sophia of your fate too, ruining my surprise."

"I know you do not wish to believe it," I calmly retort back. "But I am not stupid. I've had to fend for myself since I was a child. I learnt how to steal, to lie and to deceive people in order to survive. I've done this all on my own for years, never needing anyone's help. I had no help. I deceived James easily enough. Using his sympathetic and good nature to weave a story of how I had fought poverty to gain a place to study medicine. How I wanted to help people like he had done. It was easy. I deceived Annalise too."

"She knew exactly who you were," he hisses, interrupting me. "She knew too much about you. Torture loosens the tongue, I've learnt that over the years."

I swallow.

"Yes, she knew," I agree. "But not from the start. She worked it out of her own accord. She is also more intelligent than you give her credit for. She wanted to tell you. I forced her not to. Told her she had to stay quiet for Sophia's sake. I made her feel guilty and told her that she would be betraying Sophia if she said anything."

I close my eyes, looking down at the floor. "For Sophia's sake, she said nothing. She is more loyal to her than anyone I have met. She cares for Sophia so much that she risked everything to keep this secret. All I ask is that you let her go back to her. To help look after her and the baby. She doesn't deserve to die for being loyal to the Queen." I force myself to look up at him. He is staring at me but his face is blank with expression, leaving me with no idea of what he is thinking.

"You are an unusual man, Thomas Thornton," he says, eventually. "Most people in your position would be begging me to spare their own lives, not that of an irrelevant servant girl."

"My life ended the day you took Sophia from me. I see no point in fighting for it now." He smirks at me, the look on his face one of a man who knows he has defeated his enemy.

"I suppose that is true of what little life you had. And in a way, I admire you. For admitting your guilt. For accepting your fate. For this reason I shall allow the girl to live."

I let out a shaky breath that I didn't realise I had been holding. "Thank you."

"I'm not doing this for you. I'm doing this for my wife."

I feel my jaw clench as he says it and the smirk on his face tells me that he noticed the break in my composure too. As I am led back to my cell and they open the door, I see that Annalise is no longer sleeping and the minute I walk back in she runs into my arms.

"I thought they'd taken you to ..."

"No. No, it's alright. I just needed to speak with the King."

One of the guards walks forward, placing a hand on her arm. "Come with me girl."

Annalise looks at me, her eyes wide, and I shake my head.

"Don't be scared, Annalise. They are taking you back to Sophia. I told them you had nothing to do with it. You were just protecting her."

"What about you?"

Swallowing down my tears at the innocent hope in her voice, I pull her in tight, whispering into her hair. "There is no hope for me. But you don't deserve my fate. Just promise me you will look after her and the baby."

As she pulls back from me, I see the tears in her eyes which threaten to make mine flow. She nods as she is led away, out of the cell and I follow them to the door as it shuts behind them. She turns to look at me, managing a smile which I just about manage to return. Edmund is watching us with interest from the back of the group. And the guard holding onto Annalise turns to him as he speaks.

"Take her down to the dungeons."

My blood runs cold as I see Annalise's eyes widen in fear. She begins to struggle against the guard, screaming but he picks her up as if she weighs nothing, dragging her further and further into the darkness, until I can see her no more.

As Edmund and the other guards turn to follow them, I shout at them to let her go, wrenching desperately at the door to no avail.

"What are you doing?! You swore you would let her go free!"

Edmund stops, turning back towards me, smirking in the low light of the flickering torches. "I did and I will. I just need some insurance first."

Before I have a chance to say anything more, he strides off down the corridor in the direction of the dungeons.

All I can hear are her screams travelling down the long, stone corridors, which echo with every heart-breaking noise. There is nothing I can do to block it out, I can only sit here, imagining the horror she is going through, wondering why I ever trusted anything that Edmund said.

Suddenly, the air is pierced with the most blood-chilling wail which cuts into my heart like glass. Then there is silence and I feel sickening guilt at what I have done. The next noise I hear are footsteps walking towards my cell door, and as it opens and Edmund walks in I stumble to my feet but before I can reach him I am held back by two guards.

"Where is she?" I roar. "What have you done to her?"

"I told you, Thomas. I gave you my word that she will go free and she shall. I just needed to ensure something first. You told me that you forced her to stay quiet. Well now she will."

I shake my head in confusion as he gestures to one of the guards behind him. He walks forward holding tight onto Annalise.

Her face is deathly pale, her brown eyes full of tears, staring into nothingness. Her nose and mouth are stained with her own dark red blood.

The guard throws something to the floor and I swallow down my revulsion, as I realise that it is her tongue.

"Now she will be quiet forever." Edmund smiles, walking over to her and stroking a hand across her cheek. "No more danger of her cooking up plans with my beloved wife. She can hear everything but speak nothing. Just as a servant should."

I see the tears start to fall from her eyes and I feel the wetness of mine against my cheeks.

"Annalise, I'm sorry. I didn't … I never … I …"

"Take her to James," Edmund instructs, interrupting me without looking at either of us. "Tell him what has happened so that he can treat her. Then tell him to take her back to Sophia so she knows just how dangerous it is to be associated with this man."

All I can do is stare at Annalise's tear-stained face, as she is dragged away. Her eyes wide with pain and fear. The dark red blood at her mouth evidence of the horror she had just endured. I watch her until she is out of sight before focusing my attention back on Edmund, as he walks to stand right in front of me.

"You're a monster." I hiss, spitting in his face. The guards wrench me back, as he takes his handkerchief from his pocket and wipes his cheek.

"Maybe I am. But at least I've got my prize. Where as you? You will leave this world tomorrow with nothing. The way it should be."

JAMES

I sit at my desk working through papers. My heart and concentration are not in them though. All I can think of is Tom's impending execution and the role I played in getting him there. There is a knock at my door, but I don't look up from my work.

"Hmm?" I mumble lazily, as I scrawl my quill across the page. It is only when I hear a muffled sob that I raise my eyes and immediately feel my heart starting to beat faster in my chest as I do.

"Annalise?"

The young girl is barely able to stand, her mouth covered in blood, as the guard holds her around the waist. I rush over and grab her as her eyes flutter shut and she collapses forwards.

"What on earth has happened to her?" I ask the guard, who remains standing at the door as I carry her over to the bed. As I place her down and begin to examine her, I realise with sickening horror just what has been done.

"Her tongue has been cut," I say, looking over at the guard in anger. "Who did this?"

"The King's orders, sir. She was arrested this morning."

"On what charge?"

"Assisting the prisoner Thomas Thornton in his deception."

My heart is thumping in my chest as he casually says the words, and I feel sickened realising the price she has paid for my treachery.

"Get out!" I snarl at him, my voice stronger than I have ever heard it. "Get out and let me work."

As he leaves, I turn back to Annalise who is barely conscious, painful moans escaping her lips that make the tears prick at my eyes.

"I'm sorry child," I whisper, stroking back her hair from her face, before reaching for the bottle of laudanum in my bag and measuring out a large dose.

"I need you to take this," I say gently, placing the glass to her lips. She cries out, shaking her head, refusing to open her mouth. She's terrified yet still so strong and I hate myself as I place my hand to her nose, forcing her mouth open allowing me to tip the strong opiate down her throat.

"Sleep, Annalise," I say, stroking back her hair again, as her cries turn to whimpers and her eyes begin to flicker shut once more. "I'm going to make the pain stop soon, I promise you."

I don't even know if she hears me.

She drifts into unconsciousness guided by the laudenum, and I retrieve the instruments I need from my bag to attempt something which I have only ever seen in books. Something, I hoped I would only ever see in books, the idea too horrific to comprehend.

Yet I know that I must if I am to save her life. She never deserved this. The guilt eats away at my heart as I work, knowing that this should have been me.

I wrack my brain, wondering if I had said or done anything to place her in such danger. But in my heart I know. I know that Edmund would not have looked for facts. In his mind, social standing determines who can be trusted and who cannot. I wonder if he would ever believe such treachery of me, even if the evidence was presented right in front of him.

Yet young Annalise, who was caught up in this whole thing by accident; this innocent young child, has paid the price for my misdeed. Time becomes obsolete as I continue my work carefully, trying to save her life even though I know that I cannot save her voice.

As I finally finish, I just sit at her bedside and watch her sleeping. Wishing I could take away the pain for good; or turn back the clock to make sure this never happened at all, feeling an unfamiliar wetness at my cheeks as the tears begin to flow from my eyes.

"What is going on? Let me past!"

Sophia's voice suddenly rings out from outside the door to my chambers and I feel my heart drop. Annalise is still sleeping; for how much longer I do not know. But I did not want Sophia to see her like this, pale as death and in such pain. As she bursts through the door, followed quickly by two guards, I brush the tears from my face as her eyes immediately find Annalise and her face drops.

"Annalise."

As she rushes to her bedside I motion to the guards to step back outside and leave us.

As I hear the door click, I walk over to where Sophia has collapsed down in the chair beside her bed. "What happened?" She's looking from Annalise to me, the tears streaming down her face.

"I do not know much," I reply, honestly. "All I was told is that she was arrested this morning."

"Why?"

Sophia is staring at me, shaking her head, searching my face for the answers I cannot yet give her.

"Forgive me, Sophia, I do not know the answer to that."
"What did he do?" she whispers. "What did he have done to her?"

I swallow, suddenly unable to meet her eye or look at Annalise, remembering the pain in her eyes as she was brought to me.

"Her tongue has been ..." I stop, unable to finish the sentence, but I know that Sophia doesn't need me to. She looks as nauseous as I feel, as she meets my eyes with hers which are brewing with tears.

"Go find him," she says, and the anger in her tone is unusual to my ears. "I want to know why. I will stay with her."

"You need to be with your daughter."

"She's with a nursemaid," she interrupts me, dismissively, turning back towards Annalise and placing a gentle hand to her hair. "Annalise needs me now. Please, James. Do as I ask. I want to know why he did this."

I know that I cannot refuse her request. And that deep down, I need to know why as well. I bow to her as I leave the room to find Edmund and the answers which we both need to hear.

SOPHIA

As I sit by Annalise's bedside stroking back her hair, I let the tears fall down my face, not bothering to brush them away. I keep thinking of how I could have protected her more.. But the fact is, I never would have imagined that Edmund would do something like this to her.

She is so innocent, not a threat to him in any way. I didn't think she needed protection, like Tom did. And yet Edmund has managed to hurt them both. As she begins to shift in her sleep, I finally brush the tears from my face and take hold of her hand as she opens her eyes and looks at me. I cannot bear the pain in them. Or the pitiful sounds that escape her lips, as she tries to find the voice which has been so cruelly taken from her.

"Shhh, Annalise." I soothe, desperately trying to stop my own tears as hers begin to fall. Her hand squeezes mine tight, as I see the blood slowly appear at the corner of her mouth. I reach for a cloth with my spare hand and wipe it away as gently as I can.

"Let me tell you about that secret beach," I whisper, as I place the cloth down and raise my hand to stroke her hair once more. "I want you to try and imagine you are there."

Her big, brown eyes are wide; still so full of fear and pain, as she looks at me and nods her head silently.

"You have to walk through the forest to reach it," I begin, never taking my eyes from hers. "Then suddenly the hard, forest floor feels soft under your feet and you look down and see grains of the purest, softest white sand."

I don't know if this is helping or not but I can feel her grasp my hand becoming less and all I can do is carry on, hoping that it is helping in some small way.

"It feels warm from where the sun has been shining down on it all day," I continue. "The only sounds you can hear come from the gentle waves as they flow in and out, and the seabirds which soar above it, searching for their supper. The sea smells salty and fresh, like nothing you have ever smelt before. And it is so very peaceful."

She's finally relaxed, my hand squeezing hers now as I carry on stroking her hair, looking into her eyes and wishing she could tell me what happened to her and why. I hear movement behind me and turn to see James standing there watching us both closely. I do not know how long he has been there but there is unfamiliar sadness in his face as he looks at us.

"Well?" I ask, though I'm not sure I can bear to hear the answer.

"Edmund tells me that Annalise was arrested this morning on the same charges as Tom. High treason."

"Why?" I shake my head. "Why on earth would he…" I shake my head in disbelief at his tyrannical behaviour.

"He told me that he had sufficient reason to arrest her. And subsequently she confessed to helping Tom."

Annalise is looking at me as she once again tries to speak. I place a hand to her face, shaking my head, telling her not to.

"Annalise has some injuries to her back," James speaks again, and I look across at him. "Injuries which would indicate a beating of some sort. My guess is that she was made to confess to the crime."

"Oh, Annalise." I grasp her hand tighter. "I'm sorry. I am so sorry this happened to you." The tears are falling down her face now and I cannot bear it. I turn back towards James, shaking my head. "And this was her sentence?" His face is grave and it scares me. Then he shakes his head.

"She was sentenced to death," he replies. "She was due to be executed alongside Tom. But he …" He stops, turning his face to the ground and I already know what he's going to say. Because of course he would. "Tom fought for her," James continues, confirming what I already knew to be true. "He told Edmund that she had nothing to do with it. And that you needed her. So Edmund agreed to let her go."

"Then why?"

"Edmund says he wanted to teach her a lesson," James replies, his voice quiet as if he doesn't want to speak the words. "And…" He stops, unable to look at me.

"Say it, James."

"He told me," he begins, before sighing and shaking his head. "He told me, that he felt that it would act as a reminder to you, that this is what happens when you associate yourself with Thomas Thornton."

I thought Edmund could sink no deeper. I underestimated him. And now Annalise has paid the price.

"Will she ever speak again?" I know from the look on his face that the answer is a no before he even replies.

"The damage is too extensive," he shakes his head. "With rest and care she will get better, but no. She will never speak again."

I can taste the salt of my tears against my lips, my heart breaking for the young girl who has helped me so much. Who was forced into this life unwillingly, who became one of my closest confidants; and spoke with such wisdom beyond her years, now silent for the rest of her days.

"Sophia." As James says my name again, I turn to him and see he is looking at me carefully.

"What is it?"

"Edmund also informed me that the executioner has just arrived."

I choke back a sob as he says it, shaking my head as he walks over to me.

"It will happen tomorrow at noon."

"No." The tears are streaming down my face as he places a gentle hand to my shoulder. "I don't want him to die," I cry. "Please, James, speak with Edmund. Get him to change his mind. He listens to you, you managed to make him change his mind about Papa, please!"

"Sophia." He shakes his head as he crouches beside me. "This is not the same. You know that. Edmund believes that Tom tricked me to make his way in here. For me to now begin fighting his corner would look most suspicious and Edmund is not a fool. It would put my life in danger too. I'm sorry."

I squeeze Annalise's hand as the tears fall from my eyes, needing the comfort of someone's touch. I know he's right.

I know that I cannot ask this of him.

"There's something else."

As I turn to James I see he is once again struggling to meet my eyes.

"What?"

"The last time I spoke with Tom, he asked me to do something for him. Practically begged me."

I'm looking at him. He's hanging his head, his eyes closed as if remembering something painful and I feel my heart constrict with my own pain at the sight of it.

"He doesn't want you there ... when it happens." He swallows, finally looking up and meeting my eyes. "He asked me to find some way of keeping you away from it all."

"Edmund will make me ..." I start, but James interrupts.

"Yes, I know. And I cannot help you, or at least be seen to be helping you. However, if you were not to be found in your chambers tomorrow when they were to come and escort you there, then my feeling is that they would have to proceed without you. They would not postpone it, not when the executioner has travelled so far."

"But I should be there," I whisper. "If I cannot stop it, then at least I should make sure he's not alone." My voice catches on the last word, the tears burning my eyes again. I look at James and see he is shaking his head, the sadness in his face unmistakable.

"If you go, any happy memories you have of him will be tainted. You will be left with nothing but nightmares and he doesn't want that. He wants you to remember him as he was. As you both were before all of this."

"I'll never be happy again, James." It's true. My heart is hollow.

Edmund has broken it over and over, and over again. The happy memories of my past life with Tom are fading, like footprints in the sand washed away by the sea. He was the only thing keeping me steady here. Keeping me from breaking. Without him, I cannot do this anymore. James has stayed quiet, just watching me.

"I know how hard this is," he speaks eventually, his voice gentle. "And I know it feels like you will never be happy again. But he wants you to try. For him, and for your daughter."

I open my mouth to speak but the words won't come. Then James' voice drifts over once more.

"I promise you, Sophia. You are stronger than you realise. He knows that and so do I. And ..." He hesitates, looking at me and I manage to meet his eyes with my cloudy ones. "He won't be alone, at the end," he finally says, his voice soft. "I'll make sure that I am with him."

James lets me stay with Annalise as he carries on his work for the day. I do not leave her side. She flits between painful waking moments of consciousness and sleep, which is helped by the doses of laudanum which James comes back to give her periodically.

Whilst she sleeps, the room is silent aside from the ticking clock in the corner and the overwhelming thoughts in my head. Before he left, James spoke with me of memories of my life before all of this; happy moments which I know that Tom had relayed to him, knowing that his time was growing ever shorter, to try and help me cope. But it has just made everything seem terrifyingly real once more. I couldn't save him.

There is nothing that I can do and his time has now run out. I understand why he doesn't want me there when it happens. The thought of it petrifies me.

But can I really leave him to face his final moments alone? As much as it breaks my heart, I know that I must respect his wishes. And giving him his last request may help him find some peace. Evening has arrived without me even realising it, the room growing dimmer by the minute as my mind continues to taunt me. I light the candle at Annalise's bedside, deciding that I will stay here with her tonight, when there is a light knock at the door and a guard walks in.

"My Lady, I am here to escort you back to your chambers," he begins, but I shake my head dismissively.

"My lady-in-waiting is unwell," I reply, placing my hand to her hair again. "I am staying with her tonight, to give her comfort."

"My Lady, this is not a request." His voice is dark. "King Edmund has commanded that you return to your chambers. He wants you well rested before tomorrow."

I get to my feet and walk over to him, not wanting to disturb Annalise from her much needed sleep. The guard's face shows no flicker of emotion.

"Are you going to force me from this room?" I ask, my voice stronger than what I feel. "Am I under arrest?"

"My Lady." He shakes his head. "I do not want to force you. But if I must then I will."

I swallow, turning to Annalise one more time. I do not wish to bring her any more fear or panic than she is already going through. So, holding my head high, I brush down the skirts of my dress and allow myself to be escorted from the room. The palace is quiet as night time has set in and people have retired to their rooms. I glance around, trying surreptitiously to work out how I can somehow distract my sentry and make my escape.

But he must sense my thoughts as he suddenly takes hold of my arm, tight enough for me to know that he isn't afraid to hurt me if I do anything foolish. Still, I try and shake him off, desperation beginning to claw at my chest as I realise that I am about to be trapped and forced to watch the love of my life perish tomorrow.

"Please," I whisper, trying to appeal to any small sense of conscience he may have in him. "Please do not do this."

He ignores my plea and as we reach the door to my chambers he pushes me inside and I hear the door lock behind me. I reach for the handle in vain, tugging at it but it is no use.

"Sophia."

I jump as I hear my mother's voice from behind me. As I turn, I see her standing in my bedchamber, dressed in her nightdress and housecoat, a piece of half completed needlework in her hand. It is the first time I have seen her since my daughter's birth. After I realised what she had done, I refused all contact with her. I never wanted to see her face again.

"Get out," I hiss at her, my eyes blurred with tears, my voice harsh with how much I hate her for what she has done.

"Don't be silly, Sophia." She shakes her head. "This has gone on long enough. It is time for us to make amends."

"Never! This is all your fault."

"Sophia I only did what was right. That man took advantage of you and you were foolish enough to let him. The King is your husband and he has a right to know, and to dispense justice as he sees fit."

"The King is a monster!" I scream, as I walk towards her, wrenching up the sleeve of my dress to expose my scarred arm. "The King did this when he forced me to marry him. He had a guard hold a burning candle to my arm until I said the words because he knew I would not do it willingly. How can you defend him? How can you defend that?"

She's looking at my arm, her face unreadable and I wonder for a second if this realisation has made her see sense. Then as she shakes her head, I realise how foolish I am for hoping such a thing.

"You had a duty, Sophia," she replies eventually. "You didn't have a choice in the matter. The King had chosen you. If only you had stayed and done your duty then none of this would have happened. You would have been happy. Living here, wanting for nothing. He loves you, Sophia, this was just unfortunate. I do not condone what he did and I wish he hadn't done it. But I understand why."

I look at her in disbelief.

She is supposed to be my mother. I cannot believe that she can stand for something like this.

"Papa knew," I say eventually, wiping the tears from my eyes. "He figured it out. He knew who Tom was and that he made me happy."

"Your father was a fool." Her voice is cold as she says this. "He should have held his tongue. If you want someone to blame for all of this then you should look to him."

"No!"

"He allowed you to carry on this fantasy life you were trying to live. Allowed you to believe in what you thought was right when he should have respected his King. He is fortunate that he was shown mercy."

"How can you be so cruel?" I whisper. She has lost all the kindness in her heart.

"I love your father, Sophia!" she snaps back. "But you cannot act like that towards your sovereign and expect no punishment. At least he is alive. And for that I thanked the King for his mercy."

"He was just protecting me. And now I'll never see him again."

The tears begin to fall from my eyes and this time I don't bother to brush them away. I crave the love and protection of my father from this woman, who is becoming more of a stranger to me by the minute.

"Here." I feel her hand at my shoulder and I flinch away from her. She's standing in front of me, holding out a bottle containing a sleeping draught. "You need to take this and sleep," she says, her voice gentle now. "You will need sleep to prepare yourself for tomorrow."

"No." I shake my head, pushing her hand away.

"Sophia."

"I know what you are doing. I'm just as much of a prisoner now as he is. And I know that I cannot stop this. But I will not be made to watch as they take his head. I will not!"

"You are being ridiculous, Sophia." Her voice is bitter once again. "The sooner you accept his fate and learn to love this new life the better. He was never worthy of you, why can't you see that?"

My hand hits her cheek before I realise what I have done. I've never raised a hand to anyone, least of all my mother. Yet her words lit a flame of anger in me that I couldn't control.

"All you care about is status," I hiss. "You wanted me to marry the King because of the status it would give you. The money. The dances. The dresses. Being able to look down on people like you have all your life. You resented Papa because he wasn't like you. You resented the hard work he put in to give you the life you wanted. Tom is kind and gentle. He's never asked for anything in his life. And everything he has done has been to protect me. We had a farm back home in Lowshore and we were so happy. We were trying for a family of our own, before Edmund kidnapped me and brought me back here to live this hell. I love Tom and have only ever loved him."

I reach for the bottle in her hand and pull the stopper out of it, pouring the contents on the floor before throwing the bottle away, as she looks at me in fury.

"You stupid girl! How long before you stop living in this fantasy world inside your head? That man will die tomorrow and you will be there as is your duty, which you will follow this time. And with him gone, maybe you will finally realise your place here and start acting like a Queen."

I stumble back from her as I watch her walk over to the door and instruct the guard outside to fetch Doctor Collins immediately. As she returns, she refuses to look at me, walking back over to her chair and beginning her needlework once more. The minutes tick by, the silence deafening as we wait for James' arrival. I hear the door open and he appears. My mother looks relieved as she gets to her feet again.

"Doctor Collins." She smiles. "I am sorry to call on you so late. I'm afraid there is a problem. Sophia refuses to take the draught you gave me, in fact she discarded it, so I am in need of a new one. And I also feel that you can perhaps explain to her why this is for the best."

I'm sitting on my bed as James walks over to me and I look at him defiantly.

It was him who suggested the idea of not being found in my room tomorrow morning. And I know that he must keep up this pretence for his own safety. But I do not understand why he is here, providing my mother with the one thing that will stop me from escaping.

"My Lady, your mother is right." James' voice is stern as he comes to stand beside me. "The King expects you to be at the execution tomorrow. And you will need sleep to help you face it."

"No!" I cry out, shaking my head. "I will not watch him die, please don't do this to me, please."

"I will prepare another draught, now," he says, ignoring my statement and directing his words towards my mother. "It will take me a few minutes. Hopefully this will allow Lady Sophia the opportunity to calm herself a little. Think things through."

I don't understand what is happening. I've trusted James since the moment I met him. I want to trust him now but my mind is so full of hurt and confusion that I do not know who

I can trust anymore. I listen as my mother converses naturally with him as he works, acting like the caring mother I know she isn't, and eventually James turns back towards me, a bottle in his hand.

"Please James," I whisper, my heart aching. "I know he deceived you, I know how angry you must feel but please, please don't do this to me. I cannot watch ... I cannot."

"My Lady, you have no choice. Edmund has commanded it. He is not just your husband but your King. You must do as he says. I do not want to force you to drink this but if I have to then I will. Please."

He's looking at me carefully as he holds the bottle out to me again. In his gaze I see the man I know and trust and though I am scared, I hold out a shaking hand, choking back a sob as I take it from him. He's still watching me closely, urging me on with his eyes and eventually I take a deep breath and drink the contents. It doesn't taste like a sleeping draught. It doesn't taste of anything. My face begins to crease in confusion, as he places an arm around my neck and guides me gently down onto the pillows.

"Sleep, my Lady," he says, gently, giving me a knowing look. "That's it."

Realising what he has done, I let my eyes flicker shut as I feel him place the blanket over me.

"You are a true voice of reason, Doctor." I hear my mother say thankfully, as I feel him move away from me.

"Sometimes a gentle approach is what is needed, Mrs Reynolds," James replies courteously. "Though her affections towards that man may be misplaced, we mustn't ignore them. Instead we must help her realise the truth, no matter how long that takes. After tomorrow, I hope it will become easier but it will be a long road I fear."

I listen for the click of the door opening and then being locked by the guard who stands outside. My eyes are still shut tight as I feel my mother come and perch on the side of my bed, her hand brushing through my hair.

"This is all for the best, my darling. That man corrupted you and corrupted your father. Tomorrow will see him punished for what he has done to our family. We can all then begin again. Rebuilding the bridges he has broken."

It's taking all of my strength to keep my eyes closed, until I feel her weight leave my side as she blows out the candle.

Then I begin the long and lonely wait until I can make my escape.

TOM

I hear the jangle of keys as my cell door opens but I do not turn around. I stay sitting on the floor, facing the wall, where I haven't moved from since the moment they dragged Annalise from here yesterday, forever silenced because of me.

"Someone's quiet for once. Did they cut your tongue out too?" as the guard retorts, I huddle myself further into the corner, ignoring him, waiting for him to leave me alone.

"Funny how the thought of getting yer 'ed chopped off is enough to make someone quieten down for a change." He snorts, as he lays a tray of food at my feet. "You'd better make the most of this, it's the last meal you'll ever eat in this world."

As he walks off and I hear the door slam shut, I look down at the watery plate of food before pushing it away, the thought of eating anything sickening to me. The remaining hours of my life seem to pass by slowly.

With sleep unforthcoming and without the presence of natural light to signal night or day, I have only had the ominous tolling of the clock tower bell to advise me on the countdown to my fate.

It is as the ten o'clock bell rings, that I once again hear movement at my cell door. Knowing I am not to be executed until noon, I wonder what fresh hell they could be intent on putting me through before they take my head. I don't turn to face whoever it is that has entered the room.

"Thomas? My name is Father Daniel. I am here to listen to any confession you may wish to give before your sentence is carried out. We can also pray, if you wish."

If I had the energy I would laugh. After everything that has happened, for a priest to be visiting me, hours before my death to offer me comfort, seems like a sick joke.

"I'm sorry, Father but you are wasting your time," I say, quietly. "I don't believe in God, yours or any other."

He walks over and sits down on the bunk. I don't look at him. I'm hoping that if I just ignore him he will take the hint and leave me alone.

"I'm not sure that is strictly true of someone who married in a church." His voice is gentle and sympathetic though not full of pity. The fact that he has mentioned my marriage to Sophia, has lit a flame of anger in me that I am struggling to keep control of.

As I finally turn to him, I see that he is a kindly-looking man with greying hair and blue eyes like mine. He is dressed in simple robes, reminding me more of the village priest who conducted mine and Sophia's marriage than those who flaunt themselves around court, dressed in their finery, dripping in jewels.

Yet in a way it makes me even angrier that it is someone like him here, rather than one of those people. It feels wrong.

"My marriage never existed," I say, my voice bitter. "The King made sure of that. With some help from people like you."

He at least has the decency to look rueful at this.

"Records can be hidden," he replies, eventually, as I turn to the wall once more. "They cannot be destroyed. The King has the right to instruct the Church to carry out his wishes. The Church, however, takes its instruction from God alone."

"What does it matter though?" I move towards him, roughly brushing frustrated tears from my face. "None of it matters, anymore. I did believe, yes. It took me a long time to understand the path God had set for me, then after I found Sophia everything started making sense. But now…" I shake my head as I drop to the floor at his feet, my body too tired to carry on standing. "I don't see how any God could let something like this happen. I don't mean to me. I probably deserve this. Some of the things I have done. But Sophia doesn't deserve any of this. We never asked anything of anyone."

Father Daniel stays quiet, just listening to me, and I am glad of it. My thoughts are flowing from me like floodwater right now and I fear that if I am interrupted then the barriers will come up and I will shut down, taking all of this pain with me to my grave.

"I've done things I'm not proud of. But I did them in order to survive so I will not apologise for them. I stole to eat so that I wouldn't starve. I fought to win a bed for the night so that I wouldn't freeze to death on the streets. I came here and tricked my way into this place to try to rescue my wife, then deceived everyone to stay with her when I couldn't." My thoughts flash to Annalise, the guilt trickling into my mind.

"I have no family," I continue, forcing her from my mind. "My mother died bringing me into this world. My father sold me to the workhouse to pay off his gambling debts. I learned a trade, but nobody would ever let me work for them once they found out my background. Like father, like son they would say. I've always been alone. Until Sophia. She was my family and I've made my peace with her, so you are free of your duty to me, Father. You would be better placed comforting someone who actually believes."

He carries on watching me and I stay quiet, hoping that he will eventually get up and leave me alone.

"Are you sure you have made your peace with everyone?" he asks, gently, "What about young Annalise?"

As he says her name I look at him, feeling my chin start to wobble as I desperately try and hold back the emotion and guilt that wants to explode from me. I shake my head.

"Please," I stutter eventually, "please don't make me talk about her. I can't."

"What happened wasn't your fault, Thomas."

"Wasn't it?" I cry, the pain exploding from me. "I should never have trusted him! I was a fool to be taken in like that. She suffered so much pain because of me."

"You saved her life."

"Did I?" I shake my head, my vision blinded by my tears. "An axe to the neck would have been kinder. Quicker. All I have done is made her as much of a prisoner as Sophia is and caused her all that pain."

I break down in choking sobs, pulling my knees into my chest. I just want this to be over now.

The idea of death suddenly feels like a relief to me as I feel Father Daniel place his hand gently upon my head.

The gesture is somewhat soothing and eventually, as my tears subside, I look up at him.

"Will you pray with me, Father?"

He nods, clasping his hands over mine and I close my eyes as he begins to speak. I listen to his words, letting them wash over the pain and guilt I feel in my heart, soothing my soul, bringing me peace, closure and acceptance. As he finishes, the tears in my eyes have dried; my mind feels calm and at rest, for the first time in so very long.

I raise my head to look at him and I am grateful that he is the one who was chosen to help me unburden my soul. I know there is no judgement there. After so long being hurt and cheated and broken down, my trust is barely existent. But I trust him.

"I'm ready."

Speaking with Father Daniel seems to have stilled something in me. Though the fear of what awaits me still lingers in my heart, I feel ready to accept my fate. So when the door to my cell opens once more and the guard instructs me to get to my feet, I do it without question and only the mildest flicker of fear.

The heavy cuffs are placed around my wrists and I am led from the cell, flanked by guards as we walk corridor after corridor until we reach the gated entrance which leads to the courtyard. As the gates open, I am hit with sunlight for the first time in as long as I can remember. I blink, adjusting my vision as it warms my skin, taking me back to the time when I used to feel its warmth upon me every day as I worked.

As my eyes adjust to the brightness, I can see that the courtyard is full of people. People, I realise quickly, who are all here for the show. As I am led towards them, they begin to part, leaving a dusty pathway which I am walked down towards the wooden platform in the distance where an executioner stands dressed in black, axe in hand.

The murmurings of the crowd get louder as I walk closer to my fate and I feel myself getting spat at, smell the putrid rotten fruit as it is thrown at me. I take myself away from this place, trying to blank it from my mind as I walk on. Just as I am about to reach the steps to the platform, my attention is caught by someone in the crowd. I know it is just my mind playing tricks on me but for one brief moment; as I meet the eyes of the stranger in the tattered grey cloak, it is as if I am looking at her.

The sight of it, the feeling it stirs within me, makes me lose my concentration and I miss my footing on the steps, sending myself crashing down against the platform as the jeers of the crowd ring in my ears. I try and fail to get to my feet, the chains at my wrists and the pain in my arm making it impossible.

Eventually, I am wrenched up from the ground, desperately trying to disguise the gasp of pain which escapes my lips, not wanting to give the crowd of people any further pleasure at my discomfort.

I see the block in the middle of the platform, the masked executioner standing silently beside it. I see James standing solemnly beside a courtier who holds a scroll of paper in his hand. He doesn't look at me yet seeing him there brings me a small sense of calm.

Sophia is nowhere to be seen. He kept his promise. The courtier with the scroll comes to stand beside me. Breaking the wax seal upon it, he un-scrolls it and begins to read.

"Thomas Oliver Thornton. You have been found guilty of treason and have been sentenced to death. Do you have any last words before your sentence is carried out?"

As I look out at the crowd of spectators which seem to go back for miles, I think back to the happiest day of my life, closing my eyes, wishing I was miles away from here, back home with the woman I love in our little house with our simple, happy life.

"I wouldn't change a thing that I have done," I say, my voice strong as I try and make it rise above the jeers of the crowd.

"My only regret is that I couldn't save her. And I just hope she knows how sorry I am that I failed her. And that I will always love her in this world and the next."

Suddenly, I'm pushed to my knees and I find myself facing the front row of the baying crowd. Something in a woman's arms catches my eye and I see that it is a bloodstained basket. She catches my eye and grins toothlessly at me.

I swallow down the bile in my throat as I realise she's waiting to add my head to the countless number she must have caught in that basket before. Swallowing hard, I place my neck against the block, still wet and sticky from the blood of the last poor soul who must have lost their head here.

I give an involuntary shudder as I feel the cold sharp edge of the blade touch lightly against my neck, marking the spot where my head will soon leave my body. It's funny what they say about your life flashing before your eyes in the moments before your death.

Because it's true. In those moments I see all the times I felt the cruelty of my father, the sting of his belt against my skin as he took out his drunken frustration on me.

I see the cruelty of the workhouse and all of the years I was forced to live there, working like a slave to keep the roof over my head until they threw me out of the door at fifteen, to fend for myself. I see her on our wedding day. I see us dancing in the cornfields at sunset, our first as a married couple.

Then the whooshing sound of the axe being lifted brings me back into the present and I brace myself for death, knowing that at least it will be over quickly with hopefully not too much pain.

"STOP!"

Her voice rings out above the chatter of the crowd and I wonder for a moment if I am dreaming, until I feel her weight on top of me, shielding my body with her own from the axeman above us both. I feel people trying to drag her away and from their panicked conversation I realise that they haven't figured out who the mad woman is who has just flung herself over a condemned man, to protect him from the axe.

She shakes them off, wrenching the hood from her head. At the sight of her they step back, their heads bowed as they realise who it is.

"Lady Sophia …"

"Get the King here, immediately."

Her voice is strong as she interrupts the courtier who spoke her name. I glance up at him and see that he is still in two minds about what to do. The executioner stands beside him, his axe glinting in the sunlight. His eyes catch mine through his black hooded mask and I force myself to close my eyes.

"Now!" She screams it at the courtier and I hear his footsteps as he rushes from the platform.

"Sophia…" I manage to speak her name but I don't know what it is I want to say. I feel her press her lips to my hair.

"I won't let him do this," she whispers it, but she is so close to me that I can hear it even amongst the growing chatter of the impatient crowd.

"You cannot stop him," I reply, strongly. "He's too dangerous. What were you thinking? You could have been killed."

"I'd rather die here with you then live in a world without you in it."

"Don't you dare." My voice is harsh through frustration. "I told you Sophia. You have a beautiful baby girl up there who needs her mother. You cannot abandon her for me. It's over for me. Just … let me go."

I feel her body start to shake as she erupts into heart wrenching sobs, her face buried into the back of my head and I curse the fact that there is nothing I can do to even comfort her. All I can do is wait, hands bound, for the inevitable moment that they come and wrench her from me and make her watch as my head is taken from my shoulders.

SOPHIA

Footsteps alert me to people returning to the platform, and with a shaky breath I look up in defiance expecting to see Edmund standing there. So I am surprised when it is James that I see.

"Where is he?" I say strongly to James. "I want him here now."

"The King will not come here, my Lady," he says gently.

"You know it is considered bad luck for him to attend the place of executions."

The panic starts to rise in my chest as I feel his time running out. "I won't leave him," I state fiercely, though the tears sting my eyes. "So he can either come here or …"

James reaches into his jacket and retrieves a letter.

It is adorned with Edmund's wax stamp seal and I recognise his handwriting upon it, though from this distance I cannot make out the words.

"The King wishes you to attend him in his study," James begins, as I shake my head and open my mouth to protest but he stops me. "This is a letter from him stating no harm will come to the prisoner in the immediate future. You need to come with me now, my Lady."

"No."

"Sophia." Tom's voice cuts through the noise of the crowd, the ringing in my ears, the thumping in my head. For a moment I feel like it is just me and him.

"Go with James," he says, softly. "I know you can trust him."

I shake my head. "I won't leave you. I don't trust them, Tom. I won't leave you here."

He's smiling at me. That little half smile he always does just for me. He looks over at James, at the letter in his hands and gestures towards it with his head.

"That letter has a crest and everything, so it must be official."

James hands the letter over to the executioner who looks at it with disdain. "As you can see, King Edmund has officially given a brief stay of execution to this prisoner." James says, calmly, not looking at me or Tom. "You have orders to take him back to his cell and await further instruction."

"I'll be fine," he says gently, as I squeeze his hands. "Go with James."

I look at him as he encourages me with his eyes to do as he says. I turn my gaze towards the men standing to the side, taking it in turn to read the words upon the letter.

"Take him back first," I assert, with conviction. "I want to see him leave this platform unharmed before I go anywhere." The men just stare at me with mocking eyes which riles me.

"I am your Queen and you will do as I say. Take him now." My voice is strong, I don't back down. I stare at them until eventually two of them walk forward towards Tom.

I stumble to my feet as they wrench him up from the ground and as he gasps in pain I remember his arm is still injured. He composes himself quickly, taking shaky breaths to get through the pain as he looks at me. All I want is to take him in my arms and kiss him until I can no longer breathe, but I know that it would only put both of us in even more danger. I place a hand to his cheek as I look into his eyes. "I won't let them kill you," I whisper. "I'll find a way."

He looks at me and I know he's given up hope but still he smiles.

As the men grab his shoulders again; ready to cart him off to his cell, he places the lightest of kisses against the palm of my hand resting on his cheek before they pull him backwards and away from me. I watch until I can no longer see him, the jeers of the crowd getting louder as they realise they've been cheated out of their afternoon entertainment.

And suddenly, my legs can no longer carry me and I stumble to the floor. James is at my side in an instant, guiding me to my feet, keeping an arm around my waist to keep me upright - as he walks me in the opposite direction, to Edmund's study where I will have minutes to save the life of the man I truly love.

We reach the door to Edmund's study and I can barely stop the shake of my legs. I look to James wishing he could give me some reassurance, but I know he can't. It's too dangerous for him to show allegiance and I wouldn't want to see him hurt because of me.

He knocks at the door and we are beckoned in by Edmund. I see him sitting at his desk, reading through a book with disinterest. He doesn't look up as we enter. It feels like hours have passed before he finally utters some words.

"You may leave us, James, thank you."

With a quick glance towards me, in which I see the regret in his eyes, he extends a bow to Edmund before turning and leaving, the door shutting heavily behind him.

I don't move. I don't speak. I wait for him to make the first move which he eventually does, closing the book slowly before looking up at me, his eyes taking me in with disdain.

"Take that cloak off," he orders, gesturing to the battered old cloak I found in the scullery to disguise myself in. "You look like one of the beggars on the street, it's embarrassing."

Unhooking the fastening at my neck I do as he says, letting it fall to the ground, revealing the navy-blue dress he would see as more befitting of a Queen. His eyes continue to take me in, silently, as he gets up from his desk and walks over to me. I instinctively want to move back but I don't, forcing myself to look at him as he comes to stand in front of me.

"That was a foolish thing to do, Sophia."

"And you were a fool to bring me here in the first place!" I surprise myself with the strength in my voice.

He scoffs, his eyes wide with shock. "Excuse me?"

I swallow down my fear knowing that I have one chance to save Tom and time is running out. "You must know that I never have and never will love you."

"This is a funny way of trying to save the life of your beloved," he says, his cheek twitching with barely held composure. "Beheading him is a kindness. I can think of much more painful and drawn out ways to get rid of him."

"Edmund. Let me speak."

His eyes widen as he raises an eyebrow. Nobody ever speaks back to him or interrupts him. Least of all me.

"Well my little songbird." He grins, as he eventually replies. "It seems you have finally found your voice. Please, enlighten me."

I close my eyes. I know that by doing this I am closing the book on any dream I ever had of finding a way out of this hell that I am living in. But I have no choice.

"I will not lie to you," I say, as I open my eyes and look at him. "When you brought me here you told me that you would wait as long as it takes for me to love you. But I will never love you. After everything you have done to me. To him. To Annalise. And deep down, I think we both know that you have never loved me either. You just want me."

His face is expressionless. Proving the words I have just spoken to be true. "Why him?" he says, shaking his head. "What is so special about him?" The disdain in his voice sparks an anger in me and I know I will never get another chance to tell him exactly how I feel.

"He is everything you are not," I reply, and he scoffs again as if this is a bad thing. "He's kind and gentle. He puts others before himself. And he loves me. He loves me for who I really am."

"Hasn't done him much good, has it?" He smirks and I feel my composure falter for the first time.

"I have a proposition."

He laughs, shaking his head in wonder as he walks closer to me and I resist the urge to pull back.

"A proposition? My my, you are full of surprises today, aren't you my darling?"

"If you let him go …" I continue and I hear the break in my voice. "If you set him free and let him go back home, then I promise you I will be whatever you want me to be. I will be your possession. I will give you whatever you want, tell you whatever you want to hear. Surrender myself to you and never try to leave you. I will be yours until the end of my life. I swear it. As long as you let him go safe from here."

I feel the stray tear fall down my cheek and brush it away roughly. He's looking at me and I cannot work out what he is thinking. I've never been able to. But this is all I've got. And if it's not enough then I won't be able to go on. I force myself to look him in the eye and await his response. He carries on studying me, taking in my body with his eyes. Until finally he speaks.

"Prove it to me, Sophia." He reaches a hand towards me and I take it. Pulling me towards him he cups my breast through my dress and I try not to flinch. He's staring at me. His other hand lifts my chin so that my eyes find his.

They are dark. Cold. And there's something behind them that has always scared me.

He's waiting, I realise. Waiting for me to make the first move. I place my hand behind his head and pull him closer to me until my lips connect with his. I feel him forcing my lips open with his tongue and I am helpless to do anything but let him.

Then some primal instinct seems to hit him and he's got my hair in his hands and is dragging me to the floor. His hands rip at my bodice, exposing my breasts, before finding their way roughly under my skirts. Then he's on top of me, crushing against me with his weight so I can barely breathe.

He forces himself on me again and again, his breathing heavier with each movement, the pain soaring through my body, but I cannot scream out. I cannot let him know how much I hate him with my entire being for what he has made of my life.

"Are you mine, Sophia?" he asks breathlessly and I hate myself more and more with every minute that passes. I can barely make myself answer him but I know I must.

"Yes."

"Say it." He's looking at me, his cold dark eyes alive with a manic fire as he sweeps the damp hair from his forehead. I force myself to think of Tom dying and the idea that doing this could set him free.

"I'm yours."

Grinning, he forces himself down on me one last time, his face contorted in pleasure as he finally finishes, rolling himself off me and lying next to me on the ground, twisting a strand of my hair around his finger.

"I accept your terms," he says breathlessly, and I can hear the glee in his voice, making me feel sick. He pushes himself up onto his hands and looks down at me, his face a picture of pure joy. "Let us go and tell him the happy news."

He gets to his feet and holds out a hand to pull me up from the floor, as I feel the last part of who I really am leave my body.

If sacrificing myself means that he can live then I have no other choice. I cannot live in a world without him in it, even if it means I will never see him again.

TOM

I pace the floor of my cell, my body shaking. Partly because the fear of almost losing my head is still coursing through my veins. And partly because of how close Sophia came to being killed, risking her life to save mine. I don't want to die. But without me here he has nothing to hold against her. And maybe one day, she can find the strength to escape his clutches knowing that I'm not there for him to play his games with.

I'm still thinking of this when the door to my cell opens and two guards walk in. Without speaking, they walk over to me, grabbing my arms and pulling me forwards. I struggle but they hold firm.

I'm confused for a few moments and wonder if they are about to take me to meet my death again, until I see Edmund walk into the small space of my prison cell, followed by Sophia who I can tell from her face has been crying.

"Sophia…" I try to shake off the guards and make towards her, but Edmund stands in front of her, blocking my path.

"I'd thank you not to go near my wife," he says, his voice dripping with barely contained joy. "And you should always address Lady Sophia by her correct title, for future reference."

I scoff, shaking my head and his gaze turns sour. "Something funny? In your situation I would advise against laughing."

"In my situation, it's all I've got left."

He walks up to me, his eyes taking me in, working me out. He starts at my bare feet, filthy from pacing this dirty, stone floor. My clothes, which are just as dirty and have seen better days. My fists clench in their cuffs and I see that he notices.

"My wife tells me you are a good man. I struggle to see how she can tell me this, but she insists it's true. I just see a wastrel who wants more than he could possibly dream of having."

He's trying to rile me. I know that. Still, I can feel the muscle twitching in my jaw as I try to contain my anger. He grins. I don't think I'm the only one who wishes to have something he cannot.

"She would like me to pardon you. She was most persuasive, in fact."

I look over at Sophia and see she can't meet my eye. As I take in her appearance properly, I finally notice the ripped bodice of her dress, her grazed legs through her torn stockings and I understand what he means.

"No." I shake my head. "Sophia why? Why would you do that for me?"

I watch as she walks up to me, the tears in her eyes breaking my heart.

"Sophia."

"Shhh…" She places a gentle finger to my lips stopping my words, before replacing her finger with the touch of her kiss. As she breaks away she pulls me in close, her forehead touching mine, her hands at the back of my head stroking through my hair.

"You didn't need to do that," I whisper, my voice breaking. "I'm not worth it."

"Don't say that," she replies, her eyes bearing into mine. "You have never believed in your worth. You have done so much for me. You do not deserve to die here because of me." "This isn't your fault."

"You came here because of me. You stayed because I asked you to."

"Sophia, I came here to bring you home because I cannot live without you. He's held me against you for so long. Without me, you have a chance to somehow break free one day. So, please. Just let him do what he wants with me. Don't put yourself through this to save me."

"Tom." I can tell by the tone of her voice that her decision is made. "He will never let me go." Her voice is strong though her eyes are clouded with tears. "And the only strength I have is knowing that you are alive and carrying that piece of my heart with you, which will always be yours. Keeping that spirit of us alive."

The tears are falling down my cheeks now as I shake my head, trying one more time to make her see sense. "Sophia, please …"

"Enough." Edmund's voice breaks the air and I feel Sophia's kiss against my lips one more time before he drags her away. My eyes are still locked with hers as Edmund walks up to me, smirking. "The prisoner is free to go."

As the cuffs are removed from my wrists, I open my mouth to speak but the guards usher me towards the door.

"Wait!" Edmund's voice sounds again just as I reach the threshold and I am dragged back as he walks over to me. He's smirking at me and I force myself to meet his gaze.

"I've changed my mind," he says with a shrug. "The prisoner will be detained for trial."

"No!" Sophia screams, rushing over to him and grabbing hold of his arm. "No, Edmund, you promised me!"

"I did." He nods. "But promises can be broken." He's still staring at me, ignoring Sophia as she grabs at his arm, pleading with him, trying to hold him back. "Your conversation just then made me realise something." He grins, turning to her. "You are right, my darling. I will never let you go. So why should I agree to a deal that I will never lose anyway?"

"No! Please, Edmund, please." She is screaming at him, pulling at his arm, trying to make him focus on her. But his vicious gaze is on me. I can see the annoyance in his eyes and I am about to try to calm Sophia down, when he turns and thunders his hand across her cheek.

"Enough, woman!"

"Hey!" My punch floors him, taking him by surprise. I want to carry on but I am held back by the guards. Sophia is on the floor, her hand at her cheek as she sobs. Edmund is laughing as he stumbles to his feet, his eyes wild as he walks over to me.

"You should die for striking your King," he hisses. "But there was something that you said that actually made sense." He looks over at Sophia who shakes her head.

"Edmund, please."

"With you gone, who else do I have to hold against her?" He shrugs. "Better to keep you alive and under lock and key. Why put you out of your misery so quickly?" He nods to the guards who wrench me backwards, cuffing my wrists once more and securing them to the wall from where I can only watch, helpless, as Edmund drags Sophia from the room, her pleas echoing across the cold stone cell.

Hours pass before the door to my cell opens once more and this time James is standing there with a guard.

"Leave us." He addresses the guard, his tone dark and unusual to my ears. "I shall alert you when I am finished with the prisoner."

As the guard nods, slamming the door shut as he leaves I swallow down my nerves as James walks towards me, his face unreadable.

I wince as I try and manoeuvre my wrists from where they are chained to the wall above me, but it's useless. James still says nothing as he takes a seat on the bunk beside me. He's waiting, I realise after a beat, waiting for the sound of footsteps to disappear, waiting for the guard to do as he had commanded. As the sound drifts off and is replaced with silence he turns to me.

"I'm sorry I cannot make you more comfortable." His voice is low and full of regret. I shrug.

"It's not so bad. I've been in worse positions. At least my feet are on the ground this time."

He shakes his head at this, but I see the small smile on his lips as he opens his bag and begins rifling through the bottles.

"Has he decided what to do with me yet?" My voice is light but I can feel my heart thumping with the panic I'm trying to contain. James looks across at me thoughtfully.

"I have it on good authority that the King has signed documents handing you over to the custody of the Lowshore County Gaol. You are to be tried and sentenced there." I catch his eye but he shakes his head. "He's got the ways and means to take your head here. I do not think death is your sentence. I believe he wants to make an example of you. And send you as far away from Sophia as possible."

I laugh. "Of course he does. With me still alive he's always got something to hold against her. He's not as stupid as he looks."

James sighs, looking down at the ground. "I'm sorry it came to this," he says, sadly. "I wish there was more I could have done."

"You told me not to come. You warned me against it. Maybe you were right. Because I couldn't just come here and keep my head down. I kept pushing it and pushing it and in the end I pushed it too far. And now it's not just me who will suffer. Sophia will live with the constant threat of what he could do to me, hanging over her, allowing him to force her to do whatever he wishes. And then there's Annalise…" I daren't look at James as I say her name for fear of what it might tell me. It's something that I need to know but do not know if I want to.

"She's alive, Tom." I hear him say, softly, and I take a shaky breath, "she's in pain but she will heal. I'm taking care of her."

"I never meant …" I close my eyes, trying to rid my mind of her screams which still linger there now. James places a hand to my arm.

"I know. She knows. You must stop torturing yourself. For your own sake."

I know I will never be able to. But I nod my head, hoping to ease his own guilt even if mine will never leave me. Eventually, when the silence becomes too deafening I look up at him again and smile. "I am glad to have met you, James. And I will be forever grateful to you. For taking care of her."

As he gets to his feet he places a hand to my arm. "I will try and see you again," he says, quietly. "In Lowshore, before your trial. It is protocol for a physician to declare a prisoner fit to stand trial and I very much doubt Edmund will want a town doctor to make that decision."

"Then I shall look forward to seeing you again, my friend."

"Just try to stay out of trouble, until then?" He raises an eyebrow at me and I cannot help but laugh.

"You know I never get myself into any trouble, James."

With a shake of his head he walks over to the door and hammers on it three times to signal he is ready to leave. When the guard eventually arrives and the heavy door opens, James gives me a small smile before the warmth suddenly disappears from his face.

"I was a fool to trust you. You took advantage of my good nature and used it to trick your way in here. You should be grateful for the King's generosity in sparing you your life." He turns to the guard. "The prisoner is fine. He should be fit to be transported to Lowshore tomorrow."

The guard nods, smirking at me as James leaves my cell without a backwards glance. As the heavy door closes once more and the lamps extinguish, I sit staring into the darkness until at some point, eventually, I am pulled into sleep.

Sophia

Autumn hit the city with a flurry of colder air. From my bedroom window I can see the leaves falling from the trees in the courtyard, scattering the ground below with gemstone paths of russet and gold. I hear a knock at the door, but don't turn around. I finger the sleeves of my black dress, pulling them down to cover my wrists, the bodice so tight that I can barely breathe. My visitor has entered the room but does not speak. I stand, still staring at the falling leaves from my window, as I ask my question.

"Did you attend the trial?" My right hand grasps involuntarily at my left ring finger as I wait for the answer. The gold, ruby-studded band has never felt heavier or more like chains as it has these last few days.

"Yes," James's voice pierces the silence. "Five years hard labour. Banished from the Capital indefinitely."

I'm thankful to have the windowsill to grasp onto, else I fear I may faint. James appears at my side, his face not betraying anything of what he is thinking.

"I've heard about these labour camps," I whisper, not wanting to think about it, but unable to stop my brain from whirring. "People say they are like hell on earth." As I turn to him, I cannot stop the tears from filling my eyes. "Most people don't last a year."

He studies me carefully before smiling softly. "Most people, aren't Tom Thornton."

I look at him and try to return the smile but fail miserably. I know Tom is strong. But I know that Edmund will make sure that his time in an already hellish place is made a hundred times worse. And even the strongest people have breaking points.

"Did you manage to see him?" I ask eventually, as I find my voice once more.

He nods. "Not for long. I told them I needed to check on him, to make sure he was fit to stand trial."

I look at him meaningfully and he nods.

"I gave it to him."

"How is…?" I begin, before realising what a stupid question it is.

"He's as well as can be expected," he answers. "As usual, he is trying to make everything seem better by making a joke of it all. At least he hasn't lost his sense of humour."

I try to smile but once again I cannot muster one. A cry from the corner of the room catches James's attention, but I turn away.

"How is she doing?"

"She's fine."

He wanders over to her and looks into her cot, smiling. "She's beautiful, Sophia," he says softly. "Though I think she's trying to tell you something."

Her cries get louder and I close my eyes, trying to block it out.

"I'll call for her nursemaid," I reply, turning towards the door.

"Sophia..." I stop, as he calls my name. As I turn back towards him, I see he has her in his arms. "She doesn't need her nursemaid. She needs her mother."

I'm looking at him, biting my lip to stop the tears from falling as I collapse down into the nearest chair. He walks over to me. She's still screaming in his arms, not settling at all.

"I can't," I whisper. "I promised him I would try for her sake, but I can't. Because every time I look at her I remember what Edmund did to me, to Tom, to Annalise and I can't bear it."

He doesn't reply. Instead he walks towards me and places her gently in my arms. She instantly starts to settle, her cries slowing to snuffles before she finally closes her eyes and lies softly against my breast, her tiny lips open slightly as she takes gentle breaths.

"I named her Olivia," I tell him. "I thought if I gave her some connection to Tom it would help me."

"None of this is her fault, Sophia," he says gently, as he takes a seat beside me. "Just as none of it is yours. You must stop blaming yourself and taking it out on her. Tom was right. She needs you to carry on. She needs you to be her mother."

I look down at her. Wisps of auburn hair cover her tiny head. Her pale skin is flushed from the exertion of crying, the tracks of tears still visible on her cheeks. I see her button nose crinkle as she settles into sleep, and find myself not knowing whether to laugh or cry as I remember how Tom used to tease me about how my nose would do the same.

I've been too afraid to look at her properly since her birth. Partly because I was scared I would see Edmund staring back at me, which I am relieved to see is not the case. But partly because I desperately wanted to see some of Tom, even though I knew that was never going to be. I'd always imagined what our children might look like. A perfect mix of the two of us. My red hair and my nose. His bright blue eyes and cheeky grin.

Would they be serious like me or full of mischief like him? There can never be any of this wonder with Olivia. I just have to hope that she has as little of Edmund in her as possible. She is fast asleep now and as I watch her tiny chest rise and fall with gentle breaths, I feel that maternal feeling of protection for the first time since her birth.

"You see?" James says, with a smile. "She just needed her mother."

I manage a watery smile as I look at him. "When do you leave?" I ask, remembering Edmund's words to him about no longer needing his services following the birth. I cannot bear it. He is taking every one of my strengths from me one by one.

"I have asked Edmund if I can stay on as Court Physician," James replies, with a smile. "I told him that I am too old now to be travelling around the country. I want to settle down and I feel that I can do some good here."

"And he agreed?" As he nods, I let out a shaky breath of relief as I hold my hand out to him and he takes it. "I am so relieved," I say, honestly. "The idea of trying to carry on without you to help and guide me frightened me more than I can say."

He squeezes my hand as he looks down at Olivia once more. "You are stronger than you realise, Sophia. You brought this beautiful baby into the world when you thought you couldn't. You risked your life to save Tom's. You have suffered so much yet you are still here fighting. Never forget that."

Hearing him speak like this, right now, it feels like he is talking about a stranger. I don't recognise the woman he is speaking of. But I promised Tom that I would try to be brave, and strong. That I would carry on fighting for my little girl. James squeezes my hand once more, bringing me into the present.

"I shall leave you to get settled," he says, gently. "And I shall ask that you are not to be disturbed."

As I thank him once more and he leaves the room, I get to my feet as Olivia shifts in her sleep. I rock her gently as I walk back over to the window and watch the leaves falling from the trees once more.

"In another world ... another life," I whisper, softly. "These trees would be tall and evergreen. And Papa would go out and work hard amongst them every day, whilst we looked after the animals at the farm. And you would have Amos to look after you, just as he looked after me. And on an evening, we would all go down to the secret beach and you would feel the sand upon your feet before the saltwater washed it away. And life would be so simple and happy."

She begins to wake, unsettled once more and instinct tells me that she is hungry. I know I should call for her wetnurse. Edmund says it is wrong for a woman of my standing to feed a child by my own breast. But she is *my* child. I sit down and begin unfastening the lace of my dress. I have never done this before, yet somehow, I know what I am supposed to do. I guide her gently towards my breast and as she latches on and begins to feed, I feel the tears start to well up in my eyes as I realise that she is my saving grace. My reason for carrying on. Just like he said.

"I'm sorry I haven't been there for you," I whisper, tears dripping from my cheeks and landing upon her tiny head. "I blamed you for something that wasn't your fault and that was wrong. And I promise you, Olivia. I am going to love you and guide you and protect you just like a mother should. Because this world can be scary and cruel sometimes and I never want you to be afraid. I never want you to feel that cruelty. I will fill your life with as much happiness and magic and wonder as I can. And I will protect you until my dying day."

I wipe the wetness of my tears from her head before placing a gentle kiss against her soft, downy hair. The room is quiet and still. And for the first time in so very long, I feel safe.

TOM

As the prison cart rolls up to the camp I look through the slatted bars at my new surroundings. My home for the next five years.

The black metal gates open with a creak as I am driven through them towards a fenced-off courtyard in the distance, where I see a group of men dressed in the same uniform as the one they made me change into before transporting me here.

A long grey stone building sits beyond that with further cold, uninviting buildings in the distance. For someone like me, someone who has spent the majority of their adult life sleeping out under the stars, having the freedom to go wherever I wish, the heavy metal gates and locked buildings send my heart plummeting, bringing back memories of my time in the workhouse as a child. The cart pulls to a stop and a guard unlocks the door sending a whoosh of cold air into my face. "Out."

The thin jacket I'm wearing does little to protect me from the chill of the wind, the drizzle which is falling from the sky soaking through it within minutes. The guard walks off, seemingly leaving me to the mercy of the wolves. A baptism by fire. Within moments, I am surrounded by a group of fellow prisoners, circling me like vultures around their prey.

"Well aren't we honoured?" A man's voice pipes up. "Our famous guest has arrived."

They smirk, chuckling amongst one another and I smile at them, not willing to give them any satisfaction.

"I wasn't expecting a welcoming committee." I grin in response. "This is most kind of you."

"We've been warned about you." A tall, brutish man with close shorn black hair walks closer to me, followed by his friends. "The traitor who was having his wicked way with the Queen behind the King's back. The madman who believes she is already married to him."

I chuckle to myself, shaking my head before turning to look at him again. "Well, at least I'm in good company here," I reply. "With all my fellow madmen."

I see the anger flash in his eyes as he moves so close to me that I can smell his rancid breath against my cheek.

"You think you are so clever, don't you?" He snarls. "But you weren't so clever when the King caught you, were you? Screaming like a baby as he tortured you. Begging them to let you die."

I lose my composure a little at his words, then suddenly his hand is at my collar, grasping it tightly. "You'll be wishing they had let you die by the time you leave here," he sneers, a dark grin appearing on his lips. "If you get to leave here that is."

He throws me to the ground, spitting at my feet as his fellow thugs laugh at my expense before following him over to one of the buildings, leaving me to build up the energy to pick my broken body up from the floor.

"Thomas?"

I glance up as I hear a familiar voice, blinking in the sunlight, trying to make sure my eyes aren't deceiving me.

"George?"

It's him. I know it because I see Sophia's eyes staring back at me in the man I last saw some six months ago. Though thinner and more unkempt, wearing the same uniform as me, it is Sophia's father. And for some unknown reason our paths have crossed again. He holds out a hand to help me up from the floor and I take it, wincing with the effort, my body still recovering from the infection which had ravaged it.

"I heard they were bringing someone from the palace," he says, his hand still at my shoulder. "I didn't think ... I hoped it wouldn't be ..."

I smile ruefully at him. "My luck ran out."

"Sophia?" The pain and worry in his eyes is clear to see and I want to take it away.

"Safe," I say, before shaking my head as I realise how wrong that is. "Looked after. James is there. The King never suspected him, thank goodness. He's taking care of her, I promise."

He nods his head at this but doesn't question it further. "You look like you could use some food," he says, with a small smile. "Don't get too excited, it's not great. In fact, it's awful. But you'll need it to keep your strength up in here."

I return his smile as I follow his lead towards a small canteen filled with row after row of wooden benches. He tells me to take a seat before heading over to where the cook is serving small portions of porridge and mugs of coffee out for the waiting line. As George passes me mine I take a sip of the brown liquid and grimace. He grins at me.

"Told you it was awful. Though I suppose you have been used to finer tastes for a while now?"

"Why are you in here George?" I ask, ignoring his question. "What happened?"

He sighs, shaking his head. "When I left the Capital with nothing, I knew that the only place I wanted to be was Lowshore. I knew that it was where Sophia had last felt safe and loved. I wanted to feel close to her. Plus, it's in my blood. I thought maybe I could find some farm work, start again like my ancestors did. But we both know it's not that easy."

I nod, remembering my own struggles to find work before that fateful day when Sophia's path crossed with mine. I start spooning the bland porridge into my mouth to stop the rumble of my stomach as I wait for him to carry on his tale.

"When I finally made it here, I asked around but nobody wanted to help," he continues. "Judging by the state of me I cannot say that I blamed them. Stood there with nothing but the shirt on my back, still bleeding from the scars which

Edmund graced me with. The first few days, after realising that work was unforthcoming, I slept in the forest under the stars. Thankfully, summer had brought its warmth and I was comfortable enough with the help of some small fires I managed to build. But then came the hunger. And when it became unbearable I had no choice but to steal to survive. Problem was, I'm not that good at it." He gives me a rueful grin and I can't help but laugh.

"I thought I was doing alright for a first-time thief. Fruit from someone's orchard. Some bread and cheese from the market whilst the stall holder was preoccupied helping an old lady with her bags. I even managed the occasional egg from a chicken coop when the farmer wasn't looking. Turns out though that I had already been spotted. The police waited a few weeks before following me back to a barn I had secretly taken shelter in. I think they wanted to catch me with as much loot as they could. And they did. Enough for me to find myself in here for four months."

"I'm sorry."

"It is what it is. I'm just sorry that we have been reacquainted only a few days before I am due to leave," he says, regretfully. "Perhaps we can meet each other again when you are released? How long are you in here for?"

"Five years."

I see the look of shock on his face as I say it. "You don't need to say anything," I say, with a small shrug. "I know what these places are like. I know that most people are broken before the end of one year. These places aren't made for long sentences.

And I don't expect to survive. But, she made me promise to try. For her. And so that is what I will do. I will fight to stay alive as long as I can. Because I know that she is fighting just as hard for me."

"She chose a good man," he says eventually, placing a hand to my shoulder. "I'm just sorry you ended up in here. I'm sorry that any of this happened. I would have preferred never to have seen her again; knowing she was happy and cared for, than being reunited like we were, only to discover the horrible truth."

"Sophia gave birth to a healthy daughter," I say, once again trying to deflect the attention from myself, and I see his face light up at this. "I only saw her once but she is as beautiful as her mother."

"I wish that I could have met her." He muses, softly. "What did she name her?"

"I don't know. I was arrested the day she was born. I never found out."

"What happened, Tom?" He's looking at me carefully, but I shake my head.

"It's a long story."

"We've got time," he replies, and I look at him in confusion.

"It's Sunday," he explains. "The Lord's day. We aren't expected to work Sundays. So between breakfast, supper and bed we've got all the time in the world and not a lot to do with it." He smiles at me. "Why don't we take a walk?"

As we walk, I tell George of the happenings back at the palace, how Rebecca's actions ultimately led to my arrest and the horror which Edmund put me through. George looks shocked, almost angry at Rebecca's betrayal but admits that as man and wife they are not similar in the slightest; her heart is in the right place but she follows her head too much.

Supper is as bland as breakfast - stale bread and watery stew, but it helps to build up more of the strength which illness has taken from me these past few weeks. George shows me to my bunk in the sleeping quarters upon which lies a thin nightshirt.

The sight of a proper bed, even one that doesn't look that comfortable, is enough to make my weary bones crave sleep after so long sleeping on concrete blocks in dungeon cells. I unbutton my grey uniform and shrug it off, instantly hearing sniggers from the other men in the room who all stand staring at me. I glance down at my bare chest, still bruised and grazed from beatings, and see the raised X which Edmund branded me with, clear as day against my skin.

I see George is looking at it too, but his face is not full of mirth like the rest of them. His is a look of remorse for someone else who, like him, bears Edmund's scars. Ignoring the stares, I pull the nightshirt over my head before reaching into the pocket of my jacket and pulling something out, discreetly tucking it into the underside of the bunk. I crawl under the covers, facing the wall as sleep comes for me quicker than I expect it to, crashing over me before the lamps are even extinguished.

I realise over the next few days, that George's presence is the only thing keeping me safe from the baying mob.

I see the other prisoners watching me, muttering amongst themselves, gesturing to me when his back is turned. I am plagued by nightmares which wake me violently from sleep but he is always there to bring me back into the present; reminding me that the monsters in my head are not real.

So, when the day comes that he is to leave, my heart is heavy with regret and prickled with anxiety.

"Where will you go?" I ask, as I walk with him to the heavy iron gates which I was driven through only one week ago.

"A couple of the lads are heading up to Highshore," he replies. "Think they can get some mining work up there and have said I can join them." He gives me a rueful smile. "I never thought that I would feel regret at leaving this place," he says. "But I wish we could have spent more time together."

"I'll be fine," I say, returning his smile with more confidence than I feel.

"I know, son. But watch your back. I don't trust many of the people in here. Too many are in the King's pocket."

I nod my understanding as he holds out his hand to shake mine.

"Look after yourself, Thomas," he says, as he is called to by his fellow free men to make a move. "And keep your promise to my daughter."

I feel a lump in my throat as he says the words with a small smile.

"I will. I swear it."

He shakes my hand one more time before turning away and beginning his walk to freedom which seems like a lifetime away for me. I watch him walk away until I can see him no longer. With a deep breath, I turn and make my way over to my workstation.

"It's a shame your friend has left, Thornton." I hear a voice call from behind me, but I do not turn back. "For you, anyway. Now our fun can begin."

SOPHIA

It has been two months since I last saw Tom in his prison cell, deep below the palace on the day I believed I had set him free. I think about him every day, wondering what hell he must be going through, knowing this is only the start of his nightmare.

My mother sits by the window with Olivia in her arms, cooing over her, as I sit at my dresser letting Annalise braid my hair. I didn't want to let my mother back into my life at all. But Edmund insisted. So I put up with it.

"She favours you," my mother's voice calls, from her window seat. "I see nothing of Edmund in her at all. Which is a shame, don't you think?"

I pretend that I haven't heard her. I look up in the mirror, trying to catch Annalise's eye but she is focusing on my hair. It has only been a couple of weeks since she became well enough to work again.

My mother tried to forbid it but Edmund told her that having Annalise work for me would be a constant reminder of what happens when you deceive him. And of course, my mother agreed.

"I am sure when you bear a son, he will be the image of his Papa." She smiles as she rocks Olivia in her arms and I shudder at the thought. Annalise finishes my hair and finally looks up at me as I take hold of her hand and squeeze it.

"Thank you."

She manages a small smile but the constant look of fear in her eyes breaks my heart. She walks over to my mother, clearing away the tea tray as I turn back to the mirror, until I hear the crash of crockery hitting the floor.

"Oh for goodness sake, you stupid girl! Are you blind as well as dumb?"

"Mother!"

I can see Annalise is on the verge of tears, her hands shaking as she drops to the floor and begins frantically picking up the pieces of broken china. I run to her, placing my hand at her arm as I crouch down next to her and make her look at me.

"I'll clear this up," I say, gently, taking the piece of china from her hand before she hurts herself. "Please. Go next door and rest a while." She shakes her head as she carries on frantically gathering up the broken teacups, the tears she had been so desperately trying to hold back now flooding down her cheeks. "Annalise. Please."

She looks at me and I encourage her with my eyes, until finally she gets to her feet and curtsies to me before rushing from the room.

"I don't understand why you are so kind to her." My mother shakes her head dismissively. "Of course, I see why Edmund insisted she carry on working for you, to teach her a lesson. But she doesn't deserve your kindness. And you shouldn't be doing that." She gestures to the mess that I am clearing up from the floor. "You should leave it for her to sort when she has come to her senses."

"I can clean, Mother. I used to clean my own home all the time."

"She should have been sent away with him."

"Tom." I stare at her, waiting for her to meet my eyes with her own. "He has a name, Mother. Say it."

"Sophia, darling. He has gone. It is time you accept this and move on."

I laugh, shaking my head. "How little you know me. You can tell me to move on as much as you like. But I never will. I will never be the Queen you so desperately want me to be. I am the wife of a woodsman. I own a farm. You can take all of that away from me but you will never change who I really am. Or who I love."

She ignores my statement and goes back to cooing over Olivia who has started to wake, no doubt because of all the noise. I finish placing the broken pieces back on the tea tray and carry it over to the table.

Olivia's murmurings are getting louder and I know she is telling me that she is hungry.

"She needs feeding," I say to my mother, as I walk back over to her. "I'll take her."

She passes my daughter to me and I begin to soothe her, gently rocking her as I make my way over to the chair and undo the lace of my dress so that I can feed her.

"Sophia, what on earth are you doing?" My mother's horrified voice makes me look up just as Olivia begins to feed. "I am feeding my daughter."

"By your own breast?" She questions, appalled. "Where is her wetnurse?"

"She doesn't need a wetnurse. I am her mother and I can provide her with the milk that she needs."

"Sophia." She frowns sternly at my declaration. "You are the Queen. Queens do not feed their children by their own breast."

"I do."

"And what does Edmund think of this?"

I glower at her. "Edmund doesn't care about me. I told you this. So why should I care what he thinks? He's got what he wanted."

"Sophia you really must try to move on." She's shaking her head as she looks at me.

"Move on? Tom is my husband."

"Was …" she states. "Whatever you had with that man is gone. Over. Edmund is your husband and you must learn to accept that."

"When did you become so cruel?" I whisper. "You are my mother. You are supposed to understand me. Protect me."

The commotion disturbs Olivia from her feed and she starts to grumble. I take her gently from my breast and place her back in her crib as I fasten my dress and get to my feet. My mother is standing now too.

"Edmund had a right to know. And I gave that man a chance. I gave him my word that I would say nothing so long as he stayed away from you, then left as soon as the child was born. So when I saw him there with you, with Edmund's child ..."

"I needed him!" I scream. "I couldn't have done that without him. I never understood why he had been so distant. So unwilling to see me in those last few weeks. And it was all because of you."

"Sophia."

My eyes sting with tears as I turn away from her. "I don't want to speak to you. I don't want to look at you. Just leave me." I don't turn back until I hear the door click and know that she has gone.

As evening falls, I sit by the window as Olivia feeds happily. My mother hasn't been back all day and I am relieved. Annalise seems happier, more relaxed without her looming over us too.

I stroke Olivia's auburn hair which seems to be growing more and more by the day. I'm so focused on her that I don't even hear the door open and only look up as I feel the presence of other people around me. Edmund is standing in the middle of the room, next to him is a woman in a grey dress, apron and bonnet and my heart drops as I realise.

"No …" I shake my head, as Edmund walks towards me. I get to my feet, holding Olivia tight to my chest. "Edmund no, please don't do this!"

He ignores my pleas, taking hold of Olivia and removing her from my breast. She begins to scream and I instinctively rush to her, hastily fastening my dress.

He rocks her for a few moments, turning his back to me, shrugging me away as I try to reach for her. She will not settle and eventually he passes her over to the wetnurse, who curtsies to him before leaving the room with her.

"How could you?" I cry, as he finally turns to face me. "How could you take her away from me? She's my daughter, she's all I have." He glares at me, his dark eyes full of annoyance. He spots Annalise who has backed herself into the corner of the room, still terrified of him.

"Out!" He orders, his voice booming out like cannon fire and I see her jump in fear as she rushes out of the door, closing it carefully behind her. The room is now silent, yet the sound of my blood thumping in my ears as he stands staring at me is deafening.

"Did you really think I would never find out?" His voice is steady, yet I can hear the anger bubbling beneath the surface.

"She is my daughter," I reply strongly. "I am capable of giving her what she needs."

"You are a Queen!" He growls, charging towards me and I flinch away from him instinctively. "Your body belongs to me! And until you produce me a male heir, your job is not done. A wetnurse can provide our daughter with everything that she needs. You need to focus on my needs. On birthing me a boy that I can raise to be the future King."

"I never wanted your children." My anger at having my child ripped away from me is pushing aside my fear.

"And I was so relieved when I gave birth to a daughter. Because I knew that she would never be subjected to your cruel teachings on what life should be. Why should I give you a son, knowing the future he will have? I wouldn't wish that on any child!"

"Now, now, my darling." He strokes a hand down my cheek, making me feel sick. "You remember our deal don't you? You told me that you would give yourself to me completely if I let him live. It sounds like you are thinking of breaking that promise. But I know people in that labour camp. People who can make Thomas Thornton's existence even more of a living hell than it already is."

"Hasn't he suffered enough?!" I scream it, moving as far away from him as I possibly can.

He is silent as he follows me, backing me into the corner of the room so I cannot escape his gaze or his touch.

"Oh no, Sophia." He shakes his head. "He hasn't suffered anywhere near enough for what he did. But I am a man of my word. You do as I command and I will keep my wolves at bay. That I promise you."

After he has got what he wants from me, he leaves.

I have no more tears left to cry. I don't feel anything anymore. The only thought in my mind is how I can stop him from getting the one thing he wants. Stop him from putting his much desired son and heir in my womb.

Making a mental note to speak with James tomorrow I undress myself, slipping a cool, cotton nightdress over my head before going to sit at my dressing table.

My eyes are shadowed with fatigue and red from all of the tears I have cried. It is a stranger staring back at me. A prisoner. Trapped in this hell by a man I despise, to protect the one I love. As I get to my feet to walk over to my bed, I hear a noise at the door and see Annalise standing warily in the crack of the open doorway.

"It's alright, Annalise. He's gone. Come here."

She does as I ask, closing the door behind her as she walks over to me.

She looks exhausted too, the constant pain and fear in her eyes something I cannot bear. She has aged so much in a matter of weeks and I take some responsibility for that; the guilt of not protecting her like I should have will stay with me forever.

"It's getting late," I say gently, placing my hand to her cheek. "You should be getting yourself ready for bed."

She looks away as I say this and I know why. Since her arrest most of the other maids have shunned her, either through loyalty to the King or through fear that something like this could happen to them too.

"You can stay here with me tonight if you like?"

She nods her head without hesitation. If I had suggested this when we first met she would have been horrified. Her position as household staff making it inconceivable to her to accept such an offer.

But fear and shame can make you do things you never would have dreamed of before, as long as they make you feel safe.

I take one of my nightdresses from the closet and bring it over to her before beginning to unbutton her grey dress. I wonder for a moment if she has ever had anyone help her to dress like she has helped me every day. But deep down I already know the answer. As she slips the dress from her shoulders I have to stop myself from staring in horror. She is skin and bone. Her already slight frame has been ravaged by her inability to eat properly due to the pain of what has been done to her. I slip the nightdress over her head.

It buries her. But at least it is comfortable, more comfortable than the itchy woollen dress which she wears day in, day out. I carefully unpin the bonnet from her hair and let the locks fall across her shoulders. I always thought her hair was black. But it isn't. It is a beautiful deep brown, almost chestnut and with it flowing down her back it glows red in places where the light hits it. I take my hairbrush and brush it gently before plaiting it. I take her hand and lead her to the bed, getting her settled before coming to lie next to her.

It's at that moment that she clings to me like a child clings to her mother, telling me with the strength of her grasp not to let go.

I begin rhythmically stroking a hand through her hair until I feel her begin to settle, her body relaxing against mine.

"I won't let anyone hurt you ever again, Annalise. I swear it. I'll do whatever I have to do to protect you. To protect you and Olivia. And Tom."

I can tell by the gentle rise and fall of her chest that she is asleep. She likely didn't even hear my words. But I meant every one of them. I'm going to take strength from all of the pain he has caused me. Do as he commands, be what he expects me to be.

For I stopped being me, the moment I was taken from my home and brought here. That person is dead now. Edmund has created a new person from within me. Someone forged from fear, pain and loss. Someone who is ready to play him at his own game. Someone who is not afraid anymore.

SOPHIA

5 years later

I sit looking at myself in the mirror, I don't recognise myself. I haven't for years. The carefree girl who spent her days living off the land; riding her horse through the forest; loving fiercely, is long gone. The fire within me is going out with every punch I take.

The cut on my lip stings like hell. It was the face today. Unusual for him. If I annoy him, or displease him, as I seem to do on an almost daily basis, then I certainly know about it. But he doesn't like others to know. That would wreck his public image. The bruises that cover my body are all hidden. So I must have really displeased him today. Maybe it's because he was once again angry at the fact that I have been unable to give him a son. And I reminded him of how he mocked Tom for not being able to give me a child.

His hand thundered across my face, taking me by surprise. I could see in his eyes that he had more in store for me but thankfully Annalise arrived and instead, he marched past her and out of the room. I haven't seen him since.

If only he knew just what lengths I go to, to ensure that I never again bear him a child. James tried to dissuade me, telling me that taking the tincture of mugwort and pennyroyal too often may mean that I damage my body so much that I may never have children again. I know why he said it. But we both know that I will never leave this place. Will never be free of him. Any dreams I once had are now a distant memory.

"Mama, you are hurt." I turn at the sound of my daughter's voice. She's standing at the door looking at me, her green eyes wide with confusion, her long red hair falling in waves against her pale pink nightdress.

She is the living image of me. She looks nothing like her father, which I thank God for every day.

Annalise stands beside her. She looks concerned as she always does and it's the only time I am ever relieved that she cannot speak. Talk is dangerous in this place. I smile softly, holding out my arms to Olivia and she runs to me, cocooning herself against my breast.

"Mama just fell and hurt herself sweetheart," I whisper, kissing her hair. "Nothing to worry about, I will be all better soon, I promise." I look over at Annalise and smile. "You can leave us now, Annalise. Thank you."

She curtsies, leaving the room and closing the door behind her. I remove Olivia from my embrace and look at her as I tuck a loose strand of hair behind her ear and take her hand.

"Have you had a good day?"

She nods. "Annalise took me to feed the ducks at the pond," she says, animatedly, "there were five of them! And one of them had little ducklings following her."

I chuckle. "That's nice my love. I wish I could have been there to see them."

"Can you come tomorrow? We can all go and see the ducks and the bunny rabbits!"

I smile again. "Maybe another time," I reply, knowing full well that I cannot leave the palace walls, even just to walk the grounds. "Remember that it is your visit to see Grandmama tomorrow."

Olivia puffs out her cheeks in annoyance. Edmund provided my mother with lodgings in the palace grounds which have made her most happy.

I haven't seen her for three years. I never forgave her for what she did to Tom. For breaking her promise and for breaking my heart. She insisted on being here whilst Olivia was a baby.

Keeping her room in the palace, visiting us daily, trying to make out like nothing had happened. Suffocating me still. Then when she realised that I wasn't going to relent and become the perfect Queen she thought I should be, she told Edmund she was leaving. And of course he couldn't have that. He adores my mother.

So now she lives on the grounds in a cottage and wants for nothing. He makes Olivia visit her at least once a month and I cannot stop that.

"I don't like going to Grandmama's." Olivia sighs. "She makes me do *girly* things."

I grin, as she pulls herself into me and I gently stroke her hair.

"Ask her to teach you how to bake," I whisper, thinking back to the only happy memories I have of me and my mother. "You can bake a cherry pie and bring some back for Mama."

As she yawns widely, I place a hand to her cheek. "Are you tired sweetheart?"

She nods, her thumb going to her mouth which it always does when she's ready for bed. I get up gingerly, trying to ignore the ache in my bones as I reach out a hand to her.

"Let's get you tucked up in bed."

She's getting so sleepy, and I would love desperately to carry her, but I don't think my body could take it. So I grasp her hand tightly and walk slowly with her down the corridor from my room to her own.

"Can you stay with me tonight, Mama?" she mumbles sleepily, as we walk, and as we reach her room her maids are ready to take her from me as they normally do. I smile down at her.

Edmund left earlier on today, travelling to Westshore on royal business for two days. I trust her nursemaids not to say anything to anyone if I disobey his orders just this once.

"I will put her to bed tonight," I tell them.

"Yes, Lady Sophia."

They curtsey to me as Annalise did, then leave the room. Shutting the door behind us, cocooned in this peaceful room with my baby girl I finally feel as happy as I can be here.

"Look, Mama!" She takes my hand and leads me over to her dressing table upon which lie rocks and pebbles of various shapes and sizes.

The sight of them, something so simple yet beautiful, takes my mind back to the pretty wooden birds and flowers which Tom would carve and leave for me to find when I woke, of the seashells and pebbles I would make him carry home from the beach each time we visited.

The memories are so strong, so overwhelming, that it takes me a few moments to realise that Olivia is calling to me. Shaking myself out of my memories, I turn to her, trying to smile.

"I found this one today. Isn't it pretty?" She holds out her hand to me, dropping a pebble into my palm. It is tiny and perfectly round. It almost appears that it is made out of glass, like a pearl but even prettier.

"It's beautiful, my darling," I say softly, turning it over in my fingers. "You have many wonderful treasures here. And you must look after them always. Because your dolls and your toys can be replaced. But these cannot. These are special because you found them and you chose to bring them home. Each one is different and magical." I go to place the pebble back in her hand but she shakes her head.

"I want you to keep it, Mama," she says. "You looked happy when you held it. I like it when you are happy. I don't like it when you cry."

My eyes prick with the tears she doesn't like to see and I pull her in close to me to disguise them.

"You are such a kind little girl," I whisper into her hair. "Never change my darling." I squeeze her tight until I manage to compose myself as I kiss her hair and let her go.

"Can you tell me a story, Mama?" She's looking at me wide-eyed, the sleepiness of earlier overtaken by the excitement of her treasure chest and the promise of a fairy tale.

I nod, getting to my feet to extinguish the lamps in the room leaving only one small handheld candle which I carry to her bedside and place on the table. I settle her down into bed, the starlight beaming through the open window.

"Once upon a time, there was a young girl who lived with her mama and papa in a big city, just like this one. Until one day, she ran away and married a woodcutter named Tom."

I carry on telling my fairy tale as Olivia drifts off to sleep. A fairy tale built in real life. Except this one has the happy ending which I will never have. I look down at her, sleeping peacefully with her thumb in her mouth and I give in completely to my tears. I manage to compose myself, kissing her forehead lightly before blowing out the candle and walking over to the windowsill.

The stars, normally so dull in the sky of the Capital shine so brightly tonight, the silver and white twinkling against the dark, navy blue and purple of the night sky. I've never seen them shine so bright here before.

The pebble is cool in my hand and I roll it between my fingers, feeling comforted by it until the sound of footsteps at the doorway make me jump.

But, as I turn I see that it is Annalise. I can see her face in the light of the candle she is holding, and I beckon her over to me. As she walks to my side I offer her a place next to me on the windowsill and she takes it as I look up at the stars once more.

"Tom once told me," I begin, knowing that I can talk freely with Annalise. "He told me that if there were ever a time when he was not here beside me, that I could look up at the stars and know that he would be looking up at the same stars and thinking of me."

"It's a surprise!" He laughed, not giving anything away. "Here, take my hand and close your eyes." I must still have looked uncertain as he gave me a little half smile as he walked closer to me. "Trust me."

He was still holding his hand out to mine. With a shake of my head, I closed my eyes and took hold of it, feeling his fingers interlocking with mine.

When he finally told me to open my eyes, we were in a clearing in the forest. He had lit a campfire and laid out two blankets, one containing a picnic of bread, cheese and mead. Smiling, he walked over to the other blanket and settled himself down upon it before holding out his hand once more for me to join him.

Without hesitation this time I took his hand, getting to my knees next to him on the blanket. With a grin, he laid down before gesturing to me to do the same.

"Open your eyes, Sophia," he said, suddenly, breaking me out of my daydream. "And look up."

I did as he said, looking up into the deep blue of the night sky and saw hundreds and thousands of stars glinting bright white and silver against it. The sight of it was spellbinding and I found myself speechless for a while, as I just gazed up at it in wonder.

"The stars," I whispered eventually, mesmerised. "You don't see the stars in the Capital sky. Not like this. They're beautiful."

"I've slept under this sky so many times. After a while, it starts to feel comforting in some way," he spoke again, before looking over at me and shrugging as he shook his head.

"Ignore me, I'm talking like a fool."

"No." I shook my head as I sat up. "No, you're not. I can see why it could be."

"The way I see it, is that all of us ... each and every one of us look up at this same sky every night, and sometimes when you are so alone it makes you feel like there is someone there." He sat up suddenly, taking hold of my hands. "If there is ever a time when I'm not here beside you, I want you to know that you can look up at those stars and know that I will be looking up at the same stars and thinking of you."

I placed a hand to his cheek, confusion sweeping through me. "Tom, what are you talking about? You will always be beside me. I'm not going anywhere."

"My life has been such a mess. Sometimes I wonder how the hell I ever managed to find myself with someone like you. The fact is, good things don't happen to people like me. And sooner or later, I always find myself back where I started. Alone, staring up at the stars."

"I love you, Tom Thornton," I said, strongly, turning his face to mine so that our eyes connected. "You are all I want and all I need. And you will never be alone again. I promise you that."

He stared at me, the tears swimming into his eyes, making them look all the more vivid in the moonlight.

"Marry me." His voice took me by surprise.

"What?"

I looked at him, wondering if he really just said what I thought he did. He grinned at me through the tears that had started to spill down his cheeks.

"Sophia Reynolds, will you marry me?"

I laughed, partly through shock, partly through the fact that I still couldn't believe I was hearing this, after we had known each other a matter of months.

"Are you serious?"

He placed his hand to my cheek. "I've never been more serious in my life," he replied, as he stroked my cheek gently with his thumb. "I want you to be my wife. I want to protect you; love you and be here with you until my dying day. Marry me. Please."

I could feel the smile on my face growing as his eyes searched mine waiting for my answer. "Yes," I whispered eventually. I giggled before his lips found mine and the world disappeared around us; leaving only the two of us, together under the starry night sky.

As my mind flashes back to that moment, I'm lost in the magic for a while until I feel Annalise's gentle hand at my wrist and I turn to her, tears glistening in my eyes.

"Do you think it's true?" I whisper. "Do you think he's still in this world, thinking of me?"

It's almost five years to the day since they sent him away to the labour camp. Five years in a place which sends most people mad after one. Part of me thinks that if he were dead, Edmund would have taken great pleasure in telling me. Yet another part thinks he would keep it from me, knowing that I daren't go against him for fear of hurting Tom.

Annalise places a gentle hand to my cheek, wiping my tears away. She inspects the cut to my lip and I wince. She motions to me that she wants to take me to get it cleaned up, but I shake my head, looking up at her.

"Just five more minutes, please?"

She gives me a small smile and I turn back towards the window, gazing up at the stars, hoping he's still out there like he promised, gazing up at the same stars and thinking of me.

Tom

The rain hammers down, soaking me to the bone as I stand in a grey and dismal yard, cutting up tree trunk after tree trunk into various sizes for various uses. Mostly for firewood, though some would be used by other prisoners to make chairs and tables for the local school. I've done this every day barring Sundays, for the past five years.

The joy I used to feel from being surrounded by nature, doing the work I loved is long gone. Edmund knew what he was doing when he sent me here. Yet I've survived, despite all the odds, and I am due for release in three days' time.

"Thornton." I close my eyes as I hear Eli Fisher calling my name. He's made no secret of the fact that he gets preferential treatment here from the guards for making me suffer. By order of the King.

"Do you have nothing better to do?" I sigh, turning away from him as I lift my axe again and continue working. The next minute I am surrounded by him and four of his friends.

I snatch a glance over at the guards but as ever they are turning a blind eye.

"As it goes, no I don't." Eli is a tall, broad, brute of a man with a shock of white hair. He beat a shopkeeper half to death and yet was sentenced to just six months in this place. He holds a hammer in his hand, his fist clenched around it as he stares at me.

"Well, I'm sorry to disappoint you but I'm busy." I lift the axe above my head but it doesn't come back down again. I feel Eli wrench it from my hands and watch as he throws it to the floor. I shake my head. "I don't want to fight you. I have no reason to. I haven't wronged you in any way."

"You wronged the King though, didn't you?" He sneers, leaning in so close to me that I can smell the liquor on his breath.

"And you are so loyal to the King, are you?" I scoff, shaking my head. "Forgive me if I find that hard to believe."

"I am when it suits me," he replies with a grin. "When it gets me extra food and mead, and a better bed for the night in this hovel."

"Good for you, Eli." I turn my back on him again and walk over to the large pile of tree trunks, looking for ones small enough that I can carry from the pile and put to the side. Just until they give up and leave me alone, so I can grab my axe again. Eli's hands push me in the back and I stumble but stay on my feet.

"Don't walk away from me, Thornton!"

I ignore him, grabbing hold of a log and lifting it onto my shoulder. He carries on following me.

"How's your wife?" He sneers, and I feel my jaw twitch with anger. "Or should I say the King's wife? I hear she still hasn't given him a son and heir."

I feel the anger burning up inside of me, the familiar feeling rising, the blood pumping in my ears as I take deep breaths and keep my back turned to him.

"That either means she's barren, useless or as ugly as sin. Maybe she's all three?"

Before I know what I'm doing, the log is on the ground and I've floored him with a punch to the jaw. I keep on punching him, his blood mixing with the rain water, running onto the dirt and joining the puddles, before I'm dragged off him by his friends and then it's my turn.

The punches and kicks come from everywhere and I am in no position to defend myself. The sound of a whistle reaches my ears and suddenly the torment stops, as I am dragged to my feet and held by a guard. Eli and his friends are being held back too.

"Enough!" The prison Warden bellows as he walks over and looks at us with disdain, before speaking to the full yard. "Down tools, everyone. Make your way into the food hall for supper."

The guards let go of us and I wait for Eli and his gang to walk ahead before I start limping back towards the hall, clutching my ribs. But I am soon stopped by the Warden.

"Not you, Thornton. You'll carry on working until you've got rid of that pile of logs."

"And what about Fisher, sir?" I say, shaking my head in disbelief.

"My guards tell me you threw the first punch."

"He provoked me!" I yell, but I can already tell that it's pointless as the Warden holds up a warning finger to my face.

"Any more arguments, Thornton and I'll make sure there is no food left for you when you finish. Now, carry on."

It is almost sundown, when I finally chop the last log down into firewood, the sky a deep pink colour as the edge of the sun hovers on the horizon.

The lamps are on in the sleeping quarters, meaning that everyone else has eaten and is in there, preparing for bed. I follow the guard into the food hall. The cook is still there, the look on his face telling me that he isn't pleased about the fact. As he passes me the meagre bowl of stew, I see him smirk at me before spitting in it, much to the amusement of the wardens who stand guard in the now empty hall. I don't have the energy to fight back.

I take a chunk of bread from the basket before taking my seat and pushing the stew away from me. Instead, I break the small piece of bread into even smaller pieces and eat it slowly, in an attempt to trick myself into feeling full, which doesn't work.

Eventually, I am carted back to the communal sleeping quarters, ignoring the murmurings and sniggers of the other prisoners as I climb into bed, not bothering to undress, the ache of my body making it impossible to even consider the idea. I reach my hand under the frame of my bed and feel for the carefully folded piece of paper I hid there on my first night here.

The piece of paper which James hastily handed to me before my trial. I turn on my side, thankful that my bunk is in the far corner of the room allowing me these brief moments of respite and privacy. I unfold it quietly, letting the ring held in the middle fall into my palm. I take hold of it, my finger tracing the small emerald and the indentation of our initials against the silver band. I don't know how long I have before they extinguish the lamps, so I begin to scan over and over the words on the piece of paper. The words written in her hand, some of them blurred where her tears had made the ink run as she was writing. I know them off by heart by now. But seeing them written on this scrap of paper makes me feel close to her somehow.

As the guards call for lights off, I hastily fold the ring back into the paper, securing it once again under the bed frame as the lamps go out.

The glow of the moon through the tiny window is now the only source of light in the room. I stare at it, magical and full against the inky black night sky which is dotted with hundreds of tiny, glinting stars. Looking at them, I remember what I told Sophia on the night I asked her to be my wife. I often wonder what compelled me to say it. Maybe I always knew deep down that something would happen to tear us apart.

I never fully believed that I deserved the love she gave me. It always felt too good to be true. But I meant what I said that night. And she is the only thing that is in my mind right now, as I look up at the stars thinking back to a time long ago when life for that all too brief time, was good.

Three days pass and as the bell tolls; signalling the end of the working day, I can hardly believe that it is really happening. I am finally free. The gates of the camp are so tantalisingly close that I can see the road which leads back towards Lowshore in the distance.

I can hear the sniggers and sneers of the prison guards who are accompanying me to my freedom, annoyed that I survived the full five years, annoyed that they couldn't break me. But the truth is that they almost did. Not physically, though my body aches through beatings and injuries which they never treated properly. But mentally, I don't know if I could have survived another day.

"No wise cracks, Thornton?" The guard to my right smirks as we reach the gate. "Nothing you want to say?"

He's trying to rile me. I know that. But I don't have the energy to fight back. And I know that he is looking for any opportunity to keep me in here.

"No, sir."

He scoffs, shaking his head as he instructs the other guard to open the gate before leaning in so close to me that I can smell his rancid breath.

"You're bloody lucky," he hisses in my ear. "You should be leaving this place in a box."

He shoves me forward which I take as my cue to leave, and I begin walking as fast as my aching body can take me without looking back. As I hear the gates slam shut behind me, it is then that I finally see Jack standing in the distance. Amos is sat faithfully by his side and I have to swallow down the lump in my throat as I make my way towards him. Jack was the only one that I wrote to when I got sent here. I wanted him to know what had happened. I never expected him to write back but he did, religiously, for the full five years. I told him I was due to be released but I never asked or expected him to be here when I was. As I reach him he smiles at me.

"Alright son?"

I wrap my arms around him to disguise the emotion burning up in my throat, the tears pricking at my eyes.

"You didn't have to come." I manage to choke up, struggling to contain my emotions. He must realise, as he doesn't reply until I feel myself begin to calm.

"Don't be a fool, Tom. Of course I was going to come. We've been worried. Especially when your letters stopped coming as frequently." He pauses, as he pulls me back from his embrace, keeping his hands at my shoulders as he looks at me carefully. "How was it?"

I swallow. I know he can already tell from the state of me how it was. I've lost so much weight that my trousers are held up only by the piece of rope tied tightly at my waist. My eyes are shadowed with fatigue, my jaw now housing a greying beard.

"Hell." I answer, truthfully, and he doesn't question it further. I feel a nudge at my leg and look down to see Amos wagging his tail as he looks up at me. He's got more grey fur than the last time I saw him but he looks well and happy, and I smile as I stroke his head gently. "Hey, boy. Jack managed to keep you alive then?"

"Oi," Jack replies, a grin on his face. "This dog has lived a life of luxury, Mary made sure of that. Speaking of which; she's sent some food for you both." He holds up a bag filled to the brim with bread, meats and cheeses and I thank him gratefully. "So," he says eventually, as we begin walking back towards Lowshore.

"Where do you want to go? Mary has a room waiting at the Tavern for you, if that's what you want?"

I smile at him. He already knows my answer. "Give her my thanks. I really do appreciate the offer. But I need to go home."

"Tom." He shakes his head. "Are you sure?"

I nod. "I've been through too much to care what people think of me anymore, Jack. And besides, people made their minds up about me the minute Sophia went missing. I know the truth. That's all that matters to me now."

"Have you heard from her?" It's the first time his face has shown any sadness or pity. I know he has been trying to stay strong for me but the mention of Sophia is enough to bring down the walls of strength both of us have been trying to build.

"It's too dangerous. For her, and for James. Edmund made it clear that sending me to that hellhole was just another way of keeping her under his control. That if she didn't do what he said that it would mean I would suffer."

"And now?" There's a glint of hope in his eyes. The same one that flickers in my heart even though deep down I know it is impossible.

"I doubt he will have even told her that I'm free," I reply. "He wouldn't want to give her any sense of hope. I thought I could beat him, Jack. But he's too strong. Sophia knows that I love her. That I'll always love her but I couldn't save her. He's won." I swallow down the lump in my throat as I blink up at the ever darkening sky, trying once again to contain my tears.

"It's getting late." I hear Jack say eventually, as he places a companionable hand against my arm. "Let's get you home and settled."

Amos stays close to my side as we continue our walk back towards the home I last saw over five years ago. The dusty streets look the same. There are lights on in the windows of the houses we pass, as families settle down together for the evening. I hear the sound of conversation from the tavern which is full of men who have finished a day's hard work. I cannot bear the noise. I crave solitude in a place where I can feel close to her.

As the sun finally sets, I see the farmhouse, illuminated by street lamps and moonlight. I stop walking so suddenly that it takes Jack a few moments to realise that I'm no longer in step with him.

"Tom?" He eyes me with concern. "Are you sure you are ready for this? Why don't you come back to the Tavern, at least for a few days. Let Mary look after you, get your strength back up."

"No." I shake my head. "I need to be here, Jack. I want to be on my own."

He's still got the look of concern in his eyes and I know why. I hardly look capable of looking after myself right now. But I know that Mary's kindness would suffocate me, and I can already picture the pity in her eyes every time she would look at me.

"I'll be alright. I promise. Amos will look after me."

"He'd better." He smiles down at Amos, ruffling his head.

"You hear that, you scruffy mutt? You look after your master now, alright?" Amos barks in response and Jack chuckles. "I kept the farm going." He gestures to the barn. "Like you made me promise. I paid a young farmhand from the next village to keep an eye on things. He's happy to carry on, if that's what you want?"

I look past the farmhouse towards the barn and the stables which are now bathed in the light of the moon. I can hear the animals bleating and it takes me back to happier times; to memories which I'm desperate to keep hold of.

"No. Thank you. I'd like to do it. It'll keep me occupied. Give me something else to think about."

He nods as he places his hand to my shoulder again. "We are only down the road if you need us, son. No matter the hour, you hear? I'll pop back and see you tomorrow."

I thank him again as he hands me the key, and I make my way down the familiar path towards the first proper home I had ever known.

I turn the key in the lock and open the door. As I do, more memories begin flooding back into my mind, good and bad. Our chairs still sit by the fire, conjuring images of how we would just sit there and talk for hours until the embers of the fire burned away. The kitchen table which I made from scratch, where I imagined we would sit and eat meals with the children we were never blessed with. To the right is the door to our bedroom. A room I hadn't walked into from the moment Sophia was taken.

Part of me feels the need to finally make that step, but not yet. I shrug off the threadbare work jacket I have worn for the past five years and lay it over the back of a kitchen chair. I really should bathe and change my clothes but I haven't got the energy and the growl of my stomach is telling me that I need to eat before I do anything else. I hear Amos whining gently at my feet and see him eyeing up the bag which Jack gave me.

"Let's get you some food, boy." I chuckle softly, as I reach for the bag. "Mary is too good to both of us."

I prepare us some food before lighting a fire and finally collapsing into the old worn armchair in front of it. I had forgotten what it feels like to sit in comfort somewhere, without threat or the prospect of work hanging over you. Standing from dawn until dusk with no respite; pitiful meals eaten at hard wooden benches before sleep on an uncomfortable bunk - that was if the other inmates and guards allowed. I hear the sigh of relief escape my lips at the chance to rest my weary bones as Amos comes to rest beside me and before I know it I have fallen asleep.

SOPHIA

Another night. Another Ball. Another evening of being paraded around on Edmund's arm as though I am the love of his life when in reality we cannot bear the sight of one another. My jaw aches with the constant display of happiness that I have been forced to perform and I am grateful when he finally allows me a brief respite.

I immediately find a waiter carrying a silver platter of drinks and take two glasses before making my way over to the corner of the room where I hope Edmund will not find me again before he retires for the evening. I watch the men and women dancing, remembering how happy I was on the evening of the Spring Ball all those years ago, in the arms of my love as he spun me around this very room.

One of a few, precious moments of happiness I had managed to have before it was all taken away from me once again. That night was so magical. Despite everything happening to us, in that moment I felt free.

I felt safe and loved and happy for the first time in forever and I never wanted the moment to end.

I close my eyes, trying to take myself back to that moment, trying to feel the warmth of his touch, the safety of his smile and for a while I can...I can see him so clearly in my mind that I feel myself smiling as he takes me in his arms and holds me close.

"You're safe, Sophia." I hear his gentle voice say as I rest my head against his chest, comforted by his steady heartbeat and the familiar smell of his skin.

"I know I am." I reply, softly. "I'm with you."

"Sophia?" Edmund's voice rings out suddenly, breaking me from my daydream and I feel the warm, safe feeling leave me as I see him striding across the room towards me, holding out his arm, a broad smile across his face. "Ah, there you are, my darling. Will you join us? I'd like to introduce you to someone."

I brush down the skirts of my red dress as I drink the full glass of port in my hand before plastering a smile on my face and walking over to take Edmund's outstretched hand.

"Sophia, this is Duke Riall of Fallean. Riall, may I introduce my beloved wife, Sophia."

I curtsey, respectfully as he bows. I have heard much about Fallean, but only what Edmund has spoken of. He would often speak in great detail of his battle and subsequent victory over the King of Fallean at the start of his kingship; in truth I know that it is one of his greatest triumphs. And over the last few years he has made numerous trips to the tropical land, with its emerald green waters and warm sandy beaches, in order to build bridges between our nations.

Duke Riall is a formidable looking man. Tall and broad with a shock of grey hair and hazel eyes which seem to glow orange like flames in certain light. Though he smiles at me, seemingly affable, there is something about him that makes the hairs on the back of my neck stand on end.

"You recall, my love," Edmund continues. "That I have been making more frequent visits to Fallean over the past few months. After years of conflict and tension between our nations, I felt that it was time to put an end to it and begin a new era of peace and alliance."

"I am relieved to hear this," I say, politely, the act I have learnt to put on whilst in public now coming so naturally to me. "Conflict is no good for anyone. For the sake of both our lands we should find a way to move forward as friends."

"Precisely." Edmund grins, widely. "And what better way for us to move forward into this new and prosperous era than to join our families and lands as one." His words shake me from my well-rehearsed act and I look at him, warily.

"In what way do you mean, my darling?" I force myself to keep smiling, but the panic is rising in me at the look of sheer joy on Edmund's face.

"Duke Riall sadly lost his wife two months ago. He is now ready to marry again. His late wife blessed him with two daughters but was unable to give him a son to pass on the family name." He looks at me meaningfully. "I felt that, in order to cement the new alliance between our two nations, a joining of our families should take place. It is therefore my wish that our daughter Olivia will wed the Duke."

I feel my heart drop like a stone as he says it. I abandon all thoughts of acting the perfect wife and Queen, my love and protection for my daughter far stronger than my fear of what he could do to me. "No, Edmund. She is five years old. You cannot make this decision for her."

Edmund chuckles lightly. I know he is trying to save face in front of the Duke but I can see the glint of annoyance in his eye.

"My dear, she will not wed him now, that is preposterous. She is not able to give him a child, yet. However, she will travel back with the Duke to Fallean when he leaves in three days-time. She will be taught what it is to be the wife of a Duke in preparation for her marriage to him, when she reaches an appropriate age. The age where she is able to bear him children."

I feel sick. I bled for the first time at twelve years old. If she is there, away from me, without my protection, they will be waiting for the moment she first bleeds too. Then they will make her wed him and give herself to him. This man of fifty.

"No, you won't take her. I won't let you." I shake my head refusing the order.

Edmund excuses himself from the Duke, apologising for my behaviour, telling him that I have had a little too much to drink. He grabs hold of my arm, his nails digging painfully into my skin as he drags me over to the corner of the room.

"Please, Edmund," I beg. "She is your daughter. Your five year-old daughter. Please do not do this to her. She is too young."

"If you bore me a son, then none of this would have to happen," he hisses at me. "I have to make the most of what I have to strengthen this kingdom. It is her duty."

"She is a child! She neither knows nor cares of duty. She spends her days feeding the ducks at the pond, playing with her dolls. She is innocent. She deserves the chance of a normal childhood and the choice to marry who she wishes."

"Like her mother?" he scoffs. "She is too much like you, my dear. I see this already. If I allow her to choose a husband for herself, no doubt she will do exactly as you did and pick a wastrel unsuitable for someone of her breeding. Sending her away from you will ensure that she can grow up understanding exactly whose daughter she is and what is expected of her."

"I won't let you do this," I whisper, the tears falling from my eyes. "You won't take her from me. She is all I have." I stop, looking him in the eyes, begging him to reconsider. He loosens his grasp on my arms, his hands now lying gently against my skin. He lifts a hand to tuck a stray piece of hair behind my ear, his eyes burning into mine.

"He got out three days ago," he says, suddenly, a callous grin appearing on his face. "Your beloved. I must admit that I am impressed that he survived the full five years. I made sure they didn't take it easy on him, much the contrary. Though if you think that him being released means that he is safe, you would be sorely mistaken. I can find him, have him re-arrested and killed this time. Which do you think he would prefer? Tied up and shot perhaps? Or just stick to removing his head? I could have it presented to you, as a keepsake."

I can't speak. Tom is alive?

I can feel my hands shaking but I don't know if it is with relief at hearing that he survived or fear for both him and Olivia, knowing that whatever choice I make now, one of them will suffer. Edmund steps closer to me, his hand cupping my back, pulling me in close to him as he whispers in my ear, his breath sticky and warm against my cheek.

"You will do as I say, Sophia," he says, his voice dark. "Or he will bear the consequences. Enjoy your last few days with our daughter."

He places a gentle kiss upon my cheek as a tear falls from my eye. He smiles at me as he turns and walks back over to the Duke.

As the party slowly comes to its end, I know that I have drunk too much as I unsteadily make my way from the banqueting hall and up the stairs towards my bedchamber.

Edmund retired an hour or so before, having never been one for social gatherings. He enjoyed the spectacle and he made sure that the right people knew that he had been there, but he always retired to his room before the evening came to an end. The alcohol which I have consumed has brought me some small feeling of oblivion and I enjoy the numbness of it. I notice little or nothing of my surroundings as I pass through corridor after corridor of this opulent prison which is my home.

Yet, Edmund's words keep on reverberating around my mind. I can picture my beautiful, innocent daughter sleeping peacefully in her bed right now, completely unaware of the sentence which her father has placed upon her. And then there is Tom. He is alive. The thing that I have prayed for every evening since he was taken from me. I don't even know how he managed it. And yet, he still is not free. His fate is still intertwined with my own, still just some part of this wicked game which Edmund taunts me with.

As I walk down one particular corridor, I notice a guard standing watch outside a door and realise that I have wandered into Edmund's wing of the palace by mistake. I straighten my dress as I walk up to him and he bows as I reach him.

"My Lady."

"I wish to see my husband," I say, trying to stop myself from slurring the words, as the guard smiles, respectfully.

"The King has retired for the night, my Lady. He has requested Doctor Collins call on him once the party is over but has told me to refuse all other visitors."

I chuckle, the alcohol masking my fears and inhibitions. "But, I am not just any visitor, am I? And I think the King will appreciate my visit when he realises what it is I am here for." I raise an eyebrow and I see the young guard's cheeks blush with embarrassment.

"I'm not sure it is an entirely wise idea, my Lady. The King was not in the best of moods when he arrived."

"Ah." I nod, ruefully. "Yes, I expect that was my fault. We had a disagreement, a mild one. We got angry with one another. But, I have had time to think things through and I see that I was wrong. If I am able to go and speak with him, I feel it will make the atmosphere a lot better for everyone."

I see the guard's face relax at this. Edmund's mood had an effect on the entire palace and the staff.

Him being happy is better for us all.

"Alright. But I must stay and stand guard. Those are my orders."

I shake my head, smiling. "I appreciate your loyalty and protection. As does the King. But he is in no danger here, not tonight. There are guards stationed at the front doors due to the party. Everyone here has been fully checked. And besides …" I stand up on my tiptoes so that I can whisper in his ear. "I'm not sure the King would appreciate you hearing any … noises that may arise tonight. It would be best if what happens stays between a man and his wife."

I see his cheeks blush even redder and he cannot meet my eyes. "I … well I suppose."

"You know what would make both the King and I feel much safer? If you would join the guards at the front of the palace, making sure all of our guests leave promptly and the palace is secure."

He looks grateful at this suggestion, extending a bow to me once more before taking his leave. I wait, until I see him disappear around a corner before I knock at Edmund's door. I don't wait to be called, I walk in and find him already in his bed, reading.

He looks up with a smile, probably expecting James to be standing there. As he sees that it is me, his smile drops and he closes the book with a slam.

"I wish to discuss the matter no further, Sophia," he says, his voice dark as he places the book down on the nightstand. "And I specifically told the guard that I was to have no more visitors. Where is he and why did he let you in here? I swear I'll have him flogged."

"I sent him away," I reply, my voice strong. "I told him that I wished to speak with you. I told him to join the guards at the front of the palace, making sure all the guests leave."

"You had no right."

"I came here to apologise, Edmund." As I say it, he looks at me, closely.

"Apologise?"

"Yes." I nod. "I have been thinking, long and hard about how I have not done right by you. Haven't done my own duty to you, in giving you a son."

He doesn't speak, but gestures for me to come forward, so I do, sitting down on the edge of his bed as I start to speak again.

"I promised you that if you let Tom live that I wouldn't fight against you any longer. That I would give myself to you, do whatever you desire. You kept your side of the bargain and I feel as though I haven't done the same as I haven't been able to give you a son and heir. But we still have time, don't we?" I look into his eyes as he reaches a hand to my hair. "Let me give you a son, Edmund," I whisper, as I place my own hand to his cheek. "Let me help your legacy continue."

He stops me speaking as he places his lips to mine, flooding my mouth with hungry kisses and I feel his wandering hands making their way up my skirts.

He's in his nightshirt so it doesn't take him long to ready himself and I close my eyes as our bodies connect. He's still kissing me, his hands now pulling at my hair, trying to tear it from the elaborate updo it has been teased into. As he slows, I open my eyes and look at him as I reach up to my head and take the ruby-studded hairpin from it, letting my hair fall in waves to my shoulders. I see him grin with exhilaration as he looks at me.

"You are all mine, Sophia," he says, breathlessly. "Forever. And you will bear me a son."

I smile euphorically at him. And he's still gazing at me as I drive the hairpin into his neck. I see his eyes widen in shock as the blood begins to spill from his mouth.

He's making choking sounds trying to reach his arms forward to grab me, but it is no use. All he can see is the wildness in my eyes and boiling hatred in my blood as I twist the hairpin harder into his flesh. As he starts to fade, I lean in towards him, whispering in his ear. "I hate you with every fibre of my being. I hate the person you have broken me down to become. I'm taking my daughter as far away from this life and this city as I possibly can. And I will *never* bear you a son."

I pull the hairpin from his neck, watching as the blood begins to gush from the open wound. I carry on watching him, watching the life drain from him until his eyes stare into nothingness and I look down at the blood stains on my dress, realising what I have just done. An odd sensation of panic and fear mingled with pure relief begins coursing through my veins and I start to laugh as the tears begin to pour from my eyes.

JAMES

Glancing at my pocket watch tells me that it is drawing ever closer to midnight and I stifle a yawn, as I watch the few remaining guests of the party still talking and drinking, seemingly not wanting the night to end. All I want to do is get into my carriage and make my own way home.

But Edmund insisted he wanted to see me once the party had finished, instructing me to prepare a sleeping draught as he has not been sleeping well recently. I make the decision to head up and see him now. I doubt any of us were expecting the party to carry on this long, least of all Edmund.

I'm a little surprised that he hasn't reappeared, telling everyone to leave him in peace; after all, parties are not his favourite things after the initial introductions have been concluded. As the guards begin to try and disperse the remaining guests and the servants begin the huge task of cleaning up, I make my way up to Edmund's bedchamber and am confused when I do not see a guard outside the door.

Edmund's door is always guarded, his paranoia that one of his enemies may attack him at his most vulnerable forever at the forefront of his mind. I can hear a noise that I cannot make out coming from the room and I cautiously edge towards it until I reach the door and open it slowly.

"Sophia?"

She's standing by Edmund's bedside, her eyes fixed upon his lifeless body, tears pouring down her face even though laughter erupts from her mouth.

In her hand is a hairpin which drips with the same blood that stains Edmund's shirt; flowing from a deep wound to his neck and matching the ruby red velvet throw which covers him. Suddenly, she notices me and as her eyes reach mine it is as if she comes back to life, choking sobs erupting from her as she released her grasp on the hairpin, letting it fall to the floor.

I turn quickly, closing the door and locking it with the key before turning back to Sophia who has stopped laughing now, and just stands, pale as a ghost, staring at me as her chin wobbles with tears.

"He ... he ..."

I walk up to her and it's at this moment she clings to me, holding on so tight that I can barely breathe.

"I couldn't let him take her away!" she cries. "I had to stop him! He has done his worst with me, but I won't allow the same fate for Olivia!"

I have no idea what she is talking about and I fear there is little time for her to explain. Suddenly she lets go of me, glancing over at Edmund's body her eyes wide with fear.

"What will happen to me?" she stutters. "I will die for this, won't I? They will execute me. What will become of Olivia?"

She breaks down again and I swallow as I pull her in close to me.

"You need to leave here," I say, quickly, the words tumbling out of my mouth before I even realise what I am saying. "You need to go now, get Olivia and leave."

She pulls back from me, shaking her head in confusion.

"How, James? I cannot just walk out of here. They will find me."

"My carriage is out the back," I continue urgently, sensing that time is growing ever shorter and beginning to work things out in my head. "I instructed my driver to wait there for me as I would not be much longer. You must find a way to get to him. Take the servants' staircase. Tell him that I have sent you and that you need to get as far away from here as possible. He will ask no questions."

"James…"

"You must go now, Sophia!" I implore, taking off my cloak and wrapping it around her. "You won't have long. The guards are at the front of the palace, asking people to leave. You must go to your chambers and get Olivia before they shut the main doors and return to their normal duties."

I grab her arm and walk with her over to the door. I unlock it, looking out down the corridor with relief as I see that it is still empty. "Go now, hurry!"

"What about you?"

"Don't worry about me, Sophia," I reply. "I will sort this, somehow. Just get yourself safe, please."

I urge her with my eyes and reluctantly she turns and runs towards her chambers, but not before squeezing my hand tightly in a gesture that says so much more than words. As she disappears into the darkness, I swallow down my own panic as I walk back into Edmund's chamber, once again locking the door behind me as I walk over to him.

His lifeless eyes bore into mine and I realise the position I have just put myself in. But, I promised Tom that I would protect her. And maybe I always knew this would be my fate.

I expected it after Tom was arrested, yet he kept his promise to me, never giving me up despite all of the pain they put him through. Him, Sophia, Annalise - all of them have suffered so much yet I, as the orchestrator, the one who started all of this, have escaped any retribution because of my social standing, because of the deep-seated trust which Edmund held in me.

That guilt has eaten away at me for years.

Sometimes I just wanted to scream at Edmund, confess my sins and unburden my soul. But I couldn't bring myself to. Selfishly, I was scared of what would happen to me. I wasn't as brave as any of them.

"You brought this on yourself, you fool," I say to him, finally having the chance to say the things I had been wanting to say for years. "That arrogance of yours. That pride. It ruined the lives of so many people who did not deserve it. Including mine. You had your choice of brides, women who would have done anything to live here with you, to have been spoilt by you and treated to all the riches you aspire to own. That wasn't her. It never was. She wanted a simple life. She had a simple life and you took it from her, thinking that you could bully her and beat her into loving you. The truth is that you never could. She was stronger than you ever gave her credit for. And she has given you the justice you deserved."

I grab the bloodied hairpin from the floor and looked at it; pure gold and studded with the rubies he forced her to wear, to show that she was his. I've watched him slowly try to break her down over the last five years, trying to force her into submission; unable to do anything except support her with useless words and provide her with the medicine that she insisted upon to stop her from ever becoming pregnant to him again.

She has somehow managed to remain so strong; a strength I know that I do not possess. I do not know what it was that finally caused her to snap, but I am glad that it was this that killed him. The very symbol of his greed and stature.

I reach for a chair and place it in front of the large, mirrored wardrobe before standing on it and placing the hairpin on top of it and out of sight. Then I reach for the dagger at his belt which hangs within the wardrobe before pulling the chair over to his bedside once more.

I wonder how long I have until the guards realise that something is wrong. When they realise that his door isn't guarded and come to investigate? Then what? The fear of torture claws at my heart.

Not just the pain, but of what I would give away to make it stop, placing Sophia in more danger than she already is.

I close my eyes. I'm tired. So tired, body and soul. I never could have realised when I answered Edmund's summons all those years ago that life would turn out this way. I look at him once more, cursing the boy I knew and the wicked tyrant that he became.

"Perhaps I shall see you soon, Edmund," I say to him, wondering if my misdeeds are enough to send me to the same place to which he has surely gone, as I take the dagger and slit my own throat.

SOPHIA

I rushed to Olivia's room, relieved to find Annalise there, sitting by the fire reading a book, the shock on her face clear as she saw me.

I managed to stutter out what had happened, grateful when she took control instinctively, grabbing our cloaks and taking Olivia in her arms before taking my hand and pulling me towards a staircase I had never seen before, which led to the back of the palace.

I instantly recognised James' coach as we reached the courtyard and hurriedly explained to the driver that we needed to leave; that James had sent us. He was never going to refuse a Queen's orders, so he opened the door and threw blankets over us as we lay on the floor of the carriage. He then drove us out of the gates in the anonymity which the throng of guests leaving the party awarded us.

I do not know how long the journey took. He didn't take the open roads. The risk was too great.

Once we were clear of the Capital he exchanged the carriage for a cart, allowing us to travel through forest routes instead of through the towns, hidden under hessian sheets and surrounded by hay bales during the day as we would travel.

And by night, we would find a place to make camp, deep within the safety of the trees. I told Olivia that we were going on a secret adventure, and luckily she seemed excited by the idea, never complaining even when food was short and bed was a clearing in a forest, cuddled up close to myself and Annalise to keep ourselves warm.

The driver never asked any questions and I never once felt that he would betray us. He just told me that James was one of the kindest men he knew. And that he would do anything he asked of him, because he had looked after him so many times before.

My thoughts keep flashing back to the moment James found me, standing there, a bloodied hairpin in my hand and Edmund dead in his bed, his empty eyes wide with the shock of what I had done to him. His thoughts were of me, not him. He got me out of there and to safety without a second thought for himself and what might happen. And I cannot bear to think of what will become of him because of that.

"This is as far as I can take you, my Lady." The driver's voice drifts into my head, taking me from my thoughts and as I take a look at where we are, my breath catches in my throat as I recognise it instantly. "The forest comes to an end from here," he continues. "I must begin to travel back. But it's just before sunrise, hopefully you can find a place to…"

"It's fine," I interrupt him, kindly. "I know where we are. We will be alright, I promise. Thank you. I can never repay you or James for what you have done."

He tips his cap to me with a small smile, as I turn to Annalise who is sleeping peacefully with Olivia cuddled up to her.

"Annalise." I shake her gently until she begins to wake, blinking up at me sleepily. "We need to go now. Come along."

I help her down from the cart with the driver's assistance, Olivia still fast asleep in her arms. I thank him once more as he bids us farewell, and we watch him disappear into the forest once more.

"Hurry now," I say to Annalise, who looks at me in confusion as she glances around at our surroundings. "It is still early. We can reach shelter before people begin to wake."

The streets still look the same. The houses all quiet, the inhabitants still sleeping at least for a few hours more. I hold onto Annalise's hand as we walk through the marketplace where I first met Alice all of those years ago.

I know where I need to go. It is a foolish idea and one that I really shouldn't listen to, but my heart is pulling me towards it and I cannot make myself stop. And as we walk towards the farmhouse that I used to call home, my head is flooded with all the memories of a life that feels like a distant memory to me now. The sun is just beginning to rise, the glow of its golden hue mingling with the pink of the early morning sky.

The farmhouse itself looks quiet and cold. The chimney has no smoke trailing from it as it used to every morning at this time when Tom left for work, and I stayed and took care of the farm. I still hear the bleats and crows of animals though and I begin to wonder if it is just my imagination, until I see something in the field beyond the farmhouse which tells me it's not.

"Stay here with Olivia," I say to Annalise, who carries my still sleepy child in her arms. "I won't be long, I promise, I just need to check something."

Annalise looks at me warily but nods, walking with me to the gate of the farmhouse but staying there as I walk towards the door. I give it a gentle knock and wait, but an answer doesn't come.

Pushing down my anxieties, I take a deep breath before turning the handle and pushing the door open.

It's still the same. It is as though the whole place has stood still in time for all of these years. It's as though I was only here yesterday.

The kitchen table which he made from scratch is still laid out with plates and cutlery. The vase which I would place fresh wild flowers in every morning before breakfast remains too, but empty now.

I walk over to the table and place a hand to the smooth dark wood, my fingers tracing a pattern in the dust which has settled there before a noise from the corner makes me jump. And as the maker of the noise comes into view, I have to blink to make sure I'm not seeing things.

"Amos?" I say his name gently, the tears filling my eyes. I hear the unusual, low grumble of an impending growl from him but I am not afraid. I crouch down, still keeping my distance as I hold out a hand to him.

"It's me, boy," I whisper, unable to stop smiling through my tears. "It's Sophia."

He cocks his head to the side, looking at me curiously. I keep my hand held out in front of me, waiting for him and eventually he edges closer, until the wetness of his nose touches my fingertips. I see his tail start to wag as he realises who I am and without fear I place a hand to his fur.

"I never thought I'd see you again, Amos."

He is licking the tears from my face now and I have my arms wrapped tight around him. For a moment, the rest of the world disappears and I find myself in a place of comfort with the dog that risked his life to save mine.

A noise jolts me back into reality and I look up through blurred eyes and see the man I thought I had lost for good five years ago. He stands in the doorway to the bedroom, his favourite small axe in his hand, his eyes wide in disbelief. He's both the man I remember so well, yet also a stranger to me.

His face bears the scars of the hardship he has suffered all these years. Thinner, his blue eyes shadowed with fatigue and pain, and the strong jaw I knew so well now covered with a greying beard.

Yet, it's him. The brave, beautiful man that I loved and lost. As the axe falls from his hand I realise what is happening and I grab hold of him, easing him down into a chair before his legs buckle completely.

My hand finds his cheek and I rest it there, looking into his eyes, just about managing to smile as he takes a deep, shuddering breath and I feel the relief emanate from him. He opens his mouth to say something but before he can, I hear footsteps at the front door.

"Mama?" As Olivia's voice filters across the room, I see Tom's face crease into bafflement once more.

"Don't ask any questions," I say, quickly as Olivia's hand finds mine and I grasp it tightly. She's been quiet recently and I cannot tell if it's just because she is tired or something worse. I covered the blood stains on my dress as best I could with a shawl and cloak, but I still think she saw. Tom just sits staring at us.

I watch as she holds her tiny hand out to pet Amos's rough coat. She has a natural way with animals, I have noticed over the years, and Amos is no different.

As soon as her hand touches his fur I see him relax, licking her hand as she giggles. Then her eyes find Tom and she looks to me to explain.

"Olivia, this is Tom. He's a kind man. I promise he won't hurt us. Do you trust me?"

She looks at me with those wide, ever trusting eyes and whispers, "Like Tom, in your fairy story?"

I bite my lip to stop the tears from coming. "Yes," I say, once I manage to get my voice working again. "Yes, just like Tom in my fairy story. And Tom, this is Olivia. My little girl."

His eyes flash with surprise at her name but he doesn't speak. He sits stock still as Olivia walks up to him. She stands staring at him, her head cocked curiously to one side, until finally she curtseys.

"The Tom in Mama's story was a woodcutter," she says, inquisitively. "Are you?"

He stays silent for a few moments then looks at me before answering. "Yes." he says, with a small smile. "Though I'm sure I'm not as good at it as the Tom in your Mama's story."

"He had a horsie," she says, and I am happy to hear that she sounds more animated. "Do you?"

He nods. "I have two. They are over there in the paddock, grazing." He points to the window and she squeals in delight. I smile as she runs over and begins to watch Meg and Arthur as they graze in the early morning sunlight.

"Annalise! Annalise! Come and look at the horsies!"

I see Tom's eyes widen as Olivia calls for her nursemaid. With my mind occupied by seeing him again I had completely forgotten about Annalise, standing silently at the doorway, trying to make herself as small as possible. I feel guilty for forgetting her. Her silence is so unusual, so deafening even now. Tom is staring at her like he has seen a ghost. As she walks over to him he gets heavily to his feet.

"I'm sorry." He whispers it, shaking his head. "I didn't know he would do that to you. I just wanted to get you out of there, I should have realised, I..."

As she throws her arms around him I see the look of shock on his face, the tears brimming in his eyes as he stands as still as a statue, seemingly unwilling or unable to embrace her, until slowly I see his arms relax, his hands going to rest gently against her back.

"Forgive me." He chokes it out and I swallow down my own tears at the sight of his face; so full of pain and regret at the guilt he has carried with him for five long years. Annalise pulls back from him, shaking her head softly as she reaches for his hand and places it against her heart. He looks confused but I know exactly what it is she is trying to say.

"You don't need to ask her forgiveness," I explain, gently. "She doesn't blame you. She never has. She is telling you that she is only alive today because of you."

Annalise nods, telling us both that what I said was right, before squeezing Tom's hands once more and walking over to join Olivia at the windowsill. I watch as they both dissolve into laughter in each other's company. Looking over at Tom I see that he is watching them too.

"They've always understood each other completely." I smile softly. "It's like they have this language, just the two of them. I don't think I would have survived without Annalise being there to help me. She's right. You saved her life. And both of us will be forever grateful for that."

He looks at me, opening his mouth to speak but the words don't come. Instead, he manages a small smile and a nod of his head as he reaches for an old wooden cane which he leans heavily on as he makes his way over to me. He's wincing with the effort and I can't help but stare at his left leg which is covered in deep scars from where his trousers finish down to his ankle.

"Broke my leg in my first year at the camp." His voice makes me jump as he focuses my attention from his leg. He's smiling ruefully at me. "My own fault. Saw a wall and reckoned it was low enough for me to scale it and try to escape. Overestimated my own ability. Probably would have been in for a beating if I hadn't broken it on the fall back to earth. The wardens reckoned that was punishment enough. The surgeon did his best, but they didn't want me getting any special treatment. He was told to fix me up enough so I could work again as soon as possible. It was agony. But they wanted to see me suffering, so I tried not to give them the satisfaction whilst working. Cried like a baby a good few nights though."

"I'm sorry," I say, my voice quiet. I want to say more but I don't have the words. He's still smiling at me sadly.

"It's not so bad in the warmer months." He shrugs. "Worse when the cold gets to it."

I'm unable to take my eyes from the mess that had been made of his leg until his voice shakes my focus back to his face.

"What happened, Sophia?" He shakes his head. "Why are you here?"

My mind flashes back to everything that happened to bring me here. "He was sending Olivia away," I begin. "He had arranged a marriage for her to the Duke of Fallean. He was fifty years old, Tom! I couldn't let him. There was no way, not my little girl!"

I break down as I feel his arms encompass me. It's been so long since anyone held me like this. Since I felt safe and cared for.

"Mama?" Olivia's voice, quiet with worry, travels from across the room and as I look at her, the tears fill my eyes again.

"Shhh..." he whispers gently, stroking my hair. "Try not to cry in front of her, not now that she seems to have settled."

"Mama's okay, sweetheart." I try to smile as I compose myself a little. "Just a little tired. You carry on watching the horses with Annalise."

She looks at me uncertainly for a few moments and I manage to keep smiling to let her know I'm alright until finally she turns back to the window, Annalise placing an arm around her. I pull myself in closer to Tom, feeling his arms tighten around me.

"I k...killed him, Tom," I whisper into his chest, trying to stop my sobs. "I didn't mean to kill him. Or maybe I did, I don't know. I just saw my chance and I snapped. I hated him. I wanted to hurt him like he had hurt us."

I feel him squeeze me tighter. Holding onto me for dear life as if he never wants to let go and I'm not sure I ever want him to.

"How did you get out?" he says eventually, shaking his head as he turns to look at Olivia who still sits with Annalise at the windowsill watching the horses in awe. "How the hell did you all get out of there without being caught? How did you get here?"

"James," I whisper, and I see the realisation dawn in his eyes. I choke back another sob as I tell him the whole story of how James got me out of there, clinging to him as the memories seep into my brain like floodwater. "They'll kill him, Tom. If they think James killed the King they will execute him!"

"Listen to me." His voice is strong, as he searches my eyes with his. "He saved your life. He saved you and Olivia, and Annalise. He knew what he was doing. He must have known something like this might happen or why would he have made plans like the one that brought you here? You can't let his sacrifice be in vain."

"They will be coming to find me," I interrupt him, shaking my head. "They're not stupid. He gave me a head start but as soon as they realised what had happened they will have set off after me. I need to go. I need to get far away from here, take her somewhere safe. I just … I had to see you first. To say sorry."

"Sorry?" He shakes his head in confusion, "What for?"

"For everything that happened to you. Because of me."

"Sophia, none of this was your fault."

"I should have told you the truth when we first met. Then maybe we could have been more prepared. Moved further away where he couldn't find us. I just...I didn't want that nightmare to be a part of us."

"Sophia…"

"I just wanted you to be safe. I would have done anything to save you. I did." I break off, tears stinging my eyes, memories paining my brain, sickening thoughts of the past threatening to consume me. "Still, it wasn't enough. When I heard your sentence I felt sick. Forgive me," I whisper. "Please?"

He walks forward, shaking his head as he grasps my hands tightly. His skin is warm and soft against mine and in that moment I feel like I never want to let go again.

"There is nothing to forgive."

"Please." I close my eyes as I look down at the ground. "Just say it. I need you to say it." I can't look at him. My eyes stay fixed to the floor as I wait in a deafening silence which seems to last a lifetime until his voice breaks it.

"I forgive you."

I look up and find myself staring straight into his eyes. They glisten with tears that are soon to meet the tracks of the ones he has already shed. I try to smile and manage it, just, though it is a little wobbly. He's searching my face with his eyes looking for answers I don't know that I can give him. He dips his head towards mine, our eyes still connected. He looks unsure of himself and younger than I've ever seen him because of it. His lips reach mine and I realise how much I have missed his taste, his touch, the familiar scratch of his stubble against my cheek. I can feel myself becoming consumed by him and I know that I cannot let it happen. As I push him away, I see the uncertainty in his eyes replaced by hurt.

"I have to go." I wipe my eyes hurriedly. "Olivia, sweetheart, we've got to go, come along now." I make towards her and I feel his hand grasp mine, pulling me back.

"Wait! Sophia, that's it? You're leaving?"

"We can't stay here."

"Five years." He wrenches his hand through his hair and I see the grey at his temples, scattered through the light brown.

I open my mouth to speak but he walks over to the dresser and opens the drawer. He still has his back to me as he starts talking.

"Tom. You made me promise you that I would try to carry on for my baby girl. So I will try. As long as you promise me that you will carry on too. Knowing that you are still in this world being the man I know you can be will help me more than you can ever realise. I love you. Your Sophia."

He turns towards me, the scrap of paper I hurriedly wrote and gave to James to give him in his hand, once brand new now tattered. Worn. Well read.

"That place nearly broke me." His voice is hollow. "They pushed me to the edge of what I could stand, so many times. They wanted to break me. And the only thing that kept me going was reading that little scrap of paper over and over, until the light faded and I couldn't read it any more."

He stops, shaking his head. "I've spent the last five years hoping and praying that one day you would walk back through that door. Back to me. I pushed away the fact that it was almost impossible, because it is the only thing that has kept me going."

I look at him, not knowing what on earth I can say to make him see that the whole idea of us staying here is too dangerous to comprehend.

"Tom," I try, eventually, looking up into his eyes. "We cannot stay here. This is the first place they will look."

"Then let me come with you," he interrupts, strongly. "I can keep you safe. All of you. I love you, Sophia. I never stopped loving you. And no matter what he said…" His voice breaks and he stops, biting his lip to compose himself. "He never took you from me. Not really. I made a sacred vow to love you and protect you until my dying day. He never changed that. He thought he did, but he didn't, did he?"

I hear the ache in his voice and I look at him, my own eyes blurred with tears.

"Never."

"Then let me honour the vow I made all those years ago. Let me protect you and Olivia, and Annalise. We can go far away from here, where they will never find us."

"You would leave this behind?"

"What?" he laughs. "This village? Everyone hates me here. Ever since I was released from the camp. The only ones who still give a damn are Jack and Mary. And I think they'd have an easier life if I wasn't around anymore." I must look unsure, as he walks forward again and takes hold of my hands. "All I need is you. We can find a place far away from here, where they will never find us. We can start again. If you want to?"

As I look at him, I am transported for a moment back to a time before all of this happened, when it was just the two of us with such hope for the future. So much has happened since then. So much pain; so much fear; so much hurt. We are different people now because of it. Yet together, there is still that solid foundation of love that keeps us anchored. I nod my head, unable to speak and he smiles at me.

"You and Annalise better get changed. Your clothes are still in the bedroom. I could never…" He stops, looking down at the ground to compose himself before continuing, "I'll take Olivia and get the animals into the cart, she'll like that. That is ... if you trust me to?"

That unfamiliar unsure look has come over his face again, he looks like a little boy. I take hold of his hands in mine.

"I trust you more than anyone," I say strongly. "I know you would protect her with your life."

He swallows, looking down at his feet again before composing himself and turning to my daughter.

"Olivia?" He calls to her and she turns to him. "Would you like to come and help me get the horses ready, so we can all go on an adventure? You can meet all of the other animals too?"

She stares at him open-mouthed. "You have more animals? Do you have chickens?"

"Yep." He smiles. "Chickens and pigs and even a goat." He raises an eyebrow and she looks at me, excitedly.

"May I, Mama?"

I nod, calmed by her new found excitement that seems to have overtaken the quiet tiredness of the journey here.

"Of course you can, sweetheart. Mama will not be long. Annalise and I just need to change our clothes for the journey."

I can't help but smile at the huge grin on her face as she turns and runs over to Tom and, without hesitation, places her hand in his. He looks taken aback by this for a brief moment and the sight of them together sends a pang of painful guilt to my heart that doesn't seem to want to shift. As I watch him squeeze her hand back tightly as they walk out towards the stables, I feel Annalise's hand at my arm and I turn away, leading her towards the bedroom so we can change.

My breath catches in my throat as we walk into the room. It is like a museum, transporting me back in time to the last day I ever spent here. Thick layers of dust cover each and every surface. My nightgown still rests upon the pillow from where I folded it there just a few hours before I was taken. I swallow down the emotion in my throat, composing myself for a few moments before realising that Annalise is just standing watching me. Jolting myself back into the present, I walk over to the cupboard, to find some clothes for us both. I reach for my old blue cotton dress which feels so simple and soft to the touch, as I recall all of the happy memories I have of wearing it to tend to the farm. I hand it to her with a smile and she reaches for it warily.

"It's alright, Annalise," I say gently, resting my hand against her cheek, desperate to take away the look of fear on her face, which has been almost ever present for the last five years. "We're going to be safe now, I promise. Nobody can hurt any of us any more."

I turn back to the cupboard and take out my old, comfortable trousers and one of Tom's shirts which I know will bury me but I do not care. I never did. I would steal his shirts all the time to wear. They were comfortable and made me feel close to him. And though I'm closer to him now than I have been in so many years, wearing this, smelling his scent on the soft fabric, is making this moment that I never thought would happen feel real.

As I finish tucking the shirt into my trousers and reach for my old boots, I turn to see if Annalise is alright. She has changed into my blue dress and has unpinned her hair, letting it fall across her shoulders in beautiful dark waves. She looks so unsure of herself that I cannot help but smile. The child that I knew so well is now a young woman. She has grown up in front of my eyes without me even noticing.

"You are such a beautiful, young lady," I whisper with a smile. "You have grown so much. And I would never have survived in that place without you. You looked after me so well. Now let me look after you."

She gives me a proper smile for the first time in so long and I see the realisation dawn in her eyes that she is finally free.

I sit down on the bed to lace up my boots and my eyes catch sight of my wedding photograph on the bedside table. I pick it up, my finger tracing the people within it; people I barely remember. But we have a chance to find them again now.

I place it in a bag, along with a few more items of clothes before taking hold of Annalise's hand and making our way outside. When we reach the front door, Tom is sitting at the front of the cart, in his hands the reins of the horses. Olivia is fast asleep next to him, tucked up in the crook of his arm, wrapped in a blanket.

"She's exhausted." His voice is quiet as I climb up beside her into the cart, helping Annalise up next to me as Amos jumps up to sit by our feet. "She was watching me load the pigs into the back and could barely keep her eyes open.

She sat on the garden wall, thumb in her mouth, trying desperately to stay awake."

I smile as I stroke her hair. "That's the sign she needs her bed. When the thumb reaches the mouth that's it."

"I figured as much." He chuckles. "I picked her up and wrapped her in a blanket. She was fast asleep before I even put her back down again." He's looking at her wistfully and I feel my heart ache again. It's difficult not to think about what could have been if none of this had happened. I know he would have been a wonderful father. And I can see that he cares for Olivia. But I know it can never feel the same for him. And I can never give him a child of his own.

"Don't…"

I look up at the sound of his voice and see that he is staring at me, shaking his head. And I know that he knows exactly what I am thinking. Like he always has been able to do.

"Don't think that. She is you." He looks down at Olivia, sleeping peacefully between us, her thumb still in her mouth. "She is all you. She is intelligent and caring; and funny; and beautiful. It makes no difference to me that she isn't mine by blood. I will love her and care for her just the same. If you will let me?"

I can't speak. All I can do is nod and again I know that it is all he needs to see to understand. He reaches across towards me, brushing my lips with the gentlest of kisses, his thumb tracing my cheek. Taking off his cap he passes it to me.

"Put it on. Just until we get clear of here. That hair of yours is a pretty big giveaway."

He grins at me and I laugh. The first time I have laughed in so long. I had almost forgotten what it felt like. Pulling my hair up into a knot I take the cap from his hand and place it on my head, instantly masking the flame red curls. He smiles at me as he takes the reins in his hands again.

"Let's go..."

EPILOGUE

2 years later

"Annalise, hurry!"

I watch my daughter as she sits impatiently on a large rock outside our home, Annalise trying to finish braiding her long red hair. It now reaches the bottom of her back and it is a long job to tease it into any sort of style, which stops the cold air from turning it into a ball of knots. The climate here is so different and it took awhile for us to adjust. Making warmer clothes, buying boots, hats and scarves to keep out the chill.

"Olivia, don't be so rude to Annalise. Be patient, she's almost finished."

My daughter looks at me ruefully. "Sorry, Mama. Sorry, Annalise."

I smile at her softly. "Why are you in such a rush anyway?" At this, she grins at me excitedly.

"Papa said he is going to teach me how to chop firewood!"

"Oh ..." I say, looking over at Tom who shrugs his shoulders, a sheepish look on his face. "Did Papa indeed?"

She wanted to learn." He calls to me from where he is currently moving a large pile of logs ready to chop them into firewood. "It's educational. I couldn't say no."

I chuckle, shaking my head. "She's got you wrapped around her little finger."

It was Olivia herself who asked me if she could start calling Tom her Papa.

She barely saw Edmund as she was growing up. He had little interest in her, aside from how she could benefit him and I always believe she saw him as the King, rather than her father. I was her world. Me and Annalise.

So when we got ourselves settled and she finally saw me happy and loved for the first time; and she herself felt the love and protection of someone other than me, I guess things started to make more sense to her. She was always more mature than her tender years.

I was taken aback at first. And though I would have said yes instantly, a million times over, it was Tom who needed to give his blessing. He couldn't speak when she asked him. He looked at me as if to confirm he wasn't hearing things, the tears pooling in his eyes. He managed a nod of his head as Olivia jumped into his arms and I watched him pull her in tight to him, whispering something into her hair. I never asked what.

"Come along then, little rascal." Tom calls to her, as Annalise finishes tying off the end of her braid with a ribbon. Olivia squeals in delight as she rushes over to him and I take Annalise's arm and follow on.

The day that Tom asked us to leave with him, I was scared. I genuinely thought there was no way on earth that we could escape unharmed. I had visions of guards stopping us in the middle of the night, killing Tom and dragging me, Annalise and Olivia back to the capital to face our fate. But Tom knew the streets; he knew the night and he knew how to keep us safe. And eventually after a day and night of travel we reached the docks.

He paid some kindly sailors the vast majority of his savings, to take us away from the Shorelands and find us safe passage to a new life. They anchored up six days later at a small place which they told us was called Lillerup, far, far north of the Shorelands, the Capital and Fallean. Somewhere I had never even heard of.

The sea, somewhere along the journey had met a river which in turn had met a lake. This is where they helped us to disembark onto a grassy bank; Annalise and I getting Olivia and Amos safely down, whilst the sailors helped Tom with the horses and cart and the rest of the animals.

We thanked them again, Tom trying to give them more money which they refused, wishing us well before setting off again, their journey taking them to the east, towards discovery of new lands. This place was unlike anything I had ever seen before. The only similarity came thanks to the rich green forests which reminded me of Lowshore. But there were no dusty roads or farmhouses here. It was all lush grass leading to lakes which surrounded the entire land. And the houses here were made of deep red wood with stone chimneys, spaced so far out from one another that it gave the feeling that it could easily be your own private island. After asking some locals we discovered quickly that the people of this land were few. No more than a hundred residents. They knew nothing of the Shorelands or the Capital, or anything that may have happened there. They lived simply. Unburdened by greed and power.

Explaining that we had nowhere to live, they pointed us in the direction of a small uninhabited lake house with forests right behind and the cool, calming water in front for miles. It was dilapidated and in need of repair, but it was nothing that Tom couldn't fix. And so we started again. Living a life I never dreamed I would be able to live again. As happy and as safe as I knew we could be.

"Right," Tom says, picking Olivia up and placing her in front of an old tree stump on which he has placed a small log. "First of all, you need to know that this isn't a toy." He holds up his favourite axe which glints in the early evening sun. Olivia looks at it curiously.

"It's so small!"

"So are you," Tom replies, teasingly. "Doesn't mean you aren't capable of great things. Now. You must never play with this or take it or any of the other axes from my bag, do you understand?"

As Olivia nods he grins at her.

"Good girl. Okay ..." He places her hands around the handle of the axe before gently placing his on top of hers. "You need to mark the spot where you will chop it," he says, Olivia hung on his every word. "But you've also got to have faith and confidence that you can hit it." He guides her hands down, placing the blade of the axe right in the middle of the log before lifting it again. "Ready? Remember, you've got to believe you can do it."

"I can, Papa. I can do it." I see Tom's mouth twitch with a shy smile as she says it. "Okay then. On three. One, two, three." I watch him guide her hands back down, the log slicing perfectly in two.

"I did it!" She squeals in delight.

He grins, ruffling the top of her head as she rushes off to grab another log to chop. I feel Annalise squeeze my arm and I look at her and see she is staring at something in the distance. I follow her gaze and smile as I see the young boy from the village who has taken a shine to her.

"Off you go," I say, softly and she smiles at me. "But don't be back too late, alright?"

She nods before rushing over to him with a spring in her step that I've never seen before. She's happy. Properly happy for the first time in so long and it makes my heart soar. I watch with a smile on my face as the boy talks to her, looking at her like she is the most precious thing on this earth. He knows she cannot speak. He doesn't seem to care. He understands her as we do and that's all that matters.

"Will Annalise marry that boy, Mama?" Olivia pipes up, her voice alive with curiosity.

I chuckle. "She's still getting to know him, sweetheart. But perhaps one day."

"Then I can be a flower girl again," she says, as Tom hands her the axe once more and places his hands on hers. "Like I was for you."

I smile as I look at the thin, plain silver band on my wedding finger.

Tom still had the emerald studded one that he kept all those years, always believing that somehow we would find a way back to one another. But mine was lost to me years ago. And we both felt like a reminder of the past wouldn't help either of us. So we bought new ones so that we could marry again. A fresh start. The child at my breast suddenly begins to stir, the air pierced by his tender cries.

"Why is he crying, Mama?"

"Your brother is hungry, my darling."

I watch her roll her eyes. "He's always hungry."

"So were you when you were his age." I chuckle as I sit myself down upon a tree stump and arrange my dress to allow him to feed. "And now look at you. Big and strong, and chopping logs with your Papa. James will be able to do that when he's older too."

Tom looks over at me and smiles softly, as Olivia jokingly proclaims that her brother won't ever be as good at chopping logs as her.

Our son has now settled against my breast as he feeds hungrily. James Thomas George Thornton. Our little miracle. When I first realised that I was pregnant, I was scared and confused.

After everything that had happened; the damage I had done to my own body to ensure that I never gave Edmund a son; I never thought I would bear another child. And I spent the first few months panicking daily that I would lose this child just as I had lost our first all those years ago.

But as my stomach continued to grow and I could feel the little life inside of me moving and kicking so strongly, I started to believe that this really could happen. Tom was with me at the birth, by my side just as he had been when I brought Olivia into the world. Except this time he could touch his child, kiss his head and hold him gently in his arms; my eyes filling with tears at the sight of it as it confirmed what I already knew from the way he had cared for and loved Olivia these past two years.

That he is a natural, wonderful father who had now been given the chance to experience what was cruelly taken from him all those years ago. And just as Olivia is the image of me, James is the image of Tom. We both wanted to give him that name. In honour of the man who helped, shielded and protected us both during the worst years of our lives. The man who gave his life to save mine.

I never got news of what happened to him. And I hope with all my heart that he is still in this world somewhere, helping others. But deep down I know. I know that his decision to get me out of that place after I killed Edmund cost him his life. And it is something I can never repay him for. All I can do is promise that the child we have named in his honour will grow up to be a brave, kind intelligent man like he was.

"Five!" Olivia's joyful voice breaks me from my thoughts as I hear the axe chop through another log. James has finished feeding, so I rearrange my dress as he settles down into a happy slumber in my arms. I watch as Tom helps Olivia to chop some more logs before I see Amos make his way slowly out of the lake house, wanting to see what all the noise was about. He's getting on now, slowing down a lot. But still he carries on. I'm sure Tom was right when he said he was too stubborn to die.

"Amos," Olivia says happily, as she leaves Tom's side and rushes over to him. "Let's go for a walk down to the water, boy."

"Don't go too close."

"I won't, Mama, I promise. Come on, boy."

As I watch them walk slowly towards the lake together, I feel Tom's arms around my waist as he nuzzles his head into my neck, placing a kiss against it which makes me smile.

"Who would have thought a little princess would end up wanting to chop wood."

As I say it, he chuckles in my ear. "Well she always was different." He replies, "takes after her mother."

"She reminds me of you though," I say softly. "I know that sounds impossible, but she does. She's mischievous and resilient, and strong. She knows what she wants and she lets nothing stop her. And she makes me laugh."

"I thought you only laughed at me?" He says, raising an eyebrow and I giggle.

484

"Most of the time," I tease. "But you can be funny on occasion."

He releases me from his grasp, placing a gentle hand to his son's soft, fair hair before placing a kiss against it. "Are you happy here?" His question is sudden, taking me by surprise and as I look at him I can see the familiar lost boy look has taken over his face.

"What sort of a question is that?" I place a hand to his cheek, making him look at me from where his eyes have wandered over to Olivia and Amos at the water's edge. I know what he's thinking. His face is an open book. "I know it's hard for you to believe in anything good," I say, softly. "I know you are always going to have that fear that someone is going to take all of this away from you. But I promise you that they won't. Not again. And I am happier than I could ever have dreamed of being. I'm alive and I'm free. Living in this beautiful, peaceful place with the man I love and our children."

I see him swallow down tears as I say this and I reach up, kissing him deeply on the lips before wrapping my arms around him once more as we watch in comfortable silence as Olivia guides Amos back up to where we stand., yawning widely.

"All that hard work tired you out, rascal?" Tom asks her, having finally recovered his composure. She nods at him and he laughs, picking her up and letting her hook her arms around his neck before taking hold of my spare hand.

"Let's get you tucked up in bed. Then Mama can read you and James a story."

As Olivia nuzzles her head into his neck, closing her eyes sleepily, I feel him squeeze my hand and I return the gesture as we begin the walk back up to our home.

The End

ABOUT THE AUTHOR

Jemma Robinson is an Author from East Yorkshire. She has always enjoyed the magic of creative writing since her school days, particularly creating words with a historical or fantasy setting and characters for people to fall in love with.
When she's not writing, Jemma enjoys spending time with her numerous rescue pets and running fan sites for two of the UK's favourite actors.

Follow Jemma on social media: @jemmawrites

Website: https://jemmarobinsonwrites.co.uk/

BV - #0041 - 130421 - C0 - 198/129/28 - PB - 9781916202306 - Matt Lamination